THE
BITTER
TASTE
OF
MURDER

ALSO BY THE AUTHOR

Murder in Chianti

THE
BITTER
TASTE OF
MURDER

CAMILLA
TRINCHIERI

Published by
Soho Press, Inc.
227 W 17th Street
New York, NY 10011

Library of Congress Cataloging-in-Publication Data

Trinchieri, Camilla, author.
The bitter taste of murder / Camilla Trinchieri.
Series: The Tuscan mysteries; 2

ISBN 978-1-64129-283-2
eISBN 978-1-64129-284-9

PS3553.R435 B58 2021 | DDC 813'.54—dc23
LC record available at https://lccn.loc.gov/2020052761

Interior design by Janine Agro, Soho Press, Inc.

Printed in the United States of America

10 9 8 7 6 5 4 3 2 1

THE
BITTER
TASTE
OF
MURDER

ONE

*Gravigna, a small town in the Chianti hills of Tuscany
A Tuesday in June, 7:50 A.M.*

Ex-homicide detective Nico Doyle parked his red Fiat 500 under a cloudless sky that promised another hot day and followed his dog across the deserted main piazza. It was too early in the day for tourists. The tables and chairs outside Trattoria da Gino wouldn't be set up for another two hours. The benches where the four pensioners sat daily to exchange their news were empty. In the far corner, Bar All'Angolo, open since 6 A.M., would offer him breakfast.

OneWag rushed into the café through the open door, nose immediately canvassing the floor. Nico followed, scanning the tables. There were only a few customers. Last week at this hour, he had found the place full of students chattering with mouths full of cornetti, their colorful backpacks getting in everyone's way. School had since ended, and they were now having breakfast at home. The few locals who didn't have to travel far for work were standing at the bar counter with espresso cups in their hands, talking among themselves.

Sandro, one of the café's two owners, was manning the cash register as always. He looked up.

"Ciao, Nico."

Some locals turned to nod their hellos.

"Salve," Nico replied to all. He walked to the cash register. "How goes it?"

"So far the morning is good," Sandro replied with a smile. He was a good-looking, lanky man somewhere in his mid-forties with a small gold stud shining in one ear. "It's still cool enough, but get your fan out. We're going to fry today."

"I've been trying to convince him to air-condition the place," his husband Jimmy said. Jimmy's job was to work the huge, very hot stainless-steel espresso machine at the far end of the bar and the oven that baked the most delicious cornetti this side of Florence.

Sandro shook his head. "Costs too much. Besides, it's bad for you. Freezes your guts like that ice water Americans like."

Jimmy shrugged and turned to start Nico's Americano. There was no need to order, as Nico always had the same thing. While Nico paid Sandro, OneWag's nails clicked back and forth over the tiles, his snout a periscope sweeping left and right. The café floor was usually scattered with sugar-laced crumbs. After two rounds across the room, the dog sat and barked a protest.

"Sorry, Rocco," Sandro said. "I swept. I didn't want those floppy ears of yours to get dirty." The Italians called Nico's dog Rocco. They claimed OneWag was too hard to pronounce and that an Italian dog should have an Italian name. The dog wisely answered to both with his signature one wag, which usually brought good things. In this case, a day-old cornetto tossed by Sandro and caught on the fly.

"Bravo!" Sandro clapped.

"No more, please," Nico said. The morning the small stray had led him to a murdered man, he'd been a skinny, dirty runt. Nine months later, his long white and orange coat was clean and fluffy, and his stomach looked as if it held a full litter.

Nico walked over to his usual table by the open French doors and sat down, as he had nearly every day since he'd moved to his late wife Rita's hometown of Gravigna a year ago. In that time, he had slowly made new friends. Gogol was the first, a man who lived in a reality all his own. A good man with an incredible memory. Gogol's ability to quote every stanza of Dante's *Divine Comedy* was what had first attracted Nico to him. Having breakfast with him became another part of this morning routine.

The old man stood by the door, wrapped in his strong cologne and the overcoat he wore in winter and summer. It had first earned him the nickname of Gogol, after the Russian writer whose most famous story was titled "The Overcoat." His face was a maze of wrinkles, his long hair clean and brushed. The old-age home where he lived took good care of him. His coat had been recently mended. "Another day to live through, amico," he said to Nico.

"Let's live it well, Gogol." Nico stood up and held out a chair. "I'm glad to see you."

Gogol shuffled to the table and took the chair closest to the open door, minimizing the effect of his cologne. He held up the two crostini he'd gotten from the butcher around the corner. "Our friend made them for me especially. A man with a noble heart." Gogol placed the two squares of bread carefully at the center of the table. "'It pleases me, whatever pleases you.'"

"*Paradiso.*"

Gogol coughed a laugh. "*Inferno*, amico."

Trying to guess which section of the *Divina Commedia* the quotes came from was a new game Gogol had suggested, hoping Nico would study the poetry. Back in the Bronx, Nico had once had his ears filled with Dante by his wife, who also loved quoting the Tuscan poet. He found old Italian too difficult; it reminded him of struggling through Chaucer in high school. Modern Italian he could handle pretty well, thanks to Rita's lessons and Berlitz.

Nico took the salame crostino, knowing Gogol liked the lard best. He rarely guessed the quote. "It sounded too nice for *Inferno*."

Gogol bit into his lard crostino, swallowed quickly and said, "I begin to abandon hope of you ever climbing the slope. Also from *Inferno*. My adaptation for this occasion."

"Why abandon hope on such a beautiful day?" asked a voice with a Neapolitan accent.

Nico turned around. Maresciallo Salvatore Perillo stood outside the open French doors, chatting with a group of cyclists about to take off for the steep hills of Chianti. Perillo had been one of them until last year, having even won a few races. He was a short, stocky man with shiny black hair beginning to gray at the temples, a chiseled handsome face with large, dark liquid eyes, thick lips and an aquiline nose. He was out of uniform as usual, wearing jeans, a perfectly pressed blue linen shirt and, despite the heat, his beloved leather jacket flung over his shoulder.

Nico smiled, glad to see the man who had become a good friend since involving Nico in a murder investigation last September. They hadn't seen each other or talked in the last week. The maresciallo's carabinieri station was in Greve, nineteen kilometers away.

Nico pushed back a chair. "Join us."

Perillo stepped into the café, looked at Gogol hunched over the table and hesitated. "Gogol, am I welcome?"

Gogol grinned, showing his brown teeth. "You were Nico's Virgil through last year's journey into hell, or perhaps he was yours. Whichever it is, friends of Nico are welcome today. Tomorrow perhaps not."

"I'll keep that in mind." Perillo sat down next to Nico. Gogol made him uncomfortable. His overpowering cologne didn't help. The man was crazy, mentally disabled or putting on an act to get attention. Perillo eased his discomfort by bending down to pet Rocco, who was sniffing his suede ankle boots.

Sandro brought over two Americani and two whole wheat cornetti straight out of the oven, a Bar All'Angolo specialty. "Espresso for you, Salvatore?"

Perillo raised two fingers, then a thumb for his double espresso to be corrected with grappa. The inclusion of grappa meant things weren't going well with the maresciallo.

"That bad?" Nico asked before biting into his cornetto. The salame crostino, he pushed Gogol's way. The old man always ended up eating both.

"I will happily tell you." Perillo looked in Jimmy's direction, eager for his espresso. "No murders, may God be praised."

Sandro hurried over with the double espresso. Perillo thanked him and emptied the cup with one swallow. "Yesterday, Signor Michele Mantelli drove into Greve, found that the parking spots in Piazza Matteoti were occupied, parked his Jaguar in the middle of piazza, locked it and went off to lunch. In the center of the town! Can you believe it? There's perfectly good parking nearby. Of course, one of my men called the car removal service. What followed was Mantelli stomping into the station preceded by a hailstorm of insults directed at me. It was clear I had no brains, I didn't know who he was, headquarters in Florence would hear about this, I would be demoted and so on. You would not believe the fury of the man."

"Who is he?" Nico asked.

"A ball breaker. Michele Mantelli is considered a famous critic of Italian wines, said to have the power to make or ruin a new vintage. He runs a very successful biannual magazine called *Vino Veritas*, written in Italian and English and distributed globally. Also a blog, which he posts to monthly for thousands of readers. The pied piper and his rats, I say. If they only knew he was the head rat."

"I'm sorry he's gotten to you. Where's he from?"

"Milan, but he has an old villa in Montefioralle."

"Words aren't necessary," Gogol said. "The face shows the color of the heart."

"Well said, Gogol. My wife considers him very handsome." Perillo sniffed. "I suspect he's also a smooth talker when not shouting insults."

"I haven't seen Ivana since last year's barbecue. How is she?" Nico asked.

"She's fine. She was in the piazza getting bread."

Gogol chuckled to himself. "'The eyes of Ivana were all intent on him.' A very bad adaptation of *Paradiso*, canto one. Amusing nonetheless."

Perillo didn't look amused. He sat back in his chair and closed his eyes.

"Refreshed?" Nico asked after a minute of silence had gone by.

"It's a drug," said Perillo.

"The grappa or the coffee?"

"Love is a drug," Gogol announced. Clasping his hands on the rim of the table, he slowly stood. "The only woman I love is my mother. 'Watching her, I changed inside.' No point in guessing. Tomorrow, if I live." Gogol's mother had died when he was just a boy.

Nico stood up. "Tomorrow. I'm counting on it."

Gogol stepped through the open French doors, his powerful scent leaving with him.

"That was abrupt," Perillo said.

"I think Gogol knows he annoyed you with that quote about your wife."

"He didn't, though." Perillo had mostly been annoyed at his wife's comment about Mantelli. *"That man is very pleasant to look at, don't you think?"* she'd asked with a smile on her face. He'd answered her with a long kiss. Ah, yes, that reminded him of why he'd come to the café.

"How are Aldo and Cinzia?" Perillo asked.

Aldo Ferri, who owned the Ferriello vineyard, rented the small run-down stone farmhouse at the edge of his olive grove to Nico. "Fine. They invited me over for dinner last week. Spaghetti all'arrabbiata. Just as good as Cinzia's carbonara." Nico bunched his fingers to his lips and released them with a kiss. "I convinced her to give me the recipe."

"You can get a recipe for that from any cookbook."

"Maybe, but I'd use hers."

"Has there been any tension between Cinzia and Aldo?" Gogol's comment—*"Love is a drug"*—brought back the scene he had witnessed last night. Luckily, he hadn't been seen. Perillo felt a sudden pang of remorse. Should he tell Nico? But maybe there was an explanation for what had happened. It would only be spreading malicious gossip.

"Not that I've seen." Nico watched Perillo's expression carefully. "Why are you asking about them?"

A couple walked in and ordered from Sandro in French-tinted Italian. Perillo heard laughter and turned to look at them. They were hugging, mussing up each other's hair.

"No reason. Just that I haven't seen them around in some time." He stood up. "I'd better get back to the station. Say hello to Tilde and Enzo for me. Tell them not to work you too hard at the restaurant. Be well."

Nico stood too. "I'm not working Thursday night. Any chance of dinner?" It was clear his friend was holding something back. Maybe he was having problems with his wife? Getting out of the house for an evening might help. Besides, he missed Perillo's company.

"Maybe. If no one does anything stupid or cruel. I'll let you know." Perillo walked over to the counter and paid Sandro for his corrected double espresso.

Nico waved goodbye to Sandro and Jimmy and, with OneWag

running ahead, went to his car. Tuesday was laundry day, part of the routine he had set up for himself when he first moved to Gravigna. Back in the Bronx, he had made fun of Rita's need to follow a routine that wavered only when she fell sick. At the beginning of his new Italian life, he'd found that maintaining a routine helped him find his footing. Now that he was fully settled, it was possible he kept it up out of laziness.

There was no need for OneWag to join Nico in the car. The dog had his routine down pat. Nico would find him waiting in the heart of the medieval part of town, at the aptly named laundromat Sta A Te, which meant, "It's up to you."

Two hours later, his freshly cleaned clothes neatly folded in the back seat of his car, Nico started his work for Tilde and Enzo. His first duty was to pick up the restaurant's daily supply of bread from the grocer, Enrico. With the bread, Enrico gave him one of his coveted olive loaves and a ham bone. "The loaf is for you, the bone is for the little one. It's too hot to use it for soup. Where is he?"

"Thanks. He's gone to visit Nelli at her studio. She spoils him." Nico reached for his wallet.

Enrico raised his hand in protest. He was a small man with a pale face and thinning hair. "Friends pay for two loaves—one, no. Bring Rocco the next time. He's a good dog."

"He loves you."

Enrico chuckled. "He loves my prosciutto. The best in the area, if I do say so myself."

"Agreed. See you later." Nico lifted the large paper sack and turned to go.

"Watch out on the street. Some maniac zoomed past here a few minutes ago in his fancy car. Almost ran down one of my customers."

"I'll be careful." Nico looked down the slope. Only a few

people and a struggling cyclist were working their way up the steep hill.

Hugging the bag of bread, Nico climbed the rest of the way. At the top, diagonal to the Santa Agnese church, stood Sotto Il Fico. A white Jaguar was parked in front, fully blocking the entrance.

Nico squeezed through the narrow space the car had left and called out, "Buongiorno."

"Nothing good about it," the restaurant's owner grumbled. Elvira fanned herself with a large black lace fan she claimed was a gift from a Spanish admirer. The truth, according to Tilde, was that she'd bought it at the monthly flea market in Panzano.

"I'm sorry to hear that." Nico dropped the bread bag on one of the five indoor tables. He was used to her bad moods by now. "Is your arthritis acting up?"

She answered with a snort. A sixty-three-year-old widow with pitch-black dyed hair, a wrinkled face, a small pointed nose and pale blue eyes as sharp as a hawk's, Elvira oversaw the goings-on of her restaurant from an old gilded armchair in the front room. Today she was wearing a blue and green housedress, which meant it was Tuesday. She had seven, one for each day of the week.

"Where's Enzo?" Her son was in charge of managing the bar and the cash register and cutting the bread. Tilde, Enzo's wife and Rita's cousin, cooked the meals.

"He's on the terrace with that fraud who calls himself the world's best wine critic!"

"Michele Mantelli is here?"

"Yes, he marched in not ten minutes ago. If he doesn't remove his car in the next ten, I'm calling the carabinieri."

"He's already had a run-in with them."

"Good. He can have another."

Nico leaned toward the open door that led to the terrace. Mantelli was sitting in the shade of the huge fig tree that gave the restaurant its name and fame. All he could see was a crumpled white linen suit that matched a full head of long white hair. The man's face was hidden by Enzo, who was hovering over him.

"That man insisted on seeing our full wine list," Elvira said. "Enzo was just making me another espresso."

"I can make that for you, if you want," Nico offered. Enzo had taught him how to use the espresso machine behind the bar.

"No, I'll wait. Americans don't have the touch. That fraud claims he can teach us which wines to sell. 'I offer my expertise for free. I will mention you in my blog.' Enzo was beaming like a child being offered a yo-yo, showering him with thanks. Even offered him a free lunch!"

Tilde popped her head out of the kitchen. "A yo-yo won't get you anywhere with a kid these days. You need an iPhone." Tilde liked to correct her mother-in-law whenever she could. Elvira, possessive of her son, was often unkind to her. "Mantelli is a revered wine critic and will give Enzo some good suggestions," Tilde went on.

"*Pfui.* Enzo knows perfectly well what wines to offer. We taste each new vintage together and decide according to the price our clients can afford."

This meant, Nico knew, that Elvira decided. He pulled out a chair and sat next to her. "There's nothing wrong with hearing him out, is there?" She was at times unpleasant, but he couldn't help admiring her toughness. "And being mentioned in his blog has to be good for business, don't you think?"

Another snort in response. Elvira picked up the magazine on her lap and slipped on the glasses that hung from a chain on her neck. "I read from *Vino Veritas:* 'The 2015 ColleVerde Riserva offers hints of fruit, spices, scorched earth, espresso beans and herbs.'" She threw the magazine on the floor. "Scorched earth indeed! Who wants to taste spices or rosemary in their wine? Nonsense is what it is."

Nico picked up the magazine.

"Nico," Tilde called out. "You're needed in the kitchen."

"Throw that in the trash," Elvira commanded as he made his way to the kitchen.

"Coming." Nico took the magazine with him and, once out of sight, slipped it into his pocket.

Tilde was bent over the scarred marble counter, quickly shaping golf-ball-sized ground pork, egg, Parmigiano and ricotta meatballs in her hands. A long white apron covered her flowered dress. Her usual red cotton scarf enveloped thick chestnut brown hair.

Nico kissed one cheek. In Italy, it was usually both cheeks, but her other one was out of reach. "What can I do?"

"Take over for Enzo. Mantelli has him in his grips, and I need Alba back here."

Nico turned. Alba was wiping mushrooms clean at the other end of the counter. A sliced mushroom salad with apples and walnuts was one of the restaurants signature dishes. "Ciao, I didn't see you there."

"I'll kiss you later." Alba laughed. A pretty, round-faced woman in her early forties, she had never told Tilde her real name. She was Albanian, and so she said Alba was a logical choice. She also liked that the word meant 'dawn' in Italian. Coming here was for her the start of a new life. She'd fled the violence in Kosovo against ethnic Albanians and found her way to Gravigna. Her story was now a happy one. A good Italian man fell in love with her, and she with him. They married, and now she worked full-time at the restaurant, taking Stella, Tilde and Enzo's daughter's, place. She told everyone she met how blessed she felt.

Alba peered out the small window that looked out onto the terrace. "He's very handsome."

"And arrogant." Tilde rolled the meatballs with light fingers on a plate filled with flour, then dropped them gently in a hot sauté pan coated with oil. Once they achieved a nice brown crust, they would end up cooking in tomato sauce for thirty minutes. Eaten on their own or surrounded by buttered farro, they were heavenly. "Please, Nico, go out there and set the tables. Listen to what Mantelli is saying. I don't trust that man."

"You know him?"

"Just met him. Let's just say he gives me an odd feeling."

"Makes your nose itch?"

"Something like that."

Nico went back to the front room and filled a tray with plates, silverware and the clean cloth napkins Elvira folded every morning. She was now absorbed in a crossword puzzle in the *Settimana Enigmistica*. "Don't let Enzo make that man any promises," she muttered as he passed by.

"Of course," Nico said.

Mantelli was now sitting with Enzo at a corner table. Behind him under an overcast sky was the beautiful view of rows of vines spreading toward the horizon. In front of him was a half-empty glass of red wine and an open bottle. Enzo's own glass was empty.

Nico started setting the first table when he noticed a woman at the far end of the terrace fanning herself with a menu. He was struck by her beauty. She was dressed in tight white slacks and a spaghetti strap white top that hugged her torso. Long blond hair in a thick ponytail hung over one tanned shoulder. Huge sunglasses crowned her head. She looked very young, twenty at most.

Mantelli noticed Nico staring and waved him over. "Never

mind Loredana." His voice was surprisingly high and thin. "Come taste this excellent wine. Luca Verdini started his vineyard only ten years ago. Makes him a novice, but his 2015 and 2016 Riservas are jewels, and his regular wines are excellent. Verdini is getting a lot of attention these days, thanks to me. I spotted him first two years ago and wrote him up in my blog and *Vino Veritas*. You know it?"

"I'm afraid not," Nico said.

"Ah, you're American. Well, the Robert Parker people rated him a ninety-three. I give him a ninety-five. You must help me convince Enzo to stock it."

Mantelli poured two fingers' worth of the Riserva into Enzo's empty glass.

Enzo took a sip, swished the wine in his mouth and swallowed. "It is excellent," Enzo said, "but his wines are too expensive. We're not a three-Michelin-star restaurant. We serve simple food."

"Great wines will turn simple food into manna," Mantelli said. "Drinking great wines helps to better understand the land and its people. Besides, Verdini is eager to spread the word about his wines. I'm sure he'd be willing to give you a discount." The wine critic added a splash of wine to another glass on the table and held it out to Nico. "Please, try."

Nico took the glass and slowly rolled a sip around his tongue as he'd seen Enzo do. He felt like an idiot, but he didn't want to look like a country bumpkin in front of this man. He swallowed. The wine burned the back of his throat. Scorched earth indeed, not that he knew what that tasted like. "Excellent, thank you." He put the glass back down on the table. "I have to get back to work." Enzo shot him a glance. "I'll need your help too," Nico said, guessing Enzo had had enough of being lectured to.

Mantelli stood up, shook down his trousers and readjusted

his jacket. Underneath, he wore a blue and white striped T-shirt, the kind Venetian gondoliers favored. A tanned hand brushed back thick wavy white hair that fell below his ears. He was tall, with wide shoulders and slender hips. A swimmer's body. A face soaked by sun. A strong broad jaw, the straight nose Roman statues were known for, full lips, heavy black eyebrows that looked dyed, and black eyes to match. He was somewhere in his fifties, Nico thought. And yes, noticeably handsome.

"I have work to do too," Mantelli said. "I think I've given you enough guidance for now. Thank you for your offer of lunch. I'll take a rain check and leave the bottle, so you can enjoy the rest of the wine. You'll get hooked and buy, I know you will. And I'll see what I can do about a discount. Verdini owes me." He shook hands with Enzo. "Come, Loredana," Mantelli ordered without so much as a glance at her. He offered his hand to Nico, who shook it reluctantly.

"Not a nice man," Nico said as Mantelli and Loredana disappeared into the front room.

"Nice or not," Enzo said, "I'll have to order at least two cases." He filled his glass with the expensive wine and took a long sip.

"Because of his blog?"

"He can give our restaurant a big boost."

"Doesn't that feel a little like going along with blackmail?"

Enzo shrugged. "It's business. He probably gets a cut from Verdini and some of the others he praises in his magazine. I'll tell you one—"

Elvira's voice interrupted Enzo. She was giving Mantelli a piece of her mind about the car.

"You are correct, Signora," Mantelli answered in his high-pitched voice. "I am incorrigible, but please consider me a friend. Arrivederci."

If Elvira replied, Nico and Enzo didn't hear it.

Nico walked over to another table and set down the sheets of butcher paper the restaurant used for mats. "You were telling me something."

Enzo finished his glass and slapped the cork back in the bottle. "Your landlord, Aldo, I guess he doesn't play the game. Mantelli had some nasty things to say about Ferriello wines. 'Totally overrated.' 'Should be selling at half the price, if at all.' He said I should take Aldo's wines off my list."

"What did you say?"

"I said I trusted his judgment."

Nico looked up in surprise. "Ferriello wines are very good."

"I agree. Don't worry; I have no intention of dropping a single one of Aldo's wines from my list."

"I'm glad to hear that."

"Give me the tray, Nico. I'll finish setting the tables. I'm sure Tilde can use your help."

Nico handed over the tray and the mats. "Thanks. I have a food idea she might like."

"As long as it doesn't cost too much."

"Bread covered with scamorza and pancetta, then broiled. Sound good?"

"Yes, but Tilde's the judge."

"It will keep people drinking."

TWO

OneWag was busy smelling each of the flower pots Luciana displayed in front of her shop in the main piazza. Nico let him be, no longer worried that the dog would raise a leg.

A damp Luciana stood behind her work table and fanned her chest with the top of her dress. A small fan on the table blew hot air in her face. "We've reached thirty-seven degrees today. What is it in your temperature?"

"Ninety-eight, according to my cell phone."

"My flowers are wilting. If this keeps up, my fat will melt." Luciana laughed. A large woman with smiling hazel eyes, she pushed back thick hennaed curls that reminded Nico of chrysanthemums.

"What darlings of mine will you take from me today? The truck brought in some lovelies this morning. Most of them are in the refrigerator." She moved aside to let him see. "You always pick the ones I love best, but for Rita, they are yours."

"I appreciate it."

"She was a wonderful woman." Luciana had befriended Rita during their visits back to Gravigna, visits they had made whenever they could afford them.

Nico scanned the offerings. So many flowers: roses, daisies, poppies. Most he couldn't name. He found it difficult to choose flowers for Rita's grave. He felt ashamed that when she was alive, he'd only bought her flowers on her birthday and their wedding anniversary. She had bought her own almost weekly, inexpensive ones from the nearby deli. He had taken little notice of them then. He wanted to please her now.

"What do you think, Luciana? Roses or daisies?"

She pointed at a bright bunch of round-petaled flowers. "Anemones for Rita. She always dressed in lots of color." Luciana favored black.

"A big bouquet of anemones, then." As Nico reached for his wallet, OneWag lifted his head. Two seconds later, he took off. A car sped by. Nico rushed out the door, a yelp of pain already sounding in his imagination. His eyes caught the tail end of the car. His dog was on the other side of the road, safe in the middle of the piazza at Aldo's feet. He waited to be acknowledged, but Aldo took no notice. He was busy talking to Michele Mantelli.

On a bench behind the two men, the usual four old men—the "Bench Boys," as Perillo called them—chatted with each other. On the left side of the piazza, Carletta, the lavender-haired waitress, was setting up tables outside Da Gino in denim shorts and a sleeveless top.

Nico stayed, watching from the shop door. Aldo with his burgundy Ferriello T-shirt holding in his big stomach, stood in front of Michele Mantelli, who was wearing a now very wrinkled white linen suit. He could see that his friend's body was tense as it leaned in toward the wine critic, the back of his T-shirt dark with sweat. Mantelli seemed relaxed and cool, his hands stuffed in his pant pockets, head tilted to one side. Aldo was speaking in a tight, low voice. Nico couldn't catch the words, but understood they were angry ones. He noticed the Bench Boys had stopped chatting and were watching the two men. Carletta stood still, holding a plate against her chest like a shield, a hand over her mouth.

Should he go and say hello to Aldo to try to break the tension? But maybe what Aldo was saying needed to be said. An interruption might make things worse.

Nico stayed where he was and paid Luciana. She picked up two sheets of tissue paper to start wrapping the flowers.

"No need. I'm going directly to the cemetery."

Luciana gave her hennaed curls a vigorous shake and continued wrapping. "My clients walk out of my shop with properly wrapped bouquets." She tied a red bow around the tissue paper, handed the package to Nico and opened her arms to give him a hug, despite the heat.

OneWag's bark saved him. Luciana's giant bosom against his chest always made Nico uncomfortable. In this heat, it would have been terrible. He turned to look out on the piazza. The dog was pulling at Aldo's pant leg. Aldo had raised his arm, his hand clenched in a fist.

"I'll be right back." Nico handed the flowers to Luciana and ran over to where Aldo was standing. "Hey, Aldo."

His friend was shouting. "Leave my wife alone or I'll pulp that arrogant face of yours!"

"Cinzia is an old friend," Mantelli said calmly, "and I do what I want with my friends and with idiots like you. Read my next blog post. You'll see. No one will buy Ferriello wines again."

Aldo's fist landed on Mantelli's jaw, throwing him back against an empty bench. Aldo lunged toward him, fist ready to hit again. Nico grabbed his arm and pulled him back. "That's enough. You've made your point."

OneWag was barking himself hoarse.

Aldo struggled against Nico's hold, his eyes focused on Mantelli. "You can't ruin me, you charlatan. You can't tell a good wine from shit."

"Tell that to my thirty thousand followers."

"I'm warning you. Stay away from my wife!" Aldo's words came out wet with spit.

Mantelli leaned back on the bench as if he had always meant to sit there and slowly stroked his chin. "That's up to Cinzia, not you."

Aldo's hands curled into fists again. "Stay away or—"

"Or what? You'll kill me?"

"*YES!*" Aldo screamed.

Mantelli just laughed.

Nico caught hold of Aldo's shoulders before he could react and steered him away. "Where's your car? I'm taking you home."

"No!" Aldo tried to wrestle away from his grasp. "I want to see blood on that fucking bastard."

Nico held on tighter. "You've got to calm down, Aldo. I don't care what's going on between the two of you. You need to get ahold of yourself." He pushed Aldo toward his own Fiat. If he had to, he'd lock him in until he saw reason return to his friend's eyes. "Come on now, take some deep breaths. Just a few."

OneWag scampered behind them, tail held high. His owner had saved the day.

"Jesus, Nico, let go. I can walk away on my own. I'm not a child."

Nico held on. "That's news to me."

"Mr. Ferri," Carlotta called out. "Come inside. Have a glass of wine on the house."

"Thanks, Carlotta. Another time," Aldo yelled back. He raised his arms in the air. "Peace, Nico. See, I'm fine now." His face was no longer flushed.

"Good." Nico released his hold. "I'm still going to drive you home. I think the heat has gotten to you."

Aldo kept walking. Nico stayed beside him, aware that a small group of people, including Sandro and Jimmy, were standing outside the café, having witnessed the scene.

"My car is in front of the newspaper shop. I'll drive myself home." Aldo stopped to give Nico a pat on the shoulder. "Thank you. I appreciate what you did. If you hadn't stopped me, I think I really would've sent that bastard to the hospital."

"Always happy to help."

"The whole town will know about this by the evening."

"Not from me," Luciana said, leaning against her doorjamb and cradling Nico's anemones in her arms.

Aldo ignored her and walked to his Audi a hundred feet down the road, Nico trailing behind.

"If you ever need to talk," Nico offered as Aldo unlocked the car door, "I can be silent as a tomb, as you Italians say."

"It's an old story, not worth revisiting. That man may indeed have the power to ruin me. But again, thanks. See you around."

"Be careful, Aldo."

Nico watched the car drive away. If Mantelli had the power Enzo thought he did, Aldo might soon face an uphill battle to keep his vineyard open. Whatever it was, Cinzia was caught up in it. It was depressing, even terrifying, when power was in the wrong hands. Nico picked up OneWag and kissed the top of his head. "Thanks buddy. You're a good cop."

The dog gave him a lick on the chin.

Nico turned back to find Luciana walking toward him with the flowers. He took them from her. "Thank you."

"I worried you would forget after what Aldo did. Don't be upset with him. Being American, you probably don't understand Italian men's jealousy. It eats away at their brains. I saw Cinzia with that man the other night in Radda. I'm not saying they're more than friends, but Aldo wasn't with them."

Nico frowned. He didn't like what he was hearing. "What are you implying, Luciana?"

"Don't look at me that way. I'm not a gossip, and I'm not implying anything. I'm trying to explain how an Italian husband catching his wife chatting with another man could make him lose his reason for a few minutes."

"I see," Nico said, not totally convinced. He had worked enough cases in New York to know that jealousy could eat at the brains of American men and women too. Murders were commonplace. "I'd better get these to Rita."

"Yes, it's late. The cemetery closes at six." Luciana reached out to hug him. This time, Nico didn't mind. He had both OneWag and the flowers against his chest.

ON HIS WAY HOME from the cemetery, Nico stopped by the Ferriello office to check on Aldo. He parked the car and let out OneWag, who immediately ran in the opposite direction, to the welcome center. The double doors were wide open, all the lights on. That meant a tour group was coming for a simple Tuscan meal and Ferriello's excellent wines, followed by a talk from Aldo about winemaking. It was an idea Cinzia had come up with after a year of poor sales. It turned out to be very successful. Tonight, Nico hoped, explaining the process of winemaking to a roomful of wide-eyed tourists would distract Aldo from the afternoon's events.

Nico walked into the large, welcoming space with its beamed ceiling, terracotta-tiled floor and wide terrace bordered by red geraniums. "Ciao, Nico," Cinzia said without looking up. Aldo's wife, a pretty, petite woman just past forty, with short brown hair hugging her scalp like a cap, showed off her figure in tight white slacks and the company's burgundy T-shirt with the orange Ferriello logo. "No reason not to please the eye as well as the palate," she had once said after catching a guest ogling her.

In one swift motion, she pulled out the cork of a Ferriello Riserva wine bottle, top of the line. Behind her, several Chianti Classico bottles were lined up on the counter, already open. Arben, a short, muscular Muslim man from Albania also in jeans and the Ferriello T-shirt—not quite as arresting on him—raised a hand in greeting and continued to place chairs behind two long oak tables. He had worked at the vineyard for over twenty years. As a foreigner, he had once risked his position by challenging a Tuscan fellow worker's honesty. When he was proven right, he became Aldo's right-hand man. Thanks to his curiosity, he had also been instrumental in solving a murder last year.

"Buonasera to you both," Nico said, giving Cinzia a two-cheeked kiss.

"Buying a bottle of Riserva tonight will get you dinner with eighteen Americans," Arben said. Eighteen was a small group; they usually had a busload of thirty or more from Florence or Siena. "There might even be a pretty woman in the lot. If you leave with her, the bottle's on me."

Nico laughed. He liked Arben and his easygoing manner. "Thank you, but I've got plenty of Ferriello wines. Tonight I've been relieved of restaurant duty, so I'm staying home to test out a new idea. Where's Aldo?"

"He's with our Chinese distributor, who just flew in," Cinzia said. "He's taking him to eat at Il Falco outside Castellina."

"I don't know the place."

"All I know is, it's aptly named. Their prices prey on your wallet."

"And Aldo is okay?"

Cinzia looked up with puzzled expression. "Why shouldn't he be?"

So Aldo had said nothing to his wife. "He looked a bit tired when I saw him today."

"We all are."

"Very true. Ciao. I hope you sell lots of cases."

"May God hear you," Cinzia and Arben said in chorus.

NICO SAT ON HIS balcony with a glass of whiskey on the rocks and a late-night cigarette. He should be at peace. He'd just eaten two delicious pancetta and scamorza toasts. His vegetable garden was watered. OneWag, fed and walked, was curled up at his feet. The three swallows that had made his balcony roof a nesting home were asleep. All in all it had been a good day, aside from the Aldo-Mantelli incident in the piazza. Did Mantelli truly have the power to bankrupt Aldo? And why did he want to? What was Cinzia and Mantelli's relationship? Friends, ex-lovers, current lovers? If Mantelli ruined Aldo's business, he would ruin Cinzia too. None of it made sense, and it was none of his business, but Nico felt for Aldo.

It took him a minute to hear the car. The American tourists had come and gone by now. This had to be Aldo. He leaned over the balcony to see better, to wave to him. A silly way of conveying, "Buck up, Aldo." But the car wasn't headed home to the vineyard. Its headlights were going up the hill road, which met the main road at the top. For a second, the streetlight shone on a blue Mini Morris, turning toward town. Cinzia's car.

Nico looked at his watch, an old work habit: 10:24 P.M. Where was she going? It could only be to pick up a husband too drunk to drive.

Nico put out his cigarette, finished the few drops left in his drink and stood up. "Come on, time for bed."

OneWag beat him to it.

THREE

On Wednesday, Maresciallo Perillo walked up to his one-bedroom apartment above the station. He was looking forward to lunch. Ivana, his wife, had announced the menu at breakfast, as she did every morning—a ritual she had picked up from her mother, who had used the menu as a way to lure Ivana's father home each night. Perillo had no desire to wander from his household, but he did like knowing what Ivana was preparing. It helped boost his spirits when work was chaotic. Today's menu was arancini—fried rice balls stuffed with ground meat, tomato sauce and mozzarella—accompanied by sautéed escarole with capers, anchovies and olives, a Neapolitan specialty. For dessert, zabaglione with strawberries.

Perillo went to the kitchen, a large, pleasant room with its one lace-curtained window overlooking a magnolia tree at the back of the barracks. Small framed prints of flowers hung on one white wall. A blue tablecloth covered the square table. Ivana was lifting the arancini from the oil with a slotted spoon and draining them on a paper towel. She was a short, plump, forty-one-year-old woman with a pretty doll-like face that had instantly won over Perillo. He first saw her at the fish market in Naples, selling the catch her father had brought in that morning. He was a brigadiere then, his station not far from the market. He became a daily fish buyer until the morning Ivana accepted his invitation to go on a walk together. Their walks were followed by movies, shared ice cream, then kisses. Meetings kept hidden from her parents, who wanted better than a brigadiere of the carabinieri for their daughter. Nine years later, he became maresciallo, and Ivana's parents bowed to the inevitable. With marriage came the joy of a shared bed. Nineteen years later, he found his passion had lowered to a comfortable simmer. He still wished they had had children, but Ivana had been adamant, having lost her mother at fourteen. She had already raised five younger siblings, three brothers and two sisters in a household that barely scraped by. What she wanted from marriage was peace.

"Here I am," Perillo gave his wife a light kiss on her lips.

Ivana looked surprised. "You're in a good mood."

"All is quiet downstairs." He sat down at the kitchen table.

"No more encounters with the wine critic, then."

"None." He unfolded his napkin on his lap and poured himself half a glass of red wine. "Do you really think he is handsome?"

"Very." She dropped two arancini on his plate and placed the bowl of escarole on the table.

"What about me?"

Ivana served herself and sat down. "You're my husband, and I love you. You don't need to be handsome."

"Well, that makes me feel just wonderful." Sometimes he wished his wife weren't so honest.

Ivana leaned over and gave him a peck on the cheek. "Stop being silly and eat."

Perillo tasted his first arancino, closing his eyes to help him concentrate on the flavors. "Holy heaven, you have the Midas touch in the kitchen."

"That's why you married me." During their long courtship, she would leave carefully wrapped bundles of food for him at the carabinieri station. She was cooking for the poor, she'd told her father.

"Your cooking was only one of the reasons." The food bundles had made him the butt of jokes at the barracks until he began to share her wonderful food.

He blew her a kiss. As he put the rest of the rice ball in his mouth, the first notes of "O Sole Mio" rang out.

Ivana didn't bother to sigh. She was by now used to their meals being interrupted. She only hoped it would be a brief interruption. Rice balls just didn't taste the same reheated.

Perillo swiped his finger across his cell phone.

AT SOTTO IL FICO, the terrace was full of lunch guests despite the heat. Enzo and Alba had taken over Nico's waiter duties. Elvira greeted clients with a smile and offered menus as they passed her armchair on the way out to the terrace. Nico was happily busy in the kitchen, despite the heat from the oven. Tilde had approved his scamorza toasts idea only if he made them. Small cubes of pancetta were sizzling in a thin layer of oil beside piles of scamorza slices in a bowl. Nico was cutting bread when Alba popped her head in.

"Maresciallo Perillo wants to know if you can talk to him."

"I can't now. I'll call him later."

Orders for the toast kept coming in, and Tilde had to jump in and help. "Tomorrow, I'll get Alba to prepare them in the morning," she said. "Then we can just toast them as the orders come in."

"I'll be here early, then."

"No, Nico. Alba gets paid. You don't."

It was a sore point between them. This year, Tilde said there was enough money to pay him; she insisted he accept. He said no. He didn't need it, nor did he want it. Not from them. They were family. He explained to Tilde that if she paid him, his work would become a duty. He wanted it to remain fun, and to have the freedom to take the occasional day off. Tilde and Enzo reluctantly accepted. Elvira declared him a "sensible man." Luckily, he didn't need their money. He had his NYPD pension and the life insurance money Rita hadn't told him about until she was dying.

"Any news from Stella?" he asked. Tilde and Enzo's daughter was working as a guard at the Duomo Museum in Florence.

"She's coming home. They gave her the weekend off. She said she has news."

"What news?"

"She won't tell me. I suppose we'll just have to wait."

At 3:10, the last toast left the kitchen. Tilde took out a clean dishcloth, wet it under the faucet and wiped Nico's face. "Thank you and keep the ideas coming. I promise I won't insist you cook them all."

"That's good to hear." Nico took off his apron and the cap Tilde had insisted he wear. "I'm off now. See you tonight."

"You don't have to come."

"Of course I do. The place would fall apart without me."

Tilde laughed.

After a quick espresso at the bar with Enzo, Nico walked out of the restaurant. The street was empty. Shutters were closed to protect against the heat. It was also nap time. He looked forward to a long shower. Nico whistled for OneWag, who came running down the church steps. The dog planted his front paws on Nico's knees, reaching his maximum height.

"Good to see you're still in one piece." OneWag was still a street dog at heart. He had instantly let Nico know how he felt about being left alone at home by shredding both bed pillows and chewing a large hole in one of Nico's newest running shoes. Nico ceded defeat, and now whenever he was working, he let the dog wander the streets of the town. OneWag had also refused the leash. However, in a bout of generosity toward the man who'd taken him in, he had accepted a collar with an ID medallion.

Nico picked the dog up and reached for his cell phone.

"Sorry. I was stuck making toast until now."

"Have you got time to look at something?"

"Now? I was thinking of taking a nice long shower."

"I think you will find this interesting." Perillo sounded almost smug.

Something was up. His shower would have to wait. "Are you at the station?"

"No. Drive to the north end of Greve and take the road up to Montefioralle. It'll be on your left. It's a medieval hamlet above Greve."

"I've been there. It's very pretty, and supposedly the birthplace of Amerigo Vespucci."

"I'd emphasize 'supposedly.' You'll find me about five kilometers before the hamlet."

Nico's Fiat 500 struggled up the steep, narrow road with its many S curves. Almost all Chianti roads swerved either uphill or downhill. As Nico entered yet another turn, a small opening in the wall of trees that edged the road revealed what looked like a boom hovering in the air. Was he headed to a construction site?

After another curve, the left edge of the road opened up, the trees gone. Fifty meters in, a barrier shut off that side of the road. A carabiniere waved him down. "It's only one way for the next two kilometers, Signore. You can go, but take it slowly. No stopping."

Nico stuck his head out. "Nico Doyle." He knew Vince, one of Perillo's best men. He never stopped eating, saying he needed to keep his blood pressure up. "Maresciallo Perillo is expecting me."

Vince moved in closer. "Ah, excuse me, Signor Doyle. I didn't recognize you. Your windshield could use a little cleaning."

"Very true." Though the dirty windshield hadn't prevented him from seeing the crane truck with its boom lowered, the tow truck next to it and the ambulance with its back doors wide open. "Where should I park?"

"Just ahead, next to the Alfa. Close to the edge, though. You'll find the maresciallo further up. Terrible accident."

Nico parked the car and peered at the sheer drop just inches from the edge of the road. He slid over to the passenger seat to get out, a knot forming in his stomach. Someone had met a bad end down there. Someone he knew. Why else would Perillo call him here?

"Don't go far," Nico said to OneWag and hurried to where Perillo was standing near the crane. He was in his usual jeans, suede boots, and a gray shirt.

"Ah, Nico, there you are." Behind him, Daniele Donato, Perillo's brigadiere, acknowledged Nico with a nod. He looked upset, either because of the heat or because, after only two years on the job, he hadn't developed the thick skin necessary to deal with death.

Nico nodded back. "Who is it?"

"We don't know for sure yet. We're having great difficulties getting the passenger out in one piece. The top of the car has smashed him in."

Nico looked down the slope. The overturned car had plunged at least sixty feet down a slope covered in big sharp rocks, thin trees, bushes. Its descent was marked by broken branches, overturned rocks. It must have been going at an incredible speed. The drop was so steep, four men and two stretchers had needed the help of ropes latched onto the crane to lower them down.

"How many in the car?" Nico asked.

"Only one, we think."

"Let's hope so."

Two men were hooking the back fender of the car to the crane's boom. A man shouted up to the crane driver, and slowly the rear of the car rose. A big car, bigger than any his friends drove. Nico felt the knot in his stomach loosen. He looked back to check on his dog. OneWag was close, sniffing the spot where the car had gone over.

"Why did you want me here?"

"There's a very strong probability it's someone you know," Perillo said. "I thought you'd be interested."

"Stop playing games, Perillo," Nico said. Though his friend, the man could be annoyingly cagey at times.

"You're right, I am playing games. In my defense, I'll say that everyone has their own way of dealing with gruesome incidents. I also forget that you're used to American directness. I will comply. Dino, who has been down there for two hours with the emergency service and was wise enough to take his cell phone with him, informed me he found the car's hood ornament on his way down. A sleek metal Jaguar. Now that they've lifted the car, you can see its color."

Nico saw a strip of white metal. "Mantelli?"

"He didn't strike me as having the generosity of spirit to lend his car to someone else, so yes, I would say the person in the car is Mantelli. Unless another white Jaguar happened to be racing by and lost control. I would also say the man is dead. But until we've extracted him, I cannot be certain."

"Whoever it is, he must have been drunk," Daniele said, wiping his forehead with a handkerchief. There was no shade where they stood.

Perillo gave his brigadiere a disapproving look. Daniele quickly stuffed his handkerchief in his pocket and pulled at his shirt. Perillo's shirt was perfectly dry. He seemed not to suffer in the heat.

"What makes you say so?" Nico asked to give Daniele back his moment. He'd already noticed the swerving tire tracks.

Daniele pointed to the road leading up to where the car flew off the edge. "Those tracks. I took photographs."

"Daniele is indispensable. An expert in computers and photography," Perillo said.

Daniele blushed, unsure if he was being complimented or made fun of. The Daniele Bloom, as Perillo called it, happened often.

"I meant it, Dani." Perillo said.

The bloom intensified.

Perillo winked at Nico. "Anyway, whether alcohol, aneurism, stroke or heart attack, the autopsy will tell us."

OneWag barked. Below, someone had begun shouting. The dog and the three men leaned over to look. Dino raised his arm, index finger up.

"Just one victim," Perillo said. "May the sky be praised." Daniele crossed himself.

The body was slowly being lifted out of the car. Nico saw legs dressed in white trousers. What came next was covered in blood. He turned away. "I still don't understand why you wanted me here."

"Because yesterday, from what I heard, you were a good friend to Aldo. You can be the first one to give him the good news."

"So you were sure it was Mantelli when you called me?"

"Yes, but as a man who upholds the law, I'm supposed to wait for concrete evidence. I have always preferred intuition and a quick assessment of the scene, which luckily has not made my superiors demand my immediate retirement."

Nico forced himself not to show surprise. Perillo had just made an unsubtle reference to how Nico had lost his job as a homicide detective back in New York, but this wasn't the time to ask him how he knew. "I saw Mantelli yesterday at Sotto Il Fico. He had a young woman with him." Her sad, beautiful face came back to Nico. Would Mantelli's death bring more sadness or relief for her?

"Her name?"

"Loredana. I don't know the last name. She's much younger than Mantelli."

"He's divorcing his wife," Daniele said, always happy to impart news the maresciallo might not know. "It's making all the women's magazines."

Perillo turned to look at the young man he was quite fond of and loved to tease. "You read women's magazines?"

Daniele's cheeks reddened, as expected. "My mother does. I mentioned I'd met Mantelli at the station when I called her last night. She said he deserves to be locked up for good. She followed the whole story and thinks he's a cruel monster."

Perillo looked down at Mantelli, strapped to the gurney slowly making its way up the ravine. "He got what he deserved, then." He was being callous, but he couldn't control the dislike he had for this man, even now that he was dead. Mantelli's arrogance and sense of entitlement made him sick to his stomach. He was good at spotting people like this just by looking at them. They had a different way of walking, as if the air parted before them. When he'd been a kid living on the streets of Pozzuoli, his fingers would start itching as soon as he spotted them. He'd been an expert at unloading whatever was in their pockets.

Perillo turned to Nico. "Thanks for coming up here. Go take your shower, and don't forget to talk to Aldo."

"I won't." Nico started walking back to his car with OneWag at his heels.

"I will be at your place for dinner tomorrow night," Perillo called out.

Nico turned his head around. "Good. Bring Daniele and your wife."

"Thank you," Daniele said, hoping Nico heard him. As a child, he hadn't been allowed to be loud, and at twenty, he still found it difficult.

"My wife won't give you any of her recipes."

"I won't ask," Nico answered, laughing. "I just want you to stop hiding her."

THE FERRIELLO OFFICE WAS empty. Nico walked next door. Most of the space was a vast open work area where the bottles were labeled and packaged. All the wine was made below ground, left to ripen in steel casks and stored in wooden barrels for however long each wine needed.

Nico found Arben lifting a pallet of wine cases with a forklift. "Hi, Arben. Where is Aldo?"

"He's downstairs with the Chinese wine distributor, checking on the 2017 vintage."

The Mantelli news would have to wait. "When you see him, please tell him I need to talk to him. I'll be home for another hour, or he can call me at Sotto Il Fico after six." It would be useless to call his cell phone. There was no reception below ground.

"It will be done," Arben said with a wave.

As Nico got in the car, his phone pinged. The text read: IT'S MANTELLI.

"Wait," Cinzia called out as Nico was turning the car around. She was coming from her and Aldo's home, a small apricot-colored building that dated back to the 1850s. Practically new in Italy, Nico had thought when he'd found out the date.

Nico and OneWag got out of the car. "Ciao, Cinzia." The dog greeted her with his single wag, then sat, looking up at her expectantly. She was wearing an apron and smelled of sausages and beans and a hint of sage.

"Oh, Nico, I can't thank you enough. Aldo told me what happened. You're a wonderful friend and a lifesaver. Aldo has gone crazy for no reason at all."

"Mantelli threatened to ruin him."

"Michele didn't mean it. It was just a nasty joke. He's an old friend from my university days in Rome and a bit jealous of our marriage. Come back for dinner tonight. Please."

If Mantelli was a friend, she had a right to know. "Cinzia, I'm sorry—"

"I'm offering rigatoni with sausages and mushrooms. You'll like it."

"I'm sorry to tell you this, but Mantelli is dead."

Her face lost all expression, as if an eraser had been rubbed over it. "No, he isn't," she said. "It's not possible."

"I'm afraid he is. Perillo just confirmed it."

She didn't even blink. "How?" she asked.

"He lost control of his car on the road from Montefioralle to Greve and plunged down a ravine."

"Was he alone?"

"Yes. I was at the scene."

Her lower lip trembled. "You saw him?"

"Not enough to recognize him."

"Perillo is sure?"

"Yes."

It took her a few seconds to form the next phrase. A soft release of breath, followed by, "An accident, then."

"No reason to think it was anything but an accident."

Her face came to life. "No reason at all. How awful. He was an excellent driver, but always a speed demon."

"Perillo wants me to tell Aldo."

She let out a loud sigh. "That means he knows about yesterday's stupid fight. Of course. The whole town knows. Well, it's over with now. Don't worry, I'll tell Aldo. Your dinner invitation still stands."

"I'm on restaurant duty tonight."

"Then come afterward for cantucci and our sweet wine. Or a brandy. Please." Her eyes were brimming with tears. *Relief or sadness?* Nico wondered.

"Thank you. I'll try to come by if it's not too late. I'll let you know."

VINCE WAS SITTING AT the front desk when Perillo and Daniele walked into the Greve carabinieri station. "Was your hunch right?" he asked, as he slipped his focaccia sandwich into a drawer.

"Michele Mantelli is now on his way to the medical examiner in Florence." Perillo saw a crumb nestled at the corner of Vince's lips. "What is it this time? Let me guess: boar salame and provolone. Am I correct again?"

Vince's shoulders slumped. "Yes. How do you do it?"

Perillo gave his nose a couple of taps and proceeded down the corridor to his office.

Daniele had gone ahead and was already clicking at the keys of his computer. In the corner, a large fan whipped hot air.

"Good, Dani," Perillo said, seeing the brigadiere at his favorite post. "You know what I need." He went to the corner and moved the fan closer to Dani. "Mantelli's wife's telephone number and any other relatives he may have, in case she refuses to identify him."

"Her name's Diane Severson," Daniele said. "It says here she's American, from Boston. She's a successful textile designer, much loved by Giorgio Armani, Prada and the other Italian fashion greats. They have a fifteen-year old son, Paolo, whom Mantelli falsely tried to claim isn't his." Daniele wiped his forehead with his hand and continued to read. "Signora Severson still lives in the Milan villa she shared with her husband in Via Poma. According to her lawyer, Mantelli does not."

"Never mind. Where are you getting this stuff from?"

"An article in *La Voce della Donna*, the magazine my mother always reads. It's full of helpful information." He turned to look at his boss and saw the disbelief on his face. "Accurate information."

Perillo shook his head. He'd often been tempted to buy Daniele a pair of symbolic scissors to help him cut his mother's apron strings. What always stopped him was that his own mother had preferred men to her son. He wondered if he was just jealous.

"Does this magazine have Signora Severson's phone number, then?"

Daniele jotted something down on a sticky notepad, peeled

the sheet off and walked over to Perillo's desk. "The number is on her website. She works from home."

Perillo snapped it from him and reached for the house phone. Daniele's perplexed expression stopped him. "What?"

"You might want to know something about Signora Severson before giving her the news." Daniele straightened his back to give himself courage. "You can be, if you will forgive me, Maresciallo, a bit blunt in conveying delicate information."

Daniele was right. Anxiety made Perillo this way. He wanted the bad news quickly over with. "Perhaps I am at times. This is certainly delicate information, although I suspect this signora will jump for joy. She gets to keep it all." Perillo lifted the receiver.

"Except the husband, whom she may still love."

"Of course." Daniele Donato, Venetian brigadiere, was romantic to a fault, but also intelligent and dedicated. Perillo was lucky to have him.

Perillo dialed the number in Milan Daniele had given him. A woman's heavily accented voice answered. He slowly explained who he was and asked for Signora Severson.

"No here. Call cellular." She rattled off a number Perillo didn't catch.

"Signora, one moment please." He handed the phone over to Daniele, who asked for the phone number in soft Italian. Perillo watched him write it down quickly.

"Good job, Dani."

"Our next door neighbors in Venice are from the Philippines."

"What would I do without you?" As he dialed the number, Perillo made sure not to look at his brigadiere's face to save the young man embarrassment.

"Hello. Am I speaking to Signora Severson, the wife of Michele Mantelli?"

"Soon to be ex-wife," she said lightly, and without a hint of an accent, to Perillo's great relief. "Who is this?"

Perillo introduced himself.

"If this is about Michele and his damn car, it's no longer my business; he's made sure of that. If he's parked it in some impossible place, I suggest you tow it and dump it somewhere he'll never find."

"That is not the reason I called, Signora. I'm afraid I have sad news." Perillo told her about the accident, then waited for her to say something. When nothing came but the sound of her breath, he added, "He will be autopsied in Florence to ascertain what caused the accident. I'm afraid I don't know how long that will take. We do need positive identification. Are you in Milan?"

"No, I'm in Castellina at the Squarcialupi Hotel. Do I have to go to Florence to identify him?"

"I'm afraid so."

"I was hoping a photograph would be enough."

"If you come to the Greve station, we can show you a photograph of his face, but it won't be enough." Surprisingly, there had been little damage to the handsome face. The rest of Mantelli was a mangled mess.

"Thank you, Maresciallo. I have no wish to see him in the flesh, even if he's dead, but I will comply." Her voice was soft and steady. She could have been talking about rejecting a fabric. "Where do I have to go?"

"His body is at the Legal-Medical Institute at the University of Florence. If you have time, there are a few questions I need to ask you, relating to the accident. When you feel up to it, of course."

"Tomorrow morning. I just need some time to process this." There was no break in her voice. If she needed to grieve or exult, he couldn't tell from her voice.

"Is your son with you?"

"No, I'm glad to say. He's in Australia, scuba diving with friends. I won't ruin his vacation. He would feel duty-bound to come back. What for? We were no longer a family of three.

Buonasera, Maresciallo. I'll be there tomorrow morning at nine."
She clicked off.

Perillo sat back in his chair. Signora Severson had taken the
delicate information very well. He should be relieved, and yet her
calm bothered him.

"What questions are you going to ask her?" Daniele asked.

"I'll think of something. Her response to her husband's death
has piqued my curiosity. Now I want to meet her."

Behind Perillo's back, Daniele shook his head in disbelief.
Despite his formidable skill set, the maresciallo could have a poor
ear for people's feelings.

"I think it's time for an espresso, Dani." And a cigarette.
"Coming?"

Daniele stood up and reached for his jacket. The café next
door was air-conditioned. "Yes, Maresciallo."

"Leave the jacket, and it's Salvatore. On my birth certificate,
the name Maresciallo does not appear."

"Yes, Salvatore." Daniele took the jacket with him. He didn't
want to catch a cold.

VINCE AT THE FRONT desk held up a receiver when Perillo and
Daniele came back from their coffee break. "The substitute pros-
ecutor just called. I told him you were out on an emergency call.
He wants you to call him back. He says it's urgent."

"Which prosecutor?" Perillo asked, sensing that the good
feeling that the espresso and cigarette had given him wasn't going
to last long. All prosecutors enjoyed making his work difficult.

Vince nodded solemnly. "Him."

"Della Langhe!" The worst of them all. An arrogant aristo-
crat who looked down on anyone born south of Florence. "What
in the devil does he want?" Della Langhe had driven him crazy
during last year's murder case.

"He hung up before I could ask."

"Do you want me to call him?" Daniele asked, always wanting to help ward off his boss's bad moods. "You're still taking care of that emergency."

Perillo's dark look vanished. "And should he ask what emergency?"

"You're chasing a thief." Although he hated lies, sometimes small ones were necessary for the good of the station.

"Excellent." Perillo walked out of the station for a second cigarette.

"Who am I speaking with?" Della Langhe asked on the other end of the phone.

Daniele introduced himself.

"Ah, yes, the Venetian brigadiere. You come from a very beautiful city. I don't know why you would want to leave it. You are a good man, I hear from my assistant."

Daniele was grateful Della Langhe couldn't see the red glow on his face. "Thank you. Barbara is too kind." She really was wonderful. Last year, Perillo had tried desperately to deal only with her.

"I'm pleased to be speaking with you," Della Langhe said. "Now, to the urgent matters of Michele Mantelli's tragic death."

"Very sad, indeed." How did he find out so quickly, Daniele wondered?

"His wife is a very good friend of my wife's, and she's concerned how much time will lapse before the results of the autopsy come out. The longer it takes, the more tongues will wag. Mantelli and Diane were going through a bitter divorce. Most people are stupid and will think the unthinkable about Diane. She's a very successful woman, a star in fashion. People, as I am certain you know even at your young age, are envious. I want the possibility of any ugly rumors squashed immediately."

"That she killed him?"

"Exactly."

"But it was an accident."

"Of course, but unkind people will raise doubts after all the press their divorce received. I've ordered the medical examiner to move Mantelli's autopsy to the top of the list. We could know the results as quickly as tomorrow. I want Perillo—and you, of course—to handle this accident with efficiency and velvet gloves. And again, you are to end any rumors at once. I will not have my wife's friend's reputation sullied."

"We will do our best."

"I'm certain you will, young man." Della Langhe clicked off.

Daniele put down the phone. He had no idea how one stopped rumors from spreading. At least they would have the autopsy results quickly and could move on to other problems.

A smell of cigarettes preceded his boss. "What did he want?" Perillo asked as he walked in.

Daniele took a step back. "We might get the autopsy results by tomorrow. Signora Severson is his wife's friend."

Perillo shook his head and sat down at his desk. "What is so urgent about that? The members of that crowd are always kissing each other's asses."

"Even though he knows it was an accident, he wants us to stop any rumors that suggest Signora Severson killed him."

Perillo slapped his forehead. "Holy heaven and all the saints! That's a first."

FOUR

Thursday morning brought another hot, cloudless day. Because of the relentless sun, Nico had started watering the vegetable garden at night. After his usual breakfast with Gogol, Nico had rushed home and changed into gardening clothes to prepare another row at the far end of the garden for zucchini and eggplants. He hammered a wooden stake at each end and tied a rope from one to the other to form a straight line. The rest of the garden was doing well. The escarole was ready to pick, along with some broccoli and spinach. It was too soon for the tomatoes, although thanks to the heat, they were growing quickly. As Nico worked, OneWag watched from a corner bush covered in red roses. A sputtering noise made him turn toward the dirt road that led to the house. Two seconds later the dog ran toward the noise, barking a greeting.

Nico looked up.

The sputtering noise stopped, and Nelli appeared from behind a corner of the house with OneWag in her arms, nuzzling her face. "Ciao, Nico. I hope I'm not disturbing."

Nico stood up quickly, embarrassed by his appearance: a torn T-shirt, plus shorts that were overdue for a wash and showed off wrinkled knees. "No. I was just—" He bent down to wipe the dirt from his knees. "Getting ready to plant some more vegetables."

His embarrassment made Nelli smile. Maybe she did mean something to him after all. She hoped so. During the winter, she had invited him to dinner at her home. The evening had been awkward, but luckily, OneWag had made up for Nico's . . . what was it? Embarrassment? Fear that she expected more than he could give? Well, she didn't expect more. That was too demanding. She did hope for more, though. After that dinner, she had backed off, meeting him casually at the café to exchange daily news. She talked about running the art center, the exhibitions of local talent, her own paintings, her work at a neighboring vineyard, and in turn, Nico would talk about the restaurant, his dog, the crazy state of Italian politics. Sometimes he would mention his life back in America, rarely mentioning Rita, his late wife.

"You should show off your knees more. They're cute." All right, so she was flirting a bit. No harm in it.

Nico wiped his hands on his shorts and came out of the garden. He had first noticed Nelli last September at Jimmy and Sandro's café and had been drawn in by her serene face, the long graying blond braid hanging down her back, her paint-splattered clothes. Later she had opened up to him, giving him information that had helped solve the murder case.

"I didn't know you were such a good liar."

Nelli put down OneWag, who stayed by her feet. "It got you out of the garden, didn't it?"

He looked at her pale-blue teasing eyes and felt the usual flutter in his stomach. "It's good to see you. You haven't been at Bar All'Angolo lately."

"You only go there in the morning. I usually go after lunch." Seeing less of Nico had allowed her to make peace with only friendship between them. "How's Gogol?"

"Still in his overcoat, still cologned to the maximum, but he seems happy."

"Tourist season is starting. He'll soon have an audience for his Dante quotes. I really owe him a visit. I've been busy painting for another exhibit." Nelli was one of two people Gogol accepted as a good friend. Nico was the other. "Go back to your garden. We can talk while you work."

"Sure." He walked back and picked up a spade. Nelli watched from outside the wooden fence he had finally put up in the winter. "Anything specific on your mind?" He was being rude, but he was bad at small talk and worse at anything personal.

"I heard you were at the site where Mantelli died."

"I was. Who told you that?"

"Zio Peppino. He works for Mantelli at his villa, mostly takes care of the garden. He's not really my uncle, just a good friend of my father's, but I grew up calling him Zio. He's the one who called it in to the Greve station."

"He saw it happen?"

"No. He saw Mantelli leave home around nine in the morning. He wasn't walking a straight line. Maybe Mantelli was an alcoholic. Anyway, Zio Peppino didn't see the smashed-up Jaguar until just after one. He was on his way to the Coop in Greve."

"How did he know I was at the site of the accident?"

"You were involved in a murder case last year. It put you on the map for all of Gravigna's wagging tongues. Someone saw you. Zio Peppino found out and knows we're friends, so he told me."

Nico continued digging up earth, following the rope's straight line. He was picking up a comfortable rhythm. Either the ground was surprisingly soft, or he was getting stronger in his old age. Working made Nelli's presence easier. Nico would be fifty-nine in October. Nelli looked like she was somewhere in her early forties. Almost two decades younger.

"The car was pretty far down," he said. "The only way you could see it was if you stood at the edge of the road."

"Zio Peppino only saw it because he needed to pee. Maybe if someone had seen the car earlier, Mantelli would still be alive."

"I doubt it, Nelli." Nico straightened up. The row was tilled. He'd wait to put the plants in tomorrow. His back was beginning to ache. Nico wiped his hands on his shorts again. "How about a coffee?"

Nelli put on a smile. She would love to sit with him on the balcony, which she could see from where she stood. To sit and share something, even just a glass of water, but it would only feed the dreams she was trying hard to set aside. Nico was still very much married to Rita. "Thank you, but I have to get back to the studio."

To his surprise, Nico found himself disappointed. "Well, I guess I'd better get cleaned up. I'm due at the restaurant in an hour. You should come eat there one night. As my guest."

Nelli's smile was real this time. "Yes, I'd like that." She raised her hand. "See you."

"Yes, soon."

OneWag followed Nelli to her Vespa and watched her sputter away. These two-legged animals made no sense.

BOTH PERILLO AND DANIELE stood up when Diane Severson walked into the office. "Buongiorno," they said in unison. Diane smiled in response.

Perillo studied her as she approached. She had a model's height and thinness and wore wide slacks, the navy fabric covered in bold strokes of red, with a boat-necked white knit top. She took long, graceful steps toward his desk.

If she was a friend of Prosecutor Della Langhe's wife, he needed to tread softly, as Daniele had reminded him earlier. To his surprise, Diane Severson had a plain, wide face, with a strong jaw and equally strong cheekbones. Full lips and big, light-brown eyes that didn't look as if they had shed a tear. No makeup. Pale-blond straight hair cut at a sloping angle just above her shoulder. Long bangs covered half her high forehead. Her only jewelry was a thick silver coil on her left thumb. He'd thought Mantelli would have only married a beauty.

They shook hands. Hers was cool despite the heat.

She turned to Daniele, her hand still outstretched. "And you are?"

He stood to attention with instantly red cheeks. "Brigadiere Daniele Donato, Signora."

"Diane, please." She shook his hand and folded herself into the chair in front of Perillo's desk. "It's a pleasure to meet you both, although the reason is not a pleasure. I've done as you asked and identified my husband. They only showed me his face. He'd be pleased to know he still looks good." She sat very straight, her long hands folded in her lap. "Perhaps you expect me to be, if not happy, at least relieved that Michele is dead. I admit it will make my life simpler." From the back end of the room, the large fan oscillated, making her hair sway to its rhythm.

"I can move that," Perillo offered.

She smiled. "No need."

"I have to thank you for letting Prosecutor Della Langhe and his wife know about your husband's fatal accident."

"I actually called Signora Della Langhe to explain why I couldn't bring the fabric samples she wanted. Our appointment with her decorator was this morning in Florence. She's redoing her living room. Why are you thanking me?"

"We will get the results of the autopsy much more quickly now. Perhaps even this afternoon."

"I see. Can I see the photograph of my husband?"

"Oh, I'm sorry. Of course. Daniele?"

Daniele handed over the five-by-six he had printed out last night. He had Photoshopped it to remove the blood that had flowed from the back of Mantelli's head.

Diane placed the photo on her lap and looked down, as if she didn't want them to see which feelings appeared in her eyes. "They did a good job of fixing his face. He wouldn't have liked this photo."

Daniele noticed the slash of red fabric on her slacks jutting out from behind the photo and closed his eyes. Yesterday, at the sight of the mangled body, he had lost his lunch. "I took it at the scene of the accident."

Several minutes of silence passed before Diane looked up, her face expressionless. "I'm sorry. I was replaying the reel of our life together, both the good and bad."

"I hope there was much good in it," Perillo said, admiring her strength. He was used to tears, wails, anger.

"My son is the only good." Diane placed the photo facedown on Perillo's desk. "What pushed him off the road? Michele was an excellent driver."

"It wasn't another car. The only tracks are his. The swerves started twenty meters before he drove off the edge. It's possible he still had too much alcohol in his system or—"

"What time did it happen?"

"The gardener saw him drive off at nine yesterday morning. He said your husband didn't look steady on his feet." Nico had called last night to relay Nelli's information.

"Even if Peppino had seen him drive off at night," Diane said, "Michele wouldn't have been drunk. He was diagnosed with gout last year. No more drinking wine. Luckily, he could still do tastings—all they do is swirl the wine around in their mouths and spit it out. The only alcohol he could drink was one glass of whiskey a day. You can't get drunk on that."

Perillo raised his hands in the air. "A stroke. A heart attack."

"His cardiologist—Michele was a hypochondriac and went to all the specialists—his cardiologist gave him a clean bill of health just last month. Michele sweetly sent me the report with a note saying, 'Just in case you're hoping I'll drop dead.'"

Daniele sucked in his breath.

"I know, it sounds cruel," Diane said to Daniele. "Michele was like a child, always trying to get attention. Since he had given up trying to get it by loving me, he tried cruelty. Was he alone?"

"Yes," Perillo said. "May heaven be praised."

"I agree. He has a young girlfriend. Had. She's far too young to die."

"We will have to give her the sad news. Do you know her name?"

Daniele, now seated at his desk behind the maresciallo, picked up his pen.

"She already knows. I called her after your phone call yesterday. Michele's gardener had already told her."

"Her name is?"

"Loredana Cardi. You can find her at Il Glicine, a B&B in Montefioralle. Poor thing, she was under the delusion he was going to marry her." Diane leaned forward. "I mean it. I feel for her." She had tried to warn Loredana that Michele made it a habit of picking up pretty young things—that he collected them as he collected wine. "What money she has is what Michele gave her. He loved to feel magnanimous by giving monetary gifts to his girlfriends. Sometimes even me. Thank God I have my own career." But as it turned out, he couldn't have given her much. "Michele is practically broke. My lawyer says it's a common ploy when a man wants a divorce. He planned ahead and started using my money to woo her. When I found out what he was up to, I put my foot down and started a fight that unfortunately made all those dumb magazines."

"They're not all dumb," Daniele said, feeling his mother had just been insulted.

Diane saw she had upset this nice young man. "You're right. It's just that I wished they'd left us some privacy, at least for my son's sake." She turned to Perillo. "Did you ask me to come here just so I could give Loredana's name? That could have been done by phone."

She was right. "I apologize, Signora Severson. You are correct. I should have just called. My curiosity to meet you got the better of me."

Diane got up from her chair. Perillo and Daniele also stood. "Well, I hope I've met your expectations."

Perillo smiled. What could he say? She'd surprised him. "You've surpassed them, Signora."

"Italian gallantry," Diane said, laughing, and walked out.

AT SOTTO IL FICO, lunch service had ended. The kitchen was clean, the dishwasher was on its fourth run and the tables had been cleared and wiped. Enzo had taken his mother home for her siesta. Alba had gone to her husband. Tilde and Nico sat at their usual corner table at the very edge of the terrace, enjoying a small glass of vinsanto and the cantuccini that Alba had made. It was a ritual they tried to repeat as often as possible, usually at the end of the work day, but tonight Nico had dinner guests. Today it was after lunch, just the two of them with the memory of Rita sitting between them.

"Why did Salvatore call you to the scene of the accident?" Tilde asked, dipping her cantuccino in the sweet wine.

"He wanted me to let Aldo know."

"I heard about him punching Mantelli. Elvira clapped when one of the diners told her. Mantelli wasn't a pleasant man. So full of himself. Not that I should be speaking ill of the dead. He really put down Aldo's wines. That has something to do with Cinzia, doesn't it? Alba said she recently saw Cinzia arguing with Mantelli in that fancy car of his."

This news made Nico uncomfortable. Luciana had seen the two of them together earlier, and now Alba. Arguing this time. The florist had implied something different. "When was that?"

"Monday night. The white Jaguar caught Alba's eye. She'd never seen one. Then she heard a woman's voice and recognized Cinzia." She bit into the wine-soaked cantuccio, filled with almonds. "These are delicious. We should package them for sale."

Nico followed her example. "The best I've had so far."

"*Cantucci di Alba.* Wonderful idea, but we'd have to find another kitchen to make them and with Stella in Florence, I can't spare Alba or you."

"I don't see myself as a biscotti maker."

"We call them cantuccini, Nico. Biscotti is equivalent to your biscuit."

"Thank you. I appreciate the corrections."

"You rarely need them. Rita did a good job teaching you Italian."

"I'll raise a glass to that."

"And to her."

They clinked glasses and drank.

Nico leaned back in his chair and watched the play of light on the distant vineyards. Thick pillows of clouds had appeared, dropping shifting splashes of shade on the vineyards. "How does Alba know Cinzia?"

"Everyone knows everyone in this town. It isn't New York. There are only seven hundred of us, tourists excluded. We're a big family, and mostly a happy one. Of course an argument in the piazza between well-known men gets noticed and quickly relayed. No one is saying anything nasty about Aldo. He's very well-liked."

"You know everything that was said?"

"Yes. Mantelli told Aldo his next blog post was going to ruin Ferriello Wines. That's when Aldo rightfully punched him. Did Mantelli really think he could destroy a man's livelihood? He wasn't very well-liked here in Chianti. He went to all the restaurants, telling the owners what wines they should offer, what wines weren't up to his standards. You saw that yourself here yesterday. Don't tell her this, but for once I agree with Elvira."

"She certainly didn't take to him," Nico said, breaking the last cantuccino in half and spilling crumbs all over the table. "I was curious and looked up Mantelli. He had quite a social media following and was considered an excellent wine critic. I found an article in *ChiantiSette* talking about a vineyard Mantelli praised in one of his blogs, ColleVerde. That's the wine he wanted Enzo to buy. According to the article, ColleVerde sales went up almost 50 percent. That means he had real power."

"Now that he's dead, then, Aldo will have a good night's sleep."

"Yes, I think he will." And Cinzia—would she sleep well too?

NICO HAD SPOTTED THE old stone farmhouse on one of his runs a few weeks after he had moved to Gravigna and fallen in love with the crumbling place. It hadn't taken him too long to convince Aldo to rent the place to him at a price he could afford. The ground floor, where the animals had once slept, was now filled with Aldo's old wine barrels. The second floor, which the Italians considered the first floor, was made up of a bed-room, a small bathroom, and a wide front room with a wood stove, a small corner kitchen and windows on each side. Best of all was the balcony overlooking Aldo's olive grove. During the house's empty years, the balcony's ceiling beams had become a nesting and sleeping place for swallows. To Nico's great sat-isfaction, after a great deal of fluttering back and forth, three swallows had accepted his intrusion. They had made him feel less lonely.

At eight in the evening, the sky was still light, but the heat had let up a little. All the windows and the balcony door were open to let the air circulate. The three of them could eat on the small table outside tonight, since Perillo's wife wasn't feeling well. Nico, in khakis, a short-sleeved polo and an *I Love Tuscany* apron Rita had bought him as a joke, checked the ingredients for dinner, which were neatly laid out in small bowls on the kitchen counter. Everything already measured, chopped and cut, made cooking Rita's Summer Tuscan Risotto easier. It was his first time trying out her recipe. He'd taped the wrinkled piece of paper on the cabinet door where he could easily see it. Tilde had advised him on what shortcuts he could take. He'd substituted a jar of pureed tomatoes for skinned and chopped tomatoes. The broth slowly simmering on the back burner was not homemade. He'd substituted vegetable broth for chicken broth for Daniele's sake. The rest—chopped onion, sliced zucchini, asparagus points and peas he'd bought fresh this morning at the Greve Coop, along with the carnaroli rice.

OneWag rushed to the door and barked. "It's open," Nico called out.

"Buonasera," Daniele said at the door, holding a small package in his hand.

Nico smiled. He was very fond of Daniele, who was a gentle young man. "Punctual as always. Glad you're here." Daniele's good looks, pale skin, blue eyes and blond hair reminded Nico of Midwestern farm boys and sometimes of the portraits he'd seen in the Uffizi. Tonight, wearing pressed jeans and a white shirt instead of his police uniform, Daniele looked even younger than his twenty years.

"Come in."

Daniele stepped inside, happy to be joining Nico and the maresciallo for dinner. Eating alone wasn't much fun, but he felt awkward knowing the maresciallo liked meat. He was always worried that being a vegetarian was an imposition. "Thank you for having me."

"It's a pleasure."

OneWag jumped up at Daniele's knees. A greeting, but also a chance to smell the package the young man was holding. A quick sniff revealed no food was involved. The dog sat back down.

"I've missed our get-togethers," Nico said. The last time the three of them had been together was in March to try to cheer up Daniele after Rosalba, the woman he had fallen in love with during last year's murder investigation, broke things off. All Nico and Perillo had managed to do that night was get Daniele drunk, a first for him. "How are things?"

Daniele shrugged, his cheeks reddening.

"It will get better, Daniele, I promise. What can I get you? I've got white and red."

Daniele didn't want to be ungracious, but he couldn't drink on an empty stomach. "Just water for now, please." OneWag nudged his leg. He looked down at the dog and dangled the package. "How did you know this was for you?" OneWag acknowledged the question with another nudge. "Can I give it to him, Nico?" He'd always wanted a puppy, but his mother thought dogs were dirty. "It's a toy. I didn't know what else to bring. I didn't have time to make a tiramisù." Daniele always liked to show off Venetian specialties. The first time he'd come to dinner, he made Nico and Perillo a sgroppino, a drink usually made with lemon sorbet, prosecco and vodka. Daniele's version left out the vodka.

"A toy is perfect, thanks. Go ahead. No need to unwrap it." Nico handed over the glass of water, no ice, the way the Italians liked it. "Just throw it. He loves to tear up paper."

"Thank you." Daniele flung the package to the far end of the room. OneWag flew after it.

Nico went back to the kitchen stove to add olive oil to the hot, wide skillet. The risotto would take another thirty minutes. "Where's Perillo? Didn't you come together?"

"I'm here!" Perillo announced, walking in, brandishing two bottles of wine.

"How's your wife feeling?"

"She's fine and hopes you will forgive her. I'll explain later."

His friend was playing games again. "I'm glad she's fine, but why can't you explain now?"

"You're always in a hurry, aren't you? The American way—run, run, run."

"Well, it does get things done."

"You have a point. So, what happened is this. As the three of us were about to leave, I received some interesting information. I told Ivana I now had official business that I needed to share with you. She asked to stay home. It's a pact we made when we got married. I was to keep the unpleasant details of my work to myself."

"Rita felt the same way. Makes unloading hard. I ended up talking too much to my beat partner." Which was what had gotten him into trouble, but he couldn't blame Rita for that. "Okay, go ahead."

"We'll talk about it on a full stomach."

Nico tossed the chopped onions in the skillet and stirred them with a wooden spoon. There was no use in trying to pressure Perillo to spill the news before he was ready.

Perillo sat down on one of the kitchen chairs. "The wine, I bought from Cinzia. She looked upset and had quite a few questions about Mantelli's accident. No surprise, of course. They were once lovers." He placed the bottles on the table. "Shall I open one?"

"No, thank you. I've got the ColleVerde already open. Pour yourself some."

Perillo examined the ColleVerde label. "You're cheating on your landlord."

"Mantelli was touting it to Enzo on Tuesday. I had a taste at Mantelli's recommendation. It's a strong wine. I was curious to hear what you thought. Try it." He'd taken advantage of what Rita called the "cook's privilege," but had also opened up a white wine as his usual tribute to Rita. It was the only kind she ever drank. He'd enjoyed a glass while waiting for Daniele and Perillo to show up. "How do you know Cinzia and Mantelli were once lovers?"

"Maybe still were. Do you want some, Dani?" Perillo asked.

Daniele watched OneWag tear at the package, then toss the

pink pelican toy in the air and leap up to catch it. The dog's happiness lifted his own mood. After the medical examiner's phone call, no more calm days.

"Dani?"

"No, thanks." He lifted the forgotten water glass and took a sip. That poor pelican wasn't going to last long.

"Come on, Perillo. Tell me," Nico said. "How do you know? Your famous intuition?" He added the green vegetables and stirred.

Perillo sat down at the table, poured himself a glass and helped himself to an olive. "My eyes this time. I had Dani look up Cinzia's Facebook photos."

"Why did you do that?" Nico mixed the tomatoes in with the vegetables.

Perillo poured half a glass of ColleVerde and drank. A pause. "It's good, nothing special. Aldo's wines are far better." Mantelli's famous palate would have known that, which means he was pushing ColleVerde just to malign Aldo. He took a longer sip and watched Nico stir. "I have to thank you for offering me and Daniele the sight of a New York homicide detective wearing an *I love Tuscany* apron. You should post a photo of this on your Facebook page. Instagram too."

"Don't have either." Nico looked down at his belly. He'd forgotten to take off the apron. "A gift from Rita. Her way of reminding me to help in the kitchen."

"And did you?"

"I washed the dishes." And when the cancer started eating at her strength, he had taken over all of it. "Why did you look up Cinzia's photos?" he repeated.

"Curiosity. I saw her with Mantelli on Monday night."

"So did Alba. She thought they were arguing." He left out Luciana, wanting to shield Cinzia. "They obviously weren't trying to hide. What did Cinzia's photos tell you?"

Perillo drank down the rest of the wine. Arguing was not what he had seen. "That they knew each other some time ago. There's a photo of the two of them at a party. It's an old photo. Cinzia looks younger, and Mantelli's hair isn't all white yet."

"That doesn't make them lovers."

"Maybe not." It was best to change the subject. "Diane Severson came to the station this morning. An interesting woman. Not at all the type I thought would capture Mantelli's attention."

Daniele sat down next to his superior. Pieces of the pelican toy were now strewn across the floor. OneWag had gone to sleep with a leg in his mouth. "I think she's attractive, graceful, and very intelligent."

Perillo smiled. "Well said, Dani." His brigadiere, always the gentleman, was defending Diane Severson's lack of beauty. "What I found interesting was her ability not to show any emotion. As we talked, nothing came across on her face." He would now have to find a way to get through that façade.

Nico tossed three fat fistfuls of rice in the skillet, added lots of broth, stirred, lowered the flame and sat down. The rice needed constant stirring, but he was too curious about these new developments. "It's going to take another twenty minutes, so you might as well tell me about the phone call on an empty stomach."

"It's going to ruin your dinner."

"May I take over?" Daniele stood. "Risotto is a Venetian staple."

"Please do." Nico poured himself a glass of ColleVerde's red wine. "So?"

Perillo inhaled the risotto's delicious smell, prompting his stomach to protest loudly. "Barbara, Della Langhe's assistant, called me with the autopsy results. Mantelli was probably dead before the car went off the road."

"A heart attack?"

Daniele, who knew what was coming, worked the spoon with more vigor.

"No." Perillo reached into his jean's pocket and extracted a piece of paper. He held the paper at arm's length and squinted. "I had her repeat it to me. Mantelli had a cerebral hemorrhage, severe acidosis, and an accumulation of formate."

"Which translates to what?"

"Methanol poisoning. That's poisoning by ingesting wood alcohol, deadly and difficult to detect in hard liquor. Whiskey, for example, is the only alcohol Mantelli's doctor allowed him to drink since he had gout. At least, according to his wife."

Nico sat back in his chair and remembered reading about several tourist deaths in the Dominican Republic attributed to methanol poisoning. It had happened a few years ago. He'd never heard of it before. "Suicide, then."

"Unlikely. Takes too long to kill you. Twelve to twenty-four hours."

"But it gives you time to change your mind and get help."

"Della Langhe has decreed it murder. That's also the medical examiner's opinion. I'm not going to argue with them. A search warrant of the villa has already been issued. His wife said he was broke, which might give someone with his self-importance a reason to do himself in, but she thinks he just stashed his cash somewhere where she can't get to it. I sent two of my men to his villa to guard it while the forensic team gets there from Florence. I have also informed Signora Severson that her husband's death is now considered a murder. I will be interrogating her tomorrow morning."

Nico's tension eased. Aldo wasn't the only suspect. "You think he drank the methanol at home?"

"Who knows? I want his laptop, iPad, his notes, scribblings, anything that will give me information. His cell phone was with him in the Jaguar. It's already in our possession. Unfortunately, I

won't be in charge of the case for long. Della Langhe is sending
Capitano Carlo Tarani of the Nucleo Investigativo from Provin-
cial Headquarters to take over."

"Why?" Daniele stopped stirring. "We solved last year's case
without any interference."

"Mantelli has national fame. Della Langhe is following the
right procedure this time." He was probably also eager to protect
his wife's friend from being harassed by a lowly maresciallo from
the South, Perillo thought.

A disappointed Daniele tasted the rice. At least this dish was
perfect. It was time to add butter, Parmigiano and a last go-round
with the spoon.

Nico drank his glass down. He wasn't happy with Perillo's
news, either the murder or Tarani. "Shouldn't you be overseeing
the search at Mantelli's villa?"

"I'd just get in their way. Nico, accept reality. We have our-
selves a murder case that is going to be taken out of our hands.
At least we can already hand Capitano Tarani two people with
excellent reasons to be rid of Mantelli."

With a face reddened by the heat of the stove, Daniele
announced, "The risotto is done."

"This is bad," Nico said. "Aldo had better have an airtight alibi."
If he didn't, the capitano could make mincemeat out of him.

Perillo nodded. "I know. That's why I wanted to wait to
tell you."

Nico took the heavy skillet from Daniele and poured the
risotto in a bowl. "We'll eat outside where it's cooler. The table is
already set up. Please, let's not talk about this until after dessert.
Agreed?"

"Agreed," Daniele and Perillo answered in unison.

AFTER CLEARING THE EMPTY risotto and salad bowls, Nico
took a bowl heaped with fragoline di bosco out on the terrace.

"Oh, I wait for these every year," Daniele exclaimed. The tiny strawberries had just come into season.

"Good," Nico said curtly.

"Thank you." Daniele looked at his boss, hoping his enthusiasm wasn't out of line. No reaction from the maresciallo. It was his second attempt at breaking the tension. After a few bites of the risotto, he had declared, bending the truth a little, that it was even better than his mother's. While they ate, very little had been said. Nico was obviously worried about his landlord. The maresciallo wasn't happy he had to solve another murder. Having Capitano Tarani on his back made it worse. Daniele knew the next few days would be hard for all three of them.

Nico waited until everyone's plate was empty of strawberries to make coffee for Perillo. While they waited for the moka to stop gurgling, Nico lit his second cigarette of the day. Perillo eagerly lit his own. He'd been fighting withdrawal symptoms from the moment he'd walked in. Daniele pushed his chair closer to the railing to avoid the smoke and waited to see if the maresciallo had remembered.

Nico pushed an ashtray in front of Perillo to stop him from flicking ash over the balcony.

"Thanks. I don't need it." Perillo took a portable ashtray with a lid from his pocket. "A Christmas present from Daniele. Very thoughtful of him."

Daniele smiled. As soon as the moka was silent, Daniele stood up. "Allow me."

"I only have mugs, left cabinet," Nico said, happy to stay seated. "You said methanol poisoning takes twelve to twenty-four hours to act?"

"At least twelve, but it can take more than twenty-four hours. The medical examiner said it depends on the individual."

"That's going to make it impossible to pinpoint when and where the poison was administered."

"Hard, but not impossible because given Mantelli's age—he was fifty-four with some health issues he didn't advertise—Dottor Gianconi thinks the poison acted sooner rather than later." Daniele came back, placed the barely filled mug in front of the maresciallo and sat back down.

"Thank you, Dani," Perillo said. "Please, remind me to buy proper cups for our host." He downed the very hot espresso in his usual single gulp. "Twelve to eighteen hours at the very most, in his opinion."

"Are you going to call Aldo in first?"

"I'm going to make a list, as you advised last year. A list to clear my head. I will write down all the people I need to interview. Hoping the night brings good counsel, I'll decide in the morning. I have to proceed with slippered feet, as Della Langhe wants to keep the poisoning from the media as long as we can."

"Why?"

"His wife is a client and friend of Mantelli's soon-to-be-ex-wife, Diane Severson. She has promised Della Langhe not to say a word. I wouldn't be surprised if the real reason is that once the media knows, reporters won't leave Signora Severson alone, which will prevent her from redecorating Della Langhe's living room. I'll keep you informed, although I worry that you are too good a friend of Aldo's to remain objective."

"You have a point. I find it impossible to think that Aldo could kill anyone, much less with wood alcohol."

"A New York homicide detective with too much heart," Perillo said.

Nico said nothing. Perillo was again referring to his forced retirement. How did he know? Nico's captain had demanded secrecy to protect his own reputation. That secrecy was what allowed him to retire with a pension instead of doing jail time. "My good heart is something we should discuss another time," Nico said.

"Agreed," Perillo said. "Anytime you wish."

Daniele, who had unveiled the "why" of Nico's forced retirement, was lost in his own thoughts. Poisoning was considered a woman's crime, but so far the only woman they knew who had motive was Mantelli's wife. Daniele thought Diane Severson was too refined to use such a chancy poison. Mantelli might have felt the poison start working, gone to a doctor and been saved. If Signora Severson was about to kill someone, she would have used a revolver. A shot straight to the heart.

"There's his girlfriend to consider," Nico said. "A real beauty, and Mantelli, at least in my presence, treated her as an afterthought."

"I'll add her to my list of cats."

"Why cats?" Daniele asked.

"A Neapolitan saying: *Frije 'e pisce e gurda 'a jatta.* Fry the fish, but watch the cat. I want you to watch the cat too, Nico. You're in this with us if you can balance your friendship with Aldo with whatever facts come out."

Nico nodded, though not sure he could find that balance. "How about some whiskey before I send you two home?"

"Great idea," Perillo said with a broad smile on his face. "Hold the wood alcohol."

BACK IN HIS OFFICE at the Greve station, Perillo called Vince. "Did forensics find anything?"

"There was no laptop or desktop computer. The kitchen was clean, no garbage. No trash in wastebaskets in any of the rooms. The gardener, who lives at the back of the villa, admitted he'd done the cleaning. He said he didn't know what happened to Mantelli's laptop. According to him, Mantelli didn't like to come home to a dirty kitchen. The team took all the alcohol bottles to check for methanol. The whiskey bottle was unopened. They retrieved what he'd thrown out from the dumpster up the road.

They had to take every sack of garbage," Vince started laughing, "in case the gardener was lying about which sack was his. You should have heard the cursing."

"Are you still at the villa?"

The gardener had made him and Dino a plate of rigatoni with sautéed onions, but Vince thought it best not to mention it to the maresciallo. "Yes. We didn't know if you wanted us to seal the place."

Perillo smiled. Vince would have rushed home if there wasn't food involved. "No, you can go home after you've finished eating. Tell the gardener to be at the station tomorrow morning at nine. Buon appetito." He clicked off.

Vince looked at his partner, who was sitting next to him at Mantelli's kitchen table. "Damn it, Dino! How the devil did he know?"

Dino didn't answer. He was too busy wiping his plate clean with a piece of bread.

FIVE

Friday had started out as another sun-filled day. By the time Nico and OneWag got to Bar All'Angolo that morning, a wind had blown in from the East and was pushing a blanket of pale gray clouds across the sky. Sitting by the open French door eating his second whole-wheat cornetto, Nico watched the sun slip behind the clouds with a sense of relief. The day would be cooler.

A group of local men stood at the far end of the counter, talking among themselves in low voices. Mantelli's death had made the paper, and Nico caught Aldo's name bouncing from one to the other. He turned his head sideways to hear better. A column kept him from being seen.

"Ferri's a lucky man," a gruff voice said. "He threatens to kill the man in front of a crowd, and the next day the man saves him the trouble by running his car off a cliff." It sounded like the barber. Nico stayed hidden. If they knew he was listening, they'd immediately shut up.

"He didn't threaten to kill him, just beat him up. That's how I heard it."

"Get yourself a hearing aid."

"Got one, and it's obviously better than yours."

"If you ask me, the coincidence smells funny."

A trickle of laughter. "Come on, Sergio," the gruff voice said, "what are you saying? Ferri fixed the car so it would crash?"

"Could be."

"You're full of shit. Anyone for grappa? Sergio's paying."

Nico turned to face Gogol, only momentarily relieved. Thanks to the confrontation in the piazza, more than one of the towns-people was going to start spreading malicious gossip. Gogol was pointing to *La Nazione*, the Florentine newspaper the café pro-vided for its customers. It lay on the table between them. He said something, jabbing his finger at the lower half of the paper. The headline read: HORRENDOUS ACCIDENT KILLS FAMOUS WINE CRITIC.

"What did you say? I didn't understand you," Nico said.

Gogol swallowed the last of his lard crostino. "Not now. Never."

Nico laughed. Gogol was right. Dante's Italian was beyond him. "Will you accept almost never? What were you saying?"

"'Think how the sun's warmth mingles with the moist sap of the vine and turns to wine.'" Gogol quoted. "Death can come from the vine."

"You think he was drunk?"

Gogol shook his head. "The salame is mine." There was a hint of a question mark at the end of Gogol's declaration. He could be forceful and hesitant at the same time.

Nico pushed the crostino across the table. "All yours. What are you telling me?"

Gogol bit into it quickly, reminding Nico of the way OneWag grabbed a treat as if still not confident he deserved it. He glanced behind him to see his dog sitting in front of the cash register, staring at Sandro. Sandro was counting change for an elegant tall woman. She was wearing tight white slacks and a striking dark-blue silk shirt covered with a design of large yellow palm leaves. Nico watched her lean down and stroke OneWag's head. The dog continued to stare at Sandro as if he knew that the one who blinks first loses.

Gogol jabbed Nico's hand to get his attention. Once he had it, he showed him a crooked grin. "'Never has my ignorance made me thirst to know with such torment.'"

Nico grinned back. "I'm not even going to try to guess what canto that's from, but I'm not tormented to know what you said. Go ahead and quote away."

Gogol leaned in and slowly enunciated, "'For such pride, here one pays the fine.'"

"That, I understood."

"Both *Purgatorio*."

"I hope you're not referring to me."

"Michele Mantelli."

"You knew him?"

"My eyes did, not my heart."

"That's unfair," Nico said. "'The habit does not make the monk,' to quote an unknown. And why the thirst to know?"

Gogol gazed at Nico's face with penetrating eyes and whispered, "The reason for his death."

"In this case," the tall woman said, as her long legs brought her to the table, "Gogol is being totally fair. My husband was indeed proud, although I won't go as far as to say he deserved to pay the fine." She nestled an espresso cup in her thin, perfectly manicured fingers. "May I join you?"

Gogol took off an imaginary hat and bowed his head. Nico stood up and pushed back a chair.

"Thank you." The woman sat down and smiled at Gogol. "I've always wanted to meet the town poet." The smile did not reach her eyes.

Gogol shook his head, releasing wisps of cologne into the air around them. "They are not my words, Signora. They belong to Dante Alighieri."

"They become yours because you put such heart into them." It was hard to tell if she meant it, but Gogol beamed.

Looking at her, Nico thought Daniele was right. She was not

beautiful in the usual way, but she had an intelligent, striking face bare of makeup that demanded attention.

The woman turned to look at Nico sitting beside her. "And it's nice to meet another American." She kept her cup in one hand and extended the other to Nico. "Diane Severson, originally from Elizabeth, New Jersey, now Milan and Montefioralle."

Nico shook her hand and introduced himself. Diane then squeezed Gogol's hand. She was doing and saying all the right things, but her words lacked warmth. It roused his curiosity. "I'm sorry for your loss, Signora Severson."

"God, don't be. My husband was a mean bastard. Not from the start. The first few years we were devoted to each other, but then his penis got bored and started wandering. I shut down, which I guess didn't help. You can call me Diane, by the way." She drank her espresso in two sips and slowly blotted her mouth with a napkin. Her gaze looked out onto the piazza. Her thoughts were clearly somewhere else.

After a few moments, she said, "I apologize to both of you. I've given you much too much unasked-for information. I'm beginning to think my husband's death is actually getting to me. I'm usually very good at holding things in." She turned to Nico. "You live in this town?"

"Yes. I've been here just over a year."

"I was going to ask the cashier—"

"Sandro." Gogol interrupted. "Cashier and owner."

"I see. I was going to ask him how to get to the Ferriello vineyard."

"Your answer rests before you," Gogol said.

"You can help?" Diane asked.

Gogol tilted his head toward Nico. "My friend Nico." Gogol stood, his fist beating his chest several times. More wisps of cologne. "You take her, friend." He lowered his head. "Tomorrow, if I live."

"You're leaving?" Diane asked. "You won't let me hear the poet?"

Gogol shuffled his feet, his eyes down. "'A lady called me, so blessed and beautiful I asked her to command me. Her eyes shined brighter than the stars and she began to speak, gentle and low, with an angelic voice.'" Gogol bowed down, sweeping his imaginary hat over his head, and walked away.

"Thank you," Diane called after him. "Why did he leave? I wanted to pay him for that lovely quote."

"I don't think he would have accepted money."

"I'm sorry. I shouldn't have asked. His overcoat explains why he's called Gogol, but why does he wear such a strong scent?"

"It's the cologne his mother wore. It keeps her near him. She died when he was just a boy, and the old villagers think it was her death that sent him off to a world of his own. He never knew his father."

"It's probably a much nicer world than ours." Diane looked at her Apple Watch. "I need to get going. How do I get to Aldo Ferri's vineyard?"

Nico stood up. He had planned to visit Rita, but this woman's need to see Aldo had increased his curiosity tenfold. "I'm going right by there. You can follow my car."

"Thank you." Diane walked out with him.

Nico looked back. OneWag was still sitting below the cash register. "Come on, OneWag."

The dog gave Sandro one last hopeful look. Sandro shook his head. OneWag picked himself up and, with as much dignity as he could muster, padded out with his plume of a tail held high.

PERILLO LOOKED AT THE man sitting in front of his desk for a moment. He liked to study the people he questioned before speaking, give them time to study him back, gather their thoughts, calm down if they needed to. Daniele thought it had the opposite effect. Maybe. But taking that moment helped Perillo to concentrate.

Mantelli's gardener was a small man with a tanned, weathered face from working outdoors. He wore patched gray pants and a plaid short-sleeved cotton shirt. His hands, large and wrinkled, held a wide-brimmed felt hat between his legs.

"Your full name, please, and date of birth," Perillo said in a soft voice he hoped would undo whatever discomfort his stare might have given the man. Behind him, Daniele sat upright at his computer, fingers poised on the keyboard, ready to type every word, proud of his ability to type a hundred words a minute. The maresciallo did not believe in the use of tape recorders.

"Giuseppe Risso. Everyone calls me Peppino. Born in Monte-fioralle, March 7, 1939."

"You are Michele Mantelli's gardener, is that correct?"

"A bit of everything, I did for him. Fifteen years, from the very day he bought the villa. Well, the truth is, I came with the villa. Worked for the previous owner since I was a boy." He spoke with a raucous voice and a strong Tuscan accent, exhaling his *h*'s. "I mean, he didn't have to take me on, but he did. Nice man, Signor Mantelli. Stubborn, had a bit of a temper on him. Liked things his way even if they were dead wrong, like pruning roses in October. Roses get pruned after the final frost, everyone knows that. I gave up trying to teach him anything,"

"What's the bit of everything you did for him besides gardening?"

"Fetch things for him. Run errands. Cooked for him too. He loved my potato soup. He used to come down without his wife for a couple of weeks in the middle of winter. She didn't come down even when they were getting along. Too busy, he said. When he was here alone, he'd not go anywhere. He called it getting away from life." Peppino looked at his open hand, as if surprised it was empty. "The padrone could always count on me to take care of him."

"He didn't have a cleaning woman?"

Peppino's hand went back to holding the brim of his hat. The action seemed to reassure him, Perillo thought.

"Ida comes to clean the house three times a week when he's here. I take care of it when he's not around. He didn't trust her, said women never get things right. That was even before his marriage rotted."

"He had a girlfriend, didn't he? Loredana? Did he trust her?"

"Signorina Cardi? He liked to surround himself with beauty. I don't know if he loved her or trusted her. That's none of my business. He didn't want her to stay at the villa, though. He liked his privacy, even when his wife was around. He'd put her in a B&B."

"Not a hotel?"

"I think he was going through a bad time with money. Six months ago, he said he had to cut my pay. When things got better again, he promised I'd go back to my old wages. Soon, he said. Very soon. I told him not to worry about me. I have a bed at the villa, and I don't need much."

"Did anyone visit him on Tuesday?"

"He left after breakfast to visit vineyards. That's what he does first thing when he comes here."

Perillo picked up his pen and rolled it around his finger. Mantelli had also been at Sotto Il Fico to dictate what should be on the wine list. He would send Daniele around to the better restaurants in the area to see if he had created any feelings bad enough to get him murdered.

"When did you see him again?"

"Lunch was at home with the signorina. I made spaghetti with anchovies and capers. That's what he asked for, so that's what I made. Signorina Loredana ate only a salad. I picked apricots for them. We have two trees' full. He loved his apricots." Tears started to drop down his cheeks.

"And after lunch?"

He sniffed loudly and wiped his cheeks dry with the back of his hands. "Maresciallo, when his signorina is here, the padrone goes with her to Il Glicine after lunch. I take a nap at that time. The sun is too hot to work then. If the padrone came home and had visitors, I can't tell you. My room is at the far end of the villa, overlooking the pool. I take care of the pool too. Factotum Peppino, he liked to call me. I had to look up the word. It's Latin. 'Doer of everything.' That's what I was." He started twirling the hat with his fingers, his head lowered. "Doer of everything."

"What about later that afternoon?"

"He sent me down with a long list of things to buy. Coop, then hardware store, then to the mattress-maker. He wanted only wool. No springs, nothing but sheep's wool packed tight." Peppino looked up at Perillo with more tears in his eyes. "I warned him that kind of mattress was very expensive. He laughed and said money was coming in."

"Did he say anything else about this money?"

"I didn't ask." His fingers worked his hat again, scrunching the rim. "It's not for me to know. The padrone wasn't home when I got back."

Perillo waited to ask his next question. The man was grieving for his boss, perhaps for a lost job. For both, probably. After a minute, the hat-twirling stopped. Peppino lifted his head.

"You saw him leave the house Wednesday morning." Perillo kept his voice soft.

"Yes, I was right by the entrance, cleaning out the mandevilla that runs along the wall. He wasn't six feet away from me when he stumbled on the stairs. I ran over and asked him if he needed help."

"What time was this?"

"Five or ten minutes past ten."

Perillo looked at Peppino's bare wrists. "You don't wear a watch."

"Don't need to. I've got the sun, and if it's cloudy, the church bells."

"What did he say when you asked if he needed help?"

"'Three whiskies is one too many for my gout,' is what he said. I wish I'd tried to stop him. He didn't look good at all, but even if I'd said something, he wouldn't have listened. The padrone never did listen to anyone. Our faults can kill us if we don't watch out."

"Last night, I sent two of my men to the villa and our forensic team. I have to praise how well you keep order in the house."

"The padrone hated disorder. Lucky for him, me too."

"Does disliking disorder explain the disappearance of your padrone's laptop?"

"He must have taken it with him. A gray laptop. Pro something. The very latest model, he said. He was going to teach me to use it. 'Peppino, it's time you walk out of the Middle Ages and join the twenty-first century.' That's what he said to me just last Saturday."

Perillo wanted to interrupt, but sometimes it was best to listen. The hat was twirling again.

"He had just finished writing his wine newsletter. He was very proud of his work. Wine for the rich. I get my wine loose and refill the bottle when it's empty. It's just as good as what he drinks—used to drink. Then he got gout. I guess I can tell you that now that he's dead. He was afraid it would be bad for his reputation if people knew. He said getting gout was ironic. The laptop, he must have taken with him."

"Did you see him take it?"

"No. It must have already been in the car."

"It wasn't. When did you last see it?"

"Monday night. The padrone was out to dinner, and I turned it on and off a few times, just to see what it was like. I didn't take it." Peppino shifted his hat to his left hand and crossed himself. "Never even taken a coin off the street." He looked up at Perillo with his large blue sagging eyes. "God knows."

Perillo believed him. He stood up and held out his hand. "Thank you for coming."

Peppino got up from his chair and shook the maresciallo's hand. "My duty. The padrone always treated me with kindness and respect, which you can't say for most rich people."

"I'll probably need to speak to you again. Where can I find you?"

"Signora Mantelli wants me to stay on. She's going to keep the villa, or that's what she told me. With no disrespect to the signora, I pray she doesn't sell. Seventy years I've taken care of the villa." He widened those old blue eyes in bewilderment. "What will I do?"

"Relax, rest."

Peppino jammed his hat on top of his head. "Relax and rest is for when I'm underground. Arrivederci to the young man in the back there, and to you, Maresciallo. You know where to find me."

"Arrivederci," Daniele said, standing up.

Perillo nodded.

Once the door closed, Daniele said, "A good man. Someone else stole the laptop."

"I agree. Probably while he was napping."

"The killer?"

"Probably."

"Who's next?"

"The bartender next door. I need a coffee and a cigarette. When we get back let's make sure Mantelli's disowned son is where his mother says he is. Now come with me, I'm paying."

NICO COULD HAVE HONKED and pointed to the Ferriello parking lot, then driven on to his own home. Instead he turned and led Mantelli's wife directly to Aldo's office. Why did Diane Severson want to talk to him? To accuse him of killing her husband? To thank him? She had been clear about not being on good terms with Mantelli. Was it an attempt to divert suspicion away from herself? After all she had the most to gain. Was Aldo still worried Mantelli's blog post would come out despite his death? Nico had been surprised by Aldo's anger that day in the piazza. More than surprised. Unnerved by the unexpected display of raw emotion. It had uncomfortably reminded him of the anger he had allowed to surface when he saw his father hit his mother for the last time. Nico had grabbed the half-empty whiskey bottle on the table and aimed it at his father's head. His father walked out of the house with blood pouring down his face. That was the last they saw of him.

His mother never reprimanded or thanked him for that day. He was fourteen at the time, and for years he had wondered if she thought what he had done was right or wrong. When his mother was dying, he had asked her. When she didn't answer, he asked her to forgive him and finally stopped wondering.

Nico got out of the car and walked to the office. He wanted to give his friend a heads-up. The door was open. Aldo was sitting behind the desk. "Ciao, Aldo. Signora Mantelli wants to talk to you."

Diane brushed past Nico. "Thank you. I'll take it from here." Her arm reached out toward Aldo. "Signor Ferri, I'm sorry we are meeting under such unpleasant circumstances."

Aldo stood up and took her hand, confusion clear on his face.

Diane turned to look at Nico with an icy smile. "I did say thank you."

Nico bowed and closed the door.

NICO WAS ON HIS knees, planting zucchini in the row he had prepared yesterday. The sky was covered in clouds, but it was still too hot to plant anything. Tilde didn't want him for the lunch shift, but he needed to keep busy. Mantelli's murder and Aldo's possible involvement had his blood racing. At least Capitano Tarani hadn't appeared yet. The case was still in Perillo's hands.

OneWag barked. Nico scrambled to his feet with a quick look at his watch. Just over an hour and a half had passed since he'd left Aldo's office. Aldo was now standing in front of the fence, looking bewildered. Scared, even. "Hey, are you okay?" Nico asked.

"I don't know. I don't know what game she's playing."

Nico gathered the leftover plants and put them in a basket. "I can finish up later. Let's go upstairs and we can talk on the balcony. It's cooler there."

They sat overlooking Aldo's olive grove, each drinking from a glass of cold water. Nico had offered cold white wine, Aldo's own, but Aldo had said it was too early.

"What did she want?" Nico asked.

"Nothing. She came to reassure me I didn't have to worry about what Mantelli had written about me. She was going to make sure it didn't come out."

"The blog post would come out even now that he's dead?"

"Apparently he wrote his posts a few weeks in advance and sent them to his magazine publisher."

"How often did he write posts?"

"Once a month. He was supposed to send the July post on Monday. According to her, he finished writing it Monday night, but didn't send it in. She said she was going to delete it."

"You must feel relieved."

"I should, but I don't. Why would she do this for me?"

"Maybe she's a decent person. Maybe she thinks your wine deserves better. Or she wants to undo her husband's work, out of anger or for reasons of her own."

"She wanted to meet Cinzia, which made me uncomfortable for reasons I don't need to explain. I told her Cinzia was busy, but she insisted. I got the feeling meeting Cinzia was a must if I wanted the post gone."

"Did they meet?'

"Yes. Cinzia took her over to the welcome center. She asked me to leave them alone. They didn't talk long. Maybe ten minutes. According to what Diane Severson told Cinzia, the reason Mantelli wanted to destroy me was because I didn't pay up."

"Had he asked you for money?"

"No, that's what makes no sense."

"It makes sense if she knows he asked for handouts to other vintners and assumed you'd been asked as well."

"Mantelli was after me because I took Cinzia away from him. Two months after we got married, he married Diane."

"Maybe Diane doesn't know that or doesn't want to admit it. It's not fun thinking your husband married you on the rebound."

"Why she told Cinzia about Mantelli wanting payment for a good review and said nothing to me is beyond me."

"Maybe she didn't want to embarrass you." Nico said it, but didn't believe it.

"I don't know. I hate to say this, Nico, but I'm not sure Cinzia is telling the truth." Aldo wiped his face with his hand.

Another uncertainty. Had Diane told Cinzia that Mantelli's death wasn't an accident?

Aldo put a hand on Nico's shoulder. "I'm ready for that wine if you're still offering."

"Of course."

HALF A BOTTLE OF Ferriello Chardonnay later, normally verbose Aldo still hadn't said anything.

"When did Mantelli first meet Cinzia?" Nico asked.

"Over twenty years ago. In Rome, when she was at the university. Mantelli was an adjunct in the economics department. They were together for less than a year when we met. She left him and married me." Aldo poured himself more wine and took long, slow sips. After a few moments, he said, "She was going to be an architect. She had only two exams left when she met me. Gave all of it up for me. I often feel guilty about the life I've given her. She has to work so hard here. Maybe she would have—" Aldo looked up and gave Nico a halfhearted smile. "Thank you for listening. Of course Cinzia is telling me the truth. I'm just shaken. Punching Mantelli in the piazza, him plummeting down a ravine, now his wife telling me his last post about me isn't going to appear. Talking to Cinzia. It's all just happened so fast." Aldo stood. "Thanks for the wine. It's the best, right?"

Nico stood as well. "The very best."

"I'll send over a case."

"No need. Friends listen to friends."

"Thank you, Nico." Aldo gave him a fast hug, which Nico returned.

They walked to the door. "Aldo, I think Perillo should know about Diane's conversation with you."

"It was a soliloquy, not a conversation. You tell him."

"With your permission, I will." He opened the front door. "Take care, Aldo."

"You too."

PERILLO AND DANIELE WERE standing just outside the station's entrance when Diane walked through the gate. Perillo quickly put out his cigarette. She was wearing sunflower yellow slacks and a matching sleeveless top with purple streaks that looked like fern leaves.

"Thank you for coming," Perillo said.

"It didn't seem like I had a choice."

She didn't extend her hand this time, Perillo noted.

"I'd like to get this over with," she said.

"Of course. I thought we might talk in the shade in the park across the street. The heat in my office is brutal." He had for this occasion put on his uniform.

Diane glanced down at it. "Heat doesn't bother me in the least, but mosquitoes do."

Defeated, Perillo stepped aside. As she strode past him, he picked up a sweet flowery scent, pure manna for mosquitoes. He caught Daniele sniffing too.

In the office, the two screenless windows were opened wide, and the fan whirred. The mosquitoes would eat her up here too, Diane thought as she watched Perillo sit behind the desk he had hoped to avoid. The sweet-looking brigadiere held his back steel-rod straight in front of his computer, his fingers poised at the keys like a piano player. She would be the one to start.

Diane moved her chair so the fan would not lift her hair. "The last time I saw my husband alive was Tuesday night at Il Falco. It was a misguided last-ditch effort to try to convince Michele that he was being unnecessarily horrid about our money. I didn't get close enough to him to administer anything but anger. He shooed me away instantly."

The signora liked to take control, Perillo noted to himself. He found it irritating. "I realize you are anxious to get this necessary interrogation over with, but please wait for my questions."

Diane crossed her legs and decided the maresciallo was a pompous ass. "Of course. It's your show."

"Did anyone witness your meeting with your husband at the restaurant?"

"I'd brought a friend of Michele's for support."

"His name?"

"Luca Verdini. He owns the ColleVerde Vineyard."

"Anyone else?"

"I suppose the waiter and the other diners. I did have my back to them, so if I'd slipped something in his glass, they wouldn't have seen it."

"And the second-to-last time you saw him, when was that?"

"God, I don't remember. I guess in Milan." She'd asked him to come to her apartment to talk things over one time. He'd shown up with the beautiful Loredana. "If I had any money left," he'd said, "she'd be getting it, not you. She doesn't have your brains, but she's got looks." Diane had calmly walked to her front door and opened it. He took the hint. "It must have been just before Easter. He always moved back to the Montefioralle villa for the summer on Good Friday."

"When was the last time you were at the villa?"

She leaned toward Perillo. "Ah, you're going to like this. Tuesday morning. I drove by and saw he wasn't home, I wanted to talk to Peppino before Michele told him." She sat back in her chair to let him ask his next question.

Perillo understood she was playing with him. Usually with a suspect, it was the other way around. He glanced back at Daniele. "Are we going too fast for you?"

Daniele lifted his hands and made a show of massaging his fingers. His boss was good at this. "Ready, Maresciallo."

Perillo turned back to look at Diane. "Go on. You wanted to talk to Peppino."

"You want me to tell you why?"

"That would be helpful."

"Michele had sold the villa. Of course he wasn't going to get the money until our divorce came through, which would have been sometime this winter. I wanted Peppino to know. The sale would break his heart."

Odd. The gardener hadn't mentioned the sale this morning. "How did he react?"

"He didn't believe me. It seems Michele had promised him he would never sell. I kept telling him it was true. He decided I was telling him this lie because I was angry at Michele. I gave him a hug and left."

"When your husband stumbled leaving the villa Wednesday,

he told Peppino that three glasses of whiskey had been too much. At the restaurant, he only had two."

"I did not spike Michele's whiskey bottle with wood alcohol. I don't even know where to get wood alcohol. Any more questions?"

"Not for now. If more should come up, I'll get in touch with you. I do ask that you stay in the area."

"You'll find me at the villa. I'm moving in today."

"Thank you, Signora Severson. Daniele will now print out what we've said here. Please read it over and sign it." Perillo stood up. He needed to wash his face, take a quick walk in the park's shade. Another difficult visit was waiting for him and Daniele. "Buongiorno," he said with a slight bow and walked out.

SIX

A few miles before reaching the town of Montefioralle, Daniele followed the Il Glicine sign and turned left into a narrow
sloping road lined with cypresses. The bed and breakfast place
where Loredana Cardi was staying was easy to spot, thanks to
the enormous curtain of pale-purple wisteria blooms spreading
across the two-story stone house. Daniele carefully parked the Alfa
on the edge of the unpaved road.

"Damn these roads," Perillo said, unlatching his seat belt. The
windshield of the car was covered in fine white dust. "Our shoes
and trousers are going to get covered in it, and my wife will start
cursing."

As they were on official duty, they were both in uniform. Daniele would have liked to point out that men were perfectly capable
of brushing their own shoes and trousers. Loving his job, he said
instead, "There's a clothes brush in the glove compartment."

"Good thinking, Dani," Perillo opened the glove compartment
and took the brush out. "We'll use it before going in. First impres-
sions are important. I'm sure your mother taught you that. We
represent the law and the law must look clean, even if it often isn't."

Daniele had learned early on that Perillo cared more about
his appearance when women were involved. A little too much,
perhaps, but that was a thought Daniele wouldn't share with
anyone, not even his mother. It would be disloyal.

Perillo carefully stepped out of the car with clothes brush in
hand. Dust immediately settled on his black shoes.

Loredana stood next to the twisted trunk of the wisteria and waved to let the two carabinieri see her. It was too late to use the clothes brush. He would look foolish. Perillo handed it back to Daniele, who threw it in the car.

Perillo lifted his hat in salute. "Daniele, please, try not to raise too much dust." He made his way forward slowly, a smile on his face. Montefioralle, being high up, was at least five degrees cooler than the office.

"Buongiorno," Loredana said before Perillo had a chance to introduce himself. He was momentarily stunned. Nico had been right on the mark. She was at most twenty-five—far too young for Mantelli. But it was her looks that took his breath away. Behind him, he heard Daniele's own small gasp. Loredana Cardi had the biggest eyes Perillo had ever seen, as blue as a summer sky, rimmed by thick black eyelashes. A soft oval face with a pale complexion that hadn't been changed by the sun. Full lips the color of the shiny mauve shirt she had tucked into tight white jeans. Her long blond hair, covering her shoulders like a shawl, sparkled in the patch of sun the clouds had released.

Loredana smiled as the men mumbled an introduction. She was used to their reaction. Her smile was her best feature, she thought. Her round eyes would lengthen. Her thick lips would thin out, and she'd look happy instead of miserable. Lately a constant state. Now with another emotion she thrived on: anger.

After introducing himself and Daniele, Perillo held out his hand.

Loredana didn't take it. "I know he's dead, if that's why you came. Diane called me." She crossed her arms, a defiant look on her face. "Mica had no right to die."

"I'm afraid that is a right we cannot dispense with."

"Well, he had no right to die now. We were going to be married. Well," she unlocked her arms, gathered her hair and threw it over to one shoulder, "that's of no interest to you. Why are you here? I don't know why Mica drove off the road."

"Signorina, can we find a place to sit? Perhaps in the garden, if there is one."

Loredana looked at the time on her cell phone. She'd found lately that being rude gave her satisfaction. This morning, when the owner of the B&B told her how sorry he was for her loss, she told him to stick it up his ass. Before, she'd always lapped up the attention. Especially compliments, which had made her feel as though her soul was being massaged. Before. Now it was after, and there was nothing she could do.

She stopped looking at her phone. "Okay. There's an awning."

Perillo and Daniele followed her into the building. Loredana led the way down a long corridor at the end of which they could see a rectangle of grass lit up with sun. Perillo walked down the narrow corridor behind Loredana. Daniele trailed behind.

The opening of a door blocked Daniele from going any further.

A head stuck out.

"Don't believe a word that woman tells you," the head whispered so the other two wouldn't hear.

Daniele straightened his shoulders and pulled down his shirt. "Your name, please."

"Dario Terzini. I own this place with my wife. Accidents can be made to happen, and if that's the case with Mantelli, give Signorina Loredana a good look."

Before Daniele could say anything, the door slammed shut.

When the brigadiere stepped out into the garden, Perillo and Loredana were sitting in two white plastic chairs, smoking under a green striped awning.

"Bring up a chair," Perillo said. "Signorina Loredana is in a hurry, but I told her it was best if you were also present."

Perillo always wanted a witness when he had important news

to convey. Four eyes were better than two to assess an unusual reaction.

Loredana took a long drag of her cigarette and exhaled smoke in Daniele's direction. "Diane is picking me up in half an hour. She's taking me to lunch."

Daniele pushed his chair further away. She smiled at him, and he decided she might be beautiful, but it didn't make her very nice.

"You're having lunch with Mantelli's wife?" Perillo asked. Odd, but then, Signora Severson had seemed worried about her husband's girlfriend. Out of compassion, perhaps. Or was it self-interest?

"Yes. We're best friends all of a sudden. She probably thinks I know where Mica's money is hidden." Loredana smashed her cigarette out on the tile floor and left it there. Daniele looked away.

"You know about the money?"

"Didn't I just tell you that? Mica halved my allowance and promised he'd make it up to me once the divorce went through. That's not going to happen now, is it? Now, what is this important news you have to tell me right this minute?"

Perillo took out the portable ashtray Daniele had given him and put out his cigarette in it. To his surprise, he liked using it. What he did not like was what he now had to say to this woman, even if she was being rude. His words shattered dreams, lives. There was nothing he could do to alter the truth of someone's murder. He leaned forward and aimed his eyes at her large blue ones. "Signorina Loredana—"

The first notes of "O Sole Mio" rang out. He quickly took his cell phone out of his pocket and silenced it. Whoever it was could wait. "Signorina Loredana, your Mica's death was not an accident."

"If you think he killed himself, you are very wrong. Mica was convinced he walked on water. He loved his life. Lived it to the fullest, no matter who he hurt."

Perillo took in the clenched jaw, the pained look in her eyes. Had Mantelli not been good to her? This woman was Mantelli's girlfriend—she had a right to know. The media was going to ferret out the truth soon enough, if Signora Severson hadn't spilled the news already. "He was murdered."

Loredana threw her head back to reveal a long, smooth neck and laughed. "That's ridiculous."

"I'm afraid it isn't."

Her laugh subsided into a giggle. "It is. It's ridiculous. Not believable. You're just trying to give yourself importance. Men do that all the time, especially with me. Tell me they're CEOs of a multimillion-dollar company that doesn't exist. Or they own this or that villa, yacht, painting." Her giggles turned into hiccups.

"Get her a glass of water," Perillo said.

Daniele ran into the building.

Loredana held her breath to stop the hiccups. "Men are full of lies." Another long held breath. The hiccups continued. "Always thinking we're going to believe them. And we do. We are so stupid, we believe, but I don't believe you." Her eyes filled with tears. "We were going to get married. That's what he said, and I believed him and now he's dead." She held another long breath.

Daniele rushed back into the garden with a full glass of water.

She grabbed the glass from his hand and emptied it slowly over her face. The water dripped down her mauve top, leaving long, dark stains. "My tears for Mica. I don't have any of my own left." She sat back in the chair, the hiccups stopping as abruptly as they started. She rubbed her eyes, smudging her mascara. She knew she looked like a mess, but then, her life really *was* a mess now. No more being taken care of. No more illusion that what Mica had promised was true. "Did someone cut the car brakes?" she asked. She'd read that in a mystery novel once.

Perillo leaned forward. "He was poisoned."

She blinked once and widened her eyes. In fiction, it was women who poisoned their victims. "I hope it didn't hurt."

Perillo didn't know exactly how much Mantelli had suffered. He said, "It was quick," hoping she wouldn't ask for details. "I know this is a very painful time for you, but I do need to ask some questions."

Loredana wiped her wet cheeks with the sleeve of her shirt. "It won't bring him back, but go ahead. His wife can wait."

Daniele quietly took his notebook and pen out.

Perillo sat up very straight, the posture he considered proper for important questions, refusing Daniele's suggestion it might intimidate. "Were you with Signor Mantelli Tuesday afternoon and evening?"

She tossed her hair over the other shoulder. "He was supposed to come back here with me after we had lunch. We liked to nap together in my room."

"But he didn't?"

The smile disappeared. "No. Peppino drove me back here. Mica said he had work to do, that he'd pick me up at eight for dinner. I'd convinced him to take me to Ristoro di Lamole again. It's my favorite restaurant." A wistful expression came over her face. "I love to watch the sun go down from up there. He changed his mind."

"Where did you dine instead?"

"Il Falco, near Castellina. The food's fine, but it has no view at all. I was really disappointed and told him so." She shrugged. "I don't know why I bothered."

"Do you know why he changed his mind?"

"He wanted to see someone there."

"Did he?"

"Not that I know, but I spent a lot of time in the ladies' room. Some idiot bumped into my back just as I was about to drink from a full glass of red wine. On the way to clean myself up, I did see his wife in the back room, but I know he didn't want to talk to her."

"How long did you stay in the ladies room?"

She shrugged. "I took my time. Tried to get the stain out and made a mess of my dress. I redid my makeup. Smoked a couple of cigarettes. He didn't like my smoking. Maybe half an hour."

"Where did you go after leaving the restaurant?"

"To his house. He gave me a bathrobe to change into, then tried to fry me some leftover spaghetti, but he made a mess of it. I took over." She looked at Perillo with a defiant pout. "I can cook when I have to."

"Was he not feeling well?"

"He was fine. He's too proud to admit he needs glasses. Was."

"What did he drink at the restaurant?"

"Well, to start, he ordered the usual. A whiskey and a bottle of red wine he didn't touch. Mica believed a wine critic had to keep up appearances. A bottle of white wine for me. When I came back from the ladies' room, he was finishing off a fresh glass of whiskey."

"Did he normally have only one?"

"The doctor said that was all he could have. He'd finished eating, and I think he ordered the second one because I took so long to come back. Mica wasn't a very patient man."

"Did you stay over at the villa that night?"

She took her long hair in both hands and started twisting it. "I usually stay for a couple of hours. We make love, and then he takes me home."

"Is that what happened Tuesday?"

"No. As soon as I finished eating, he asked Peppino to bring me back here. He said he was tired, but I think he was mad at me for ruining my dress. He'd bought it for me."

"Was anyone else in the house besides Peppino?"

"It's a big house, but I don't think so. Mica has always been very private about the villa. That's why he didn't want me staying there. If he had to meet someone, it was always somewhere else."

She looked at Daniele, then at Perillo, without speaking. Then she said, "Why would anyone want to hurt Mica?"

"We will find out, Signorina," Perillo answered. "I promise."

"I don't believe in promises." Loredana stood up. "It doesn't really matter who hurt him. He's gone."

"I do need to ask you one more question," Perillo said, getting up from his seat.

She frowned. "What now?"

"Signor Mantelli's laptop was not in his home. Do you have it, by any chance?"

"No. I use my iPhone. He bought it for me." Her lower lip trembled. Perillo feared another outburst. "He was always so generous to me." Loredana tossed them both a smile and headed for the door.

Perillo stopped her with, "One last thing. Brigadiere Donato here will type out our conversation, but you will need to come to the station in the morning to sign your statement. I also have to ask you not to reveal to anyone that Signor Mantelli was murdered. The prosecutor in this case doesn't want the media to know. Only you and Signora Severson have been told."

"Well, there's no two without three, is there?" Loredana tossed them both a smile. "I have to get ready for my lunch with his signora. You know what's funny?"

"What is?"

"She was on her way out, but now, here she is, still his signora. I could laugh until I cry." Loredana gave them a little-girl wave. "Ciao, ciao."

Watching her go, Daniele regretted his earlier assessment of her. He felt pity for her. "She's going to tell, isn't she?"

"I think so, but is she well?"

"I think she's . . . if you'll forgive me, I think she's a fragile woman."

Sensitive Daniele always understood more about people's emotions. Perillo, thanks to his painful youth in the streets of Pozzuoli, had worked hard to shut down his own sensitivity. Sometimes being corrected annoyed Perillo, but he was grateful Daniele made up for what he at times lacked. "Of course, she's grieving. She just lost her lover to murder. It is also clear Mantelli wasn't always good to her, but Loredana Cardi does have a strange way of expressing grief."

"Signora Severson called her a lost lamb."

"Or she's a skillful actress." The disappointed look on Daniele's face made Perillo regret having voiced the possibility. "I'm sure you're right. She's just fragile."

"I could be wrong," Daniele admitted reluctantly. "The owner here stopped me in the hallway and told me not to believe a word she says. He mentioned that accidents can be made to happen, and that we should give her a good look."

Perillo raised an eyebrow.

"I couldn't tell you in front of her."

Perillo checked his cell phone for the time. "Damn it. It's late. Ivana is making us both Pasta alla Norma."

Daniele's stomach groaned. He loved Signora Perillo's cooking. "We could eat quickly and then come back?"

"Excellent idea, Dani. Tell the owner we'll be back at three. After that, you'll go to Il Falco and talk to the maitre d', and I'll tackle Aldo Ferri. It's going to be a busy day, and we'll need all those Pasta alla Norma calories."

"You aren't waiting for Capitano Tarani?"

"I'll stop for good food, but not for someone taking our job away. You, Nico and I make a great team—we've proved it once and we can prove it again, damn it! By the time the capitano gets here, we might already have solved the case."

Walking to the car, Daniele tried to calm the maresciallo's anger by asking, "Isn't Pasta alla Norma a Sicilian dish?" As far as he knew, Signora Perillo stuck to cooking from her and Perillo's home region of Campania.

"It is Sicilian, but it's a good one. Penne with eggplant, salted ricotta, tomato sauce, basil, and a little garlic." Perillo kissed the fingers of one hand. "Divino!"

Now, for a more important question. "Maresciallo, shouldn't you check your cell phone?" The earlier phone call could have been from Capitano Tarani.

"I was just about to," Perillo said. "The thought of food always distracts me." The truth was he'd completely forgotten about the call. He looked at his phone. "Good. Not Della Langhe or Capitano Tarani." He pressed the callback button. "Ehi, Nico. Sorry, but I was in the middle of telling Signorina Loredana her boyfriend was murdered. Her reaction was interesting, to say the least. I'm not saying it was a guilty one. Just a little crazy." He filled Nico in on what she'd told them. "What's your news?"

Nico told him of Diane Severson's private visit to Aldo and what Aldo had relayed to him. "I had his permission to tell you."

"I hope you would have told me anyway."

"Yes, but this way I feel better."

"That's right. You are a kind man, like my good brigadiere here. A good trait, but it can get in the way of a murder investigation. Thanks for the news. Now we know who made Mantelli's laptop disappear. Ciao." He clicked off.

"Signora Severson took it," Daniele declared as he swerved to avoid a pot hole.

Perillo gaped at him. "How the hell did you know?"

"She would want to find out where her husband hid his money."

"Good thinking, Dani." Perillo was pleased his brigadiere was clever as well as sensitive, but he couldn't help being a bit annoyed with himself. Fifty was looming just ahead of him. Was his mind slipping? "Of course, I suspected that too, but Loredana could have also taken it. Or even Peppino. Well, we'll invite Signora Severson to explain herself tomorrow morning. For now, Pasta alla Norma." He reached over and honked the horn, startling a dog on the side of the road.

Daniele gave the maresciallo a quick, questioning look.

"A honk to life, dear Dani."

AS SOON AS NICO opened the gate of the cemetery, OneWag ran ahead to Rita's grave site. Usually, he followed Nico to the water fountain to gulp down some running water while Nico took one of the empty glass vases lined up on a stone shelf, and filled it with water. Today, quenching his thirst could wait. He had spotted a friend and rushed over to say hello.

Nelli picked up the dog and moved further up another aisle, hoping Nico hadn't seen her standing in front of his wife's grave. She buried her face in OneWag's neck to cover her embarrassment.

Startled, Nico stopped halfway up the path, the vase of pink peonies held tight against his chest. "Nelli," was all he could say. He had stopped himself from adding, "What are you doing here?" Her presence in the cemetery made him feel awkward.

Nelli straightened up and showed her face to Nico, still holding the dog tight against her chest. She hadn't stopped to think that he might show up. It was foolish to have come here, hoping that standing in front of Rita's grave, looking at her photo, would give her some insight into the love Nico still felt for her. "Please, let him go," she had whispered to Rita's smiling face, as if it was Rita holding him captive.

"Ciao, Nico. We seem to have picked the same time to pay our respect to our loved ones."

He nodded.

"Those are gorgeous flowers," she said as he walked to Rita's grave. OneWag squirmed and she put him down. He lay down next to Rita's grave, his ears at attention.

Nico bent down and placed the vase next to Tuesday's flowers. "They're Luciana's darlings. Whatever I pick, they're her darlings. If she could, she would keep them all." He looked up. "Who are you visiting here?"

"My cousin," she lied. All her relatives were Panzanesi and buried in the Panzano cemetery.

"How is Zio Peppino? Mantelli's death must have been a shock for him. And a tragedy."

"Yes, it's very sad. He keeps repeating to my mother how good Mantelli was to him, how he didn't deserve to die. I imagine he's also worried his wife will sell the villa. He'd be devastated if she did. Taking care of that place has been his whole life."

"Let's hope she doesn't." Nico took last week's still-perky anemones and added them to the peonies. He leaned back and surveyed the flowers. "They don't look very good together, do they?"

"Pink and purple complement each other," Nelli said. "They just need a little rearrangement. May I?"

He straightened up. "Please. You're the artist."

Nelli walked over quickly, her heartbeat rushing, and knelt. She removed the anemones and carefully inserted them one by one between the bushy peonies, making sure they didn't get crowded out. She hoped Rita would forgive her intrusion, but helping felt good.

Nico watched. The combination of flowers now looked wonderful. His awkwardness faded. Nelli making Rita's resting place more beautiful somehow brought together his wife and this woman he admired. Had they known each other, he was sure they would have been friends.

Nelli looked up at Nico. So did OneWag. "What do you think?"

Nico smiled. "A work of art. Thank you."

Nelli smiled back. "Exaggeration is an Italian trait, not an American one."

"My mother was Italian."

"That explains it, then." Nelli stood up. Nico held out his hand to help her. She took it briefly, then used both hands to pull down her paint-splattered shirt. She had been unsuccessfully painting clouds, a new obsession of hers, when the need to express her feelings for Nico to his dead wife overwhelmed her. "Ciao, Nico. Ciao, Rocco. See you around."

"Sure. Thanks again."

"One thank-you is enough."

Nico and OneWag watched Nelli walk down the gravel path to the iron gate. In that moment, Rita was forgotten.

PERILLO AND DANIELE DIDN'T get back to Il Glicine until four o'clock, thanks to a delicious leisurely lunch followed by a phone call from Capitano Tarani saying he was at the tail end of a murder case in Montespertoli and wanted to know if Perillo had any good leads. Perillo answered that it was hard to seriously interview people without letting them know that Mantelli had been murdered. He had, of course, told Signora Severson and Mantelli's girlfriend. Della Langhe had objected to Loredana being told, but Perillo had insisted it was the right thing to do. Capitano Tarani agreed, which gave Perillo hope that they could work together well. Perillo added that he needed to know the contents of Mantelli's will.

"That's for me to know," was Tarani's answer, followed by what sounded like a chuckle. "Don't worry, Perillo. I'm in the habit of sharing. I'll be with you tomorrow, or at the latest Sunday."

"How bad is he?" Daniele had asked afterward.

"Too early to tell."

Now, Dario Terzini, the owner of Il Glicine, was sitting across from Perillo and Daniele under the green awning in the same white plastic chairs the two of them had sat in with Loredana.

"Has Signorina Loredana come back from lunch?" Perillo asked.

"She moved out," Terzini said. He was a short, round, balding man, with an equally round face, a bulbous nose, thin lips and eyes set so deep it was impossible to know their color.

A cartoonish face, Daniele thought, the kind that would have scared him as a child.

"Did she leave an address?" Perillo asked in a brusque tone. He did not appreciate possible suspects slipping away.

"La Vigna d'Oro."

"And where is that?"

"The Mantelli villa."

No one had mentioned that the villa had a name. Calling it the Gold Vine made sense. Mantelli had made a lot of money with his wine expertise and perhaps the bribes, unless that story was the invention of an angry wife. Perillo lit a cigarette. It helped him think. Diane Severson and Loredana getting together was an interesting development. Had they been friends before Mantelli? Perhaps plotted his murder together? Did Diane think Loredana knew where Mantelli had stashed his money? These were possibilities. A lot to sort through. Nico would help.

"As far as we know, Mantelli's death was an accident," Perillo said. "But I am curious to know what led you to say we should take a good look at Signorina Loredana, apart from her beauty."

"She wasn't in love. She was after his money."

"How do you know that?"

"Early in the afternoon each day, they went to her room to fuck. Why they had to do it here and not at his luxurious villa is a mystery to me. I was embarrassed for my wife, for my guests. This is a stone house, but we added the guest rooms only ten years ago when we got the idea of turning this place into a B&B.

The walls separating the rooms aren't thick. We could hear them. Animals. In the early afternoon, guests nap. We lost one couple because of them, but I made Mantelli pay for that extra room for a whole week in order for me not to kick his girlfriend out. The couple was only going to stay two more days, but after all that noise, a week's rent was only fair."

Not liking what he was hearing, Daniele turned to look at the garden. A gray striped cat sat crouched underneath boxwood. He could hear chirping. Without thinking, he clapped his hands hard. The bush released two sparrows.

Perillo was staring at him. Terzini too. He answered them with, "It was only fair."

"Not to the cat." Perillo flicked his ash into Daniele's Christmas present, which now sat on his knee. "Signor Terzini, you are telling me that they were passionate lovers, nothing more."

"I heard them fight last week up in her room. She was screaming at him. He made promises he never kept, where was the money she was supposed to get, the diamond ring. The screams turned into screeches. I knocked on the door to make them stop."

"You say them. Did he answer her?"

"What I heard at the door was the sound of a slap."

Daniele flinched. "Did you go in to help her?"

"The door was locked. I asked if she was okay. She told me to fuck off, so I did."

Perillo took a last drag of his cigarette. Was the slap heard by Terzini the first or one of many? Had Mantelli and Loredana's relationship been an abusive one? That could be good motive for murder.

"Is there anything else you can tell us, Signor Terzini?"

"This morning, I told her I was sorry for her loss. She answered that I could shove it up my ass. I am very glad to be rid of Signorina Loredana Cardi." Terzini leaned forward, elbows on his knees, and looked at the young brigadiere. A man who saved birds did not lie easily. "I've told you the truth, now you tell me the truth. Accident or murder?"

"Accident or murder, you ask," Daniele said to gain time while he fingered the crease of his slacks and prayed he wasn't blushing. He looked up at Terzini. "Which is yet to be determined."

Perillo shot up from his chair, unable to keep a smile from his face. He held out his hand. "Buongiorno, Signor Terzini. Thank you for your time. Come, Daniele, we have much to do."

As they walked to the entrance, Perillo squeezed Daniele's arm. "You'll make maresciallo one day with a clap of your hands."

This time, Daniele blushed.

SEVEN

Nico was in his car, consulting a map of the Chianti vineyards. The possibility that Mantelli wanted money in exchange for a good review of wines made him wonder about the excellent reviews Luca Verdini's wines had received in *Vino Veritas*. It took him a minute to find it. ColleVerde was at the end of a road southwest of Panzano. It would take him at the most twenty minutes to get there.

Nico folded the map and tossed it in the back seat, then started the car and opened the passenger door. OneWag, who had gone off to do his business, leaped in and curled up in the space under the dashboard.

The ride was bumpy once Nico left Panzano and the short stretch of road that led to Mercatale. The road marked white on the map was a one-lane stretch of white dust that challenged what few shock absorbers the small car had. Thankfully, no car came from the opposite way. As Nico turned a curve, a narrow wooden plank hammered to a tree announced Vigneto ColleVerde. A painted arrow pointed right. A row of young cypresses led him to a small graveled space and an open gate.

Nico parked. OneWag jumped up on the passenger seat, his tongue panting with anticipation. A man in worn jeans and a frayed red T-shirt appeared from behind a shed next to the gate. Large shears dangled from one hand. The caution Nico had learned as a young man patrolling the streets of New York made him stay put. "Buongiorno," he called out. OneWag stared, ears perked up. The man came closer. His T-shirt was stained with sweat, and dirt covered his jeans and one side of his face. "If you're here to buy wine, we're closed. If you're here to see the place, you're welcome. I could use the break." He wiped sweat from his face with his arm, leaving more dirt. "Which is it?"

Nico relaxed. OneWag stayed alert. How many times had he been kicked after a pat on the head? "I wanted both. I'll happily accept a visit. Do you mind my dog?"

"Not if he doesn't mind my Contessa. She's very friendly."

"So is OneWag." The dog followed Nico out of the car.

"Feel free to take a look around while I clean myself up a bit. I've been at it since five this morning, cleaning up the old vines. I'm Luca Verdini, by the way. I'd shake your hand, but," he opened his hands, covered in dirt.

"Nico Doyle. I thought this was a fairly new vineyard."

Verdini's face broke out into a big smile. "You're American!" Nico's accent in Italian always gave him away. "I love the United States. It's my best market. Welcome to my vineyard." Verdini began walking with Nico and OneWag down a geranium-edged path toward a square three-story stone house. "I bought it from an old man ten years ago. His family had owned it for two generations. He was the only one left, and he'd had enough of the business. He did warn me that it was a tough one and was generous enough to hang around for another six months to teach me. I've been lucky enough to be able to add new vines. Where are you from?"

"New York City."

"Exciting and exhausting." He pointed opposite the house to a partially enclosed area next to a shed. "That's where we do our tastings and selling in good weather. We keep the wines in the shack. Make yourself comfortable. I apologize for the chairs. I've got to replace them. I'll be right back."

Nico watched Verdini hurry into a side entrance of his house.

The man was simpatico. For some reason, he hadn't expected that. Maybe he could ask Verdini point-blank. On the far side of the shed, Nico discovered an old table surrounded by several chairs. Grape vines wove in and out of a trellised roof and gave a lacy shade. Nico sat down on a hard, stiff-backed chair and looked at the shallow valley dissected by countless neat rows of vines, the grass in between spattered with red poppies. In the distance, a quilt of vine patches went in different directions. It was the standard Chianti vista that brought so many tourists to this part of Italy. The wines, they could buy in stores all over the world—it was the view that delighted people. It had certainly delighted him the first time Rita had brought him to her home-town. It still did. And above all, it made him feel at peace.

Nico noticed OneWag sitting next to his feet. The dog usually took every opportunity to explore new territory. "Go." The dog looked up. "Find Contessa. You're not scared of her, are you?"

OneWag didn't budge.

"I'm glad to see you talk to your dog too." Verdini walked quickly toward Nico. "My ex-wife thought I was being ridicu-lous. I apologize for taking so long. I was covered in grime." He stopped next to Nico. Verdini had changed into clean jeans and a yellow cotton shirt with rolled-up sleeves. His tanned face, a plain, friendly looking one, was now clean. What had looked like graying hair was wet, dark and neatly combed back. He couldn't be more than thirty-five. "Hello, little one." He bent down and offered his hand to OneWag, who barely gave it a sniff, apparently unconvinced. "See, no shears. You're both safe here." Verdini straightened up and whistled. A flash of red at the far end of the garden attached to the house turned into a beautiful Irish setter bounding toward them. "Contessa, come greet our guests."

OneWag ran out to meet her. They sniffed each other for a bit. "She's very beautiful," Nico said.

"You should have seen her mother. She was the best. Having

to put her down was extremely painful." The sadness showed on his face. "Contessa doesn't quite fill her shoes."

"Was it old age?" Nico knew that losing OneWag when the time came would leave a hole in his life too. The dogs were now leaping at each other, twisting and turning.

"Regina was riddled with cancer. She was only six."

OneWag started running down the lawn in front of the house. Contessa outpaced him with a few leaps. OneWag followed as fast as he could on his short legs. A minute later they were out of sight.

"While they're having fun, what's your preference?" Verdini asked, unlocking the shed door. "Red or white? My white is good. I grow Vermentino, but my reds are what ColleVerde is known for."

"Red, then. Michele Mantelli thought very highly of your reds."

"Ah, you read Mantelli's blog?" Verdini disappeared inside the shed, leaving the door wide open. "Do you subscribe to his magazine, *Vino Veritas*?"

"I just did." He'd subscribed right after Aldo's visit. He'd wanted to read a few recent issues to ferret out who else had received stellar reviews. If Mantelli demanded money regularly, someone may have gotten tired of paying. Verdini for one, but he wasn't the only vintner Mantelli had praised. "But Mantelli praised your wines in person on Tuesday at a restaurant in Gravigna where I work."

Verdini came out of the shed holding two stem glasses and an open wine bottle. "He just died, you know. Horrible accident."

"Yes, I heard."

Verdini sat down and poured a generous amount of wine in each glass. "He deserves a toast. I owe my start to him." He raised his glass. "Thanks, Michele."

Nico raised his glass and drank with his host. He'd just been offered an opening. "There are rumors going around that

Mantelli wanted to be paid for his reviews. I'm not suggesting you were involved, as your wine merits all the praise it gets, but I'm curious." God, he was turning into a devious liar, but he was worried for Aldo. "Was there any truth in that?"

Verdini took another sip of his wine, his eyes fixed on his guest's face. Nico felt he was being assessed.

After what felt like a full minute, his host put his wine glass down on the table. "You're not a reporter, are you?"

"No. An ex-policeman, now a waiter and helper at a restaurant owned by my late wife's cousin."

"I understand that it's the policeman in you who wants to know, but why?"

"I'd like it not to be true." Another lie.

"You wish to see Italy as an uncorrupt country. So do I, but all countries are corrupt, including yours. Italy is just worse at hiding it. And I'm sorry to disappoint you, but Mantelli did ask for payment, at least from me. I was happy to pay. He had the power to put me on the map."

Nico was surprised but tried to keep the expression on his face neutral. He hadn't expected Verdini to be so open.

"You may scorn me, but necessity is a powerful motivator," Verdini said. "Should I feel guilty? Yes, but I have no regrets. I needed him. Once my wines were praised on his blog and in his magazine, other wine critics, important ones in the States, discovered me. Anthony Galloni in *Vinous*, James Suckling, the Robert Parker people, started giving me high marks. You cannot imagine how wonderful and gratifying that was. I had always thought my wines were good, but paying for praise chipped away at my confidence. I was right from the start. My vines produce excellent wines."

"Did you stop paying him?"

"No, and he deserved every euro. Last year he even came by and joked about it, admitting that my wines deserved praise for free." Verdini looked at his watch and finished the wine in his glass. "I'm afraid I must go. I have clients to call, paperwork to deal with. But stay, finish your glass, even the bottle if you want. The sunsets here lift the spirit." Verdini stood and held out his hand.

Nico got up and shook it. "Thank you for the wine and letting me enjoy the view. And answering my doubts about the rumors. It will stay between us." A smaller lie this time.

"If you want to buy, come back in the mornings. Ginevra is here from nine to one." He turned to leave, then turned back around. "You may want help getting your dog back. Contessa can be very possessive." Verdini put his two forefingers in his mouth and whistled. The sound was ear-shattering.

It didn't take long for Contessa to come loping up the path, ears flying, feathered tail held high. Half a minute later, OneWag appeared, his short legs running like a frenetic hamster's on a wheel. Contessa jumped on Verdini. He ruffled her fur. "Bad girl. Where did you take our guest?" She smelled strongly of manure.

Nico turned to look at OneWag. The dog was filthy.

"I can give you a towel to wrap him up in," Verdini offered. "It will cut the smell."

"No need for that. I'll keep all the windows open. Thanks again. I'll come by next week and buy a case of your Riserva." He'd give half to Tilde and Enzo.

"Good. It's been a pleasure chatting with you. Ah, we're usually closed on Sundays."

"I'll keep that in mind." Nico walked along the red geranium path to his car. OneWag followed with his tail between his legs, now conscious of how dirty he was. In the car, Nico cranked down all the windows and opened the door. The dog jumped over the front seat to the back and curled up on the floor into the smallest ball he could manage.

BY THE TIME PERILLO and Daniele got back to the station, Loredana Cardi had announced her boyfriend's murder on Facebook and Instagram. The news was speeding across the airwaves and whatever other waves the media used to glean information.

"Good," Perillo said when Vince gave him the news. "Now we can fully begin the investigation. If Della Langhe calls, I'm still up in Montefioralle, and you haven't been able to reach me. And get rid of that gum. My carabinieri don't chew gum."

Vince rubbed his stomach. "Please, be reasonable, Maresciallo. It helps with my hunger."

"Take up smoking. You'd lose ten pounds in a month."

"And my life."

"That would take longer."

Vince walked away with his bear gait, shoulders hunched in protest.

Perillo noticed Daniele looking down at his feet. The foot gaze meant he disapproved. "I was joking, Dani. Understood? Just joking."

Daniele looked up, his face tight with determination. "I am very proud to be working with you, Maresciallo, but I need to say something at the risk of getting transferred."

Perillo raised his hand. "You don't need to go any further. I know I'm always after Vince for eating on the job, but chewing gum is just as bad. We need to be strong and dignified. How else are people going to respect us?"

Out of respect, Daniele lowered his eyes and said nothing.

Perillo looked at his brigadiere for a long moment, then reached over and patted Daniele's shoulder. "Understood, Dani. Strong, dignified and kind. Tell Vince he can go on chewing, but only at the station."

Daniele's face lit up. "Right away, Maresciallo."

Perillo raised a finger. "Wait. I'm going out for a smoke and another espresso. While I'm burning a hole in my stomach and slowly killing myself, I want you to call Aldo Ferri and tell him I'm coming to talk to him. You go to Il Falco and find out who was dining there Tuesday night. We need to find out who Mantelli was meeting with."

"You think he drank the poison that night?"

"When he went home with Loredana, he was having trouble with his eyes. The first symptom, according to the medical examiner, is visual disturbance. And he didn't make love to his gorgeous girlfriend that night, something they always did. I think yes."

Perillo turned and strode out of the station, slamming the front door.

"What's with him?" Dino asked, walking by.

"Della Langhe is going to put his head on a plate and have it for dinner. He didn't want the media to know about the murder." Daniele also suspected Perillo was annoyed he'd given in about the chewing gum.

Dino spread out his arms dramatically. "How else were we supposed to investigate?"

Dino had never even investigated the disappearance of a cat. All Daniele said was, "With God's help," before he went to find Vince and give him the good news.

"WHERE'S STELLA?" NICO ASKED Tilde. They were in the kitchen of Sotto Il Fico, preparing for dinner. A kitchen barely big enough for three, with pots and cooking implements covering one full wall. A marble counter for rolling dough was at one end next to the stove, with a small window giving a partial view of the terrace. Another wall held two ovens and, after Nico's insistence, the new addition of a microwave. "I thought she'd be here."

Out on the terrace, Alba and Enzo were setting tables. Elvira was ensconced in her armchair, lightly snoring. OneWag was out, wandering the town. Nico had been tempted to keep him home as punishment for rolling in manure, but the dog had given him such a pleading look that he couldn't bring himself to do it.

"Wasn't she coming home tonight?"

"She's taking the last bus." Tilde bent over and put the large pan of carciofi gratinati in the oven. Artichoke hearts covered in bread crumbs, parsley and Parmigiano was the special of the night, along with rollatini di melanzane.

"I can't wait to give her a hug." Nico rolled the last thin slice of baked eggplant around a fat tablespoon of ricotta and fit the rollatino in with the rest. He ladled the tomato sauce Tilde had made that morning over them and slipped the pan in the second oven to heat them. Two other pans were already in there. "The last time she emailed me, she seemed happy."

"She's excited about something and being very mysterious about it."

"It would be nice," Nico sucked the ricotta off his finger, "if she's found a boyfriend."

"Just like a man to think like that," Tilde said, giving Nico a sharp look. At forty-three, her once-beautiful face had hardened. Her adult life hadn't been easy. "Having a man doesn't solve any-thing. Stella is just fine without one."

Nico walked to the sink to wash his hands. "I'm sure she is." He knew he had touched on a delicate subject. Stella's last experience with a boyfriend had been very bad. "What do you want me to do next?"

"You out on the terrace and Alba in here." She leaned over and gave his cheek a peck. "Don't mind me. I'm nervous."

"I'm sure Stella's news will be wonderful."

Tilde smiled and gave him a push.

Nico raised his hands and walked to the door. "I'm done. Gone. Never to come back. Then you'll regret it."

Behind him, Tilde laughed.

THE TERRACE FILLED UP quickly. Nico, Alba and Enzo wove tirelessly between tables, keeping the customers happy with wine and Tilde's good food. It was tiring work, but Nico liked the cheerful atmosphere. Liked being out in the open in the company of a hundred-year-old fig tree and an endless vista beyond the terrace. Most of all, he was happy to be helping Tilde and Enzo.

As Nico hurried by a table with two plates of the restaurant's signature mushroom, apple and walnut salad, a hand reached out and stopped him. He almost dropped the plates.

"Oh, I'm sorry."

He turned to look at the table Alba had been serving.

Diane Severson was smiling at him. "I wanted to say hello. I was rather rude with you this morning."

"Not at all. Excuse me, people are waiting for these." Nico hurried off to a table at the edge of the terrace. He hadn't expected to see her. Unfortunately, he didn't have time to talk. He would like to hear her side of things straight from her mouth instead of Perillo's. He knew his friend didn't quite trust him with this case. He had told Perillo he'd been forced to retire because he'd broken the law. Now it seemed the maresciallo also knew the reason he had broken the law was to protect someone. Perillo probably thought he would do the same for Aldo.

Nico walked by Diane's table on the way back to the kitchen and acknowledged her with a nod. She responded by raising her full wine glass in a toast.

When Nico reached the kitchen, Alba was leaving the kitchen with three plates on her forearm and two in her hands, a talent Nico had tried to master and failed. "Alba, I need a favor. Can you take table seven and let me serve three? There's four of them at seven. I've just given them wine. They haven't ordered food yet."

Alba laughed. The plates didn't move. "You want the lonely lady, eh?" She winked. "Done. Ciao." Off she went, back straight, elbows tight against her waist, hips swaying. He'd thank her later. In the States, four diners instead of one meant a larger tip. Not in Italy. Tipping wasn't expected here, as service was added to the bill. At the most after excellent service, a waitperson was left a two-euro coin.

"What can I get you?" Nico asked Diane.

"Just that delicious toasted bread slathered in olive oil and rubbed with garlic. A double order. I have to absorb my wine." She had a bottle of Panzanello Riserva on the table. "You look like a calm, sensible man. Am I right?"

"I suppose I am," Nico said. What was she getting at?

"When the place quiets down, I'd love to talk to you. I would enjoy the company of an American for a change." She raised her dark, perfectly arched eyebrows. "Possible?"

"I'm not sure. I have to help clean up too."

"That's all right. I've got nowhere to go."

"IS THIS JUST A chat, or am I being interrogated?" Aldo asked as Perillo walked into the Ferriello welcome center a few minutes after 7 P.M.

"Buonasera," Cinzia said behind the counter, forcing herself to be polite. She was shifting wine bottles from one shelf to another to steady her nerves. She was scared.

"Buonasera. So you both know."

"Yes," Aldo answered. "According to the last news bulletin, Mantelli was 'seemingly brutally murdered, although there has been no official statement from the carabinieri in Greve-in-Chianti.' Since you're here, I assume it's true."

"It is." The news had spread quickly. Perillo found himself inundated by calls from RAI, the Berlusconi news channels and various papers. The only call he'd answered was from Della Langhe's assistant, expecting to hear that he was in real trouble for having insisted that Loredana be told about Mantelli's murder.

Barbara had instead reassured him that he was in the clear of any blame, since Diane Severson had also posted about her husband's murder. The timing suggested they had let out the news together over lunch.

"Come on out, Aldo. The air is cooling down." Perillo picked up a chair from the long table and carried it out to the open side of the large terrace. Outside there were benches he could sit on, but he liked back support. "Nothing like open air."

"Well, which is it?" Aldo asked again. "A chat or an interrogation?"

"I came alone, which means it's a chat to start with." He had sent Daniele to question the Il Falco restaurant staff. "Cinzia, you too."

"A chat, I can handle." Aldo came out on the terrace with three wine glasses and a bottle of his regular red. Cinzia followed with a platter of cheese and focaccia.

Aldo poured wine into the three glasses, sat down on one of the benches facing the table closest to Perillo's chair. "Now that he's dead, I wish him no ill will. I did hate him, but I didn't kill him."

Cinzia offered Perillo the platter, her way of underlining that this was a friendly chat. "The pecorino is from Piacenza, and I made the focaccia." It was what they offered to their wine tasting guests.

"Thank you." Perillo turned his attention to Aldo. "You punched Mantelli in public the day before he died. Why?"

"He wouldn't leave my wife alone."

Perillo looked at Cinzia. He wanted to hear the "why" from her too.

Cinzia took a long drink of her wine before answering. She had to be careful with her words.

Perillo studied Cinzia's face. He hoped, for both their sakes, that she would tell him the truth.

Cinzia put her glass down and looked up at Perillo. "Michele thought he had the right to anything and anyone he wanted. At first, he couldn't get over the fact that I'd left him for Aldo, but then he forgot about me for years. Unfortunately, I ran into him last year in Montefioralle. He told me he was divorcing his wife and suggested we get back together. I laughed in his face. That was my mistake."

"You told Aldo?"

"Yes. Mistake number two."

"Why a mistake?"

Cinzia popped a cheese square into her mouth. Shit. Why had she said that? She needed to protect Aldo, not make things look worse for him.

"Because my wonderful husband accused me of ruining his chances of getting a good review from Mantelli."

Perillo noted Aldo's look of surprise, quickly squelched. "He had never given me a good review, but after that, he threatened to ruin me."

"He wasn't going to ruin Aldo," Cinzia said. "It was just a bad joke."

"How do you know that?" Perillo asked.

"Because I called him and told him to stop being a bastard. He told me he was only joking, that all he wanted to do was get me upset."

Perillo looked at the cheese and homemade focaccia. Pecorino from Piacenza was the very best. His stomach grumbled. It was almost dinnertime. How could he eat their food when he might end up arresting Aldo? He couldn't. A cigarette would help. He took one out of the pack and fingered it. "This was over the phone?"

"Yes, and in person," Cinzia said. "I ran into him Monday night in the piazza in Greve. He assured me it was just a joke. Too many other wine critics consistently gave Ferriello wines high marks. He wasn't going to ruin his reputation by going against them."

Perillo pulled the ashtray closer and lit his cigarette. She was lying. What he had witnessed Monday night was much more than a conversation. He turned to Aldo. "Did you believe it was a joke?"

Aldo nodded. "A very bad one."

"Then why did you hit him?"

Aldo propped his elbows on the table and leaned forward. "Because he deserved it, because I can't control my temper, because, because—" he dropped his head in his hands.

Cinzia put her arms around Aldo and waited.

Perillo took a deep drag of his cigarette and waited too. There was something about this picture of upset husband and consoling wife that bothered him. Too emotional. Dramatic. Maybe Loredana had been enough for one day. "You are trying to tell me something, Aldo. Go on. What's the third 'because'?"

Aldo looked up and rubbed his eyes. "I was afraid Cinzia would leave me."

Well, that made sense, Perillo decided. Mantelli was rich. Cinzia could finally stop working herself to the bone. It explained what he had seen Monday night; Mantelli and Cinzia in a tight embrace.

Cinzia held her husband's face in her hands. "I would never leave you. I love you." She kissed him on the lips, then the nose. They hugged.

Very endearing, Perillo thought, but why didn't he believe them? Too bad Daniele wasn't here to read the scene. He stood up. "Just one more question and I'll go. The question applies to both of you."

Both untangled themselves and looked up at Perillo with wide eyes.

"Where were you Tuesday night?"

"I was at home," Cinzia said. "I was alone."

"And I took a client out to dinner. After dinner, I dropped him off at his hotel and came home."

"Where did you and your client have dinner?"

"Il Falco."

"At what time?"

"Eight o'clock."

"Your client is still here?"

"He flew back to China this morning. I have his email if you need confirmation."

"Mantelli was also dining at the same restaurant. Did you see him?"

Aldo's face froze. Cinzia clenched her fist.

"Tuesday night, did you see Michele Mantelli?" Perillo asked again, his face and voice neutral, as though nothing was riding on the answer. "Maybe you even spoke to him."

Aldo shook his head. "No. No, the last time I saw him was that afternoon in the town piazza."

Cinzia released her fist. "Il Falco has three dining rooms."

"I hope you are telling me the truth. This case is now being taken out of my hands. Capitano Carlo Tarani will be in charge. Before he comes, I need separate statements from each of you. I'll be at the station tomorrow morning at nine. You decide which one wants to come in first." He reached down and took a square of pecorino from Piacenza and stood up. "Thank you. See you in the morning."

In the car, he called Daniele. "Any luck at Il Falco?"

"Yes. The maitre d' told me Aldo Ferri was there at the same time as Mantelli, but in another dining room. Mantelli's wife was in the third dining room."

He'd called Luca Verdini, who confirmed he'd accompanied Diane to the restaurant and also confirmed that she hadn't gotten close enough to Mantelli's table to pour anything in his drink. For the moment, he accepted that Verdini was telling the truth.

"Anything else?"

"No one saw either Ferri or the wife with Mantelli," Daniele reported. "Yunas, the waiter who served Mantelli, isn't working tonight, but the maitre d' gave me his phone number. Should I call him now? I'm still here going over the night's guest list."

"Wait until the morning. Good work, Dani."

"Just doing my duty the way you taught me, Maresciallo."

Perillo clicked off, feeling satisfied both with the compliment and with what he'd learned this evening.

THE SPLASH OF RED and orange that the sun had left in its wake was now gone. Only pinholes of light punctured the black sky. Alba was in the kitchen cleaning up with Tilde and Nico, at the same time keeping an eye on the terrace from the small window above the sink. Only a few diners were still there, nursing the last of their wine, the light of the table candles flickering on their faces. Diane Severson, sitting alone, was dipping Alba's cantuccini in a glass of sweet wine.

Alba nudged Nico with her elbow. "Go out there. She's waiting; I'll finish cleaning."

"Alba's right," Tilde said, as she hung the cleaned pots back on the wall. "This is your chance to find out if she killed her husband."

Alba gasped. "She didn't!"

Tilde shrugged. "Maybe not. The spouse is always the first suspect. Go, Nico. Stay as long as you like. Think of it as a favor to your friend Salvatore. You've got the key to lock up. You'll see Stella at breakfast tomorrow. Eight o'clock at our apartment."

Most of the people in the town referred to Perillo by his first name. For Nico, the maresciallo, although a friend, would always be Perillo. He'd gotten used to using only last names while working in Homicide.

Nico removed his apron and dropped his dish towel in the dirty laundry bag. He had no idea why Mantelli's wife wanted to talk to him. He didn't believe his being a fellow American had anything to do with it. But whatever her reasons, he might be able to learn something interesting for Perillo.

"I'm sorry I've kept you waiting," he said as he approached her table. She had moved to an empty table at the edge of the terrace that gave her a dark view of the hills in the distance, now sprinkled with lights.

"Don't be. It's so beautiful and peaceful out here. I've been looking at the lights of Montefioralle, trying to spot my villa. No success, but I've enjoyed every minute. Please, sit with me."

Her invitation was delivered in a low seductive voice that made Nico hesitate.

She pulled out the chair next to hers. "I don't bite men I don't know."

Nico sat. "Maybe we should remain strangers, then." God, why had he said that? She was going to think it was flirting. He looked out at the view. "Peaceful is good for me too."

"At least your wife wasn't murdered." She saw the sudden flinch of Nico's arm. "I'm sorry. Please forgive me. I'm both furious and devastated, which makes me say terrible things." She was sure a hole had grown in her heart. "I'm not trying to find an excuse for being insensitive. I've always liked to state things plainly. And right now, I am self-involved and unpleasant. Please do forgive me."

"I understand." He had watched too many fall apart or lash out in fury at the news a loved one had been murdered.

Diane rested her chin on her hand and set her large eyes on Nico's. "But didn't losing your wife to cancer feel as if she'd been murdered?"

She'd just said a horrible thing, but he wasn't angry. "No, murder involves another person. An ugly, hateful, or greedy person. Cancer is neutral—something out of our individual control. How did you know about my wife?"

Before she could answer, Nico's cell phone rang. He looked at the screen. Perillo. "Please excuse me for a moment. I have to take this." He walked to the other side of the terrace. "I can't talk now. I just sat down with Diane Severson. She wants to talk to me."

"Maybe now that she's a widow—"

"I'm not laughing, so stop it. I don't know how long this will take. I'll call you in the morning."

"Wait, I'm the one who called. We need to get together before Tarani arrives. I'm getting statements from Aldo and Cinzia in the morning. If you're not working, my office at one in the afternoon. Agreed?"

No lunch duty tomorrow. He was free. "Okay."

"Tell her I know she's got Mantelli's laptop and I want it. Ciao." Perillo clicked off. Nico put the phone back in his pocket and walked back to Diane's table. "Sorry for the interruption."

"It's part of modern life. You were asking me how I knew about your wife."

"I was."

"Small towns only hide secrets, and you're no secret." Diane dipped her last cantuccino in the wine. Should she go on or hold back? Would he believe her? Find it embarrassing? She liked the man. He could help her. What the hell? Why not open up? She lifted the cantuccino, bit off the soft part and dropped what was left in the glass. What this man thought of her was up to him.

She leaned away from the candlelight, even though she knew her face would show no emotion. She had mastered that ability years ago. It used to make Michele furious. He'd slapped her once to see a reaction. She'd faked one to calm him down. "Right now, I feel the protective armor that helped me grow up, that made me withstand Michele's infidelities, the strength that made me successful in my field, is gone. I feel stripped naked."

"Wouldn't your son's presence help?"

"I called him to tell him he'd lost his father. His response was, 'I never had one.' He wanted to come home for me, but I said no. That I didn't need him."

"And you don't?"

"No. He would fuss, and I can't stand being fussed over. I know you won't fuss over me. You are very popular, I've discovered, which says a lot about you. It made me curious. Small towns don't easily embrace foreigners, especially so quickly."

"My wife was from here."

"Yes, but you are not your wife."

Two glasses and an open bottle of Ferriello Riserva appeared at his elbow with a fresh plate of cantuccini. He looked up to see Alba's swinging hips as she quietly retreated.

"You seem the opposite of me at this moment," Diane said. "Steady and calm. I felt I could use an hour of that. As I mentioned, I'm self-involved. I hope you're not finding it unpleasant."

"Not unpleasant. Just a bit . . . strange. Want to switch wines?"

"No, thank you. I like the sweetness of this Dolce Amore. And its name. Sweet love."

He half filled a glass with the wine Alba had brought. It was his first glass of the night. "I should warn you that Maresciallo Perillo and I are good friends."

Diane leaned into the table. The light from the candle at the center of the table lit up her face, and her eyes seemed to be smiling. "And I'm probably suspect number one and should watch my words?" She raised her glass. "Thanks. I appreciate you telling me, although I knew already. I've heard you were instrumental in solving last year's Gravigna murder."

"A great exaggeration." He hadn't done much more than make suggestions, but Perillo, overjoyed the case was solved, had insisted on giving him additional credit.

"I probably won't watch what I say. I find you easier to talk to than the maresciallo."

"Because I'm American?"

"No, because I don't think you'll jump to conclusions as easily."

Nico put his glass down and stood up. "I think you're the one jumping to conclusions. Maresciallo Perillo does not. You'll excuse me, but I need to go and help in the kitchen."

Diane grabbed his hand. "Please, stay." She didn't want to be alone. She'd hoped that the presence of Michele's girlfriend at the villa would make her feel better, but Loredana was wrapped up in her own anger and grief. She had no warmth to offer, whereas this man did. "Just for a few more minutes."

The emotion in her voice caught Nico by surprise. He stood still.

"I'll tell you things that could help your friend."

He sat back down and took a sip of his wine.

"I'll start by saying I did not kill my husband, although lately I've often dreamed of doing so." She stirred the wine-soaked cantuccino in her glass and watched it fall apart. What more to tell him that would cause no harm? "I took Michele's laptop before the carabinieri arrived. I'm still looking for his money—that's why I took it. To my great disappointment, there was no trace of where it is."

"What about Loredana? She might know something."

"You think that's why I invited her to stay with me?"

"It's not unreasonable." Why else invite her former rival?

"Well, I did think she might know something. Then I realized that what I needed was her company. We are two women who both loved the wrong man. There was the possibility that we could console each other."

"Did you?"

"No. I guess you have to grieve on your own. And she says she knows nothing about the money. It was dumb of me to think she would. Michele didn't trust women, thanks to his own mother farming him out to an aunt when he was three, so she'd be free to party." She took a spoon and fished out the wet cantuccino crumbs from her wine glass, then slipped them into her mouth.

Nico watched her close her eyes as she enjoyed the wine-soaked sweet. A tough woman who now needed consoling. Because she had lost the man she loved? Because Mantelli's money might be gone forever? Or because she was feeling guilty? She certainly struck him as capable of poisoning her husband.

Cantuccino gone, Diane opened her eyes and smiled. "There's heaven in small things."

"Maresciallo Perillo needs that laptop."

"Of course he does. I'll take it over to the station in the morning. His technical team might be better than I am. They might find the money and the murderer."

Perillo's technical team was Daniele, and he *was* good. There was a chance he could find at least a hint as to where the money was. "How would they find the murderer?"

"Michele kept a sort of diary of all his business dealings, about which I doubt your maresciallo knows anything. For instance, a list of the new vintners who paid him for a good review. One of them might have gotten tired of paying for what he thought wasn't a good enough review, or simply tired of paying at all. It's a possibility. Your landlord is on the list."

"How do you know they're bribes?"

"A sequence of sums next to each name. What else could they be?"

"Who else besides Aldo?"

"From Tuscany, only him and Luca Verdini. The other two are small-timers from Piedmont and Sicily. Four names in all. I'm surprised Luca agreed to the bribe. I thought he had a great start without Michele's help. A lot of other vintners were starting to praise him, but I guess he couldn't resist the great Mantelli blessing."

"Aldo said he was never asked to pay anything." Nico believed him.

"He would, wouldn't he?"

"You think he's the murderer?"

"He certainly had good reason, but I don't know anything beyond that. It's up to your friend to find out, with your help."

"After you spoke to Aldo, he told me you had a private conversation with Cinzia."

"Yes."

Nico sat back in his chair, keeping his eyes on her.

Diane met his gaze, then laughed. "Is that your interview-room stare? I'm supposed to confess under your penetrating gaze. My Siamese cat used to do that when I didn't give her the food or the toy she wanted. She'd jump on my lap and stare me down. She could stare for hours. You probably can too." Diane raised her arms in surrender. "All right, I'll tell you what I told her. That she was the only woman Michele had ever truly loved. He'd told me that only once, on a night when he was very, very drunk, way before the gout stopped him from binging. I believed him and still do. Cinzia leaving him that abruptly hurt him so deeply that he found refuge in being mean and selfish. He apologized for that, but said he couldn't help it."

"In other words, blame the woman. First the mother, then Cinzia."

"Yes, the usual out for many men, but in his case he had reason. I believe he did love only her. At least he believed it."

Nico wondered if Cinzia believed it now too. He hoped she wouldn't blame herself for his actions or his death in any way. He wanted to talk to her. He drank more of his wine. "Why did you erase the bad Ferriello wine review from your husband's computer?"

"I erased everything, not just that review. It gave me great pleasure to undo my husband's meanness, his fraudulent work.

There will be no more 'Michele Mantelli Wine Critic' blog. No more *Vino Veritas*." She picked up a cantuccino and bit into it. "Mmm. Delicious, even dry. These are the best cantuccini I've ever had."

"Alba, who waited on you, was the one who made them."

"She should go commercial with these."

"She's thinking about it." Or at least, Tilde was.

"Don't think about it, go Nike. Just do it. If she needs any help with packaging or marketing, she can count on me."

Nico rested his arm near the candle so he could see his watch.

Diane caught him looking. "It is late, and I've kept you here too long. I hope I've earned your time."

She hadn't told him anything he didn't know, but he was telling the truth when he said, "I enjoyed talking to you." Looking at her, he determined that she didn't need looks to be attractive. Her intelligence was enough.

"Good. You've made me feel infinitely better. Thank you." Diane stood up and double kissed his cheeks.

Nico watched Diane Severson walk away with a model's long-legged stride. He wasn't quite sure what to make of her.

EIGHT

Saturday morning, Tilde ushered Nico and OneWag into her kitchen. This room was a first for OneWag. He had already greeted Tilde with his single wag. Now, it was time to explore the brand-new smells.

Nico stayed in the doorway. He had many memories attached to this kitchen. He and Rita had eaten countless breakfasts in the wood-floored room that belonged to a previous century. Two old, mismatched armoires and a fat bureau stood against the walls in place of cabinets. Under the one window, a long oak table that had once been in a refectory served as counter space. Now, it displayed two cakes. One wall held a vast array of pots and pans so clean they gleamed. A waist-high fireplace was wedged into the corner. In the center of the room, a round table covered by a white lace tablecloth was already set for breakfast with Tilde's good china. The stove and refrigerator were the only modern appliances in sight.

Tilde noticed the softness in Nico's eyes. She patted his arm. "They were happy times."

"Very," Nico said. He turned to give Tilde a quick embrace for understanding him. "Today is happy too. Where's your beautiful daughter?"

"Doing her granddaughterly duty. Elvira always has to come first. You know that."

"She isn't having breakfast with us?"

"No. She isn't very good at sharing Stella. Sit down, I've just

made coffee. Enzo has gone to pick Stella up." Elvira lived near
the restaurant, Tilde and Enzo in the other half of the old town,
a good fifteen-minute walk from Elvira's home. Nico suspected
the choice of location was Tilde's.

Nico sat in one of the chairs around the table. Tilde poured
coffee into a delicate cup.

Enzo walked in. "Ciao, Nico."

Nico stood up. "Buongiorno."

The doorway filled with a sudden splash of bright blue. "Zio
Nico!"

Nico opened his arms, and Stella rushed into them.

"Ooh, I've missed you." Stella said, looking at Nico's strong
face with its deepening wrinkles and the smiling eyes. She
stroked his cheek. Good, solid Nico, who was always so kind
to her. When she'd moved to Florence at the beginning of the
year to start her job as a museum guard at the Opera del Duomo
Museum, he had written long weekly emails encouraging her and
giving her strength. He'd wanted to call, to visit, as had her parents, but she'd asked them not to. She needed to be alone, but the
emails were more than welcome.

OneWag looked up at Stella and barked. She picked him up,
burying her nose in his fur. Everything at home seemed the same,
and yet it wasn't, or at least, she wasn't. She was stronger and
more independent now.

"Sit down everyone," Tilde said. She led Stella to the table.
When she had come home last night, Tilde couldn't keep her
hands off her beautiful, sweet daughter. Almost six months had
passed since she'd left. Staying away from Florence had been
painful. Many times she had been tempted to drive to the city and
hide somewhere in the museum simply to watch her daughter,
breathe in her presence. She realized what a silly thought it was.
She never would have been able to just watch. The need to hug
Stella, to talk to her would have overwhelmed her. She had since

made peace with talking to her in emails. Stella would email back at most a paragraph, reassuring her all was well. Once a week, Stella would call on FaceTime, telling them about the people she met at the museum, going into details on the art and signing off with, "Don't worry, I'm fine. I love you."

"Sit," Tilde said. "The coffee's getting cold."

"And I'm starved." Stella sat between Nico and Enzo, the only two men in her life now. She was beginning to feel uncomfortable with all the attention she was getting at home, though loving it too. "I hear there's been another murder."

Tilde's sharp voice cut her off. "Please, Stella!" Last year's murder had weighed heavily on all of them.

Nico squeezed Stella's hand. He hadn't seen her in almost six months. She had called only twice, when she was worried about her parents. She looked tired and too thin. "I hear you have something special to tell us."

"I'll tell you after I've filled my stomach with Mamma's cooking." As Tilde poured coffee for the four of them, Stella brought over the two cakes that had been sitting on the refectory table. "My favorites! Mamma, thank you. I'm going to get fat this weekend."

"You need it," Enzo said and took the two cakes away from her. "Tell us the news now, please, if you don't want your mother to have a heart attack."

Stella laughed. "Mamma's too young for that." She sat back down and pushed the cakes back in front of her. "I'll only tell you if I can talk with my mouth full."

"At twenty-two, you can do whatever you want," Enzo said. "Just remember not to do that in front of your grandmother. Did you tell her?"

"No, Babbo. You come first." Stella cut a slice of semolina cake dotted with raisins and crystallized fruit and offered it to Nico. He pushed the plate back. "Eat and tell us."

Stella dug her fork and held it up in front of her. She wasn't being fair to them. "My good news is that I've been promoted. I even got a small raise." The loaded fork went into her mouth.

Enzo hugged her. Tilde clapped a hand over her mouth to stop herself from tearing. Nico patted her back. "So soon. That's wonderful."

"I'm not surprised," Enzo said. Tilde nodded. Her daughter deserved much more and would ultimately get what she deserved. Tilde had no doubts.

Stella continued to eat. She had taken it upon herself to be more than a guard for the area she was in charge of. She entertained the visitors with her knowledge of the works: *The Penitent Magdalen* by Donatello that had moved her to tears the first time she had seen her, Ghiberti's *Gates of Paradise* restored to a golden sheen, each panel a story all its own. The most moving of all was Michelangelo's *Pietà*. The director of the Duomo had noticed her involvement with visitors and promoted her to guide.

After polishing off two slices of each cake, Stella turned to Nico. "Someone you know has come to visit the museum several times. You'll never guess who."

"Gogol."

"No, although he would love it. You should book a tour with me and bring him."

"Not a bad idea. I'll suggest it."

Tilde stood up to make more coffee. "Gogol has only ever gone as far as Panzano. Florence would terrify him."

"Show him pictures of the *Gates of Paradise*," Stella suggested. "That might convince him."

"Who, then?" Enzo asked.

"Daniele, Salvatore's brigadiere. He only knows about Venetian artists, so he's full of curiosity about our art. He's a wonderful listener and can be quite funny too."

"Good for him," Nico said, noticing a slight frown appear on Enzo's forehead.

"You've seen him outside the museum?"

"Yes, we had coffee after work." She regretted having mentioned Daniele in front of her father. Daniele had been involved in last year's murder investigation, but then, so had Nico.

"He's a nice boy," Tilde said to put Enzo at ease. "Am I right, Nico?"

"Daniele is a piece of bread," Nico said, using the Italian expression he had learned last year. It meant Daniele was good and kind.

Enzo looked at his watch. "Ehi, it's time we got to the restaurant." He stood up and took his plate to the sink. "Nico, I need a favor."

"I'm yours."

"The other day I ordered three cases of ColleVerde wine thanks to Mantelli's recommendation. I got a bill, but the wine won't be delivered until Monday. I could use a case tonight."

"I'll pick up all three cases this afternoon."

"Thanks."

"You'd better hide the bill from your mother," Tilde said. Elvira's hawk eyes examined every invoice, and her arthritic hand wrote the checks. "She'll burst a blood vessel if she knows you listened to Mantelli."

"I've already taken care of it."

"Good." Tilde started to clear the table.

Stella stopped her. "Stop, Mamma. I'll clean up. I'll see you at the restaurant. Tell Alba she's got a helper for the weekend."

"She knows." Tilde dropped a kiss on Stella's head, waved to Nico, took off her apron and was out the door. Enzo blew a kiss at Stella and followed.

"I'm glad Daniele is taking advantage of what Florence has to offer," Nico said as he helped clear the table.

"He seems very eager to learn."

Nico wondered if that eagerness had more to do with Stella

than the art on display. Stella was just as beautiful. But he said nothing. Stella seemed lost in thought.

Stella threw out the coffee grinds and rinsed the two mokas. She liked Daniele's company, his enthusiasm, his innocence. The second time they had coffee together, she didn't want him to leave. She walked him to the bus depot behind the Santa Maria Novella train station. As he got on the bus, she had reached up and kissed his cheek. The redness that bloomed on his cheeks had made her smile.

NICO STOPPED AT THE Ferriello vineyard before going home. OneWag jumped out, looking for Arben.

Cinzia heard the car and came to the open door of the welcome center to see who it was. "Ciao. Nico. Aldo's not here. Salvatore asked us to give official statements about our whereabouts on the day Mantelli was poisoned. He wanted us separately, so Aldo went first."

That explained what she was wearing: a simple loose beige dress that covered her arms and knees. Cinzia's usual uniform was tight slacks and even tighter Ferriello top.

Nico walked over and kissed her cheeks. "I came to see you, actually. Do you have a moment?" Behind him, OneWag leapt after a tennis ball flying across the parking lot.

"That's a happy dog," Cinzia said stepping back inside. "I wish I could say the same for me."

"You're worried?"

"I'm definitely scared. Did you know Aldo and Mantelli were at Il Falco at the same time Tuesday night?"

"I did."

"Thank God Mantelli's wife was there too. She has a much stronger reason for killing Mantelli than Aldo does."

On the selling counter, Nico noticed an open bottle of wine and a half-empty glass. It was only ten-thirty.

Cinzia caught him looking. "Wine calms me down. Join me."

"No, thanks." He took both her hands and sat her down next to him on the bench. "Did Perillo tell you that the investigation is going to be in the hands of a captain from the Nucleo Investigativo?"

"Yes, he did. It makes things so much worse. Salvatore, Daniele, all the carabinieri at the station know us. We're good people, and Aldo would never kill anyone."

"I know that, but you have to tell the truth now. Both of you have to."

Cinzia took her hands back and sat up straight. "We have."

"I wish I'd come earlier, before Aldo went to the station."

"He told the truth yesterday. Salvatore will remember what he said, and Aldo will tell the truth today."

"What about you? Have you been telling the truth?"

Cinzia reached for the glass and took a long sip. "Of course I have."

"Omitting something is just as bad as lying, Cinzia."

"Since when have you picked up a judge's gavel?"

"I'm not judging anyone. It's not my place. I'm trying to help. If you don't tell the whole story about you and Mantelli, Capitano Tarani will find out. Perillo would have found out too. It's just a matter of putting two and two together."

Cinzia finished her wine and started pouring herself another glass. Nico tried to stop her. She slapped his hand away. "Fuck off, Nico. What do you know about anything?" She filled her glass and held it to her chest.

"Maybe nothing. Maybe I have it all wrong, but this is what I think may have happened. The name Ferri is on Mantelli's list of vintners who paid him for a good review. Mantelli could never give the man who stole his love a good review, but as long as he got paid, he wouldn't give him a bad one, either. Aldo is not a man who bows down to threats. He would have risked losing his vineyard rather than pay Mantelli."

Cinzia said nothing.

"You paid in his place."

Cinzia opened her eyes wide. "I did? If I paid him, why would Michele write that terrible review? His wife read it aloud to me, you know. He wrote that Aldo cheated, used grapes from another region. Why would he do that if I'd paid him?"

"This past winter, Aldo had to buy new harvesting machines, and suddenly there wasn't enough money to keep paying Mantelli. That's when he wrote the review, but he never sent it in. He knew that ruining Aldo also meant ruining you. You were his great love, and so he offered you an out. Leave Aldo, and Aldo would become rich from his praise."

"I would never do that."

"Did you make a counteroffer?" Not her heart, but her body? "Tuesday night, I saw you drive off at around ten o'clock. You don't have to tell me where you were going. I'm asking you to tell Perillo."

Cinzia was on the verge of tears. "And what? Tell him I was willing to sell myself to save our business? That would only give Aldo even greater reason to kill Michele."

"Why would Aldo have to know what you were planning? You can tell Perillo you wanted one more chance to change Mantelli's mind."

"By talking?"

"Yes. Let Perillo think what he wants."

"He'll think I killed him."

"I doubt he will. For one thing, he knows you, and from what the girlfriend told Perillo, it looks like Mantelli was already sick by the time he got home after dinner. What about Tuesday afternoon? Can someone vouch for your whereabouts?"

"I took Hua Chen to Florence in the morning. He wanted to buy his wife a present. After shopping, we had lunch. We got home around four o'clock. Aldo wasn't there, but Arben saw me. I worked with Arben the rest of the afternoon."

"That's good news. Now tell me about Tuesday night."

Cinzia finished her glass and pushed the cork back into the bottle. "Aldo wasn't going to come home anytime soon, so I decided to go to Michele's house to make him an offer he might accept. If he wasn't in, I was going to leave a note. I stopped halfway up the front steps when I heard a woman's angry voice. The windows were wide open. I got closer to get a peek and saw his girlfriend standing in the middle of the kitchen. She had her back to me, but I recognized the long hair. She was yelling at Michele for being drunk, for spoiling her evening, for making promises he wasn't going to keep. I couldn't see him until I moved closer. He must have been sitting. I only saw his head. He was holding it up with his hands."

"Did you touch anything?"

"No. I parked the car on the street and found the gate open. I just walked through the front garden, heard the voice and moved to the window."

"Good, let Tarani put you on the suspect list but not find fingerprints to place you at the scene. You'll tell Perillo everything?"

She nodded slowly. "You won't say anything to Aldo, will you?"

"There's nothing to say. I know you can count on Perillo and Daniele too."

"I guess I've no choice but to believe you." Cinzia walked slowly to the wine counter, picked up her handbag and took out her car keys. "I'm going there now. Ciao, Nico."

Nico stood up and linked his arm in hers. "Let me drive you to the station."

"That's the wisest thing you've said today."

WHEN NICO WALKED INTO Perillo's office for their one o'clock meeting, he was greeted by a colorful spread of food laid out on a low filing cabinet: thinly sliced grilled vegetables brushed with garlic and pepperoncino-infused olive oil next to a platter of different salamis, prosciutto and mortadella, surrounded by olives and slices of unsalted country bread. A large bowl of apricots, peaches and pears completed the picture. To one side were three cloth napkins and silverware.

Nico nodded his greeting to Perillo and Daniele, his eyes on the food. It looked like a modern art painting. "What a bonanza."

"Thank my wife," Perillo said, filling his plate with the meats. "I was going to order from the bar, but she said I would be insulting my guest." He pointed a fork at Nico. "You're a guest now. Help yourself, but leave some vegetables for the vegetarian."

Daniele, with fork and plate in hand, said, "Take all you want, please."

"I'm already full. I had a big breakfast with the family to celebrate Stella." Nico made a point of not looking at Daniele, who was right behind him. "She's here for the weekend."

"That must make you happy," Daniele said.

"It does. Stella makes everyone happy." Nico took a few slices of each offering and sprinkled salt on the unsalted bread that Tuscans favored. "She's a lovely woman."

Yes, she is, Daniele thought, feeling the heat rise from neck to cheeks. Thankfully, Perillo was behind him and Nico's back in front of him. Would he have a chance to see her while she was here?

"Give her my regards." Perillo sat at his desk and started eating.

"Mine too," Daniele added, hastily filling his plate.

Perillo forked a slice of salame and pointed it at Nico. "Cinzia left half an hour ago. Interesting what she had to say."

"I hope you believed her."

"There's no reason not to believe her, although . . ." Perillo left the rest unsaid.

"I know. She has a good motive, but the timing is wrong."

"You think Mantelli had already been poisoned by then?"

"I do."

"I'm afraid the timing is not that clear-cut, but I am inclined to rule Cinzia out. Tarani might have a different opinion. You had something to do with her candor, she says."

"She needed some encouragement." Nico sat in the chair facing Perillo's desk.

"I've asked for Mantelli's phone records," Perillo said, "but they haven't come in yet. According to his girlfriend, Mantelli was going to meet someone at Il Falco that night. We don't know who or whether they showed up. The waiter may tell us."

"A mystery appointment?" Nico asked before spearing a couple of slices of grilled sun-bright yellow peppers. "Definitely worth pursuing." The phone records or the laptop should tell them more, unless the appointment was made in person, he thought as a slice went into his mouth. It was soft and sweet, coated in an olive oil with a peppery bite. Why did they have to discuss murder over food like this?

"I've decided to add Loredana to the suspect list," Perillo said after swallowing his salame. "Although Daniele thinks she's too beautiful to kill anyone."

Daniele pulled up a chair and rested his vegetable plate on a corner of Perillo's desk. "That's not what I said."

"I know you didn't. I meant it as an affectionate tease, Dani."

"If you say so, Maresciallo." He thought it was an odd way to show affection, but he did know his boss meant well. What he had told the maresciallo was that Loredana seemed too fragile to have carried out the murder.

Perillo asked Nico, "What did you learn from Signora Severson last night?"

In the back of the room, the fan whirred, cooling off nothing.

"Not much. She's having a hard time with Mantelli's death, either out of love or because of the missing money. Maybe both. She admitted to taking the laptop. Mantelli apparently kept detailed notes on it. The only two Tuscan vintners paying him off were Aldo and Luca Verdini."

"Yes, we know. She dropped the laptop off this morning," Daniele said. "Including the password, which made things much easier. She left a note, wishing us good luck in finding the missing money."

"No mention of the murderer," Perillo added and bit off half a rolled mortadella slice.

"Interesting that she knew his password. What is it?"

Daniele dug into his pocket, took out his small notebook and flipped through a few pages. "Here it is. It's in English and I think German. Greenhill&Grünhügel. She explained that Mantelli kept all his passwords in an agenda locked up in his desk drawer. She found the key taped behind a picture on the wall."

"Forget the password," Perillo said with a wave of his hand. "What do we have?"

"You tell me," Nico said. Perillo may not be interested in passwords, but he found it intriguing that the password translated into Italian was ColleVerde.

"Four suspects: the wife, the girlfriend, Aldo and Cinzia." Perillo counted them off by picking up olives and lining them up around the rim of his plate. "The son is still in Australia. We checked. Aldo is the most solid suspect. He has a motive, means and opportunity, since he was at the restaurant at the same time as Mantelli."

"So was Mantelli's wife and whoever her date was."

"Luca Verdini."

"How did you find out?"

"She told me. I've got it in writing."

Nico was annoyed. Perillo didn't trust him. "You didn't tell me that. What else is in writing?"

"She tried to talk to Mantelli, but he told her to leave. She says she didn't get close enough to the table to put anything in his drink. Verdini confirms that."

"I'm glad I asked. They could both be lying."

Perillo threw himself back on his chair with a defeated look on his face. "You're right. We're in this together and I should have told you. I apologize. I'm upset, nervous. I hate the idea of this capitano taking over. Just hate it."

"It's okay. I understand. Everyone likes to be their own boss. Did anyone see Aldo and Mantelli together at the restaurant?"

"Not so far. The waiter who served Mantelli wasn't on duty last night. He's coming to the station this afternoon on his way to Il Falco to give a statement. He's not on duty for the lunch shift. And may I remind you that Aldo didn't have to be anywhere near Mantelli? All he needed was to be near the bar when the waiter was preparing Mantelli's whiskey."

"You're assuming the poisoning took place at the restaurant. It could have happened earlier."

"We have a statement from the gardener," Daniele said, eager to interrupt the ill feeling that had crept into the conversation. "Peppino Risso. A nice man. Mantelli also had a housekeeper, Ida. We haven't talked to her yet."

Daniele had put a slight emphasis on "yet" as a way of nudging his boss. Nico suspected Perillo hadn't seen the need to call her in.

"She could have interesting information," Nico said.

Perillo shook his head. "She's only part-time help." He was perfectly aware that he had done a lousy job with this murder investigation from the beginning. He was letting his intense dislike of the victim get in the way. Michele Mantelli reminded him too much of Substitute Prosecutor Riccardo Della Langhe. And knowing Capitano Tarani was taking over certainly didn't help.

"She works three days a week, according to Peppino." Daniele swept his bread across his plate to soak up the last of the pepperoncino-infused olive oil. "Always according to Peppino, Signor Mantelli didn't trust her. Maybe we should find out why."

Perillo raised his arms in exasperation. "All right, I heard you. Call her in!"

"Call who in?"

The three men turned to look at the door. Capitano Tarani, in full uniform, saluted.

Perillo scrambled to his feet. He was wearing cotton slacks and a short-sleeved shirt. Daniele shot up from his chair and saluted back. Not knowing exactly when Capitano Tarani would arrive and being cautious by nature, he was in uniform. Unfortunately, a dark spot of oil now marred his crisp blue short-sleeved shirt. He placed his hand over the spot. Since Perillo seemed dumbstruck, Daniele answered for him. "The housekeeper, Capitano."

Tarani took off his hat. He was a very tall, trim man with slicked-back dust-colored hair, a pointed face and small eyes that reminded Nico of the school hamster he'd played with as a child.

Tarani aimed his eyes at Daniele. "You are?"

"Brigadiere Daniele Donato."

Tarani shifted his gaze at Perillo and Nico. "Which of you is Maresciallo Salvatore Perillo?"

Perillo stepped forward. Tarani held out his hand. Perillo shook it, hoping his fingers were clean.

"You were aware I was coming?"

"I thought it was tomorrow, Capitano."

Nico stepped forward. "Domenico Doyle. I'm a friend." He caught Perillo about to open his mouth and stopped him with an icy stare. Tarani did not come across as someone who would welcome the interference of an American ex-homicide detective.

"I see." Tarani walked back to the filing cabinet and picked up an apricot. "You were celebrating something?"

"No," Perillo said. "My wife wanted to return the favor of Nico's hospitality the other night. As our kitchen is only large enough for two, she suggested I invite him here."

Daniele tried not to blush. The maresciallo's kitchen table could easily seat four, even six.

Clever, Nico thought, but again, blaming the woman.

"By the looks of what's left," Tarani juggled the apricot from one hand to the other, "you have had enough to eat. Now it's time to do some work. We have a murder to solve." The capitano gave Nico a pointed look.

"And I have work to do," Nico said. "Buon pomeriggio, Capitano. A pleasure to meet you." *The man hasn't even bothered to introduce himself*, Nico thought as he turned to Perillo. "Please thank Ivana for the wonderful meal." As he passed the filing cabinet, he picked up a pear and bit into it loudly.

As Nico opened the front door of the station, he was greeted by a little yelp. He looked down, thinking he had hit an animal. He was met by a pair of red high-heeled sandals.

"You hurt me."

Nico looked up to see Mantelli's very beautiful girlfriend, dressed in a long lacey white dress. "I'm sorry."

Loredana remembered to smile. "You didn't really. I'm just a little nervous. I know you, don't I?"

"I was at Sotto Il Fico on Tuesday, when Signor Mantelli was going over the restaurant's wine list."

"Yes, my Mica was still alive then. It seems so long ago."

Nico noticed her comment did not erase her smile. He also noticed that her pupils were reduced to pinpoints. She was high on something.

Loredana tossed her hair to one side. "I'm here to make a statement. Why are you here? You're not a suspect, are you? You look too nice to have killed anyone."

"Thank you. I'm a friend of the maresciallo's."

"That awful man? How could you be his friend? I'm sure he thinks I killed Mica."

"I'm sure he doesn't. He's a good man just trying to do his job."

"Well, it's a horrible job. Ciao, ciao."

Nico watched as she entered the station and stopped at the

front office. Vince appeared in a nanosecond, palming his hair, his stomach sucked in. By some innate Italian male instinct, Dino and another carabiniere came out of another office. "Signorina," all three said, almost in unison.

Nico grinned and shut the front door.

"COME ON, LET'S GO." Nico had driven home to pick up OneWag before going to Verdini's vineyard. "Enzo needs his wine."

The dog didn't even lift his head. He was comfortably lying in the vegetable garden beneath the bean plants. The earth was still cool from the morning's watering.

"OneWag!"

The dog didn't move. Nico knew this was payback for having left him at home while he met with Perillo. "Okay. I'll go without you. I'll come back smelling of manure, then you'll be sorry."

One ear perked up. "Ah, you remember your roll in manure with Contessa."

OneWag's head lifted. Nico started laughing—at the dog, at himself. During the winter, a bleak one with bad weather that had kept the restaurant almost empty, he'd started one-way conversations with OneWag. Maybe it was only his imagination, but the dog seemed to listen. He had unloaded years' worth of feelings and memories, both sad and happy. He found it comforting.

A whiff of cologne reached Nico's nose. He turned around. Gogol was slowly walking toward him, holding a crostino.

"Buongiorno, Gogol. What brings you here?" The only other time Gogol had been to his house was last September, when Nico had thrown a lawn party to celebrate the closing of the murder case with his new friends.

Gogol looked up at the sun. "The sun says it is now buon pomeriggio. I wish that for you."

"Thank you. The same to you."

"I was in the woods, looking for mushrooms."

"It hasn't rained in weeks."

"Where there is a heart, there is hope." He looked at Nico with gray rheumy eyes. "It is believed that only a lonely or a crazy man speaks to animals. Saint Francis found it a necessity. Crazy, he was not. Lonely, perhaps yes. I was alone this morning."

"Oh, shit! I'm sorry, I forgot to tell you. I thought I was going to see Stella last night. I saw her this morning for breakfast instead. Please forgive me."

"There is nothing to forgive. I was not alone for long." He shook a finger at Nico. "The poet says, 'I am one who, when love breathes in me, takes note.'"

"Whether *Inferno*, *Purgatorio* or *Paradiso*, I have no idea. But I think you're trying to tell me it was Nelli who kept you company this morning." Lately, when love came up, it always had to do with Nelli.

Gogol pointed to his boots. OneWag was sitting next to them, looking up at the two men and listening.

"A gift from Nelli." Nico guessed. "She loves you." He'd been told she had always been generous with Gogol. For years, she had offered to buy him a new coat, but he always refused. He claimed his coat had his soul in its pockets.

"And you?" Gogol asked.

"I am your friend."

Gogol shook his head with impatience. "'You think like a child, your foot does not yet trust to step on the truth.'"

"What truth?"

"Love is in your heart. You do not hear for you are steeped in the whys of that man's death. Keep your gaze on his fair-haired beauty."

"Loredana? You think she has something to do with Mantelli's murder?"

"She is one who has death in her heart."

"What are you saying? What do you know?"

"I know only the poet's verses. I go now. Monday, if I live. Sunday, I am in church with the Holy Mother."

Gogol loved being enigmatic. Nico occasionally thought it was a ploy for attention. "I'll be there Monday, but let me drive you home. I'm going to pick up some wine at the Verdini vineyard."

"Nelli's boots will walk me home." He bent down to scratch OneWag's head. "Go with your master. Keep him safe."

OneWag padded over to where the car was parked and waited for Nico to open the door.

NICO PULLED INTO THE ColleVerde parking lot and parked next to a Prius and a Mercedes. As soon as he opened his car door, OneWag leaped over his lap and sped down the path, looking for Contessa. "No manure," Nico called out just in time to see Verdini's Irish setter greet OneWag. They checked each other's smells, and then off they went. Nico took his time walking down the path, wondering if he should line his vegetable garden fence with geraniums. A slight welcome breeze stroked Nico's face. The house and selling shed sat on a crest. The vineyards lay below. He looked down to see Contessa running between fenced vines, OneWag chasing her. His dog would come back filthy, tired and very happy. Gogol's words returned to him. Was his friend right? Was he being childish by not acknowledging the warmth he felt in Nelli's presence? For choosing loneliness over the complications of a new relationship? Maybe love or something close to it was in his heart, but he was scared. And being scared was more than childish—perhaps it was stupid.

"Buongiorno," said a man walking up the path toward Nico, carrying a bag full of bottles.

Nico greeted him back.

"Here, taste the '15 vintage." His German accent was strong. "It is superior. There are only a few bottles left."

"Thanks for the tip."

The man hurried past him, bent to one side from the weight of his bottles.

Nico continued to walk down the path. As he reached the selling shed, he heard a woman's voice. "You were friends."

"Only business friends."

Nico recognized Verdini's voice. "Buongiorno," he said, stepping inside the small veranda.

Loredana, seated in a chair, looked up at him with her large blue eyes. "You again." Even frowning she looked beautiful, with her long lacy dress draped over her chair.

"I hope I'm not disturbing you."

"Not in the least." Verdini stood up and shook hands. Nico thought he detected relief in his voice. "Signorina Cardi was just about to leave."

"No, I wasn't." She stared at Nico's face. "You're not following me, are you?"

"No. Why would I?"

"You're friends with the maresciallo, and he thinks I killed Mica. That's why." Her words came out slightly slurred. She was still high.

"I'm here to pick up three cases of wine for Sotto Il Fico," Nico said.

"Of course." Verdini stood. Nico was sure now of the relief on his face. "I'm sorry I couldn't deliver. I'll go get them."

Loredana watched Verdini's back as he crossed the path and hurried into the house.

"Did all go well at the carabinieri station?" Nico asked.

"I'm still free. So is Diane, who has more reasons to want him dead than I do."

"What reason would you have?"

"I loved him. He was going to leave me. I saw the signs. I'm good at catching on to the bad stuff. I've had a lot of that in my life."

"I'm sorry to hear that."

"Thank you." She turned away from Nico and looked down at the vineyards below. She felt herself tremble. She wanted to shut up, but the pentobarbital l had torn down her usual barriers. She felt free, which was good. Scared too. Maybe she'd taken too many. She'd been able to hold herself together with that maresciallo, who was eating her up with his eyes. The young one was nice. He'd smiled at her as though they were friends. "Everyone only sees my looks and fawns over me. No one bothers with what's inside. Mica certainly didn't. He just wanted to show me off." She turned around and pointed a finger at Nico. "You know what's funny?"

Nico shook his head.

"Diane. His wife. She caught on right away that I had a suitcase full of crap inside me. She advised me to leave Mica. I thought she just wanted him back. But no, she was worried for me. She took me in, her husband's girlfriend. Even gave me some money. Does that make any sense to you? I like her and all, but I'm getting out. I've got other plans."

Nico looked at his watch. Verdini was taking his time getting those cases.

"He's hoping I'll leave."

"Why would he?"

Loredana giggled and leaned over the table. "He's attracted to me. I can tell, but he doesn't want to be disloyal to Mica. They were very good friends."

Nico tried to keep his eyes away from her chest, now in full display. "What makes you think they were friends?"

"All those wonderful reviews. That's what you do for a friend."

"When did you meet Mantelli?"

"Easter last year. I came to Greve for the weekend with a girl-friend. Mica was eating at the same restaurant, at the table next to mine." She sat up, excitement in her face. "And guess who was sitting next to him?"

"Luca Verdini?"

"Yes, yes. See? They were friends." A proud smile on her face. She reminded Nico of a child who'd just found a lost toy. "And you think he knows about the money."

"I know he does. I'm good at catching on to these things. It helps me survive."

What a sad, beautiful woman. And no, there was no way to exclude "beautiful" when thinking of her. "Did Diane send you here?"

She tossed her long hair from one side to the other. "No one sends me anywhere. I have my own plans. Ah, here's Luca."

Verdini came out of the house pushing a cart loaded with the three cases. "I apologize for taking so long," he said, avoiding Loredana's gaze. "I'll walk this to your car."

Nico could easily have taken the cart, but he sensed that Verdini was trying not to deal with his female visitor.

"Can you whistle for Contessa? My dog went off with her."

Verdini put two fingers in his mouth and produced a piercing sound. Two minutes later, Contessa came leaping up the path on her long graceful legs, her ears flopping with each leap. It took another minute for OneWag to scramble into view, panting hard. "Good boy," Nico said. No bad smells this time.

Nico turned to Loredana and said, "Arrivederci."

Loredana gave him her best smile and wiggled her fingers at him. Now she had Luca to herself. He was handsome, divorced. He had money. They could share. A new life with Luca. She blinked at the Irish setter, who stared back at her, sniffing the air. Did she stink? She widened her eyes to see better. The dog was dancing. She blinked again. The dog became fuzzy. Sleep. She needed sleep.

Loredana rested her head in her arms and closed her eyes. Mica was dead. At least he couldn't leave her now. Luca, alive. Nothing wrong with dreams. She heard the buzz of a bee. Footsteps. The squeak of the cart. Then nothing.

"I don't know why that woman came here," Verdini told Nico as they both pushed the cart up the path. "I don't understand what she wants. She keeps saying I was Mantelli's good friend and now that he's gone . . . and then she stops there and looks at me with those big pleading eyes as if I'm the solution to all her troubles."

"I'm pretty sure she's high on something."

"Oh, yes, that's clear. I'm sorry for her loss, but I can't help her." They reached Nico's car. Nico opened the door, pushed the seat forward. Verdini handed him the crates one by one. Nico dropped them in. OneWag jumped up on the passenger seat, rewarding himself for deserving a "Good boy" from the boss.

"A Fiat 500 was my first car," Verdini said. "I wish I'd kept it."

"What do you drive now?"

Verdini pointed to the blue Prius, the only other car in the lot. Nico had assumed that was Loredana's car. "How did she get here?"

"Diane dropped her off. I'm now going to call her to pick her up."

"Ah, that's right. You know each other."

A questioning look appeared on Verdini's face, quickly dismissed. "I do, thanks to my ex-wife. They're in similar businesses. Diane does textiles and design, Mirella furniture."

"You had dinner with Diane the night before her husband died."

"Yes, I did. At Il Falco. Mantelli was there too. Diane was hoping to have a word with him. I was there for support."

"She spoke to him?" Nico wanted to hear Verdini tell him what happened, in case it varied from what Perillo had said.

"Yes, I went with her. He was in a foul mood, kept saying his whiskey tasted like shit. She lectured him about drinking making his gout worse. He told her to fuck off. I pulled her away. In his mood, he might have struck her. Women are funny. After what he did to her, you'd think she wouldn't care if he drank himself to death."

"What did he do to her?"

"He cleaned out his bank account and probably stashed it in Switzerland, Lichtenstein, or some Caribbean island. She knew he'd written her out of the will, but that money also belongs to their son."

"If she finds it."

"I told her to get the Italian finance officials involved. They're so hungry for tax money, they'll ferret it out." Verdini punched some numbers into his cell phone. Nico waited.

"Diane, please, come and get your sick friend. She needs help." He clicked off.

Nico held out his hand. Verdini shook it. "I'll come back next week to pick up some wine for myself."

"I can get it for you now."

"No. It will give me an excuse to come up here again. Your vineyard is a feast for the eyes, and my dog has found a friend."

"I just hope this heat doesn't keep up, or it's going to hurt us." His expression was grim. "You're both welcome to come any time. No need to buy. Arrivederci."

"See you soon." Nico got in the car and watched Verdini walk away. As soon as he was out of sight, Nico called Perillo. "How's it going with Tarani?"

"I can't talk right now. He's bringing us up to date. Tonight, after dinner. I'll come to the restaurant."

"Good. Don't let him get to you. You'll solve this right under his nose."

"Thanks. We'll talk later." They clicked off in unison. Nico started the car. "Off the seat!" he ordered.

After a pleading look that got him nowhere, the dog obeyed with a low grumble.

CAPITANO TARANI WAS CIRCLING the room again, his boots hitting the floor hard. The room had been cleared quickly of all food by Vince and Dino, who happily helped themselves to Perillo's leftovers. Loredana Cardi had made her statement, signed it and left over an hour ago. Not even her beauty had softened Tarani's grim face.

"I've read Mantelli's will, notarized exactly two weeks ago. He left his wife nothing, which of course is against Italian law. Wives and children cannot be disinherited. Mantelli hadn't yet divorced her, nor had they filed for a separation. She will get what is due to her. To his son, he leaves the bulk of his money, except for two thousand euros that go to a Giuseppe Risso."

"That's his gardener," Daniele said.

Tarani continued, clearly not interested to know more about Giuseppe Risso. "There are no other codicils. We've spoken to the manager of the bank where Mantelli had a joint account with his wife. He confirmed there were only a few thousand euros left in it." Round and round the room he went, like a circus horse. "I pressed him to work backward to pinpoint when big sums of money were withdrawn. I said it was of the utmost urgency. Mantelli might have been the victim of a blackmailer, but blackmailers don't usually kill their victims, so I'm not giving that theory much weight. He'll get back to me soon. We have also contacted the department of finance to look into where Mantelli's money ended up. However, his money is only of tangential importance to our case."

Then why the utmost urgency? Perillo wondered. His fingers kept twirling a cigarette. He was ready to sell his soul to the devil for a smoke. And it was way past his afternoon coffee break. "You don't think he might've been killed because he wouldn't reveal where the money was?"

"Seems pointless, but it is a possibility. Now, I want a factual account of what happened between this Aldo Ferri and Mantelli on Tuesday afternoon. Only the facts, please. Leave the interpretations to me."

Perillo, seated at his desk in the middle of the room, was getting a neck ache trying to keep eye contact. "I was not present at the dispute between the two. What I know was referred to me."

"By whom?"

"Connor Domenico Doyle, who was here when you came in."

"The American who walked out loudly chewing a pear?"

"He goes by the name of Nico," Daniele chipped in.

"He left out Connor when he introduced himself. A man who has refused his first name. Odd."

"His father was Irish, his mother Italian."

"A volatile combination, I've been told. So he chose the mother. How long has he been here?" He looked at Daniele for the answer, since the young brigadiere knew the man's nickname.

"One year, Capitano."

Tarani turned to Perillo. "Could he in any way be involved in Mantelli's murder?"

"No. He happened to be in the piazza when the incident took place. Aldo Ferri is his landlord."

"So Doyle will give a biased account. Were there any other witnesses?"

"Yes, quite a few." Perillo was groaning inside. He hadn't bothered to get the names of the people in the piazza. He'd relied solely on Nico's account. Tarani was going to give him an ulcer. "Aldo Ferri is a respected man in Gravigna. Everyone will be biased in his favor. Mantelli was not well-liked. Ferri himself described what happened in his statement. I have it here. It's a straightforward account." Perillo held out the two sheets.

Tarani read the statement as he continued his walk about the room. Once done, he threw the stapled sheets at Perillo. They landed on his desk.

"Good throw, Capitano," Daniele said.

Tarani rewarded Daniele with a surprising smile. Daniele made a mental note of it. Tarani warmed to compliments.

"I was the captain of the basketball team at the University of Pisa."

"A fast, difficult game," Daniele said.

"Yes, indeed." The circling continued. "It seems to me that we have three strong suspects in the murder of Michele Mantelli. His wife, Diane Severson, Mantelli's girlfriend, Loredana Cardi, and Aldo Ferri. What about Ferri's wife? She had a motive, saving her husband's business."

"We have her statement. She has an impeccable alibi for Tuesday during the day. At ten o'clock that evening, she drove to Mantelli's villa hoping to talk to him, but she saw from the open window that Mantelli's girlfriend was with him. She left without speaking to him."

"And you believe her."

"I do, since the girlfriend stated that the only people in the villa were herself, Mantelli and the gardener. I think the girlfriend would have been only too happy to add another to the suspect list."

"Any other possible suspects?"

Daniele spoke up. "The gardener lived with Mantelli and therefore had access. He might have known about the two thousand euros in the will, but he's a simple man who wouldn't know what to do with that money. He just wants to take care of the house and the garden until he dies."

"I agree," Perillo said. "Mantelli also had a part-time house-keeper, Ida."

"The one you were going to call in?"

"The very one."

"Bring her in tomorrow. I presume you don't mind working on the Lord's Day."

"Murder does not pray." Perillo looked back at Daniele, who was already on the phone dialing Peppino for Ida's phone number. Poor Daniele would have to miss Mass. Perillo looked at the time on his cell phone. "We have half an hour before the Il Falco waiter arrives. I suggest a coffee break. There's a café next door."

"Excellent idea. What can we bring you, Brigadiere Donato?"

Daniele felt heat rise on his cheeks. He wasn't used to being left behind. "A fruit juice, thank you. Apricot if they have it."

"It shall be done."

Perillo looked back at Daniele and winked. "You will forgive me, Capitano, but it is my habit to have Brigadiere Donato accompany me to the café."

Tarani stiffened. "Of course. My apologies."

"Come on, Dani. We all need a break."

With a bright-red face, Daniele rushed to open the door for his two superiors.

NINE

Enzo helped Nico unload the three cases of ColleVerde into the front room of Sotto Il Fico. As they entered one after the other, Elvira sat up in her armchair and peered at the front door like a hawk that had just spotted a sudden movement. She was neatly dressed in her Saturday outfit, a loose green shirtwaist that covered most of her. Tomorrow, on Sunday, she would wear white to honor Jesus.

"Buonasera, Elvira," Nico called out.

She ignored him. "Enzo, did you get a receipt?"

"Yes, Mamma. All done. Go back to sleep." Enzo set down the first case behind the bar.

"I sleep in my bed. Here, I keep my eyes wide open. That terrible wine you ordered behind my back belongs in the basement. I don't want it anywhere near me. I can't believe my son listened to that terrible wine critic, God rest his soul."

All three cases were now behind the bar. Enzo and Nico straightened up and wiped their shirt fronts.

"Mamma, I'll move the cases later. We've got a full house tonight. Tilde needs us." Enzo walked over to his mother and gave her a kiss. "Don't upset yourself."

"I don't upset myself. I get frustrated with terrible decisions." She waved at Enzo. "Go to your wife and let me talk to Nico. Getting old is not easy. I used to be the ship's captain, and now . . ." she said, waving her hand in the air as if pushing the thought away. "Nico, come sit by me. I don't like to shout."

Nico pulled out a chair and sat next to her. He had learned there was no denying Elvira's requests if he wanted to feel welcome here.

"Has the maresciallo found the killer yet?"

"Not that I know of."

"And you would know. Good." She sat back in her gilded armchair. "What I have to say might help. This morning I went to my beauty parlor in Panzano, as I do every Saturday."

"You look very nice." Her black hair, pulled tight in a low bun, was now blacker than a crow.

Elvira patted her hair and smiled. "Thank you. Now, you must know that when women get together, they like to talk, exchange opinions. At the beauty parlor, we chatted quite a bit while getting our hair done. Of course, Mantelli's murder came up almost right away. While we talked about it, I noticed a woman I'd never seen before listen very intently to what we were saying, but she didn't join in. I thought that was curious and asked her if she hadn't heard about the murder. She said she certainly had and that she knew who killed Mantelli."

Nico nodded politely. A murder always got people clamoring for attention, spreading gossip. He needed to get out on the terrace and help serve already.

"Aren't you going to ask who?"

"Tell me."

"She wouldn't say. There were five of us in the shop, begging her to tell us. She claims she's decided not to tell anyone because she's glad he's dead. He was a nasty man who treated women badly. She asked us to forget what she'd said."

"Did she tell you how she knew this?"

"I had to go under the hair dryer and couldn't hear anything more. When I came out, she had left. I didn't miss anything because she'd stopped talking, but I did ask the owner of the shop who she was. She'd never been in the shop before, but fortunately she had made an appointment that day. Ida Crivelli."

Mantelli's housekeeper. Perillo hadn't gotten around to interviewing her yet. Did she really know who had killed Mantelli? Or was she just trying to get attention, to feel important? He would tell Perillo about the encounter when they met later tonight. Nico got up and kissed Elvira's forehead. "Thank you. You're still captain here. Keep listening. Every little bit helps."

Elvira's chest puffed up like a pigeon's.

When Nico walked into the kitchen, Alba slipped past him with a "Ciao" and four plates in her hands. Tilde was bent over the counter, cutting into a wide dish just out of the oven: a gratin made up of barely cooked spaghetti sautéed in browned butter, to which she'd added Parmigiano, the zest and juice of many lemons, topped with bread crumbs toasted in olive oil and shoved in a hot oven.

"Sorry I'm late. Elvira had something to tell me."

"I'm glad you listened. She's feeling neglected. Stella can't spend the whole day with her."

Alba was back. "I need four gratins and one grilled vegetables." She gave Nico a quick kiss. "It's busy out there. We could use your help. Tell your lady friend she'll have to wait."

"She's back?" He slipped five plates on the counter for Tilde to fill.

"Half a bottle of Antinori already gone. And two orders of my cantuccini." Alba filled her hands and arms with the plates. "She's at table six."

"It just means she likes eating here," Nico said.

"She asked for you."

Nico watched in admiration as a loaded-down Alba floated off to deliver her orders.

"It takes practice," Tilde said as she handed Nico two mushroom, apple and walnut salads. "Hand these to Stella. She knows where they go. Don't mind Alba. If talking to Mantelli's wife helps solve the murder, please do so. There's so much nervous gossip going around."

Nico picked up the shallow bowls. "I'm sure her presence here doesn't help."

Tilde laughed. "Wrong. The diners love it." She went back to cutting more portions of the gratin. "Stella says it's buzz, buzz, buzz out there. The rest of us would like a resolution. So it's up to you and Salvatore. Now go, get out of my kitchen."

Diane Severson waved at Nico as he handed Stella the salad bowls. She was seated on the far side of the fig tree with only a citronella candle illuminating her face. He acknowledged her with a nod.

"Thanks, Zio," Stella said. "Your friend is very anxious, and for good reason. She's been waiting for you. Please be nice to her."

Nico picked up a stray menu. "I'm always nice."

With hands full, Stella had to nudge him with her shoulder. "Most times. Ciao." Stella went off to deliver Tilde's signature salad.

"The mosquitoes are on the warpath tonight," Diane said in English as Nico walked to her table. She was holding a small electric fan to her face. It made her hair dance.

He dropped the menu in front of her, reverting to his waiter role. It made approaching her easier somehow. "Can I get you something to eat?"

She smiled at him. "Something that's not pure sugar?"

"It wouldn't be a bad idea."

"Widows of murdered husbands thrive on sugar."

The people at the nearby table obviously understood English, because they turned to look at her. She looked right back. They quickly turned away.

"I'm not drunk yet." She had lowered her voice. "Do you have time to chat? I need to ask you something."

He answered her by pulling out a chair and sitting next to her. "Ask away."

"Loredana says she saw you at Verdini's place. Why were you there?"

"I was picking up some cases of wine for the restaurant."

"You don't think he's involved in any way, do you?"

"Why would I?"

"You're a policeman. When there's been a murder, policemen are suspicious of everyone."

"Well, I handed in my shield back in New York. Do *you* think Verdini might be involved?"

Diane combed long fingers through her blond hair. "Why kill the goose that laid the golden egg? Too bad you gave up policing; I could use your help, I'm sure the maresciallo could use it too."

"It's not his case anymore. A Captain Tarani of the Carabinieri Investigative Unit has taken over."

"Good. Maybe I'll get results. I can spot your surprise, even under candlelight. Sure, I considered Michele a despicable human being, but I still want his murderer caught. That's another despicable human being removed from society."

Nico watched her face as she spoke. Did she believe what she was saying, or was it just for show? He couldn't tell. Her face revealed nothing. "Are all murderers despicable?" he asked. He was thinking back to the woman he had saved from a lifetime in jail. It had been the one impulsive act in his entire career, and it had forced him out of the police department. "Sometimes a person kills to survive."

"You can always walk away. I did."

"You're lucky your husband let you."

Diane took a small sip of her wine. "Loredana should have, but then she got lucky."

"You're not suggesting—"

"That she killed him?" Diane threw back her head and laughed loudly. Again heads turned. "Sorry," she said. "Sono americana." She leaned forward and lowered her voice again. "Have you noticed how Italians don't laugh like we do in restaurants? You barely hear them. I find it odd. It doesn't go with their open personalities. No, Loredana adored Michele. He was her lifeline. She thought she'd finally had it made. An important, wealthy man making her shine, giving her the life she'd always dreamed of."

"According to her, you encouraged her to leave Mantelli."

"To save her future pain. She'd been with him less than a year. Getting dumped for someone else would have come later, but it would have come. Well, she's been dumped a little earlier than I expected, and, as I feared, she's falling apart, popping pills and worse. I'm trying to get her to stop, but she won't listen."

"Did you drive her to Verdini's vineyard today because she wasn't fit to drive?"

"That was one reason. She asked about him this morning. Michele must have mentioned that I knew Luca. She perked up when I said he was divorced. She asked to meet him, using the excuse that Michele had talked about him a lot, which I doubt. I thought it was a great idea and offered to take her to his vineyard right away. Luca would make a wonderful replacement for Michele. He's good-looking, divorced, successful. A nice man, a little dull, but Loredana wouldn't notice. And Loredana is beautiful, young, sexy—and she needs help. She was very eager. I am too. I'd like to get her out of the house and settled elsewhere."

Was she really concerned about Loredana's future? Maybe having the young woman living with her hadn't worked out. It seemed bizarre to pawn off her late husband's girlfriend to one of his friends.

Diane peered at Nico's face. "You don't approve? I do have a reputation of manipulating my clients. If they want to cover their upholstery with beige fabric, and I think that's boring, I push until I can get them to adore blue and green or bright yellow. I refuse to deal with boring or bad taste. And I will admit that

I don't think Loredana has very good taste, despite her looks." Her eyes smiled. "There. I've bared my ugly soul."

Really not a pleasant woman, Nico decided, but he couldn't help admiring her. He still wasn't exactly sure why. Her gumption, perhaps. Or her not caring about how she presented herself. "Bare your soul just a bit more, please. You saw your husband at Il Falco, didn't you?"

"Yes, I was with Luca for support."

"Luca is a good friend?"

"No, but I know his ex-wife. I ran into him in Piazza Matteotti in Greve Tuesday morning. We were in the same bread shop. On the spur of the moment, I invited him to dinner that night. He said he had another engagement, but I wouldn't take no for an answer." Diane took a deep swallow of her wine. "It turned out to be a waste of time, which I knew from the start, but when I'm angry, I don't think straight. Michele was positively bestial to me that night." She looked up with a toss of her head. "Hardly the first time." Nico was looking at her with an intense gaze. "If you're thinking I'm the one who poisoned Michele, you're wrong."

Nico blinked. "Do you have any idea who did?"

"No."

"No suspicions?"

"I'm the only logical choice, aren't I? I certainly had motive, and I suppose means, but I know I didn't do it."

Nico stood up. "If you had killed him, you would never know where he put the money that rightfully now belongs to your son." *Unless she's already found the money.* "Forgive me; I need to get back to work."

Her eyes smiled. "Thanks for your time. I'm sorry I can't be of help. I mean that."

"Should something strike you that doesn't square with the rest of what you know, please relay it to me or the maresciallo."

"I will." She looked up at him. This man stirred something

inside her, something she hadn't felt in a long time. "How do I get ahold of you?"

Nico saw hunger in her gaze. He was flattered, but felt nothing else. "You'll find me here. Goodnight."

Diane felt a tug as she watched him walk away, as if he'd caught a stitch inside her.

VINCE KNOCKED ON PERILLO'S office door and, as usual, didn't wait for a "Come in." He popped his head in. "The waiter from Il Falco is here."

"Well, send him in," Capitano Tarani said with impatience.

"Buonasera," Yunas said, walking in with a smile spreading across his face. He was a small, thin Black man, already dressed in his waiter uniform—dark slacks, a white shirt and a burgundy jacket with the head of a hawk, the restaurant's logo, embroidered on the front pocket.

"Hello," Daniele replied. Perillo, in a foul mood for having had Tarani take over his seat and desk, acknowledged the waiter with a nod.

Tarani stared, eyes wide in surprise. "You are?" he asked sharply.

The waiter kept his smile. Used to sharp questions and much worse, he stood taller. "I am Yunas Mengistou, originally from Ethiopia, now happily in Italy—legally. I served dinner to Signor Mantelli Tuesday night and was told you have questions for me."

Tarani was taken aback for an instant. He had little experience with fancy restaurants, but an African waiting on well-to-do, important clients was unusual.

Yunas saw the doubt in the capitano's face. "The owner of Il Falco, Signor Falchetti, employed me because I am a good waiter."

"What I need from you is a good memory," Tarani said.

"That is a waiter's asset."

"Sit here." Tarani pointed to the chair in front of the desk.

"Just answer the questions." Tarani looked over at Perillo, standing against the far wall, arms crossed in front of his chest. "Stop hovering and sit down too."

Perillo lifted the chair next to Daniele and set it down a few feet from Tarani. "I'm Maresciallo Perillo, in charge of this station." he said to Yunas. He would not tolerate rudeness in his station. "Capitano Tarani, from the Investigative Unit, is leading the investigation in Signor Mantelli's murder. Brigadiere Donato will transcribe the interview."

From his computer post in the back of the room, Daniele nodded. Yunas nodded back.

Tarani frowned at Perillo, then looked down at the list of questions he had prepared in advance. Without taking his eyes off the list, he asked, "Brigadiere Donato, are you ready?"

"Yes, Capitano." Daniele turned to face his computer. Tarani had already fed him the questions. He just had to type in the answers, which made the work easier. With the maresciallo, he never knew what question would come next. By the time he typed in the question, the answer was already said. Nimble fingers and acute hearing was a must on this job. He was proud to have both.

Tarani looked up at the waiter. "How many tables did you have to serve Tuesday night?"

"Six."

Tarani checked off the first question. "Did you have all six tables in your sight?"

"I did, except when I went to the kitchen to pick up the dishes or had my back to some tables while I served others."

"Do you know who the clients at those six tables were?"

Perillo leaned forward. "We already have their names. The answers to these questions are in the file." Daniele had called each one of those parties. No one had paid any attention to their surroundings.

Tarani checked off the question without commenting or looking at Perillo. "Did Signor Mantelli order anything to drink?"

"A glass of Johnny Walker Gold Label Reserve for himself and a bottle of ColleVerde Riserva and ColleVerde Vermentino, which the lady with him enjoyed. He only drank the whiskey. Later, he ordered another."

"Who poured the whiskies?"

"The owner, Signor Falchetti. He supervises the bar."

Perillo suppressed a groan. Daniele had already spoken to Falchetti, a man beyond reproach. Before retiring and going into the restaurant business, Falchetti had been a prestigious Florentine lawyer. At this rate, they were going to be here until nighttime. Perillo was looking forward to dinner. He could almost smell the chicken sautéing with peppers and sausage. After dinner, a much-needed whiskey with Nico.

Tarani checked off the last two questions. He sat up tall for the important question. "Did you tamper with Signor Mantelli's whiskey?"

Yunas looked up at Tarani's stern face. A white face staring at a Black one with mistrust. Yunas saw it clearly. He mentally shrugged. A poor man, this capitano with such a closed mind. He remembered a line from an Ethiopian poem: *There are those who are dead even while they live.*

"I did not. The first whiskey came from an open bottle that served many clients. The second bottle was opened by Signor Falchetti. He filled the glass himself and poured himself a shot. Last night, Signor Falchetti was still on his feet."

Perillo forgot his hunger pangs, his instinct to take over from Tarani too strong. He leaned forward. "Signor Yunas, did anyone approach the table besides you?"

The waiter was happy to answer this man, who had preceded his question with "Signor Yunas." "Yes. I had served the first course when the signorina spilled wine on her dress and went, I believe, to the ladies room. After she left, a very tall woman and a younger man approached Signor Mantelli. From one of her remarks, I understood the woman was his wife. I don't know who the man was. They did not get close to the table, because as soon as Signor Mantelli saw them, he raised his hands in front of his face and told her to leave him alone. 'I am not going to change my mind. Get out of here,' is what he said." He did not add the expletives used.

"How did she answer?" Perillo asked.

"She said, 'I'll find it.'"

Tarani leaned over his desk. "They were how far away from the table?"

"A meter or more. I was standing next to him. They did not touch anything."

"You are certain?" Tarani asked.

"Yes. On my mother's head."

"Did anyone else approach Signor Mantelli?" Perillo asked.

"Maresciallo," Tarani warned, sottovoce.

"Yes," Yunas said. "When I served him his second whiskey."

SOTTO IL FICO WAS closed. The tables had been cleared; the last run of the dishwasher was churning away. Enzo had taken Elvira home. Tilde was catching up on Stella's life in Florence while they both wiped down the counters. To give them privacy, Nico went to the bar and poured himself a small whiskey. It was almost midnight, and Perillo still hadn't called. Nico had sent him a text, but no answer yet. Drink in hand, he stood in the open door and let the cool night air wash over him. Across the street, the blue light of a TV filled a window. When he stood to one side, he could make out two flickering figures. A man's voice, then a woman's. "Amore" floated out of the open window, followed by sighs, heavy breathing, long groans of pleasure. Two people making love. How long had it been for him? Over two years. Once Rita got sick, he had only been able to hold her in his arms, kiss her lightly on her lips, her face, her hair, her hands. Bare touches because she hurt so much. When it was over and she lay on the bed with her hands folded over her chest, he had kissed her feet and said goodbye for the last time.

"There you are!"

For a moment Nico thought the voice came from the TV set.

"Nico!" The voice came from down the hill. He couldn't see who she was, as the street lamps down the hill weren't lit. What little light there was came from open windows.

Nico closed the door of the restaurant behind him and walked down toward the voice.

"I was worried something had happened. I couldn't find your car."

"Nelli!" She was holding OneWag. The dog saw him, squiggled out of her arms and ran to him.

"I knew you wouldn't abandon Rocco."

Nico leaned over as OneWag planted his front paws on Nico's legs, his head reaching up as far as it could go.

Nico leaned down and ruffled his fur. "Hey boy, you miss me?"

"He missed you so much, he came to my studio and would have stayed with me all night." Nelli stepped into the pool of light from the restaurant lamp. She was in her usual work outfit: wide-legged jeans and a man's shirt several sizes too big for her. Both were splattered with paint, Nico noticed, as were her hands and her lovely open face.

"This hill is going to keep us young or kill us. Where did you park your car? I was going to leave Rocco inside. I don't like him wandering in the dark. He's small, and cars won't see him." Nelli walked up a bit more and sat down on the church steps. OneWag dropped down in front of her feet.

The sight of the two of them sitting together, both looking at him, made Nico smile. "You two are picture-worthy."

Nelli reached down and tugged at OneWag's ear. "We are a pretty pair, aren't we, Rocco?" OneWag tilted his head toward her hand to give her a better grip of his ear. "I guess that's a yes." She looked over at Nico, who was still standing by the restaurant door. "Now that I see you didn't rush off with Perillo on the hunt for a murderer, where did you park your car?"

"Next to the church, in Don Alfonso's parking spot. Can I get you something to drink?"

"You'll end up in hell, and yes, a limoncello, thank you."

"That's cough syrup."

"Cough syrup to you, delicious to me."

Nico stepped inside and went around the bar to open the small refrigerator. The bottle of limoncello was kept in the freezer.

Tilde heard him in the kitchen and called out. "Why are you still here?"

"I'm getting Nelli a drink." *And waiting for Perillo to get back to me.*

Stella let out a squeal. "Nelli!" She came running out of the kitchen and rushed outside. Nico poured limoncello into a small glass. He took advantage of the two women catching up on their news to text Perillo one more time.

"Nico, come out here," Stella called.

The two women were kissing each other's cheeks as he walked out.

"I'll come to the studio tomorrow," Stella said. "I can't wait to see your work. And I'll come to the show, I promise."

Nelli pointed a finger at Stella. "See the work first, and no favors. I need your honest opinion. Saying you love it when you don't is no help at all. Only the truth."

Stella laughed. "That will be easy. I love your paintings. Ciao. I have to get back to the kitchen." Another kiss on the cheek and she slipped back inside.

As Nico handed Nelli her limoncello, he heard his phone

chirp. "Excuse me." He took the phone out of his pocket and clicked into his messages.

SORRY. I CAN'T MAKE IT. I'LL EXPLAIN TOMORROW.

Nelli noticed Nico's brow furrow. She sat back down on the church steps, sipped from her glass and gave him time to digest whatever news he had just gotten.

Nico looked at the time on his phone, turned it off and slipped it back in his pocket. Perillo's response didn't convince him. Too abrupt. It was already twelve-fifteen. Why hadn't Perillo called earlier? Something must have happened.

"Come sit with me and Rocco. We like company."

Nico walked over and sat down. "I was supposed to meet Perillo tonight. He wanted to talk things over with me. He canceled just now."

"That worries you?"

"Yes, it does. It's unlike him to do that so suddenly."

"There could be an emergency."

"That's what I'm worried about. I hope he's okay. His wife, too, and Daniele."

"Maybe he was just in a foul mood. Another murder investigation can't be fun."

Nico leaned over and kissed her cheek. "Of course! It's Capitano Tarani. Thank you!"

Nelli drank the last drop of limoncello. "Who's he?"

Nico explained. Nelli listened as she licked her glass clean.

"Poor Salvatore," she said, resting the glass on the step. "He's such a proud man. He's become a good friend, hasn't he?"

"Yes. I've been lucky. Just over a year ago, I came to Gravigna only knowing Tilde's family, and now I need two hands to count my friends. You're one of them, in case you don't know it. OneWag, what are you doing?"

The dog had jumped up on the step and was licking Nelli's empty glass. "Silly dog, you'll get drunk." She took OneWag in her arms and kissed the top of his head, glad for the interruption. She wanted so much more than friendship.

"I'm very worried about Zio Peppino," she said, latching on to something that had been on her mind since yesterday.

"Mantelli's gardener?"

She let go of the dog. OneWag settled himself on her lap, licking his mouth looking for the sweet taste from the glass. "Yes. He's beside himself, saying that his life is over, that he might as well end it. It's heartbreaking to see him like this."

"This is about Mantelli's death?"

"It's the villa. He just found out Mantelli sold it a few days before he died. His wife has been trying to explain to Peppino that she can't stop the sale from going through. It was Mantelli's house before they married. I feel for him; that place is his life."

"Maybe the new owners will want him to stay on."

"Signora Mantelli tried. She introduced Peppino, and the owners told him they were sure he was a hardworking man, but the time had come for him to rest his tired body."

Nico wondered what possessed some people to hurt for no reason at all. Did it make them feel superior? He couldn't understand it. "I'm sorry, Nelli. For him and for you. I know he means a lot to you."

"He's a good, sweet man."

"Someone else will hire him."

"I've started asking around. The sad thing is, Peppino doesn't want a new job. He wants the one he's had all his life. He was much more than a gardener. He ran the house. It was his home. Where is he going to live?"

"I'm sure Mantelli left him some money in his will."

"He did. He told Peppino that the chances he would outlive his employer weren't good, but just in case, Mantelli was going to leave him two thousand euros."

Nico did a mental multiplication. At the current rate, that meant Peppino would receive just over twenty-two hundred dollars. "Mantelli was a stingy man."

"Peppino doesn't want money. He wants to stay and die where he has worked and lived for over sixty years. And now he can't." She buried her face in OneWag's fur. Tears started falling. For Peppino; for Nico, who wouldn't let her in; for feeling suddenly old and alone.

Nico watched her shoulders tremble. He didn't know how to help. Women's tears always made him freeze up. "I'm sorry, Nelli," he said. "I wish I could help."

Nelli looked up, her wet cheeks shining under the light of the restaurant lamp. "You can." She lifted his arm and wrapped it around her back. They sat in silence on the church steps for a few minutes, OneWag curled on her lap.

Nico leaned into Nelli's shoulder, embarrassment forgotten. It felt good to hold her.

Tilde and Stella came out of the restaurant, locked the door and said goodnight. Both smiled and muttered something to each other as they walked off.

Nelli watched them go. A few moments later, she dropped the dog into Nico's lap. "Your dog has more sense than you do." She kissed Nico lightly on his lips and stood up. "Goodnight, Nico. See you around."

"Do you want a ride home?" Nico asked, already missing the weight of her shoulder against his.

She waved, not looking back. "No thanks. I live down the hill."

Nico knew that, and Nelli knew he knew. He really felt dumb now. "Buonanotte," he finally managed to call out, although she was already halfway down.

OneWag jumped off Nico's lap and headed for the car with a bounce in his step. At last, progress had been made.

CINZIA WAS PACING IN front of the small farmhouse when Nico and OneWag got home. She rushed to the car. "God, where have you been? I've been calling and calling."

"I'm sorry. I turned my phone off. What's the matter?"

She punched his arm, hard. OneWag growled softly. "Nico, you know perfectly well what's the matter. I thought we were friends. God damn you and Salvatore, and may that bastard Tarani get bitten by a viper." OneWag growled as she tried to slap Nico.

Nico took her hands down from his face and held them. "Cinzia, come upstairs. We'll sit down and you can tell me what happened."

"Come on, Nico; don't pull that I-don't-know-anything crap on me."

"All I know, from the state you're in, is that whatever happened involves Aldo."

"In the middle of dinner, Tarani, Salvatore and some men I've never seen before showed up at the house with a search warrant. No explanation offered. The men slipped on gloves and started going through the rooms, our closets, drawers, everything. I followed them and kept asking, 'Why are you doing this? What do you think you're going to find?' It was horrible. I felt violated. How dare they!"

"I'm sorry you had to go through this."

"Oh, sorry? You haven't even heard the end. Your friend Salvatore is a coward, didn't want to own up that he was part of this charade."

"He didn't have a choice."

Cinzia hit Nico's arm with another punch. The dog bared his teeth. "Don't defend him, Nico. Not now. I'm too upset. Do you know what Salvatore had the stomach to say to me?" She didn't wait for an answer. "'Don't worry, Cinzia. They have to do this. It's part of the investigation. I know they won't find anything.'

It was perfect timing, like something right out of a movie. Salvatore says that and one of Tarani's men comes into the kitchen. 'I found this in the tool shed.' He was holding an opened can of antifreeze."

"'What did you use this for?' Tarani asked Aldo. Aldo told him it was for our cars. Tarani's answer was like a stiletto plunged right into my heart. He smirked and said, 'It's also useful for killing people.'"

She started crying. Nico tried to hug her, but she pushed him away. Gulping air to calm down, she sputtered, "Tarani is detaining Aldo on suspicion of murder. They're on their way to Florence now. I wasn't allowed to go with him. God, why is this happening? What are we going to do? I curse the day I met Michele Mantelli. Aldo, my sweet Aldo. They think he's a murderer. I don't know which way to turn. It's not true. You know it's not true." She clasped his face with both hands and shook it. "It's not true."

Nico took her hands and held them against his chest. "I know that." Would the Italian justice system be fair to Aldo? It hadn't been fair to Amanda Knox. Now he knew why Perillo had canceled. "Come with me." He unlocked the front door and led Cinzia up the stairs.

Once inside, he sat her down in his one large armchair. "Wine or whiskey?"

"I don't care." Cinzia sank into the big armchair and closed her eyes.

Nico opened the whiskey bottle, filled two shot glasses and handed one to Cinzia. She looked ravaged.

He sat across from her on the two-seater sofa and watched Cinzia take a deep swallow with her eyes still shut. "There has to be more than an open bottle of antifreeze to detain him. There has to be some new evidence. What is it?"

Cinzia let out a long breath. "Aldo is like a child. He's

convinced that if he keeps something to himself, no one will find out about it." She looked at the glass cradled in her hands. She seemed reluctant to go on.

"What something?"

"Aldo didn't tell the whole truth in his statement."

"What did he leave out? Perillo hasn't said a word to me about Aldo—we were supposed to meet tonight, but he canceled. So please, tell me what you know."

She sat back up, her eyes meeting Nico's. "The waiter who served Mantelli Tuesday night told Tarani that Aldo and Hua Chen, our Chinese buyer, walked up to Mantelli's table and talked to him, a fact Aldo didn't bother to tell me and omitted in his statement to Salvatore."

"Not a good move, I'll admit, but talking to Mantelli the night before he died isn't evidence of murder."

"There's more. The waiter said he had served Mantelli his second whiskey a few minutes before Aldo and Hua Chen came over to his table. After they left, Mantelli called him over complaining that the whiskey didn't taste right. How Tarani can think Aldo poured antifreeze in the whiskey right in front of Mantelli makes no sense. It takes more than a drop to kill someone, doesn't it?" She looked at Nico with pleading eyes.

A tablespoon was enough to kill a man, Perillo had told him. "I'm sure it takes much more. Let me drive you home. You need to get some rest, because tomorrow morning you need to get back to being the feisty, fighting Cinzia I know."

"Yes, I'm going to Florence the minute I wake up. Our lawyer is there."

"Good. He'll take care of all the rigamarole the Italian legal system requires. Next, get ahold of your Chinese buyer. Call, text and email. If Aldo didn't get close enough to Mantelli's table to alter his drink, he can clear Aldo." If the prosecutor was willing to believe him. It wasn't going to be easy, not with Della Langhe in such a hurry to close the case. He wished he understood the Italian Code of Criminal Procedure better. The Penal Code, written during Mussolini's government, was clear. It made good bedtime reading. The Code of Criminal Procedure, recently rewritten, he found unduly complicated. He couldn't make heads or tails of it.

Nico stood and held out his hand. "I'll drive you home."

She handed him her empty shot glass. "I prefer to walk." It was no more than a ten- or fifteen-minute trek. "I need to clear my head. Thanks for listening and caring. I guess Salvatore let you down too."

"I think he was worried I'd warn you."

She cocked her head. "Would you have?"

"Yes, but I would also have stayed with you to make sure the two of you couldn't skip out. Running away would have only made things worse."

"I know that, but it would have been hard to resist. One day all is going well and then, with the snap of a finger, it's gone. I'm having a hard time making sense of it."

"I know."

"Yes, you do. You lost your wife." Cinzia raised herself on tiptoe and leaned toward Nico. OneWag stood up on the sofa with an almost inaudible growl, ready to jump off if needed. "Goodnight, Nico." She kissed his cheeks. "You are a good friend. Tell your dog I won't hit you again."

"He was just showing off for you. We'll come downstairs with you. I need to water my vegetables."

Nico and the dog stood by the vegetable garden fence and watched Cinzia walk away. Aldo was in trouble, and it wasn't going to be easy to get him out of it. The only way was to find the real killer, Nico realized. And Perillo was going to help him, like it or not.

TEN

Perillo swerved to the side of the road and stopped the car. He leaned over the passenger seat and rolled down the window. Nico, on his daily run to town, recognized the car and ran past him.

"Ehi, Nico, stop. Get in the car. I was coming to see you."

Nico kept running.

Perillo slapped the horn in frustration. Nico was angry. Perillo couldn't blame him. Well, he was angry too. If Nico had a perfect right to display his feelings—displayed childishly, in Perillo's opinion—then the maresciallo had a right to explain himself. He put the car in first gear, slipped back onto the road, shifted twice and raced past Nico, spewing gravel from the back tires.

Juvenile, Nico thought, slowing down. His knees hurt, and his breaths were getting shorter and shorter. He didn't want Perillo to see the sorry state he would be in if he kept up his normal pace. Slow was good, slower even better. Let the maresciallo wait.

"I'M GLAD TO SEE you took your time." Perillo was sitting on Nico's doorstep, smoking a cigarette. Nico had walked back. His breath was back to normal, even if his knees still hurt. OneWag, who had learned that his short legs were no match for Nico's long ones on a morning run, now ran to greet him.

"You know our saying," Perillo said. "*Who goes slow—*"

"—*goes far and goes with health,*" Nico finished for him. "Daniele?"

"In church."

Nico kept his distance. Besides being covered in sweat, he wanted to avoid the cigarette smoke. "When I got home last night, Cinzia was waiting for me. She was not a happy woman. Are you here to tell me why?"

Perillo met Nico's look with wide eyes. "She must have told you."

"Not that. The bigger why."

Perillo took a long drag of his cigarette before answering. "Aldo was arrested under suspicion of murder. Yes, I'm here to tell you everything Yunas, the waiter, witnessed at Mantelli's table." He told Nico about the two whiskies poured by the owner, the second one from a new bottle and tasted by Falchetti, who was still alive. Perillo hesitated, taking another drag of his cigarette. "Aldo may be a good man, but he is stupid."

"Go on."

"In the statement he signed in my office as to his whereabouts on Tuesday evening, he didn't mention that he went to Mantelli's table with his Chinese buyer."

"Cinzia told me. Did the waiter claim he saw Aldo put something in Mantelli's whiskey?"

"No, but right after Aldo left, Mantelli complained about the taste."

"Don't tell me Tarani considers that proof Aldo tampered with the drink?"

"I don't know about Tarani. He's a closed book. Della Langhe thinks it proves Aldo poisoned him."

"Did Aldo explain why he went to Mantelli's table?"

"He claimed the buyer found out Mantelli was in the next room and wanted to meet the famous Italian wine critic. Aldo said the buyer is a very good customer and he felt obliged to please him."

"Have you or Tarani called the Chinese buyer to hear what he has to say?"

"Cinzia gave us his number and email. No answer on either. Can we continue this conversation upstairs? You look like you could use a shower, and I owe you an explanation, which will be easier with something soft under my ass. I'll even put out my cigarette."

Nico looked down at the T-shirt sticking to his chest. "A shower would be good, and an espresso will make you explain even better than a soft seat. You can make it while I shower." Nico pulled the plastic bracelet with his keys from his wrist and unlocked the door. "I only hope your explanation makes sense."

"I can answer that right away. It does, with regrets."

THEY DRANK THEIR ESPRESSOS on the covered balcony with the balcony door and the window opposite wide open to create a draft. At nine o'clock, the heat was already gearing up to offer a stifling Sunday.

Nico, in shorts and a T-shirt and still wet from the shower—he hadn't bothered to towel off, knowing the air would dry him quickly—put his cup down and sat back in his chair.

Perillo understood it was time to deliver. "Here's the reason I didn't show up last night. Before coming down, Tarani looked into my record; I suppose to get a sense of who he was dealing with. He complimented me on my successful investigation of last year's murder, but he added that he'd heard rumors you had helped me. He'd looked you up too, learned that you'd been a homicide detective in New York, and that sealed it. The rumors were fact. When he saw you in my office yesterday, he understood we worked together. He was incensed. 'The Carabinieri is an esteemed branch of the army, over two hundred years old, and should know how to solve their own investigations. We need no outside help.' I of course immediately thought of the ribbings we get from the police. Want to hear one of their jokes? Two carabinieri have their car stolen. The capitano asks—"

"Not now."

"You're right. In any case, I was ordered not to contact you until we had made an arrest."

"He referred the waiter's statement to Della Langhe?"

"Who pounced at what he considered excellent news. He wanted Aldo arrested and brought to Florence immediately. He seemed convinced that Aldo would flee. He showered congratulations on Tarani and added that he was going to make sure the media would know an arrest had been made. All that arrogant dickhead wants is to boast the renowned Italian wine critic's murder has been solved in record time."

"Shit. That's terrible."

"I agree. Tarani knows we're only at the beginning of the investigation. I was slow getting started, I'll admit. I let my dislike for the man get in the way. I should have gone after the waiter right away, not waited for him to come to me when it was convenient for him. I should have gotten a statement from the housekeeper. Questioned Diane Severson more thoroughly. Questioned the gardener a second time. The first time, Mantelli had just died, and he was upset, so who knows what he left out?"

"Blaming yourself doesn't get us anywhere. Is Tarani out of the picture now?"

"For the time being. It depends what happens with Aldo. The judge has to decide if there's enough evidence to proceed to a trial. If there isn't, and we know there isn't, Tarani will be back."

"But this means we have a few days to do our own investigating."

"Aldo has twenty days to file a defensive brief."

"Good. I'll let Cinzia know he should take the whole time allotted, even if it means more jail time. We need time and active minds," Nico got up and went inside. He came back with a pen and notepad.

Feeling better now that he'd explained the why of Aldo's arrest,

Perillo smiled at the sight of the notepad. He remembered the advice Nico had given him last year: *Put order in your brain by making a list.*

Nico wrote down the names of the people Perillo needed to talk to again. "What about the owner of Il Glicine? He may have more to say about Loredana."

"I don't think so, but add him anyway."

"And Luca Verdini."

"Why him?"

"He's connected to Mantelli and his wife. Now Loredana is interested in him. In the mornings, he has an assistant taking care of business. She might be able to tell me something about him. I'll ask some quick questions when I go over and buy a case of wine."

"We'll divide up the questioning. You start, and if you find anything solid, you pass it on to me. I like and respect Aldo, but I can't afford to lose my job trying to help him."

Nico studied Perillo's face for a moment. The maresciallo met his gaze. "What's the matter?" Perillo asked.

"You do believe Aldo is innocent?"

"You have to admit there's a possibility he isn't."

"A possibility so thin I can't see it."

"You're letting personal feelings cloud your judgment."

"All right, I'll proceed alone so you don't put your job at risk. Most of the town knows Aldo's my landlord. It won't seem strange if I ask questions."

"They also know you were a policeman."

"A patrol cop. Only you, Daniele, Tilde and now Tarani know I worked in homicide. Which reminds me. How did you find out the reason I had to retire?"

"Working backwards. I knew your retirement date and asked Daniele to look into any trials within a two-year period after that."

"That's absurd, wasting Daniele's time that way. Why did you bother?"

"He's the one who suggested it. Dani knows I don't like mysteries. He offered because he has nothing to do at night. No girlfriend or friends, and he's Internet-crazy. I did a good thing. Made him happy."

Perillo was an expert at justifying his actions. Nico was convinced Daniele wouldn't have suggested the search if Perillo hadn't complained about not knowing. "And what did Daniele find out?"

"A murder trial in which you testified. You and your partner were the first on the scene of a man shot dead in his home. His wife called it in. The woman showed signs of abuse on her body. The district attorney was convinced the wife had killed him, even though the man had big gambling debts. The jury found her not guilty. An important piece of evidence was missing. The gun. You have a big heart, my friend. It took courage to throw the gun away. In one of New York's two rivers, I suppose."

"What I did was instinctive, not courageous. My mother—"

Perillo stopped him with a raised hand. "No need to go further." The sufferings of a mother belonged only to the family. "You're lucky you got away with forced retirement."

"My captain didn't want another black stain on his record. He had many. As I told you last year, the price was silence."

"The silence will continue, rest assured. The silence of a tomb."

EIGHT-THIRTY A.M. MASS WAS over. Ivana Perillo linked her arm with Daniele's as they slowly walked out with the others who had attended, mostly old women and a few old men. The sudden brightness of the day stunned them. The women squinted and removed their head coverings. Some covered their eyes with their hands.

"It's a nice church," Ivana said. "The priest gave a good short homily. Ours goes on forever." They had always met for the early Mass at the Basilica di Santa Croce in Greve, but this Sunday, Daniele had wanted to attend Mass in Gravigna. Curious to know why the sudden change, she asked to join him.

Together, they walked down the two ramps of stairs edged with terracotta pots of pink geraniums. "I hope you'll be happy with lunch today," Ivana said.

"It was very nice of you to invite me, and anything you feed me makes me happy, Signora."

"Thank you, but please call me Ivana. We're Salvatore and Ivana." She knocked gently on his forehead. "Lock those two names in your sweet, stubborn head." They reached the bottom of the stairs. She could see the sign for Sotto Il Fico thirty meters further down. "That's where Salvatore's friend works, isn't it?"

"Yes, it is."

Ivana stopped and unhooked her arm. "One day, I should invite him for a Sunday lunch." She was taking time she didn't really have, and Daniele's head was swiveling from right to left and back. He was clearly looking for someone.

"I think he would like that very much," Daniele said.

"Good. I'll invite him after the case is solved. I don't want talk of murder at my table."

Daniele wasn't listening; his eyes had found the person he was looking for at the top of the church stairs.

"This is no stairway for old people," Elvira grumbled as she tugged at her white Sunday dress to hide her expansive stomach and linked arms with Stella. "If Don Alfonso does nothing about it, he's going to have an empty church on Sundays."

Stella slipped on her sunglasses and tightened her grip on her grandmother. "Mamma told me the church committee is going to have pizza parties to raise money."

"Pizza! I don't like pizza."

"You don't have to eat it." They were taking the stairs one step at a time. "Just give them some money." She knew Nonna didn't part with money easily. "They're going to put in a chair that will ride you right up. That should be fun."

"I'm going to church, not a Luna park."

Daniele was looking at the nice young girl, Ivana realized. She was pretty. "Do you know her, Dani?"

He nodded.

"Go and say hello. I'm not in a hurry." She crossed herself mentally for the lie she'd just told. The pasta for the cannelloni was made, but she still had to prepare the mushroom cheese filling and the green parsley sauce, which involved a great deal of chopping.

"I'll be right back." Daniele walked the few steps to the bottom of the church stairs. Elvira and Stella had reached the second ramp. "Ciao, Stella."

Stella stopped and looked down. "Ciao, Dani. How nice to see you."

He pushed his hair off his face and smiled, "Me too. I mean, nice to see you too." He could feel the blush rising on his cheeks. "It's awfully hot, isn't it?"

Stella waited until she had brought Elvira down to solid ground to answer. "Yes, it is hot," Stella said, knowing his red cheeks—they made him look adorable—had nothing to do with the heat. He was dressed in pressed tan slacks and a checked blue and white long-sleeved shirt with the cuffs and collar buttoned. He'd added a navy-blue tie. When she had seen him in Florence, he hadn't been dressed so properly. She suspected this was his church outfit. "Why don't you roll up your sleeves? You'll be cooler."

"Yes, of course. Good idea." Daniele fumbled with the buttons, reluctant to take his eyes away from Stella. Luck had blessed him. Ever since he'd heard from Nico that she was back for the weekend, he had hoped to run into her. He'd even thought of the possibility of having lunch at Sotto Il Fico to see her, but that was before Signor Ferri got arrested. Now the case took precedence over his personal wishes, but he was always allowed Mass. Why not in Gravigna instead of Greve? He rolled up his sleeves and half-bowed to Elvira. "Buongiorno, Signora. Daniele Donati."

"I know perfectly well who you are, thanks to last year's horrifying events." She turned to Stella. "This young man is right," Elvira said, giving Daniele a nod of acknowledgment. "It is far too hot to linger. Take me to the restaurant, please. I have work to do, and so do you."

Stella obeyed.

Daniele stayed at the bottom of the stairs, watching her go with a heavy heart. She looked so pretty in that light-green dress that matched her eyes. Even her feet were pretty in raw leather sandals.

At the door of Sotto Il Fico, Stella let go of Elvira's arm and walked back to Daniele. "I'm taking the last bus to Florence tonight. I'd love to have an ice cream with you before I go."

Daniele's heart skipped a couple of beats. His cheeks bloomed. "I can take you to Florence on my motorbike."

"That's wonderfully generous of you, but no. It's too far away."

He started to protest. She shushed him with a finger on his mouth. "Just ice cream. Okay?"

Daniele nodded, wishing he had kissed that finger.

"Bar All'Angolo has the best. I'll call you." He had given her his number on his last visit in Florence.

"You have work to do," Elvira called out.

"Coming! Ciao," Stella said. Daniele watched her go, his heart now light.

"Daniele." Ivana tried to hide that big smile in her heart that was sure to show on her face. "If you want lunch, you'll have to drive me home now."

"Of course, Signo—Ivana."

NICO AND PERILLO WERE drinking their second espresso when OneWag, who was outside, started barking. Seconds later, they heard a motorbike approaching.

Perillo looked at his phone. "Mass is over."

The barking stopped.

Nico went inside his living room/kitchen and strode to the far window. Daniele was trying to get off his bike, but OneWag was jumping up on his legs, body wriggling in welcome, making a nuisance of himself.

"Ciao, Daniele. Ignore OneWag. He's just happy to see you. The door's open."

Perillo joined Nico at the window. "Ehi, Dani, where's my car?"

"I parked it in your spot at the station."

Perillo turned to Nico and in a low voice said, "Just like him to worry about using up my gasoline."

OneWag ran in with the satisfied look of a job well done. Daniele followed, holding a folder in his arms.

"You're looking happy, Dani," Perillo said. "I'm afraid going to Mass never did that for me. I hope you said a few prayers for us."

"Only for Signor Ferri."

"Good for you," Nico said. "Your boss seems to think he might be guilty."

Daniele looked at Perillo, then Nico, then back to his boss. "We don't know that yet, do we?" He lifted the folder he was holding. "Capitano Tarani left a folder with his notes in the office last night when you left to arrest Signor Ferri. I assumed we would continue the investigation and made copies."

"Ah, that explains your happiness."

Daniele did not correct his boss.

Perillo crossed his arms over his chest and grinned. "Bravo, Brigadiere Donato."

"Good thinking, Daniele," Nico said. "Have you had breakfast?" Rita, a devout Catholic, never ate before Mass if she was taking Communion.

Daniele hugged the folder. The compliments embarrassed him. "I'm fine, thank you."

"Food sounds good," Perillo said. "How about a nice American breakfast? Bacon and eggs, or those flat round things with streams of syrup on top."

"No pancakes, eggs or bacon. And no cornetto. All I can offer is toast, mortadella, caciotta and some prosciutto bought two days ago. What shall it be?"

Perillo and Daniele answered together. "Toast." Daniele added, "please." Eating cheese and prosciutto for breakfast was too odd.

Nico was still eating his melted caciotta sandwich and Daniele was crunching on the last of his buttered toast when Perillo put his empty plate aside and opened Daniele's folder. "Our dear capitano didn't mention he already had Mantelli's phone records. Incoming and outgoing." He should have asked about them. He was letting Tarani take over too easily.

Perillo traced his finger down the few numbers and names. "The usual suspects." Daniele had looked up the numbers and jotted down the names next to each. "Many to and fro with Loredana, the wife calling him four times. He didn't call back. Three restaurants. A couple to the gardener."

A meek bark from OneWag, seated at the maresciallo's feet, made him look down. Perillo had purposely released a shower of crumbs to the floor. They were now gone. "Go to your boss, he's still eating."

OneWag changed feet. "All done, kiddo. Sorry. Wait, I forgot to feed him." Nico stood up. OneWag barked and ran to the kitchen. "If you must, light a cigarette. You're going gray from withdrawal. Use your ashtray." He followed his dog.

Daniele wet his finger and raised it in the air. Good. The breeze was moving away from him. He moved his chair, just in case the air switched.

"I'll raise my voice so you can hear, Nico." Perillo quickly lit a cigarette and continued. "Ah, here's one call to Luca Verdini last Sunday. Verdini called back the same day. Called on Tuesday too. You were right to put him on the suspect list. And the housekeeper called Mantelli twice—once on Monday, once on Tuesday. So Ida goes on our list."

"She's already on it." Nico took cooked rice and raw hamburger meat out of the refrigerator, mixed in an egg yolk and warmed the bowl for thirty seconds in the microwave.

Daniele shifted in his chair. He had an idea he wanted to share. "Signorina Loredana told us the reason they went to dinner at Il Falco that night was because Mantelli was going to meet someone. Maybe it was Verdini."

"Could be," Perillo said. "Or it was just an excuse to eat where he wanted to eat and not where she did."

"He was going to meet someone?" Nico asked. "You didn't tell me that."

"I forgot to. I'm not sure I believe much of what she said that day. She was a little crazy," Perillo sensed Daniele's back straighten. "I've misspoken. She's a fragile woman, and I'd just let her know her boyfriend was murdered."

"She also told us someone knocked into her from behind and made her spill wine on her dress," Daniele added. "She had to leave the table to clean it up. Maybe someone did it on purpose so Mantelli would be alone."

"That's a possibility." Nico took OneWag's food out of the microwave and spooned it into his bowl. The dog did a happy wiggle. "I think I'd like to have a conversation with Signorina Loredana. Thanks for telling me, Daniele. I won't hold it against you, Perillo."

Perillo mumbled, "Good," his attention absorbed by the phone records. "There are several calls to a Diego Serretti."

"Serretti is the Banca Commerciale manager Mantelli dealt with," Daniele said. "The information is on a different piece of paper. Capitano Tarani said Serretti was going to let him know what withdrawals Mantelli made in the past year. If you want, I can call him tomorrow and ask if he has the information. Tarani told him it was urgent. I'm sure the manager worked on it this weekend."

"It's risky to reach out," Perillo said. "Officially, the investigation is no longer in our hands."

Across the table, Daniele leaned closer to his boss. "Forgive me, Maresciallo, if I don't agree. Capitano Tarani was conducting the investigation from the Greve station, and we are the Greve station. I will call the manager from the station phone. Whatever information the manager gives me, I will of course share with Capitano Tarani. I will say I called of my own accord. I am a young brigadiere with little experience in murder investigations. At most, he will yell at me. Or he may be happy I saved him a phone call."

Perillo looked over his shoulder. Nico was walking back. "What do you think?"

"We don't know if the missing money is what motivated the murder, but since we don't know, let's find out as much as we can. Thank you, Daniele. You're shining today."

Yes, Daniele thought. *Shining*. That's exactly how he felt.

Nico sat back down. "What time is it in China?"

"Six hours ahead of us." Daniele looked at his phone. "Four-forty in the afternoon. The buyer's number is in the folder. On the second page."

Perillo put the page on the table in front of Nico. "The call is on you."

Nico took out his cell phone. "You're covering your ass, but I'll happily do your job for you."

"He will certainly speak English, not Italian."

"Let's hope he can understand me." Nico clicked the numbers. A voice answered in Chinese after the third ring.

Nico walked inside to hear better. "May I please speak to Mister Hua Chen?"

"Yes. Yes, I am Mister Hua. Who are you?"

Nico introduced himself. "I need to ask you a few questions about your dinner Tuesday night with Aldo Ferriello. I'm doing this at his request."

Nico explained as briefly as he could about Mantelli's accident, leaving murder out. The carabinieri needed to corroborate what Aldo had told them about their meeting with Mantelli.

"Why did carabinieri not call me?"

"They tried, but got no answer. They also don't speak English."

"I speak a little Italian also. Italy is in my heart."

"When you approached, Mr. Mantelli was drinking something. Were the two of you near the drink? Did Aldo touch the glass?"

"We touched nothing."

Nico felt his stomach muscles release. "Thank you, Mister Hua."

"No problem. If carabinieri need me, I am here now."

"I will tell them, but as a favor to Aldo, please don't mention I called you. They don't like people who are not police to interfere. They might not trust what you say."

"Yes, yes, I understand. Our police are difficult also. No trust at all. Tell Aldo now I will open a bottle of his Riserva to wish him a good vintage this year."

"I will, and thank you again. Goodbye." Relief prompted him to bend down and give his dog a hug. OneWag, who had his priorities straight, went back to licking the now-empty bowl.

"Good news," Nico announced, walking back to the balcony. "Hua says Aldo wasn't near Mantelli's drink. Now you have to tell Tarani to call him. Hua won't mention my call."

"I'll tell him, but we'll have to see if Tarani believes him."

"Tell him not to mention Mantelli was murdered. I didn't. Hua doesn't know, or he would have said something. Tarani should claim he's calling to try to understand what led to the accident."

"I don't believe Capitano Tarani is willing to take advice from me. I will suggest that calling Hua Chen for corroboration might be a good idea."

"He'll need a translator," Daniele said.

Nico sat back down. "Hua Chen speaks some Italian. What's the waiter's name? He's next on my list."

"Yunas Mengistou," Perillo answered. "He's from Ethiopia. Tarani was surprised a restaurant as fancy as Il Falco would hire a Black waiter. Before Yunas left, Tarani explained to him that he'd meant no disrespect, but that it was unusual. Yunas answered that thankfully, things in Italy were changing for the better, and Tarani agreed."

"Then he's not all bad. I met a Yunas last year during the Chianti Wine Expo. He was a waiter at Bar della Piazza."

"The same man. He brought in his résumé."

"Then I know where I'm having dinner tonight."

"It'll cost you," Perillo warned.

"I'll eat a big lunch. I want to see the layout of the place."

"And Ida Crivelli, the housekeeper?" Daniele looked at Perillo, who was having the last drag of his cigarette.

"Call her in. Tomorrow morning at nine."

"Perhaps best to visit her?" Daniele suggested. "I have her phone number and address."

Perillo slapped his knee. "Bravo, Dani. Always keeping those young brain cells working. We'll pay Ida an unofficial visit."

"Good." Nico stood. Perillo and Daniele understood and got up too. "I'll go to Verdini's vineyard in the morning. We'll keep in touch. Now it's time I switch to my real job, waiting tables."

"Too bad," Perillo said. "Ivana has prepared a fantastic Sunday lunch for me and Daniele. Homemade cannelloni. I'm sure there's enough for four."

"Thanks for letting me know what I'm missing."

Perillo gave Nico's shoulder a friendly slap. "We missed those bacon and eggs."

The three of them walked to the door. OneWag opened one eye to see them go from his place on the sofa. A full stomach made him sleepy.

"How about your cooking?" Perillo asked. "No new recipes?"

"Too much on my mind."

"Of course, the murder."

That wasn't all, Nico knew. He opened the door.

A "ciao" came from Perillo with a wave of a hand.

Daniele said, "Arrivederci. Thanks for breakfast."

"Eggs and pancetta next time. We'll talk tomorrow."

Nico sat back down on the balcony and propped his feet up on the low wall that acted as a railing. He was going to get Aldo out of this mess, with or without Perillo's help. And once that was over?

Back to his Tuscan family, to the work he enjoyed, to his Gravigna friends. Why did he feel it wasn't enough?

Nico took out his cell phone and called Il Falco. He had Sunday night off.

DANIELE HAD JUST GOTTEN back to his room from Ivana's big Sunday lunch when he heard the first notes of Vivaldi's "Spring." He picked up his cell phone and swiped.

"Why did you arrest Aldo Ferri?" Stella's voice was icy. Nonna had just told her Aldo had been taken to a jail in Florence. She knew Aldo was innocent, a good man. When the restaurant was having a hard time a few years ago, he had lent them money interest-free. The money was paid back, but the kindness remained.

"I didn't arrest him," Daniele said. "The investigation is no longer in our hands. The Special Investigative Office stepped in. Capitano Tarani arrested Aldo Ferri."

"Your boss was with him."

"Maresciallo Perillo had no choice."

"Do you believe he's guilty?"

"Stella, I'm a carabiniere. I can't discuss the case."

"You just said it's not in your hands anymore. You can discuss it. I want to know if you think he's guilty."

"Why does it matter what I think?"

"Because it says something about you. If we're going to be friends, I want to trust you and your judgment."

How he would love to be friends with Stella, but he knew he needed to say this. "My idea of friendship is respecting your opinion, even if it differs from mine."

"That's not what we're discussing. Just answer yes or no. Do you believe Aldo killed Michele Mantelli?"

Daniele sighed. He couldn't lie. "No."

Stella felt a warmth in her stomach. If Daniele had said yes, she would have to erase him from her life, even though he was only a very little part of it for now. A nice part.

"I CAN'T REMEMBER THE last time I wore a dress," Nelli said as Nico opened the door to Il Falco. She didn't think Nico would care when she last had worn a dress, but she was flustered and a little anxious.

"You look nice." He meant it. When he picked her up in the main piazza, it had taken him a minute to recognize her. He had only seen her in paint-spotted jeans and oversized shirts.

"Thank you." She'd taken a great deal of time trying to look as nice as she could manage. A little makeup on her eyes and cheeks. A five-year-old white cotton shirtwaist dress she hadn't worn more than two or three times, colorful espadrilles on her feet, her long graying hair gathered in the usual braid hanging down her back.

"You look good too," Nelli said, her shoulder brushing against his chest as she walked past him. Nico looked exactly as he always did, slightly disheveled, dressed in a blue shirt and tan slacks that needed another go-through with a hot iron.

When Nico had called earlier to invite her to dinner, she'd felt a wonderful, welcome wave of happiness. Nico went on to warn her that all he was offering was dinner, very little company. Her wave of happiness receded when she had realized he would have to concentrate on talking to the waiter who had served Mantelli the night before his death.

"Because Aldo was arrested?" she had asked.

"Yes. I need to help him."

"That's very nice of you, but can't you go alone?"

"I could, but it would be more pleasant to have you sitting with me."

That had felt nice. Not a wave, just a lap. As Nelli rinsed paint off herself in the shower, she wondered if he'd been telling the truth. It was true that a man sitting alone and questioning the waiter might raise eyebrows. Bringing a woman along was a much better cover-up. But he'd chosen to invite her.

They followed the maitre d' through a medium-sized room with a beamed ceiling, oxen yokes turned into lamps, floors covered in dark leather-looking tiles and rows of wine bottles on three walls. The far wall was all glass panels, now open, overlooking a small olive grove. The sun was still fairly high, but trees were starting to inch their shadows across the lawn.

The artist in Nelli took in all this and more: the ochre-yellow tablecloths, the few elegantly dressed foreigners who liked to eat this early, the flowering rosemary branches on each table, the candles in round glass bowls, waiting to be lighted when it turned dark. An expensive restaurant, she thought. She'd have to be careful ordering.

A skinny young Black man dressed in black trousers and a

burgundy jacket with a falcon head embroidered on the breast pocket strode toward Nico and Nelli. He was smiling. "Signor Doyle, Signora, I am Yunas, your waiter."

"Buonasera, Yunas. We met last year at the Chianti Wine Expo. It's nice to see you again." Nico held out his hand.

Yunas's eyes went from Nico's hand to the maitre d'. After a moment's pause, the maitre d' nodded. Yunas's smile widened, and he shook Nico's hand. "Your dog was thirsty. You too. Water, no gas."

"That's right. Good memory."

Nelli kept her eyes on the waiter's angular face, his deep rich brown skin, his friendly eyes, the wide cheekbones. She would love to paint him.

"A good memory is a must for a waiter. I will take you to your table." They walked into a smaller replica of the room they had just left. This room's open glass panels revealed a walled-in garden filled with roses.

"I apologize. I guess I wasn't supposed to shake your hand," Nico said, his eyes on Yunas instead of the roses.

"It is uncommon, but the respect is most appreciated." Yunas indicated the corner table. "Signor Mantelli sat there." Seeing Nico's questioning look, he explained in a low voice, "Some diners have curiosity and wish to see; others stay far from this room, fearing it might bring bad luck. You asked to be seated in this room, so I made a presumption."

"You presumed well. Your instincts are correct. I am a friend of Signor Ferri. I'd like to ask you—"

Yunas stopped Nico from going any further by lifting his hand. "I serve this room, and the next reservation is for eight o'clock. For thirty minutes, I am yours alone." He pushed back the corner chair and looked at Nelli. She hesitated, preferring the chair with the view of the roses.

"It's best this way," Nico said, though he was sorry for it.

She understood and sat looking out at the other tables. This way, Nico would have his back to whoever sat down or looked in. Yunas started to unfurl her napkin. She took it from him before he was finished and opened it on her lap. "Thank you," she said. She didn't want to offend him, but she was perfectly capable of opening her own napkin.

Yunas bent over Nico as he unfolded his napkin. "I am sorry for Signor Ferri. I'll go and retrieve your menus."

Nelli waited until Yunas was out of the room to ask, "Questioning him here is a bit awkward, isn't it?"

"It is, but if anyone is looking, I'm hoping to pass it off as just me being curious about the murder. I also wanted to see the place."

"Who would be looking for you here?"

"Capitano Tarani doesn't want me to be involved in any way. He knows about my ties to Perillo. I don't want to get him in trouble. So it's just me taking a friend to dinner and asking a few questions." It wasn't the whole truth. The need to talk to Yunas had given him the courage to ask Nelli to dinner. This way there would be no long, awkward gaps in the conversation, but she would still be dining with him.

So there it is, thought Nelli. She was a prop.

Yunas came back with the menus. He gave an open one to Nelli first. She chuckled. Obviously, rich people were incapable of doing anything but making money. Her eyes widened when she saw there were no prices. She held out the menu. "It's all free?"

Yunas tilted his head at her. "Signora?"

"The prices aren't marked."

Nico leaned toward her. "The guest shouldn't see the prices so she feels free to order anything she likes without worrying about the cost." The one time he had taken Rita to a restaurant with guest menus, she had protested too, though not as aggressively.

Nelli handed her menu back to Yunas. "This guest would like to see the prices. Thank you."

"Of course." Yunas said.

"I know the restaurant is trying to be fancy to justify the prices," Nico said.

"I find it demeaning."

"I'm sorry."

"Don't be." She was ruining the evening. "I'm not used to fancy."

"Neither am I." Her smile told him she wasn't angry.

Yunas slipped her the regular menu without opening it. This lady clearly wanted to be in charge. He moved next to Nico with the pretense of adjusting a fork. "I did not see Signor Ferri put anything in Signor Mantelli's drink." Yunas spoke softly. "They were at least two meters away from where the signora now sits."

"You said that to Capitano Tarani?"

"I did." Yunas straightened his spine. "What would you like to drink?"

"Water, no gas," Nelli said, with a smile. "And a martini, please." She was going to be an expensive prop. Besides she'd always wanted to taste one.

Nico looked surprised. "I was going to order a bottle of wine."

"Of course," Nelli said. "I'll have some after my martini. I like red." She wasn't rich or sophisticated and didn't know the rules of high society, but three things she did well were painting, drinking and sticking to her opinions.

Nico ordered a bottle of Ferriello Riserva, the 2015 vintage—a very good year, according to Aldo. Yunas took the order and left.

"I'd like to raise a glass to Aldo," Nico said. "Will you join me?"

Nelli's head was buried in the large menu. "Maybe more than one." Filet mignon was expensive enough. Maybe that was what she should order.

"I didn't picture you as a big drinker," Nico said, surprised.

Nelli lowered the menu. "How do you picture me, Nico?"

"I don't really know. You're a wonderful painter. I like being with you. Seeing your face. It's open and friendly and curious. And if you're overly fond of alcohol, that's your business, but I hope you aren't. I don't want to worry about you."

Nelli laughed. She did so like this big loyal man. Prop or not, she forgave him. "I'm not overly fond of alcohol. I drink on special occasions. And this *is* very special. Ah, just in time."

Yunas entered carrying a silver tray with the martini and the bottle of wine. But Nico was still staring at her. He'd never seen her laugh. She simply glowed.

Yunas started opening the bottle. "Go on, Nico," Nelli said. "Ask your questions."

Nico shook his head as if just waking up. He turned to Yunas, who was standing by his shoulder. "The signorina who was sitting with him in the seat where I am now. She said someone bumped into her back and made her spill wine on her dress. Did you see that happen?"

"I did." Yunas popped the cork out and offered it to Nico.

"I presume there is more to that," Nico said. Yunas poured a couple of centimeters of the wine into Nico's glass. Nico took a long sip. "Wonderful."

Yunas filled his glass. He wiped the wine bottle and set it on the table. "The signore offered me twenty euros to bump into the signorina at the correct moment. I took the money and did as he asked. Her eyes went to the stain on her dress, so she did not see me. I regret it now."

Nelli looked up at Yunas's face. There was real dismay there. She hoped he wasn't ashamed. Despite having a steady job, twenty euros could still seem like a great deal of money for a man who must have struggled to get to Italy, to find a job as a Black immigrant. A beautiful one, but still so foreign to some people.

"Did he give a reason?" Nico asked.

"He wished to be alone."

Because he was expecting to see someone here, Nico thought. At least, that was the reason he had given Loredana for changing restaurants. But who? Not his wife or Aldo. And why send Loredana away? "Did anyone talk to Mantelli besides his wife and Signor Ferri with his Chinese buyer? Anyone at all."

"I did not see anyone. If I was not in this room, it was only for two, three minutes, no more. Once the signorina left, he looked at his cell phone a few times."

"No staff besides yourself?"

"I took care of the signore myself. I am sorry I cannot help you. I have told you my truth. What I saw. No more."

"The truth is exactly what I'm after," Nico said. "Thank you for giving me yours."

Yunas acknowledged Nico with a nod. "Have you decided what you would like to eat?"

Instead of the filet mignon she had planned to order, Nelli chose a much more affordable dish. "I'll have the stuffed paccheri."

Nico found the names of different pastas very confusing. They changed by region. Same pasta, different name. "What are paccheri?"

Nelli answered before Yunas could. "Big rigatoni. They're typical in Campania, Maresciallo Perillo's region."

"We stuff them," Yunas added, "with a ragu of beef, mushrooms, kale, finely chopped, with a pink béchamel sauce."

"Sounds delicious. Two orders of paccheri, then."

"Will that be your first course?"

Nico glanced at Nelli. "My first and second," she said.

"For me too." Nico said. He waited for Yunas to take the menus and leave before saying, "I hope the prices aren't stopping you from ordering more."

"The prices are ridiculous, but no," she lied. She raised her martini glass. "Let's toast to Aldo coming home soon."

Nico raised his glass and clinked it with hers. To Aldo, to being here with her.

"Is what Yunas is telling you helping?"

"Yes. He's cleared Aldo."

"But he told Tarani what he told you, and Aldo got arrested anyway."

"A stupid, hasty arrest to please the prosecutor. Now they have to prove he did it, and there's no proof. They're assuming the poison was administered here, but maybe it wasn't. Yes, methanol gives a bad taste to the drink it's in, but it could also alter the taste of food and drinks consumed later."

"His wife was here that night too, wasn't she?"

"Who told you that?"

"The online grapevine of Gravigna. There's no need to gather in the piazza to gossip anymore, which is a shame. It was a much better way of connecting."

"Face to face is always better, like tonight."

Nelli set her martini aside. As it turned out, she much preferred wine. "With Yunas."

"Yes. I already knew what Yunas had told Tarani, and Perillo had already relayed that to me, but I wanted to ask my own questions."

His answer wasn't quite what she'd hoped. Nelli raised her empty glass. "I'd love some wine now."

Nico raised the wine bottle. Yunas took it from him and poured into Nelli's glass. "The eight o'clock reservation is now in the front room. More answers will be difficult."

"One last one before they come in. When my friend was here, the signore complained that his second whiskey tasted bad."

"He did. I offered to have Signor Falchetti open another bottle or change whiskies. He said no. I reminded him his first dish was a raw artichoke salad. I do know wine and artichokes are bad partners. Maybe also whiskey and artichokes."

"The owner poured the whiskies himself, is that right?"

Yunas looked over his shoulder. Signor Falchetti had stopped to talk to the four people he would soon be serving. "Yes. He trusts no one else with the alcohol. He was not happy the carabiniere came to ask questions wearing his uniform. The murder is much talked about. He does not want clients to be upset."

"Thank you," Nico said. "No more questions from me. You have been very helpful."

Yunas's face shined with pleasure. "Your paccheri will be here shortly." He left them to greet the new diners.

"Do I have you all to myself now?" Nelli asked.

"Yes. I'm sorry." Was she upset? She didn't look it. Her face was radiant, as always. "I did let you know."

"Yes, you did, which didn't stop me from being annoyed at first. But it passed fairly quickly."

"You made the evening much easier for me. Thank you. I really appreciate you and your patience."

"I believe in looking ahead, not backwards." She was looking beyond Nico's shoulder. "Now, *that* is a masterpiece."

A different waiter wearing a waist-length burgundy jacket instead of the more distinguished blazer approached their table with their paccheri. Instead of being served in a loose mound, the paccheri, eight of them, stood tall on each plate, like roman columns.

"A specialty of the house." The waiter lowered the tray and handed out the dishes. "Buon appetito."

"Thank you," they both said. Without another word, they cut into the first pacchero.

With her mouth still full, Nelli started fluttering her hand in front of her chest, her way of saying the pacchero was incredibly delicious.

Nico swallowed before agreeing with her. "I have to tell Tilde about this dish. Do you remember what's in it?"

"I do. I'll be happy to write it down for you, but stuffing the cooked pasta without breaking it is time consuming. This place probably has at least ten or more in the kitchen putting food together for the chef."

"I have to tell her."

They went back to eating, while Yunas took care of the two German couples sitting at the table behind Nico. The two German men had strong voices they seemed happy to show off. Nico wasn't good at small talk, and if he was hoping to know more about Nelli, tonight was not the night. They would have had to speak too loudly.

"How is your Zio Peppino doing?" Nico asked after there was nothing left on his plate. "Is he still mourning his boss?"

"He's both furious and devastated."

"He's double-mourning. The loss of the house and Mantelli's violent death." He'd witnessed many different reactions as the past bearer of bad news. Dumbfounded disbelief. Quiet tears. Screams and wails. One father, whose gay son had been murdered by a gang, had reacted by attacking him and breaking four of his ribs. "Any luck on finding Peppino another job?"

"Signora Severson found him one, but he'd have to start right away, and he doesn't want to leave until the new owners come. It's sad. He's such a good man."

"I'd like to talk to him."

"I'm sure he told Salvatore everything, but you don't need me to see him. Ask Mantelli's wife. He works for her now." At the mention of her name, Nelli felt a pang of jealousy. According to the grapevine, Signora Severson and Nico were spending a lot of time together at Sotto Il Fico. She had no right to feel jealous. She had no claim to Nico. She knew she was being ridiculous, spoiling a perfectly nice evening, but jealousy was what she felt. "I think I need to go home. I've got a lot of work to do tomorrow."

"Of course." Bringing up Peppino had upset her. He was sorry for that. He paid the bill with cash, leaving Yunas a large tip.

Nelli was silent on the drive to her house. She looked sad, and Nico didn't know what to say to comfort her. In front of the gate of her small home in the newer part of Gravigna, she thanked him and kissed his cheeks. "I hope you find the real murderer."

"We will, and Zio Peppino is going to be okay. Grief just takes time."

"Yes, it does. I know." She stepped out of the car. Feeling awkward, Nico stayed put.

Reaching into her bag for her keys, Nelli walked up the short path to her door.

"Nelli," Nico called out as he scrambled out of the car. "I'd love to take you out to dinner again. I promise the only questions I ask will only be about you."

She turned around and felt a smile rise from her chest. "I'd love that too. Sleep well."

"How about Thursday night? I don't work on Thursdays."

"Thursday it is. Now go home. Rocco misses you."

"Buonanotte, Nelli."

"Buonanotte."

AS SOON AS STELLA walked into Bar All'Angolo with Daniele, Sandro stepped out from behind the counter to give her and her backpack a hug. "Bella Stella, we miss you. You're leaving again?"

"Yes. Work calls!"

"When are you dumping the big city and coming home for good?"

"When you offer me a job with decent pay. Do you know Daniele?"

"By eyesight only. You're Salvatore's right-hand man." Sandro raised his hand in salute. "Ciao, I'm Sandro, married to Jimmy, who's in the back stocking supplies when he isn't napping."

Daniele raised his hand in return. "Ciao."

"What can I get the two of you? It's on the house."

"No," Stella protested. "We'll each pay for our orders."

"I'll pay for both of us," Daniele said. He'd made sure to bring enough money in case she wanted more than ice cream.

Sandro shook his head, his one gold earring picking up the light. "It's no use, Daniele. Stella doesn't like to be indebted to anyone."

"That's right," Stella said. "Sorry, Dani. Only the Roman way for me."

He gave in. "Okay." Whatever she wanted was fine with him. It was nice just being with her. She was so full of life, he felt as if some of it rubbed off on him.

"My bar, my rules," Sandro said. "Without taxing my brain too much, I say you," he pointed at Stella, "want two scoops, one salted caramel and one coffee on a cone."

Stella laughed. "Brilliant deduction."

Sandro turned to Daniele. "And you?"

"Dark chocolate and stracciatella, please. In a cup."

Sandro prepared the ice creams and handed them over. They thanked him and walked with the overly full cup and the cone to one of the benches in the piazza.

"You're good friends with Sandro?" He missed having friends.

"I'm friends with more or less everyone," Stella caught a descending bit of caramel with her tongue. "Gravigna is a small town. Sandro gave me my first real job. I've helped at the restaurant in the summers since I was twelve, but since it belongs to my family, that doesn't count. When I was sixteen, Sandro offered me my first real job at the café for the summer. I blew all my salary on ice cream cones. Salted caramel and coffee. It's a great mix. Want to taste?" She held up the unlicked part of her cone.

Daniele hesitated. He'd already used his spoon.

"Hurry up, Dani. Lick away. It's melting. Your germs won't kill me."

Daniele allowed himself one lick, then quickly backed off.

"Now I'll use your spoon to taste yours so our germs get to know each other."

Daniele offered her his cup. "That would be nice."

"I think so." Stella dug the spoon in deeply and quickly scooped a small mound of stracciatella into her mouth. "Mmm. That's good." She handed his spoon back.

"Why only the Roman way for you? What's wrong with a man treating you to ice cream?"

"If we both pay, we're equal. It's better that way."

"I know it's the way now, but I think it's too bad. Trust has gone missing."

"Yes, it has. For good reason, though."

"I'm not like that."

"I know. That's why we're having ice cream together."

"You didn't trust me earlier."

"Aldo is a good friend of my family."

"They don't have enough evidence to hold him. He'll come home soon."

"I hope you're right. When I'm upset, I lash out. I'm sorry."

"It's okay. What time is the bus to Florence?"

She glanced at her phone. "In twenty-eight minutes. I hope you'll come visit me again."

"I want to. I don't have any friends around my age yet."

"Sure you do. Me."

Daniele was grateful they were sitting in the dark side of the piazza so she wouldn't see his red face.

"We're friends, right?" Stella asked.

"Yes, we are." He was happy.

"Good."

They finished their ice cream in comfortable silence. The only noise came from the chatter and laughter from Da Gino's crowded outside tables and the occasional car driving by.

ELEVEN

Monday morning, Nico and Gogol were finishing their usual breakfast at Bar All'Angolo. OneWag, having scoured the floor for crumbs, had left, sniffing out what goodies and smells the piazza might offer. Beppe, the newspaper seller's chubby nineteen-year-old son, shuffled into the café to deliver two copies of the Florentine daily.

"You're late," Sandro said from behind the cash register. "What's your excuse this time?" In the past half-hour, a steady stream of customers, regulars and tourists had been coming in.

"Come on, Sandro," Beppe spread out his arms. The papers fell to the floor. "What's time when you're young and happy?"

Gogol nudged Nico with his lard crostino. "'Oh, you who have a healthy intellect.'"

"I heard that." Beppe picked up the papers and flung them down on the nearest table. "Well, dear Signor Gogol, my intellect is just fine. My class grades were posted on the school bulletin board. I passed. You can go see for yourself if you don't believe me. I'm finished with school."

A few regulars clapped. Last year, Beppe had been sent back.

"Congratulations, Beppe," Nico said. "Well done."

At the back of the bar, Jimmy was unloading the dishwasher. "You're going to work at the news shop?"

"I'm going to be a reporter. Exciting things are going on here. Two murders in the area in less than a year. Who better than me, a native, to spin the story, eh?"

"God help us," someone behind the pillar muttered.

"In fact, Signor Nico, you are a friend of the maresciallo and the murder—" He was stopped midsentence by Gustavo bursting through the open door.

"Is it true?" Gustavo asked Nico. "Ferri killed that wine critic?"

The news would probably be in tomorrow's papers, but to Nico's regret, their grapevine had caught the news first. He now found himself surrounded by the Bench Boys, retired men in their late seventies and eighties who spent their days sitting together in the piazza, expounding, arguing and usually getting along. They carried flip phones in their pockets so their wives could call them home for lunch or dinner.

Gogol grinned at Gustavo. "You wish to know the truth. 'It is right you should be gratified of such a desire.'" Any excuse to quote the master poet, even only partially, was a good one.

"That's worth ten cents, not a euro," Gustavo said.

Gogol shrugged. "It's free. Sometimes I need to adapt."

"Please sit down, all of you," Nico said.

Gustavo pulled a chair from the next table and sat down next to Nico. Ettore did the same. The other two pushed the table closer and leaned on it, their necks craned toward Nico to hear better.

"Aldo Ferri didn't kill anyone," Nico said, directing his words at Gustavo. "The prosecutor wanted to question him in person. That's why he's in Florence."

Ettore grimaced. "Anyone who works for this government should be fed to the boars. They think their balls are made of gold and we're cow shit."

"Oh, that's good." Beppe waved at Sandro. "Quick, give me a pen and some paper."

Sandro shook his head. "Your mother is the one who sells pens and notebooks. I sell food and drinks."

"Nico, don't say anything!" Beppe yelled as he ran out.

"It looks bad if they want to question him," Gustavo said. "He did punch the man and threaten to kill him."

"He didn't mean it," Ettore said.

The rotund man behind Gustavo said, "Maybe he carried out his threat."

"How well do any of you know Aldo Ferri?" Nico asked the foursome.

"I know his wife, Cinzia," Ettore said, as always running his hand over his bald head as if he hoped to find a full head of hair. In contrast Gustavo had a mane of pure white hair that stood high around his sharp angular face. "Always has a nice word for us, asks about our families." The other two, whose names Nico didn't know, nodded in agreement.

Gustavo pointed a bent finger at Ettore. He always seemed to have a rebuttal to anything his friend said. "The wife isn't the husband. You have to keep things and people separate. Nico, you do the same. Ferri's your landlord, your friend. You helped him in the piazza, calmed him down. We all saw that, so we understand if you defend him. Ferri works hard, makes a good wine. I don't want to think he killed anyone."

Ettore nodded. "He gave you a bottle when his wife found out it was your birthday. You didn't share."

Gustavo waved the words away. "Stop harping about that. I told you I would have, but my daughter took it for the party she didn't give me."

"Do you see him as a murderer?" Nico asked the four.

"Given enough reason," Gustavo said, "all of us could kill, and Ferri thought he had a very good reason. A wife is sacred."

"Not mine," Ettore said with a laugh.

Gustavo looked at him sharply. The laugh stopped. "If you think that," Gustavo said, "you are cow shit. She feeds you, makes the bed, and sends you out with clean clothes. That makes her sacred."

Ettore lowered his head. The other two men nodded their agreement.

Gustavo turned to Nico. "Americans always think the best of people. With our history, Italians have good reason to be skeptical. I hope you are right, Signor Nico. From my heart, I hope Ferri is as honest as the wine he makes."

"Me too," Ettore said.

The four stood up. "Arrivederci, Nico. Have a good day."

"You too."

Beppe ran back into the café, pen and a notebook in hand. The Bench Boys walked past him on the way out. "Wait," he called out. "What did he say?" He turned to Nico. "What did you say?"

"Aldo Ferri did not kill anyone. And you can quote me on that." Nico got on his feet. "See you tomorrow, Gogol."

Gogol gave his usual answer. "Tomorrow, if I live."

"You will." Nico said. "Ciao to all." Stepping out on the sidewalk, he was met by a blast of sun halfway up in the sky. He took out his phone and sought the shade of one of the linden trees in the piazza. The flowers were in bloom and gave off a sweet, pleasant smell. He dialed Cinzia's cell phone.

"Hi, Nico." Her usually cheerful voice was flat. "I hope you're calling with good news."

"Not yet, I'm sorry. Hold on tight. We'll find the real culprit." He hoped he wasn't making an empty promise.

"I've gnashed my teeth to bits, but I'm holding on as tight as I can."

"Where are you?"

"At work with Arben. Aldo didn't want me to stay in Florence. There's still work to do here."

"Is there anything I can do to help at the vineyard?"

"No, we've got everything under control."

"Listen, Tarani thinks Mantelli was poisoned at the restaurant. I've read that how quickly methanol kills depends on the individual, which means it could have been administered any-where from a full day before to right before. In case they start looking at it from that angle, is there someone to vouch for Aldo after the fight in the piazza Tuesday afternoon?"

Cinzia let out a long exhale. "Yes, God be praised! A very good alibi. He was here at the vineyard with me, Hua Chen and Arben until it was time for them to go to dinner."

"I'm glad to hear that."

"Tell Perillo to push that angle with Tarani. I want my hus-band back where he belongs."

"He'll be back. Ciao, Cinzia."

"I'm counting on you, Nico."

"I won't let you down." *May it be true.* He clicked off.

Nico whistled for OneWag. Before paying a visit to Ver-dini, he wanted to visit Rita. Nelli's warm presence had stayed with him through the night, making him feel guilty and con-fused. Maybe sorting those feelings out in Rita's presence would help. She'd always been good at seeing these things clearly. He checked his watch. Luciana's shop was open, and she was prob-ably feeding cookies to OneWag. He would buy yellow roses this time.

PERILLO LOOKED UP AT the steep, winding steps that would take him to Ida Crivelli's apartment. She lived in one of the towers of the medieval castle that had once helped keep the Sienese army at bay.

"I hope this is worth it," Perillo grumbled, bending down to massage one knee. It had started to hurt during the winter. The severe June heat hadn't helped so far.

"Want me to go up first to see if she's home?" Daniele asked. As this was ostensibly an unofficial visit, they had forsaken their uniforms for jeans and short-sleeved shirts.

"Didn't you call first?"

"I did, but we're late." The maresciallo had insisted on having a second breakfast at the café next to the station. Two espressos, a cream-filled cornetto and a cigarette outside the bar that, to an always punctual Daniele, had taken forever.

Perillo checked his cell phone. "Thirty minutes isn't late. Let's go."

By Daniele's watch it was close to forty-five minutes, but he said nothing and followed his boss up the first ramp. The stone steps were cracked, the center of each worn down to satin smoothness by three centuries of use.

After the second ramp, Perillo stopped to rest, his knee pulsing with pain. "If you want to climb stairs like this until old age, Dani, don't take up cycling."

Daniele resigned himself to being even later. The maresciallo wasn't so young anymore. Almost fifty. "Vince said you were a great cyclist."

Perillo took his weight off his bad knee and leaned against the wall, happy to rest. "I cycled for years up and down these hills. Chianti is known for its killer hills. Professionals come to train here. You think going up is going to kill you. As you climb, you think your lungs will burst, and then you arrive at the top and down you fly, arms wide, the wind drying the sweat on your face. It's a glorious feeling."

"Ehi," a sharp voice called down. "Are you through reminiscing? I've got to go to work."

Perillo looked. He could see a small, round face staring down at him. "Please accept my apology, Signora."

"Well, hurry up. These stairs didn't kill me; they won't kill you either."

"Of course not." Perillo didn't like admitting to weakness. "We're coming."

Perillo finally heaved himself up the last step and was met by a compact barrel of a woman in a flowered housedress and a blue apron that almost reached her ankles. Her sharp face was surrounded by a cap of yellow hair.

"Finally," Ida said to him, standing by her door with a piercing look. "Don't bother to introduce yourself. I know who you are. Your brigadiere too. He's more handsome in uniform. Come in." She moved aside to let them pass.

They walked into a large, hot kitchen, immaculately clean. A delicious smell filled the air.

"Keep going."

"You're baking something," Daniele said, overcome by the aroma.

"A chocolate crostata for Signora Severson. She pays me extra. She didn't wait long to take over the villa—two days. Good for her, I say."

"Could I bother you for a glass of water?" Perillo asked, his chest still heaving.

Ida pointed to the wide stone sink, partially filled with flowering plants. "Help yourself. The glasses are next to the sink. The brigadiere can come with me. You'll find us on the balcony."

Perillo went to the sink with a smile, surprised that Ida's lack of respect for a maresciallo of the carabinieri didn't anger him. It was almost admirable.

Daniele followed her. They passed a small room with an armchair and a sewing machine; two small tables holding ceramic figurines and more flowering plants; and a bed piled high with crocheted pillows and covered in a flowered fabric that matched Ida's house dress.

Beyond the small room, they walked onto a narrow balcony. "This is my joy," Ida said, stepping on a stool so that she could look over the castle parapet.

"Dio mio!" Daniele exclaimed. He had never seen the Golden Valley from such a height. Many years ago, it had been full of wheat. Now, it was kilometers and kilometers of perfectly aligned rows of vines, each patch going in a different direction. A splotchy blanket of poppies covered the ground underneath.

Perillo joined them and looked out at the view. It faced west, meaning she could see the sunset. "Dio mio indeed. You are a lucky woman."

"My grandfather was lucky. I could sell to some foreigner and retire, but it would break my heart." She put her forearm on the parapet and turned to face Perillo. "Now, Signor Maresciallo, I have things to say about that man's death. What took you so long?"

"Why didn't you come to the station, then?"

"You asked Peppino to come, but you didn't ask me, so I didn't come. I've worked for Signor Mantelli for over three years, three times a week when he was in residence. I am a woman and I see things Peppino does not."

"Can we sit down and talk? Brigadiere Donato needs to take notes."

"No, I just finished baking. It's too hot inside, and talking about a murder is best done in the open air. I don't want evil in my home."

"Then you should have come to the station."

"Well, I didn't, did I?"

Have patience, Perillo told himself.

Daniele took out a pen and small notebook from his pocket. He placed the notebook on the thick parapet. It was a perfect desk.

"Signor Mantelli didn't like me because I notice things. He loved Peppino. Peppino is a good man, but he doesn't know how to add one thing together with another and maybe yet one more thing to see the truth."

A lot of things, Perillo thought, *probably leading to nothing.* "And what truth was that?"

Ida stepped off the stool and sat on it. She had to look up to see the maresciallo's face. "The truth that Mantelli's girlfriend killed him."

Perillo leaned down. Now they were face to face. "Loredana Cardi?"

"Yes, Signorina Loredana. Who else? His girlfriend—one day, his wife, is what she had on her mind. A poor girl from a small town, she thought she'd climbed the mountain and reached the sky. I feel sorry for her."

"Why do you—"

Ida stopped him with a raised hand. "No. This is my story; I'll tell it my way. I know I'm only a maid and not considered worth listening to, but you are in my home and you will listen. If not, I tuck my story in my bra like it was money." She furrowed her brow for a few seconds, then grinned and slapped her knee. "It did not come to my mind before. My story *is* money. The newspaper would be very generous if I told them what I knew."

Perillo didn't take her threat seriously. She seemed too proud a person, but he admired her gumption. "I could take you down to the station and make you tell your story there, but you've made a good point. We all have a right to be listened to, no matter who we are." He was quoting his adoptive father, the carabiniere who had plucked him from the streets of Pozzuoli and offered him a home. "The story is yours. Go ahead."

Ida nodded her approval. "Monday night, I had finished my work and was getting my purse from the closet in the entryway, when a great crash made me jump. I ran through the dining room to the living room. Signor Mantelli was sitting on the sofa, laughing. The signorina was standing in front of him, her pretty face looking like a rabid dog's and Signor Mantelli's precious Venetian vase, the one he wouldn't let me clean because he was sure I would break it, was in pieces on the floor. A glass shard had cut her leg. Blood was trickling to the floor. I don't think she was aware of it.

"'You're bleeding, Signorina Loredana,' I said. 'Come with me, let me clean you up.' I felt it was my duty, woman to woman.

She didn't hear me, but he did. He stopped laughing and snarled, 'Get out of here.' I did as he ordered. It was none of my business, I told myself, but as I'm sure you know, curiosity has the fangs of a snake—once it bites, your body fills with poison." Ida leaned a shoulder against the parapet and sighed.

Daniele took advantage of the pause in her story to shake out his writing hand and sneak another look at the view.

Perillo leaned against the doorjamb. His knee had stopped throbbing. He knew not to interrupt. She was getting there, he thought. Soon, he could thank her and take her information with him, then puzzle it together with the rest of what he knew.

"The windows of the living room were wide open. Signor Mantelli didn't believe in air-conditioning. Let me tell you, I sweated liters cleaning that house."

Daniele loosened his grip on his pen. Perillo thought of Cinzia peeking through Mantelli's open window. Maybe the very same one. He was glad he lived on the second floor, facing the street and the park.

Ida lifted her shoulder off the wall. "Never mind. I stood underneath one window. They couldn't see me. Being short has its advantages. 'You can break everything in this house, but it won't change anything,' the signore said. 'Our relationship is over. As of next week, I will no longer pay for your room at Il Glicine. I will no longer see you.'

"She started screaming. 'You can't do this. You made promises. I'm not shit you can just wipe away.' Things like that. She was crying and screaming at the same time. It was hard to understand what she was saying. I heard the sound of a smack followed by silence. He must have slapped her. I'd had enough. I started to tiptoe away when she said, in a loud, calm voice, 'If you leave me, I'll kill you.' I guess he thought that was very funny, because he just laughed hard. When he got tired of laughing, he said, 'Well, my dear, you have a week in which to do it.'" Ida crossed herself. "That's the truth, God's truth."

Perillo straightened up. "Thank you, Signora Ida."

"Signorina, and proud of it. I'm not finished."

Perillo sat back down.

"The Friday after Signor Mantelli's death, Signora Severson had moved in, and so had the girlfriend." Ida lifted both hands, showing Perillo her calloused palms. "A strange arrangement, but not for me to judge. Signora Severson has a kind heart, but she didn't understand what she had brought home with her. I caught the signorina going through Signor Mantelli's desk, looking for money, I'm sure. I stopped her. Not an hour later, I saw her going through his closet. This time I said nothing. My hours were done, and I wanted to go home."

"Did you tell Signora Severson?"

"I'm going to tell her today. She should know who she has in her house. All right, I'm done with my story now. It's the truth. Do with it what you want."

"A very interesting story."

"A true one," Ida corrected.

"Yes. Thank you. Before I go, I need you to answer one question. You called Signor Mantelli last Monday and also on Tuesday. Can you tell me why?"

"It wasn't me on Monday. The signore sent Peppino to Panzano to get two steaks from Dario Cecchini. Peppino's phone had no charge, so he borrowed mine. I guess he called him from Dario's to let him know, because he came home without the steaks."

"And Tuesday?"

"I told him I needed to switch Wednesday for Thursday. I needed to see Dottor Berti for my sciatica. He said he didn't care when I came in, as long as I got the work done without disturbing him."

Perillo remembered something Peppino had told him. "Did Signor Mantelli lower your wages last year?"

Ida laughed. "He tried. I told him he could do the cleaning himself then."

"He didn't lower them?"

Ida shook her head.

"He could have found another housekeeper."

"He wouldn't do that."

"Why not?"

"Because I know two and two doesn't always make six or even four."

Perillo let out a sigh. "Is there something else you know that has bearing on this case?"

"No." Her expression was sincere.

Daniele put his pen and notebook back in his pants and gave a last look at the valley below. A billowing cloud had just covered the sun, staining some vineyards with its shadow.

Perillo offered his hand. "Then thank you again."

Ida popped up from her stool with a smile and shook it. "Maresciallo, Signorina Loredana is not well. Please treat her with gentle hands."

"We will. I need to go back to the station now."

"Yes, of course. I'll accompany you to the door." She pushed past him and walked toward the kitchen. Perillo followed, casting a longing glance at the crostata, now cool enough to eat. At the front door, as Daniele followed Perillo out, Ida tugged at his sleeve. "Come back anytime. The view is best at sunset."

Daniele thanked her. The invitation warmed his heart.

"Tarani needs to know about Loredana," Perillo said as soon as they reached downstairs. "I want you to check that Ida did go to the doctor on Tuesday, and tomorrow, you're going to climb back up there and find out what she means by two and two doesn't always make four."

"I'll be happy to," Daniele said. He'd go at sunset.

ONEWAG STARTED WRIGGLING WITH excitement as soon as Nico entered the Verdini parking lot. Nico opened his door and the dog scrambled over him, barking in joy. Nico had to laugh as he watched OneWag shoot down the path to find Contessa. "I've got a smitten dog," he would tell Nelli. She would laugh that throaty laugh of hers that managed to undo whatever knots he had in his stomach. "I like her a lot," he'd confessed to Rita as he arranged the yellow roses beneath her picture. He'd stood there a good half hour. Slowly, the confusion and guilt he'd been feeling since last night evaporated. Was Rita giving him permission to live his new life? He knew he was the one who was afraid of being disloyal, of opening up and caring for a woman again. Afraid to suffer a second time. It was easier to put the burden of his emotions on Rita, as he had done when she was alive.

"Buongiorno," a young voice called out halfway up Verdini's path.

Nico got out of the car and waved at a slim young woman in a ruffled long white skirt and red top.

"Buongiorno. I'm here to see Signor Verdini."

They walked toward each other. "I'm afraid he's gone to Siena for the day." As she reached Nico, she extended her hand. "I'm Ginevra."

He smiled and shook her hand. "Nico Doyle." Ginevra here with Luca gone was exactly what he had hoped to find.

"Luca told me you might be coming by. How can I help you?" She had a pretty round face behind glasses, with a girl-next-door quality that he instantly liked. She looked no more than thirty.

"I'd like a case of his red, 2015 if available, but I'd also like to taste his white wine." That would give him a chance to sit by the shed, enjoy the view and fish for information.

"Of course."

They walked down the path edged with geraniums. Her top was the same red as the flowers. "I've always loved geraniums," she said. "I used to think they kept vipers at a distance, but Luca told me it's not true. I was miffed." She shook her head. "Very childish of me."

"They're still nice."

"I prefer red roses now. Luca has lots of those in the back garden."

Nico wondered if this was her usual welcoming chitchat, a way to put nervous wine buyers at ease. "How long have you worked for him?"

"Three years. I used to work for another vintner, but I prefer it here." They had reached the shed. "When there's no work, I just sit here and look out at the valley. It's heavenly, isn't it?"

"Yes, it is." He walked to the edge to see where OneWag had ended up down below. He covered his eyes with his hand and finally spotted the two dogs chasing each other along the fence of one large area of vines. "They're not going to get electrocuted, are they?"

Ginevra joined him. "They're fine. We only turn the electricity on at night. Please sit down while I open a bottle of Vermentino. And forgive the chairs. Luca's getting new ones. At least, that's what he's been saying since I started working here." She smiled as she slipped into the shed.

Nico sat in the same chair he'd sat in before. It had the best view. The sprinkling of poppies from a few days before had thickened. The sun, midway in the sky, had already made the air too hot, but up here, a slight breeze gave a little reprieve. "I found out about ColleVerde thanks to Michele Mantelli."

"It's so sad about his death," Ginevra said from inside the shed. The door was halfway open. "He was a nice man. I can't believe he was murdered."

"You knew him?" He heard the air pop of the cork being released from the bottle.

"Yes." Ginevra came out of the shed holding the bottle of

Vermentino and a white wine glass. "He came here several times, looking for Luca. The last time I saw him was exactly two weeks ago. I'm sorry Luca wasn't here. Signor Mantelli was upset not to find him."

"He wasn't upset the other times he came and Luca wasn't here?"

"The other times he waited for him. I'd try to keep him happy by asking questions about his work, his life. He would sit where you're sitting now and chat about how much he loved the wine-growing business, how he liked to help struggling vintners whenever he could. He heaped praise on Luca, saying his wines deserved every bit of praise he gave." She poured two fingers' worth of wine into the glass and offered it to him.

"Thanks." Instead of taking the customary wine tasting sip, he drank it all down. "I like it. I know I should go on and say I taste the hint of cooked apples or honey-coated white peaches or some such"—he'd been reading Mantelli's blog—"but 'I like it' is as far as I'll go. I'll take two bottles of this too." He'd uncork them for his dinner with Nelli on Thursday.

Ginevra gave him a sideways smile. "'I like it' is just fine. Here, let me pour you some more."

It wasn't lunchtime yet, but why not? Maybe he could get her to keep talking. "Thank you." She filled the glass. "Please join me, Ginevra. I don't like to drink alone, and I'll pay for the bottle."

"In that case, I will. Thank you." She got another glass from the shed, sat down next to him and poured herself three fingers' worth. "Now, tell me about you." She clinked her glass against his.

"I don't need to talk about myself to be happy. I want to know about you and the vineyard."

"I have nothing to say except I love this work. Luca is a wonderful boss. My last boss liked to put his hands all over me, that's why I quit. Luca is a gentleman."

"I've met Mantelli's American wife, Diane Severson." This time, Nico took only a small sip of his wine. "She knows Luca's ex-wife. I think that's how Mantelli found out about this vineyard."

"I didn't know that. Mirella was the one who hired me. When I came here, they were at the tail end of their marriage. She left about six months later. I liked her a lot, and that's all I'll say."

"Diane is a nice woman. Has she ever come by?"

"Not that I know of. You're full of questions, aren't you? Is it because of the murder?"

"Doesn't it make you curious?"

"No, it makes me sad. And it's none of our business really."

"You don't want the murderer caught?"

She tilted her head to one side, her eyes studying his face. "I do, but I expect the carabinieri will catch whoever it is. I prefer to worry about the vineyard." She stood up and polished off her glass. "If this heat keeps up, we'll have to harvest early. Luca says climate change is going to change the wine business in a big way." She stood up. "Let me get you your bottles."

Nico stood up. It was clear Ginevra had gotten suspicious and wouldn't be offering any more information, but he was satisfied. One thing she'd said seemed promising. He whistled for OneWag. Once home, he'd consult with Perillo.

PERILLO'S OFFICE WAS UNCOMFORTABLE, the oversized fan distributing only hot air. Perillo suggested the three of them convene again in the small park across the street from the station. Nico found him sitting on a bench under the shade of an oak tree.

"You should move your desk out here." Nico sat on an adjacent bench next to Daniele. "It's much more bearable." OneWag, after his usual sniffing examination of Perillo's boots, sat in front of Daniele and stared.

Perillo was clicking a number on his cell phone with his

cigarette hand. "What do you want from the café? If you're hungry, Vince says the best is the focaccia stuffed with mortadella and provolone. Dani's getting an apricot juice. You?"

"Nothing thanks. My stomach is sloshing in wine."

"Then you have to eat." Perillo spoke into the phone. "The usual for me and my brigadiere, plus one La Marinella. We're in the park. Don't wait for the pope to die, okay? Ciao." He clicked off. "The housekeeper Ida says she's given us Mantelli's killer. What did Verdini give you?"

"As I expected, he wasn't there." Nico pulled out his shirt to let some air hit his chest. "I spoke to his assistant, Ginevra. You first. Your news sounds more substantial."

OneWag, his eyes still focused on Daniele, whimpered. Daniele bent over to scratch his head. "No toy this time. I'm sorry." OneWag lifted a paw, which Daniele took. "Next time, I promise."

Nico snapped his fingers at his dog, who took his paw back, got up and headed off to the farthest part of the park. "Pay no attention to him, Dani. He's a ruffian. It's my fault. I've spoiled him."

"You need to spoil a woman, not a dog." Perillo put out his cigarette against his shoe and slipped the butt in his portable ashtray.

Spoiling OneWag was easy, Nico thought. His needs were plain to see. "Who killed Mantelli, according to Ida?"

Perillo sat back on the bench and spread out his arms in hopes of losing some body heat. "The week before Mantelli died, Ida overheard Loredana threaten to kill him. Apparently, he'd just told her their relationship was over. He was going to pay for her B&B for one more week, then she was on her own."

"Do you believe this woman?"

"I do," Daniele said. "What reason would she have to lie?"

"Loredana might have treated her badly," Nico answered. "Ida could be getting back at her."

Daniele jumped to her defense. "She's a nice woman."

Perillo smiled. "She took to our Dani. I think he may have found a Tuscan mamma. And there's no need for your Dani bloom now."

A red-faced Dani lifted his shoulders with a helpless expression on his face. "I can't help it."

"It's nothing to be ashamed of," Nico said.

"Some woman is going to fall in love with you for that blush, heed my words. My wife, for one, thinks it's adorable. Ah, here comes Renzino."

A chubby teenager with a shock of white-blond hair crossed the street with a penguin waddle. The tray in his hand held steady.

Perillo took one look at him and slapped his forehead. "Holy heaven, what have you done to your hair now? Two days ago, it was fire-engine red. Did you fall into a tub of bleach?"

Renzino laughed. "Naw, my girlfriend wants to go blond—" he jumped back at seeing a dog at his feet. Having caught an appetizing smell in the air, OneWag had returned. "Does he bite?"

"No," Nico reassured him. It always surprised him how many Italians were afraid of even the sweetest-looking dogs. Tilde had explained that a lot of mothers didn't let their children touch dogs, saying they were dirty or they'd bite. That fear seemed to stay with some of them as adults.

Perillo picked up his double espresso and drank it down. "So your girlfriend wants you to be blond too?"

"No. She just wanted to make sure she was going to like the color for herself." Renzino lifted his wide shoulders. "It's okay. I got tired of the red. Put the order on the station bill?"

"That's right."

Nico reached for his wallet. "Let me pay."

"No, this one is on the carabinieri. We're working."

"Should I come back for the tray?" Renzino asked, keeping an eye on the dog.

OneWag was now sniffing the tray's aroma from a polite distance. He'd learned that frightened humans often kicked.

"No, I'll bring it back," Dani said.

"Ciao, then." He ran off.

"Someone should tell him that if he's afraid of dogs, he shouldn't run." Nico turned his attention back to the murder. "Perillo, do you believe Ida?"

"She's a proud person. Made a fuss about not being interviewed, so she could be trying to get attention, but I do believe she heard the fight. Now we have to find out if Loredana followed through on her threat. I know you wanted to talk to her, but at this point, it's best if you leave her to me."

"I agree."

"I don't think Ida has told us everything," Perillo said.

"I checked about her call to Mantelli on Wednesday," Daniele said, eager to defend her. "She did see her doctor that day."

"I'm convinced she knows something about Mantelli that she's not telling us," Perillo said. "Daniele will further charm his way into her heart and find out what it is. It may have nothing to do with the murder, but as she said, curiosity's like the fangs of a snake once it bites." He left the rest unsaid and picked up the tissue wrapped sandwich. "Here, have your La Marinella. Buon appetito."

Nico unwrapped it. "It's enormous." There was more than an inch of mortadella and cheese in between two layers of thick focaccia.

"It'll absorb the wine."

"It'll absorb me." Nico opened his mouth wide and took a bite. It was luscious. From the corner of his eye, he could see OneWag stealthily approaching again, snout and tail held high in the air.

"All the café's sandwiches have women's names. The owner named each sandwich after one of his five daughters," Daniele said, after taking a short sip of his fruit juice. "My favorite is L'Ar-abella. That's with mozzarella and pesto. I have it for lunch a lot."

"The beyond of the beyond, according to Dino, is L'Isabella. Focaccia with layers of salami, prosciutto and mortadella, topped with arugula salad between the layers of meat."

Nico swallowed. If he didn't bring them back to the matter at hand, talk of food might go on until sunset. "Have you told Tarani yet?"

"I did as soon as we left Ida's place, without mentioning the something we might not know. He has spoken to Aldo's Chinese buyer and now agrees that Aldo couldn't have slipped the poison into Mantelli's whiskey at the restaurant."

"In fact, the poison could have been administered before Mantelli went to the restaurant. Just before or even a few hours earlier." Nico took another big bite.

Perillo nodded reluctantly. If that were the case, a lot of time and energy had been wasted. "Forensics reported the alcohol bot-tles they took from Mantelli's villa had no trace of methanol. The one whiskey bottle was unopened, and all the glasses had been thoroughly cleaned. I guess giving him the poison at the villa would have been easier for Loredana."

"Or anyone else." Daniele still found it hard to accept Loredana as a killer. "Signora Severson was at the villa Tuesday morning."

"But Mantelli wasn't."

"She could have spiked something, then asked or paid Pep-pino to get rid of it after Mantelli had a drink," Daniele said. "With Mantelli dead, she gets the money from the sale of the villa."

"I'm not dismissing the possibility," Perillo said, "and we'll call Peppino in again, but first I have to ask Loredana a few pointed questions."

"Is Aldo going to be released now?" Nico asked.

"Not yet. Della Langhe still thinks everything points to him.

His threat in the piazza, the bribes he paid Mantelli to keep him from ruining him—of course, for our prosecutor, it's the vintners who offered bribes. Mantelli was only guilty of ceding to temptation. According to him, if Aldo didn't do it at the restaurant, he did it earlier that day."

"Aldo has an airtight alibi for earlier in the day. And it was Cinzia who paid Mantelli," Nico protested. "Aldo knew nothing about it."

"It doesn't matter who paid. The fact is, they had to pay, or he'd put a big dent in their business. Did Ginevra offer anything of interest?"

Nico tore off a piece of his focaccia and gave it to OneWag. Delicious as it was, there was no way he could finish it. Some for his mutt, the rest he'd take home. "She made it clear that Mantelli had come over several times recently. When Verdini wasn't there, he'd wait for him. Last Monday was different. He was upset Verdini wasn't around. I think maybe Daniele is right. Mantelli could have gone to Il Falco to meet with Verdini. They exchanged phone calls on Sunday. Mantelli then went to visit him on Monday, didn't find him and got upset."

"You think Verdini would have shown up at the restaurant alone, but then gotten stuck doing Mantelli's wife a favor?" Perillo said. "Or that her being there was part of the plan?"

Nico shook his head. "I don't know what purpose that would serve. According to Yunas, there was no exchange of information. Mantelli shooed her away immediately. If Verdini was the man he was waiting for, her presence must have been a nasty surprise."

Daniele moved closer on the bench. "Maybe Verdini owed Mantelli money. There was no May ColleVerde payment listed in Mantelli's computer notes."

"How much was he paying?" Perillo asked.

"Eight hundred euros a month. Ferriello Wines paid four hundred euros until two months ago."

Perillo raised his hands in the air in surprise. "How do you remember that? I read the same notes and remember nothing." There it was, the realization that haunted him. He was getting old. His memory had started playing hopscotch and missing the squares; he was muddling through this case, letting Nico, Daniele and Aldo down. "Don't mind me. My two espressos haven't kicked in yet."

"I reread the notes this morning," Daniele lied. Lies were a sin, but if they made someone happy, God would surely forgive him.

"What about the other vintners?" Nico asked. Something Ginevra had said made him want to know more about them.

"Only two. The last payment for the one in Sicily was April, same as Verdini. The one in Piedmont paid the first of June. They paid much less. Two hundred euros each."

"Please email me their names," Nico said. "I'd like to talk to them."

"I have their phone numbers too."

"Good, that's even better." Nico rewrapped his sandwich and stood up. "I'm going home to harvest some vegetables. I skip a day, and the zucchini turn into footballs. If Ivana needs any basil, let me know. I've got enough to make a kilo of pesto. I'm taking this sandwich with me."

"Don't feed it all to Rocco," Perillo said. "He'll get indigestion."

"And I won't? Let me know how it goes with Tarani and Loredana. I'm working at the restaurant tonight, but text me, and I'll call you back when I can."

Daniele stood up. "Arrivederci, Nico."

"Ciao, Daniele. Perillo."

Perillo waved and jiggled a cigarette out of his pack.

Nico shook his head. "One day we'll get you to quit."

Perillo laughed. "One day."

"Maybe tomorrow. Come on, OneWag. Let's go."

The words "Let's go" usually prompted OneWag to run ahead of his boss, eager for a new adventure. This time, he stayed behind and followed La Marinella.

TWELVE

Perillo and Daniele came back from their focaccia lunch at the café to find Capitano Tarani in uniform, seated at Perillo's desk. The oversized fan whirred hot air in his face. Not a hair on his head moved.

"Here you are," Tarani said on seeing them, with what looked like a smile.

Daniele saluted. Perillo was too surprised to salute. He nodded instead.

"I prefer to arrive early rather than late," Tarani said by way of explanation.

Perillo stole a glance at his watch. Forty-five minutes early. Was Tarani checking up on them? "Didn't one of the men tell you where we were?"

"The chubby one believed you and the brigadiere were having lunch with your wife upstairs."

Good for Vince, Perillo thought. Vince knew Ivana had gone off to visit a friend in Panzano. He'd just earned himself a paid trip to the café.

"I did not wish to interrupt. Lunchtime, after all, is the highlight of the day." Tarani stood up and moved away from Perillo's desk. "I'm afraid I've warmed your seat." He took a chair from the back of the room and placed it facing the desk.

Perillo and Daniele were still by the door, both surprised by the change in Tarani's manner. Daniele was worried about not being in uniform. Perillo wondered what had happened to change the man's attitude.

Tarani waved them in. "Please. It's your office, not mine."

Daniele walked to his desk at the far end of the room as quietly as he could. Perillo squared his shoulders and walked quickly to his desk.

Tarani sat up straight in his chair. "I have an admission to make. When you opposed arresting Aldo Ferri on suspicion of murder, I did not listen to your reasons. I thought you were objecting because you resented my being in charge, or even that your American friend might have influenced you to protect Signor Ferri. After reexamining all the facts, I see that I acted hastily."

Tarani's admission was so unexpected that Perillo had to stop himself from grinning with satisfaction. "You were under pressure from the prosecutor," he offered, feeling generous.

"That is an excuse made by many to cover up their mistakes. I am not one of them. I have spoken to Prosecutor Della Langhe and suggested that we release Signor Ferri today. His response was, 'For that to happen, you need to find the real guilty party.' I will not be made to look like a fool."

"Holy heaven," Perillo exclaimed. "Aldo Ferri is innocent."

"It is wiser not to comment," Tarani admonished gently. "From what you tell me, we have the guilty party, if Mantelli's housekeeper is to be believed."

"We believe she heard Loredana Cardini threaten Mantelli," Perillo said, "but threats are not always carried out, as Ferri's situation has proven." He was aware he was being a bit pompous, but sitting back at his desk in Tarani's presence felt too good. "Daniele called Loredana on the way back from the café. His manner is gentler than mine." Perillo turned back to look at Daniele. "What did you tell her?"

Daniele pulled down his shirt. "I told her Maresciallo Perillo wanted to ask her some questions about Signor Mantelli's activities in the past few weeks." The maresciallo had dictated the words.

"Good," Tarani said. "You sent her off track."

"I'm not sure, Capitano." Loredana wasn't a strong woman, but he didn't think she was easily fooled. "She did say she loved Mantelli and would never hurt him. She agreed to come if I picked her up. She has no means of transportation."

"Where is she?" Tarani asked.

"She's back at the B&B in Montefioralle. Signora Severson has paid for her to stay there instead of the villa. I'm to pick her up at two-thirty."

"Off you go then, Brigadiere Donato. It's good that you are not in uniform this time. You give off a casual air that I'm sure will reassure the young lady."

Daniele walked out of the room quickly, before the bloom set in.

"There are a few things I need to go over with you," Tarani said after the door closed. "The manager of Mantelli's bank in Milan called me this morning with the information I requested."

Perillo nodded, thinking it was a good thing that Daniele hadn't called the very same manager this morning as planned. Ida's accusation had made them both forget.

"As we know, Mantelli and his wife had a joint account," Tarani continued, "but three years ago, Mantelli opened a separate account and started transferring money from the joint account to the new one. Signora Severson called the manager at a certain point asking about the dwindling funds. As the new account was in Mantelli's name only, he could not tell her the whole story. Two years ago, which coincides with the breakup of Mantelli's marriage, he started to take sums of money out of the new account on an irregular basis. Always in cash. The amounts differed, but they were generally no more than five or seven hundred euros at a time. The manager says this is often the method used to get money out of the country. Small sums can be carried to Switzerland without suspicion. Sometimes couriers are employed, but Mantelli had a perfectly good reason to go to Switzerland, as they, too, have wine producers."

Perillo's eyes widened in disbelief. "The Swiss make wine?"

"Since Roman times, apparently. The bank manager asked me to share this information with Signora Severson. She has been inundating him with questions he's not allowed to answer. May I ask you to take care of that?"

"Certainly."

"The carabinieri in Milan were able to enter Mantelli's apartment only this morning. He had changed the lock before coming down here, and no one had the key. The portiere sent them to the locksmith who had done the job. The search unfortunately yielded no new information."

"A lot of time and trouble for nothing," Perillo said.

"That often comes with our job, don't you agree?"

Perillo nodded. "Daniele and Signorina Loredana won't be here for another twenty minutes at least." He needed another espresso and a few puffs of smoke. "May I offer you something at the café?"

Tarani stood, seemingly relieved. "Good idea, but it's on me. That's an order."

An order that for once, Maresciallo Perillo was happy to accept.

THIS TIME, FOR LOREDANA'S convenience, Daniele parked the Alfa in front of Il Glicine. He was sure she wouldn't appreciate having her heeled feet covered in dust.

The owner, Terzini, was at the front desk. Seeing Daniele, he asked, "What now? I've told you everything I know."

Daniele smiled politely. "Buongiorno, Signor Terzini. I'm here to pick up Signorina Cardini."

"You'll have a hard time doing that. She's gone."

Was she waiting for him at the turnoff? He thought he'd been clear about picking her up directly at the front of the B&B. "When did she leave?"

Terzini started going through his reservation ledger and didn't look up. "Half an hour ago, I guess. Maybe more. I'm not in the habit of looking at the clock every time a guest leaves."

Daniele looked at his watch: 2:16. "I'm early." Fourteen minutes early, to be exact.

"She won't be back. She took her suitcases with her." He looked up at Daniele as if to note what effect his words had on the brigadiere. "Are you moving her back to the Mantelli villa? The room's paid up for the week, but if she's not coming back, I'll re-rent it. No point in keeping it empty."

"Did someone pick her up?"

"A taxi from Greve."

Maybe she didn't want to wait for him and was on her way to the station. "Did you hear where she was going?"

"Where my guests go is none of my business."

Not to the station. Not with her suitcases. Daniele felt a chill travel down his spine. "I need to see her room."

Terzini unhooked a key from the board behind the desk and tossed it to him. "Second floor, third door to the left."

Daniele caught the key and took the stairs two at a time. She had left in a hurry. The drawers were pulled out, the armoire doors left wide open; two wooden hangers lay on the floor. Daniele knew he needed to call the maresciallo—he reached for his cell phone—but first, just in case, he punched in Diane Severson's phone number. His heart was pounding so loudly, he was afraid he wouldn't hear her answer.

"Yes?" a sleepy voice answered.

"Signora Severson, Brigadiere Donato here. I'm looking for Signorina Loredana. Is she with you?"

"Sorry, I was napping and had my earplugs on. What did you say?"

Daniele repeated his question.

"No, she's not here."

"Excuse me, but you were sleeping. Are you sure?"

"No, I kicked her out and told her to stay away from here. I got tired of her drugged-up rants."

"Please, could you check? It's important. The maresciallo is waiting for her at the station."

Diane heard the panic in his voice. Poor kid. "All right. I'll have Peppino look around. I'll look for her too." There was no way Loredana was here.

While Daniele waited, he put the phone on speaker, covered one hand with his handkerchief and searched the room. The two drawers and the armoire were empty. Underneath the bed, he found a black slipper covered in dust. In the tiny bathroom, she'd left the butt of an aromatic candle on the edge of the bathtub. Two towels were on the floor. The wastebasket yielded only used tissues and makeup wipes.

Diane's voice came back into the room. "No, she's not here."

"The villa is big. Are you sure?"

"Yes. She wouldn't give me back the keys to the villa, so I had the locks changed on Saturday. She would have had to come in through an open window. Do you want me to give you her mother's number? She called here yesterday asking for her."

"Yes, please." He took out his pen and wrote the number down in his small notebook. "Thank you." The thought that she might be going home to her mother eased his panic for a moment. They would find her. He had obviously frightened her. He thought he had been as gentle as possible over the phone, but not gentle enough. Or maybe *too* gentle.

Downstairs, he tossed the key back at Terzini. It fell on the desk.

"There are two taxi services in the area. Do you know which one she called?"

"I'm sorry. You'll have to find that out for yourself."

In the car, he called Perillo and explained what had happened.

"Shit!"

"Do you want me to call the taxi services?" Daniele asked in a shaky voice.

"No, I'll do it. First, find out from Terzini what she was wearing, then come back to the station."

"Signora Severson gave me Loredana's mother's number. I'm going to call her now. Maybe she's on her way home."

Perillo heard the hope and the dismay in Daniele's voice. "Okay." His brigadiere was going to somehow blame himself for Loredana's flight. "Listen, Daniele, this has nothing to do with you. Loredana Cardini is smart. She understood we were onto her, and she ran. Wherever she went, we'll find her. We need to know what she was wearing." Perillo clicked off.

Daniele got out of the car and went back into the B&B. Terzini was still at his desk.

"Excuse me Signor Terzini, but can you tell me what Signorina Loredana was wearing?"

Terzini looked up with a spark of excitement on his normally inanimate face. "You're going after her, eh? You think she's the killer, isn't that right? You want to know what she was wearing so you can track her down. It should be easy to find her. She likes to be noticed. Her black pants were tight enough to show a pimple on her ass, and her white top showed half her melons. I didn't look at her shoes. As for the suitcases, Gucci, my wife told me. That's the kind of stuff that catches a woman's eye."

"Thank you." Daniele walked out, hoping never to deal with

Signor Terzini again. He drove the Alfa to the end of the street and stopped to text what he had just learned to Perillo. When that was done, he called Loredana's mother.

"Coming here?" the woman asked in a raucous voice. "Not a chance. I've got better things to do than take care of that tramp."

Daniele squeezed his eyes shut, as if momentary blindness would erase those ugly words.

"And for your information, she's not my daughter. She belonged to my husband. He dropped dead, and all I got after eight years of working myself to the bone for him was her."

"Why did you call her yesterday?" His eyes were now wide open.

"She hasn't sent me my money."

"She sends you money?"

"She sure does, and tell her it better show up quick, or else I'll tell that fancy man of hers what she used to sell for pocket money."

"That fancy man is dead," Daniele blurted out, his disgust now wrapped in anger.

Loredana's stepmother reacted to the news with one word. "Fuck!"

Daniele clicked off, nausea rising to his throat.

AT FIVE THAT AFTERNOON, Nico and OneWag stood in front of Enrico's shop, waiting for the owner to lift the rolling shutter. While picking zucchini and first string beans earlier, he'd noticed how lush his chive bush was. That gave him an idea.

OneWag barked. Something had hit the shutter from the inside. Enrico liked to take his afternoon nap in the back room of the store. He said the aroma of food calmed his soul.

"Ciao, Enrico," Nico called out. The shutter came up and Enrico came out.

"Ehi, Nico." He looked down at the dog. "I already know

what you want. Come on in, Nico. You, Rocco, have to stay out here."

OneWag instantly sat.

They walked through the multi-colored beaded curtain that kept the flies from entering. "First, let me cut off a slice of Norcia prosciutto for my small friend. You'll get the fresh second slice." Enrico picked up a thigh of dark prosciutto and sliced it by hand. The second slice he cut by machine. He held both out over the counter.

Nico lifted them off his finger. "You spoil us. Thank you." He parted the curtain and tossed the drier slice out to OneWag, who caught it on the fly.

Enrico rested his soft, kind eyes on Nico's face while he enjoyed his delicious snack. "You're a good customer, and I like what you did for Aldo the other day in the piazza. If he's a murderer, than I'm the pope." He shook his head several times. "This whole world is going crazy." He sighed. "So what do you need?"

"A kilo of grated Parmigiano Reggiano, please."

"I've got half a kilo grated from this morning. Give me a minute and I'll feed the other half to the grater in the back."

Nico's phone went off while he waited. He clicked and stepped outside. "How did it go with Loredana?"

"It didn't," Perillo said. "Daniele went to pick her up and she was gone. Packed her things, called a cab at 1:36 and now we don't know where she is."

"Where did the cab take her?"

"All the way to Lamole. Dropped her off at the restaurant there at 2:22. When I saw her at Il Glicine to give her the bad news about Mantelli, one of the things she mentioned was how she loved the view from there. We went up there looking for her. The head waiter there said she wanted to eat lunch on the terrace, but the whole restaurant was booked. He recognized her from previous visits and was very apologetic about not being able to accommodate her. He said she didn't look well. He offered to seat her in the back on a makeshift table. She laughed and said only the terrace would do. She said she'd come back another time and left. Another waiter said he saw her pick up her suitcases and walk up the road, and that was the last they saw of her. I sent my men up there, and Tarani added some of his. Beyond the small town, the area is full of woods and hikers. No trace of her so far. She couldn't have walked far carrying two suitcases. Someone must have picked her up."

"Is anyone knocking on doors?"

"Daniele, Vince and Dino are doing that now. So far, nothing. With her looks, if anyone else had seen her, they'd remember."

"She must have parents, relatives she might have called. Do you know who they are?"

Perillo repeated Daniele's conversation with Loredana's stepmother.

"No love there." That must have contributed to Loredana's drug use, Nico thought. "What did Diane say?"

"She claims the first she'd heard of Loredana having left the B&B was when Daniele called her. She says she has no idea where she could have gone."

"What about Verdini?"

"According to Ginevra, he's at a meeting at the Casa Chianti Classico in Radda. I called him in case he'd heard from her. He says he has no idea where Loredana is and doesn't care. I'll check with the Casa later to make sure he was there. We've contacted all the carabinieri stations in the Tuscan area, the Florence and Pisa airports, train stations. We're sending out the only picture of her Daniele found on Mantelli's computer. Della Langhe is screaming his throat raw, but it looks like he'll release Aldo."

"Great. Do you know when?"

"Anytime, was Tarani's answer. For all I know, that could mean a week from now. Not Tarani's fault. He's on our side."

Nico heard the sound of cascading water. "Where are you?"

"At the station. In the bathroom. Tarani is in my office, coordinating the search with his men. You're still persona non grata."

"To him, but not to you. What can I do to help?"

"Talk to Diane Severson. She likes you. I'm not sure she's telling the truth. Also, tell her the bank manager told Tarani he's convinced Mantelli's money is now in Switzerland."

"I will. Text me her phone number. I'm sorry this happened, but I know you'll find her."

"American optimism. I like it. I'll keep in touch. Ciao."

"Ciao." Nico slipped the phone in his pocket and went back inside the store. The kilo of Parmigiano Reggiano was sitting on the counter in two large transparent plastic bags with a knot on top and a torn piece of butcher paper telling him what he owed.

"Everything all right?" Enrico asked. "Not bad news, I hope. Please forgive. I don't mean to pry."

"A few complications, that's all." The news of Loredana's flight didn't sit well in his thoughts. Guilty or not, Daniele had read her correctly. She was in dire need of help. Where was she trying to go? Who was helping her, if not Diane?

"Complications give heartburn, so I hope they dissipate quickly."

As Nico paid, he heard the ping of a text arriving.

Enrico handed over the receipt. "May I ask one question?"

"Sure."

"What are you going to do with a kilo of Parmigiano? I hope you don't freeze it. It won't taste anywhere near as good."

"I'm going to make frittelle for the restaurant today. Frittelle sprinkled with raw chives from my garden."

Enrico's smile reached from one end of his face to the other. "Frittelle with a glass of red. Excellent idea. I'm tempted to come by after closing time and try them out. Luciana hasn't made those in years. Bravo, Nico. You've become one of us."

"Thank you, and to the next time." Nico took his cheese and walked out of the store with a lighter heart. Enrico had just paid him the highest compliment. For now, he would keep his misgivings about Loredana at bay. He had frittelle to make. "Let's go, OneWag!"

The dog responded with a bark and ran ahead like a kid playing whoever-gets-there-first-wins. Tilde always had a scrap of meat waiting.

"THAT SMELLS GOOD," NICO said, his back to Tilde. "Something new?"

"You saw what I was making."

He was bent over a baking sheet, tamping down small mounds of grated Parmigiano into flat rounds with the back of a spoon. This was the fifth batch he was making. Each fritella, once roasted, was carefully lifted with a spatula and just as carefully added to a tray and sprinkled with chopped chives. "That's right, I did. Yellow pepper stuffed with rice, sausage meat, onion, pecorino and tomato sauce."

Tilde turned around and tapped Nico on the shoulder. "What's wrong, Nico?"

He turned to look at her. She seemed concerned. "Nothing's wrong."

"I made yellow stuffed peppers at lunch."

Nico went back to his frittelle. "So you did. They were good too. So what smells so good now?"

"Freshly picked rosemary for chicken alla cacciatora. Nico, please stop making your frittelle for one second and talk to me. You told me Aldo was coming home soon. All of us toasted the news not even half an hour ago. We were happy. Even Elvira cheered. I thought you'd be relaxed."

Nico reluctantly stopped. The repetitive motion of making frittelle was calming. He turned to meet Tilde's kind, alert gaze.

When he had first come to live in Gravigna, she had been his rock. He loved her as a sister and would be forever grateful to her. "This stays between us."

"It always does, unless you tell me otherwise."

"I'm worried about Mantelli's girlfriend." He told her what he had learned from Perillo.

"You're worried they won't find her?"

"I don't know. I can't figure out why I'm worried, and that worries me even more. Did she run because she's guilty, or did she just panic? Was she drugged up when Daniele called her? Did she know what she was doing, where she was going?"

"You care for her."

"She needs help." Before Nico could say anything more, Alba popped her head into the kitchen. "Our first customers are here. A group of six men. Spaniards. Two, gorgeous. They ordered three wine bottles, which Enzo is taking care of, and six orders of frittelle that I need from Nico."

Glad for the interruption, Nico carefully placed an equal amount of frittelle onto six plates and handed them to Alba. "No stealing," he said. Alba winked, blew him a kiss and disappeared. "I better make more. I think they're going to be a success." He gave Tilde a reassuring smile.

Tilde cocked her kerchief-covered head at him. "I'm sure they will be." She knew he wasn't going to tell her anything else. He was generous toward others, always willing to help, but mostly kept his feelings to himself. Her heart had warmed with hope seeing him with his arm around Nelli on Saturday night. "Wouldn't it be nice?" Stella had whispered. "Wonderful," she had answered.

Tilde went back to salting and peppering the chicken pieces. "Diane Severson made a reservation for tonight. Nine-thirty. Late for her."

"I asked her to make it late so she doesn't have to wait until I'm done here."

Alba popped her head in again. "Two more orders of frittelle—they're divine, by the way—and your American lover is here. I put her at her usual table."

"Alba!" Nico spun around, dropping a spoonful of chives on his shoe. "She's not my lover."

"She sure would like to be. Albanians can spot desire across a room like an owl can spot a mouse in the dark." Alba did her happy gurgle as Nico slapped full plates in her hands. "Love you, Nico. Ciao."

Nico watched her sway a few meters and turn the corner to the terrace before returning to his frittelle. Alba was always happy, always teasing.

Nico took off his apron. "I'd better find out why Diane came so early."

"Of course. Go do your police work. I'll take over your kitchen duties."

Nico kissed her cheek. "There's no need for sarcasm, and your pay is lousy."

"You're right on both counts. Take a few frittelle to Elvira, or she'll sulk for days."

Nico filled a small plate and winked at her. "I'll give Elvira your love."

Tilde threw her kitchen towel at him. "Get out of here!"

It was only six o'clock, the hour people came to the restaurant to enjoy the view with an aperitivo. Dinner started at seven for the foreigners. Eight-thirty or nine was the preferred Italian dinner hour. A few more couples had come in since the group of Spaniards, Nico noticed as he walked onto the terrace. Diane was sitting under the fig tree. She saw him and waved, mouthing a "ciao."

Nico walked over. "Hello, Diane. Is everything okay?"

"Well, besides my husband murdered by his mistress and our empty bank account, everything is fine."

"I'm sorry." He sat down opposite her. "I asked because you were supposed to come at nine-thirty."

Her shoulders dropped. "I know. I got bored and tired of seeing sadsack Peppino dragging himself around the house. A woman came by to try to cheer him up. At least, that's the reason she gave. Said she was a family friend and added she knew you, which I found odd."

"It must have been Nelli."

"So you do know her. She has one of those open faces, but you can't judge anyone by their face. She could have been lying."

"She wasn't, and I don't agree with you. In my previous line of work, I discovered that faces reveal a great deal. As Gogol said just the other day, quoting Dante, 'The face shows the color of the heart.' You just have to care enough to pay attention."

"You sound annoyed. Nelli must be a very good friend."

Nico decided not to favor her with an answer. He was in fact annoyed, and his relationship to Nelli was no business of hers. "Do you have any idea where Loredana might have gone?"

"I'm sure not to her stepmother's, and she's never mentioned other relatives. Have you called Luca? Maybe he offered to help her."

"He's in Radda organizing a wine dinner at the Casa Chianti Classico."

"Once the Santa Maria del Prato monastery. We should have lunch there sometime. It's a gorgeous place. Does he know anything?"

"No, and he added he hopes never to know anything more about her."

"I guess he saw right through her manipulative ways, but it's not easy to stop Loredana when she sets her eyes on something or someone. I learned that lesson quickly. Tell your maresciallo to look for her at Luca's vineyard. She's desperate to find a replacement for Michele. I tried to help, but once I saw that her needs are the size of the Grand Canyon, I backed off and sent her on her away. Now I'm feeling guilty, an emotion that's new to me."

Alba walked by, five full plates balanced on her arm. "We're running out of frittelle."

"Go on with your work," Diane said. "Come by the villa after you're finished, and I'll tell you the little I know about Loredana. You should see the place before it's torn down. It's very beautiful."

Nico felt his stomach tighten. He hadn't bargained for this.

The expression on Nico's face amused Diane. "Don't worry. I'm not trying to seduce you, but company doesn't hurt. Something tells me you could use some just as much as I could. We'll have a nightcap by the pool and think of where Loredana might be." She tore off a piece of the butcher-paper placemat and wrote down her address. "It's about two kilometers before you get to the town. The gate is topped by cast-iron wine bottles, the only tasteless idea I let Michele get away with."

Nico nodded. Diane might think she didn't know much about Loredana, but he'd learned, through years of listening to people, that sometimes words spoken without forethought led to a clue. It was worth a try. He slipped the address in his pocket. "Okay. I'll get away as soon as I can."

"I can wait. Bring your cute dog." Diane slipped a pair of sunglasses over her eyes and watched him go. Company was fine, but sex was better. She'd give it a try.

Instead of going back to the kitchen, Nico walked out of the restaurant. He stopped a few meters away from the door so as not to be heard by Enzo, who was manning the bar, and called Perillo. "Diane says she doesn't know anything, but she suggested looking for Loredana at Verdini's place."

"I'll go there now with Tarani and a couple of men. So far we have nothing. We've canvassed every home in Lamole. No one noticed a car or a woman with suitcases."

"Text me if you find her."

"I will. I hope Diane is right."

"Me too."

"You look worried," Enzo said as Nico walked back into the restaurant. "And tired."

"I am, but I've got to make more frittelle."

"Yes, please do," Elvira encouraged from her armchair at the far end of the room. "We mustn't disappoint our diners." As he walked past her to reach the kitchen, she grabbed his hand. "You keep surprising me, Nico," she whispered, pulling down his arm.

He bent down to hear her. "If you keep coming up with ideas that sell, I might allow you to buy a small share of my restaurant." She put fingers to her lips. "But shh, that's just between us."

"That's very kind of you." He kissed her cheeks, as she expected. "You honor me." He'd get a share of the restaurant when the sun stopped rising. This was just Elvira's perverse way of paying a compliment.

"DANIELE, THERE'S THE SIGN," Perillo said, sitting in the passenger seat of a blue Alfa Romeo with CARABINIERI printed in white across the doors. Daniele slowed down and turned into the ColleVerde parking lot after thirty meters. Vince and Dino followed in the second Alfa. They had kept the siren off, not wanting to alarm Loredana if she were hiding out here. Perillo got out first, and the others followed. Perillo had never met Verdini and regretted that there had been no time to put on his uniform. Finding a runaway murder suspect was serious business, and their appearance should convey that. Instead, their jeans and shirts were wrinkled, dirty and sticky with sweat. "Stay a few meters behind me and Daniele," he told Vince and Dino as they walked down the path. "Be ready to pounce if you see her."

Perillo stopped at the tasting shed. Verdini was seated in one of his uncomfortable chairs facing the view of his vineyard below, his legs stretched out, bobbing his head to whatever music his Bose headphones were feeding his ears. He was alone.

Perillo tapped his shoulder. Verdini turned around and pulled his headphones down to his neck. "I'm sorry, I didn't hear you coming." He smiled apologetically. "I'm afraid we're closed now. I keep forgetting to add our hours to that sign."

A friendly face. Athletic-looking. Young. Perillo held out his hand. "Maresciallo Perillo from the Greve station with three of my men." He introduced them.

"Luca Verdini. I'm the owner, but I guess you know that already." Verdini shook Perillo's hand while scanning his face, shifting his gaze to Daniele and ultimately flickering his eyes at Dino and Vince, who were standing further back. "Ah." Verdini's smile vanished. "This looks serious." He gestured to the chairs surrounding the table. "Please, sit down. Forgive the unwelcoming chairs."

The man seemed perfectly relaxed in front of four armed carabinieri. A good actor? Perillo had always prided himself on being a good judge of character, but lately, he felt he was slipping. Maybe it was better to play down the seriousness of the situation.

Dino and Vince started to come forward. Perillo stopped them with an almost imperceptible shake of his head. They retreated a few paces.

"Not serious at this point, but worrisome." Perillo sat with the view behind him. He wanted no distractions. Daniele instead stood at the edge of the drop, looking for places where she might be hiding. No sheds. No boulders. Only a wide, flat field divided by long rows of vines. As he scanned the area, he caught a flash of movement at the corner of one eye. He turned to follow it. An auburn-furred dog was chasing something he couldn't make out. He hoped the something would get away.

"Loredana Cardini has gone missing." Perillo dropped his elbows on the table and leaned forward. "She had an appointment with me at the station and didn't show up. Is she here, by any chance?"

Verdini looked perplexed. "No. I already told you I don't know anything. Why would she be here? I thought she was staying with Diane Severson at her villa."

"Signorina Loredana has since gone back to living at the B&B."

"I only met the woman once. Diane drove her here on Saturday. She kept telling me I was Mantelli's good friend and I should help her. I asked her if she needed money. No, money wouldn't help her. What she needed, she said, was someone to take care of her. Thank the heavens that a client came by and interrupted her. I had to call Diane to pick her up. It was a great relief on my part when she left. She'd snorted or injected something and was in woo-woo land. I can see why you're worried."

"We are."

"Doesn't Diane know where she is?"

"Unfortunately, she doesn't."

"Poor woman. Stunningly beautiful and yet so miserable. Pitiful too. Mantelli's death really hit her hard." Verdini's gaze went to the sky beyond Perillo's shoulders. A sad gaze, Perillo thought. Maybe he had lost someone too.

Verdini seemed to shake himself back to the present. "Look, all my workmen have gone home, and I just got back here myself. I don't really know whether she's somewhere on the property or not. I don't see why she would be, but since you're here . . . The house is open. There's a giant vaulted basement where I keep the bottled wines, as well as two floors of living quarters. And here," Verdini shifted his weight to one hip and reached into a pocket in his jeans, "are the keys to the winery. It's behind the house. There's no place to hide down in the vineyard, but you're free to look there too. The dog is friendly."

Perillo took the winery keys and tossed them to Dino. "Daniele, you and Vince check the house." He trusted Daniele would make sure the house search was proper and thorough. He stood. "Signor Verdini, would you show them the way?"

"None of the doors are locked. They can manage by themselves. I trust the carabinieri."

Perillo acknowledged the compliment with a smile. The door of the shed was shut, he noticed. "Do you mind if I stay here?"

"Not at all. You must be even more exhausted than I am. I find that sitting here and taking in the view brings peace. I don't imagine you've had much peace or rest since Mantelli was killed."

"That is a fact." Perillo sat back down. "Would it be possible to have a glass of water?"

"Certainly. I'll have to get it in the kitchen. The key to this shed is with the winery keys."

Disappointed, Perillo stood. "Please, I'll go."

"If you prefer. The kitchen is to the left."

Perillo walked across the path and went inside the house. He stopped behind the front door to watch what Verdini would do in his absence, if anything. Verdini's nonchalance about searching his home and winery without his presence was bothering him. The only movement Perillo saw was Verdini punching a number on his phone. Half a minute later, he clicked off and dropped the phone on the table.

A couple of minutes later, Perillo came out of the house and sat next to Verdini.

"I just called Diane," Verdini said. "She didn't answer."

"You thought she might have information she wasn't eager to divulge to the authorities?"

Verdini turned his head to look at Perillo. "Well, she was trying to help the woman, and now I'm wondering how far her help might go. Your eagerness to find Loredana makes me think she's a suspect in Mantelli's murder. She is, isn't she?"

"Not at the moment, but she might have some information about Mantelli that would help us solve this case."

"Then I hope you find her."

"We will." Perillo took a deep breath and closed his eyes. He was tired and suspected his men would come back empty-handed. After a few moments, he reopened his eyes and gifted himself with a long look at what was in front of him. "This view is indeed peaceful." The deep blue of the sky was fading to a softer, cooler shade. The perfectly straight rows of vines with their new bright green leaves gave a sense of order, the only contradiction coming from the spattering of poppies. Here it was peaceful and cooler by several degrees.

"You were friends with Mantelli despite the fact that you had to pay him a monthly fee of eight hundred euros," Perillo said in a quiet voice. "I find that odd."

"I suppose it is, but I owe my success to him. I no longer needed to pay him. I got enough good reviews from others, but when he said he was in trouble and needed help, I continued to pay as a way of thanking him."

Perillo sat up. "What trouble?"

"Mantelli was a soccer fanatic and liked to bet on the games all over Europe and South America. He said he was good at it for a while. Around the time his marriage was in trouble, he started losing. He blamed Diane, of course. Last week he told me he didn't have much money left."

"Signor Verdini, you should have given us this information as soon as you knew Mantelli had been murdered."

Verdini lifted both his hands in the air in a gesture of surrender. "You're right, I should have. But all I know is what Mantelli told me. At first I believed him, but then doubts crept in. Was it the truth or a scheme?"

"Why a scheme?"

"Mantelli had a devious mind. He had asked me to meet him at Il Falco Tuesday night, but luckily Diane needed help in facing him, and I preferred obliging her. I had the feeling, from a few hints he'd dropped, that he was going to ask me to tell Diane about his gambling habit. If she thought he had lost his money instead of stashing it in a Swiss or offshore bank, she'd stop holding up the divorce."

"Isn't it more probable that he wanted his May payment?"

Verdini turned to look at Perillo. "No. I told him two weeks ago I wasn't going to send him any more money because he'd only gamble it away. I was trying to get him to see reason."

"How did he react?"

"He looked at me with a helpless expression and said, 'It's taken over my life.'"

Perillo tried to control his anger. It would only fall on deaf ears. "You still should have considered it your civic duty to tell us. It gives the case a whole different angle to look into."

"Please forgive my presumption, Maresciallo, but I don't agree there's a new angle. Whoever killed him had nothing to do with gambling, if indeed Mantelli gambled his money away. If he owed some unsavory characters, why would they kill him? To prove a point? To whom? His wife, who also wants his money? Once he's dead, that money is gone forever. Or more likely in some bank, you pick the place."

Perillo had to admit Verdini's argument was reasonable, but he was still angry. "You are persuasive, Signor Verdini, but it does not excuse your behavior. You withheld important information. That is a grave error, and I may have to cite you."

"Do whatever you have to. I can only apologize."

"Maresciallo," Dino called out.

Perillo and Verdini turned in their seats to see Dino walking up the slope, swinging a bunch of keys.

Perillo went to meet his brigadiere. Dino shook his head. "She's not there." While Perillo took the keys and walked them back to Verdini, Daniele and Vince came out of the house.

"Nothing," Daniele said, his face pale with worry.

Vince shook his head, looking as abashed as someone of his happy nature could. "Like we Tuscans say, Maresciallo, it's one thing to run; it's another to get there. You should have come with us, though." He walked up to Verdini, who was now unlocking the shed. "Great place you have here. I'd sell my nonna to have a kitchen like yours. And the smell . . ." He kissed his hand. "I hope you'll forgive, but I took a peek inside your oven. Lemon cake crusted with shaved almonds. Am I right?"

"You are."

"My nonna still makes it, but yours smells richer."

"I would share, but I'm bringing it to a friend's dinner tonight." Verdini disappeared inside the shed. Perillo moved closer to see inside. Passing Vince, he gave his arm a squeeze meant to shut him up, but when it came to food, it was as if his young briga-diere was running the 1000 Miglia without brakes. "She won't give me the recipe."

"Then you'd better not sell her."

Vince shuffled his feet, raising dust. "I was only kidding."

Verdini came out of the shed carrying a bottle of wine and four glasses. The door remained open. "I can offer a glass of good wine."

"No, thank you," Perillo said as he stepped closer to the shed. The room was empty, big enough for two people, three at the most. One wall showed a large calendar open to the month of June. Most of the days were filled with penciled notes. Sundays were crossed off. A single shelf held different glasses for red and white wine. Below was a small refrigerator. No Loredana. "We need to go, Signor Verdini. I appreciate you letting us search your property without a warrant."

"There was no need for one. I hope you find her."

"We will." In his mind, he added, *I hope.* Perillo turned around and walked back up to the car with Daniele beside him. Dino followed dutifully. Vince dragged his feet, trying to recall the taste of his nonna's lemon cake in his mouth.

The frittelle had sold out, and now Nico was back on the terrace serving tables. The sun was about to cede the day when his phone vibrated. He served two orders of pollo alla cacciatora at table twelve and went back inside to check who it was. Perillo. He quickly walked out to the street and called him back.

"Two hikers saw her," Perillo said. "She was sitting on one of her suitcases by the side of the road that leads down to 222. She was holding the heel of one of her shoes in her lap. They asked if she needed help. Loredana just shook her head. They left her there and continued on . . ." Nico noticed how quickly Perillo was speaking, and in an out-of-breath voice, as if he'd been the one hiking that steep road. "Slow down."

Perillo took a deep breath. "Continued on their hike, but the woman was worried about Loredana. They went back. Loredana and her suitcases were gone. She says no more than twenty minutes had passed since they saw her. The road is visible for about four kilometers. They didn't see any cars."

"Too bad, but not surprising. A car would eat that distance in three minutes at the most."

"It's worse than too bad. We have to figure out how she disappeared. Did someone drive by, see her and pick her up out of kindness, or had Loredana arranged to be picked up all along? She did refuse the hikers' help despite having a broken heel? I say the prearranged pickup. What do you think?"

"What time did the hikers see her?"

"They ran into her around three. The woman couldn't pinpoint the time any better than that."

That would have given her time to eat at the restaurant if they'd had a table. "If it was prearranged, it would have to be for a specific, recognizable place like next to a sign or a particular vineyard."

"I would think Loredana herself was specific enough."

"You've got a point," Nico said. With her looks and that long blond hair, she'd be instantly spotted. He hoped that whoever picked her up, prearranged or not, did it only out of kindness. "It's going to get dark any minute. She could be far away by now."

"We'll find her. I'll call as soon as we do. Ciao. No, wait! Verdini came up with an interesting theory. Mantelli could have lost his money gambling on soccer. Ask Diane what she thinks."

"I will. In the mouth of the wolf." This was the odd Italian way of wishing good luck.

"May the wolf croak. Ciao."

IT WAS JUST PAST midnight by the time Nico banged the brass lion's head knocker of Villa Vigna d'Oro. A small old man opened the door. OneWag sniffed his shoes.

"Buonasera," Nico said. "I'm here to see Signora Severson. She said I could bring the dog."

The man stepped aside, leaving only a narrow space through which OneWag slipped through easily. Nico had to enter sideways. Hardly a welcoming gesture, Nico thought, but understandable. This man, with sagging eyes and a face webbed with wrinkles, was mourning. "You must be Peppino. I'm a friend of Nelli's. Nico Doyle." He extended his hand.

"Good woman, Nelli," Peppino said with a gruff voice, ignoring Nico's hand. "The signora is by the pool." He pointed a bent finger toward a large room on his right. OneWag was already there, exploring all the new smells. "Straight through. You'll find it." His face was expressionless, and his words had no life to them.

Nico didn't move, remembering the feeling of having lost everything that gave life meaning. "Nelli *is* a good woman, and she's worried about you. She cares for you very much."

Peppino shrugged his stooped shoulders. "What's the point? It's over."

"I know it feels like that now, but time helps." He was spouting platitudes, but time had helped him. "Look, Peppino, I have no right to tell you what to do, but I know something of what you're going through."

"You lost your wife. Nelli told me."

"Yes."

"Time hasn't helped you."

Is that what Nelli thought? "It is helping."

"A wife you meet at twenty-five, thirty," Peppino said. "You marry, you work, maybe children come, friends, voyages. Your life is full of many things, not only your wife. Me, I came to work in this villa to help my uncle the very day I turned twelve. Four years later, he was dead and I took over. Eighty-two years-old I am now, and what is left of my life has been erased with a signature." Peppino lowered his head to rub his hand under his nose and sniffed. He looked back up, not at Nico, but at some past moment. "He sold without telling me. He said I would die on this property. He should have told me himself." His sagging eyes brimmed with tears.

"How did you find out, then?"

"The signora told me when she came here Tuesday morning. The signore was out looking at vineyards, so I let her in. She wanted me to know. You'd better go to the signora. She doesn't like to wait." Peppino turned his back to Nico and shuffled back to the kitchen. On his feet, Nico noticed the same kind of soft felt slippers Rita used to wear to keep the shine on the floors.

Nico entered the room Peppino had indicated. It was huge, at least twelve hundred square feet. White sofas, armchairs, ottomans and low tables with many-colored tile tops were scattered around the space in a haphazard way. Black and white photographs of vineyards spread across the walls.

"There you are. I thought I heard voices." Diane strode toward him, dressed in a long, flowing turquoise robe flecked with green.

OneWag cautiously approached her bare feet. She stopped and looked down as he quickly sniffed her toes, then the hem of her robe. "Hello there."

OneWag went back to examining the rest of room. "I guess he doesn't like my scent. You were talking to Peppino?"

"I was trying to cheer him up." Nico met her halfway on a tile floor that looked like dark burnished leather. "I didn't succeed."

Diane kissed his cheeks. "I'm afraid he's inconsolable." She took his hand and led him through another large room. "Has Loredana popped up?"

"She isn't at Verdini's place. Perillo has uncovered an interesting possibility regarding the missing money. He's designated me as the messenger."

"A very welcome one, but no money talk now. Let's have a drink first." She walked him down a few stone steps to a pool area surrounded by flowering plants. She had a firm grip on his hand. He wanted to take it back, but didn't know how without being impolite. OneWag followed.

"Welcome to my favorite spot," she said, with a wave of her silk-sheathed arm.

Nico needed to turn to see it all. Three sides were fenced in by honeysuckle-covered trellises. The fourth side ended with a turquoise-tiled infinity pool. Brightly covered pool furniture was scattered here and there. Large terracotta pots spilled fuchsia bougainvillea all the way to the dark stone slab floor. "I can see why it's your favorite spot."

"If you want to take a dip, there are several bathing suits in the pool room, or you can go naked. I wouldn't mind. I might even join you." She purposefully did not look at him as she made the suggestion, in case she was embarrassing him.

The infinity pool was tempting after weeks of unbearable heat, Nico thought, but he didn't like what her offer implied. "Thank you, Diane, but I'm afraid I'm not here to have fun."

A brutal answer. "That's too bad." She let go of his hand. She was foolish to have hoped the evening might turn out differently from all her other evenings. She could use some romance. She hadn't felt a man's touch since Michele had left her. There had been offers—enticing ones too—but at the last minute, she hadn't been able to go through with it. Michele still had his hold on her. Now that he was dead, she finally felt free.

"I'm sorry, Diane."

She turned around and beamed him a smile that didn't look the least bit sincere. "Don't be. You have a murderer to catch. Come, sit." She walked over to a grouping of lounge chairs and floated down onto one of them. She had such a refined grace. "I'm having a gin and tonic. What would you like?"

Nico sat in a cushioned chair next to her. "Just plain tonic would be nice."

"Sober to the end. Behind me is the bar. Help yourself."

As Nico stood up, she handed him her half-empty glass. "Top this off for me, please. Just gin." She might as well drink. While Nico filled her glass and got his tonic, she said, "You and the maresciallo think Loredana killed Michele, don't you?"

He handed her the refilled glass. "What do you think?"

"Please don't play that game with me. I asked a direct question. I'd love a direct answer."

"I believe so."

"Why? Because she ran away?"

"I'm not at liberty to discuss."

"Of course not. You're a loyal man. Loyal to your maresciallo friend, and I suspect still to your dead wife. I know, that's none of my business. What's this new possibility about the whereabouts of Michele's money? He didn't stash it away in some secret bank?"

"That's still possible. Tarani finally got an answer from your bank manager." Nico repeated what the manager had said.

"I've said that all along. What I need to know is which bank." She took a long drink of her gin and tonic.

"The other possibility is that he lost it all gambling on soccer." Diane sat up. "Who came up with that idea?"

Nico shook his head.

"All right, it doesn't matter who." She took another slow sip. Michele did like to gamble. Nothing could tear him away from soccer home games or the TV set on Sunday. But most Italian men were soccer fans. From there to losing all his money . . . was it possible?

Diane rested back on the lounge chair. "It seems a bit far-fetched, although it would explain why he sold this house out of the blue. I only found out about the sale thanks to my lawyer just a few days before he died. Michele loved this place, considered it his real home. He would have lived here full-time, but he felt he needed to keep a presence in Milan. He needed to show he had money, that he was as important as those hotshot industrialists. Poor Michele, he was so insecure. His arrogance was just armor. He was afraid people would see him for who he really was."

"Who was he?"

"A small-minded boy. And a fraud." She finished her drink. "Why is Tarani pursuing the money? I'm sure it's not for my sake."

"If Mantelli was a big gambler, maybe he took out a loan he couldn't pay back."

She curled up her legs on the chaise, propping her head up with her arm to face Nico directly. "I like that possibility. It would mean Michele didn't hide his money to spite me. That's the reason I fought him. My spite against his. It was never about the money. In the past five years, my business has been very successful. I have enough on my own for myself and my son's future. And now, my son will get the money from the sale of the villa. The possibility that a despicable loan shark murdered

Michele is much more preferable than thinking Loredana killed him. Have you met her?"

"I saw her twice."

"Poor, gorgeous thing. I tried to help her, but she was unreachable. She'd been abusing drugs since she was twelve. Uppers and downers. Some crazy doctor had prescribed her pentobarbital to get rid of her anxiety. She's had an incredibly difficult life." Diane finished her drink. "If Loredana was going to kill somebody, I would think it would be herself. Too much of that stuff, and you're gone."

"That's what I'm afraid of. She took a taxi to Lamole, was unsuccessful in getting a table at the restaurant there, then walked off with her suitcases. A couple of hours later, she was spotted on the south road by some hikers. She was sitting on one of her suitcases with a broken shoe heel. When they went back to check on her, she was gone."

"Someone must have picked her up."

Maybe you? "It looks that way. Can you think of who might have? Verdini is accounted for."

"I don't know. I'm sorry, I really don't." Diane noticed Nico hadn't even taken a sip of his tonic water. He looked uncomfortable, sitting up straight at the edge of his chair. A nice interesting man. A keeper. "Peccato," as the Italians said. Too bad. Funny that the word also meant "sin." She laid her head back on the chaise and closed her eyes. "Forgive me; I think the gin has gotten to me." Gin and regret.

Nico stood up. "It's been a long day for everyone."

"Yes, it has." She kept her eyes closed. She didn't want to see him leave. "I wasn't any help, but I hope you find her. Please let me know."

"I will. Good night. I'll see myself out."

"Please do."

OneWag, who had warily kept watch on his boss and the woman, let out a bark of joy and rushed to the door.

—

NICO HAD JUST SQUEEZED himself into his Fiat 500 after OneWag and buckled up when his phone vibrated. *Damn!* He'd forgotten to get his phone out of his pants pocket and slip it in the door pocket when he'd gotten in. The car was so damn small. He knew he'd gained weight, but this was ridiculous. Nico unbuckled, got out of the car, slammed the door shut and took out his phone. "Did you find her?"

"We found her suitcases halfway down on the same road the hikers saw her. They were hidden behind some bushes. Her shoes were there too. She must have kept the broken heel for some reason."

If the need occurred, Nico thought, a stiletto heel could make a good weapon. "If she left the suitcases, she wasn't picked up by a car."

"It must have been a motorcycle. If she was on foot, we would have found her. Tarani left two men on a stakeout near the suitcases in case she comes back for them. I sent my own home. Let his men do the night. She could be halfway to the Swiss border by now."

"Why the Swiss border? Do they extradite?"

"I was thinking of Mantelli's money. The housekeeper caught Loredana riffling through Mantelli's desk and closet on Friday. What if she found some Swiss bank information?"

"Or his overdue laundry bill. Perillo, you're tired and grabbing at straws. Get some sleep. We'll talk in the morning. Buonanotte."

"Let's hope it's a good one. Ciao."

THIRTEEN

When Nico walked into Bar All'Angolo with OneWag, Gogol raised both his arms and exclaimed, "'The time was the beginning of morning, and the sun was rising accompanied by three stars from when divine love first made these things of beauty.'"

"That's a good one," Nico said as he sat down facing his friend. The sight of Gogol welcoming him with an enthusiastic quote lifted his spirits. Being in the café also helped. Sandro at the cash register, Jimmy manning the espresso machine, clients elbowing each other at the long counter. Life was back to normal here. Worried about Loredana, he had tossed and turned most of the night, driving OneWag to seek peace on the sofa.

"Dear Gogol, I understood every word, and I'm going to surprise you by guessing correctly. Since Dante is seeing the sun, it can only be from the first canto of *Inferno*."

With a brown-toothed grin, Gogol lifted his hand for a high-five. Their hands clapped.

"He came in half an hour ago," Sandro said, bringing over Nico's cornetto. "Kept fidgeting and muttering until he saw you. Jimmy claims he can tell when something is wrong before it happens."

"Thanks." Nico took the plate. "That sounds like a bit of folklore to me."

Sandro lifted one shoulder, "Maybe," the other shoulder came up. "Maybe not."

Gogol paid no attention to Sandro, his eyes intent on Nico's face.

"You must be hungry." Nico pushed the plate across the table. "I'll get another one."

"Coming up," Jimmy said from the far end of the café. "Along with an Americano for you and an espresso for the seer. Come get them."

Nico walked to the back. OneWag followed. Today's pickings on the floor had been meager. Nico swept up the cornetto flakes and powdered sugar on the counter and let them fall to the floor. OneWag started licking.

Jimmy noticed. "Thanks. No one bothers to clean up after themselves." He put the cornetto and two coffees on a tray. "What Sandro told you isn't folklore." He spoke in a low voice. "The morning my mother died of a stroke, I rushed over to her house, and there was Gogol walking back and forth on the sidewalk. When my sister broke her water three weeks early, who was outside her home but Gogol with a flower in his hand. He feels things, like animals just before an earthquake."

Nico wasn't convinced, but he played along. "I'm glad he can also feel good things coming, not just bad."

"We all are. Otherwise someone might get it in his head to run him out of town."

Nico took the tray back to the table and sat back down. "Did you enjoy that?" he asked. Nico's first cornetto was gone.

Gogol shook his head and wiped the crumbs off his lips. He drank his espresso before looking up at Nico. "'Charon, don't torment yourself.'"

Nico guessed a sleepless night showed on his face. "I'm not ferrying anyone to hell, Gogol, so I can't torment myself."

Gogol huffed and used his chin to point to Perillo walking through the open French doors. Dressed in his usual jeans and a crisp shirt, Nico watched him walk over to a group of cyclists and start chatting. What the hell? He'd expected Perillo to come straight over to him and share whatever news he had. Even if there was no news.

Gogol clasped his hand over Nico's wrist. "'Don't torment yourself. It is willed where the power resides to will it.'"

Nico freed his wrist. "Gogol, please just say it in plain Italian. What are you trying to tell me?" Gogol's chagrined face made him instantly regret his outburst.

Perillo walked over, sat next to Gogol and leaned in. "He's trying to tell you," he said in a barely audible voice, "that God willed her death."

"Loredana?"

Perillo nodded, his face drained of any visible emotion. "I need a cigarette," he said in a surprisingly steady voice. "Signor Gogol, would you mind lending me your friend while I smoke outside?"

"He is yours to keep today. I wish you both buoyed spirits. The day is full of sadness." He stood up with them. "Tomorrow, if I live."

"God wills it, Gogol. See you tomorrow." Nico called out to Sandro, "I'll pay you later." Sandro raised a thumb.

Outside Perillo lit his cigarette and watched Gogol walk away. "It's odd, but the dogs in the kennel don't bark at him. Vince sees him there often, hears him quoting Dante to them, and not a one barks."

"They sense he is gentle. Tell me about Loredana."

Perillo started walking along the grassy edge of the road. Nico kept pace. "Dino found her—that is, his dog did."

"Where?"

"In the woods behind the kennel where most of the hunters around here keep their dogs. It's almost at the end of the south road that leads to Lamole."

"The road where the hikers saw her?"

"The very same, except five kilometers further down. Dino

goes to the kennel at five-thirty every morning to walk his German pointer before coming to the station. As soon as he opened the cage, the dog ran off into the woods. Dino thought he'd spotted or smelled a hare and went after him." Perillo jabbed the cigarette in his mouth and sucked the smoke in. He took his time blowing it out. Sucked in more smoke, taking it down all the way to the bottom of his lungs. Perillo's mind was replaying his visit to Loredana at Il Glicine. How breathtakingly beautiful she was, how wild and yes, how fragile.

Nico didn't press him.

"She was curled up as if she'd fallen asleep," Perillo finally said. "Fully dressed. Only her shoes were missing. She had the broken heel in her hand. She'd used it to start writing a suicide note on the ground. I AM SOR. That's all she managed to write before whatever she'd put into her body took over."

"You are sure it was suicide?"

"It certainly looks that way. There was a syringe not far from the body."

"She could have overdosed," Nico said. "According to Diane, a doctor had introduced her to pentobarbital. It's an anti-anxiety drug. You get the dosage wrong, and you're dead."

"Overdose or suicide, the result is the same. An ugly, sad, useless death." Perillo looked at his watch. "The medical examiner took Loredana and the syringe with him. They should be in Florence in half an hour. We'll have a definitive answer on Loredana in a few days, depending on how many other bodies he has to deal with. We should know what was in the syringe by tomorrow." Perillo started walking again. "The idea of that beautiful woman being cut up makes me want to throw up."

It was nauseating when it came to all victims, Nico thought, keeping up with Perillo's pace. Nauseating but necessary. It gave answers, which in turn gave peace to the family. "Have you called her stepmother?"

"Daniele has that job. The good news is that Aldo is coming home tonight."

Nico tapped Perillo's shoulder. "That's wonderful. Let's try to focus on the good news."

"I will when we close this case," Perillo said, "and I hope that happens when we get Loredana's autopsy report."

"You have doubts she killed Mantelli?" Perillo had seemed convinced before.

"I'm full of doubts these days. The autopsy should clear some of them."

"NELLI'S OUT ON THE terrace," Enzo said when Nico walked into the restaurant with Enrico's bread for the lunch service. "She heard about the suicide. Awful, isn't it? She was so young and beautiful."

Nico dropped the bags on the first table. "It's awful even when they're old and ugly."

"You're right, but somehow it just hits you differently. Thanks for the bread." Enzo was in charge of slicing it.

Nico walked to the kitchen, saying buongiorno to Elvira on the way.

She was in her armchair in her blue and green Tuesday dress, folding napkins. "I appreciate you saying that about the old and ugly. I never had the luxury of beauty, and I certainly have no intention of committing suicide. It's a selfish act. No thought to the pain she caused."

"She had no one, Elvira."

"It's not possible to have no one. She didn't suddenly appear in a cabbage."

"Her father and mother are dead. So is her boyfriend, and there was no love from the stepmother."

Elvira crossed herself. "Suicide is a sin, but I hope the Lord will forgive her."

Nico continued walking, popping his head in the kitchen. "Ciao, Tilde. Nelli's on the terrace. Do I have time to talk to her?"

"Take all the time you want. She's upset about Mantelli's girlfriend committing suicide. I sent Alba to her with a plate of your frittelle. Go and cheer her up. Even better, invite her to have lunch with you. Alba and Enzo will handle the lunch crowd. Go."

"Thanks." Walking out on the terrace, he crossed paths with Alba, who gave him a quick double kiss. "Sad day." Nico nodded, his eyes searching for Nelli. She was seated at the least popular table, one far back against the building wall.

"I tried to get her to move to a seat with a view," Alba said. "She wouldn't, so I brought over your fritelle. She looked in need of cheering up. So do you. I know, I heard. If the American lady shows up, I'll tell her you're not here. Nelli's nice."

Nelli spotted him and smiled.

He walked over to her table and sat down facing her.

"Ciao, Nico. Your frittelle are very good. I wasn't hungry, but I finished them all. How are you?"

"It's been a sad morning, but it's nice to see you."

"Why did she do it, do you know?" Nelli saw his face shut down. "I'm sorry. If you know, you probably can't tell me. I didn't come here to get information about her. I wanted to know how you are. It must be horribly sad and also frustrating for you and Salvatore. She was running away, wasn't she?"

"The usual rumor mill told you?"

"Who else? Thanks to the Internet, the news—false or not—takes flight. The cab driver wrote something on his Twitter feed, and it spread from there. How are you?"

"Okay. I had no emotional attachment to her. I only saw her twice. The second time, I exchanged a few words with her, that's all. Suicide is always sad—it's devastating for the family, for friends."

"Theories are already sprouting about her death," Nelli said. "I thought you should know."

"Such as?"

"That she overdosed by mistake. Or was kidnapped by a hiker or a tourist, raped and killed. Or that she knew where Mantelli's money was, and his wife or someone else forced the information out of her, then killed her. Or that she was blackmailing Mantelli's killer, and he or she shut her up."

"Perillo should cede his job to these people."

"No one likes uncertainty, so people come up with possibilities. I think it makes them feel in control."

"As long as it doesn't harm anyone."

"Sometimes it does."

"It will take a few days to know what really happened to Loredana. I'd like to put her aside for now and concentrate on lunch. Will you keep me company? I'd like that very much."

"You don't have to work?"

"Tilde kicked me out of the kitchen, thanks to you. If you'll join me, I'm going to enjoy every minute of it."

Nelli didn't feel like eating. The young woman's ugly death had shaken her. She had come to console Nico if he needed it, but realized she was looking for consolation too. Nico's presence did that. "I would like lunch with you very much. Thank you. What's on the menu besides frittelle?"

"The best pappa al pomodoro in all of Tuscany, for one."

"All of Tuscany?"

"You'll see."

BEFORE GOING HOME AFTER lunch, Nico drove by the Ferriello welcome center for news of Aldo.

Arben was lying down on a bench, eyes closed. OneWag nuzzled his ear. "Ciao, Nico." He kept this eyes closed. "You've heard the good news about Aldo?"

"I did. I'm sorry I interrupted your nap."

"I give myself twenty minutes each day on a bench. It reminds me of how lucky I am that I'm sleeping in a bed again. Today, I gave myself an extra ten to celebrate." Arben opened his eyes and sat up. "You just missed Cinzia. I wish you'd seen her. She was gushing like a badly popped champagne bottle. I've never seen her so happy." Arben was one big smile too. "She asked me to tell you she's having me and the rest of the workers here to celebrate. She wants you to come."

"I didn't work at lunch, which means tonight is a must, unfortunately." Nico knew he could get out of the dinner shift. Tilde had made it clear that, since he insisted on working for free, he had no obligations to her. Celebrating Aldo's freedom would have been fun under different circumstances, but Loredana's death sat heavily on his chest. "I'll drop in and give Aldo a hug before I go. I'll celebrate with him another time."

"She's going to be upset." Arben wiped his face with his hands. "I should be working now." He stood up. "I heard about Mantelli's girlfriend. I guess she didn't want to spend the rest of her life in jail. I would have done the same, although I hear Italian jails are much better than the stinkholes in Albania."

"Ciao, Arben. I'll tell Cinzia myself. Enjoy tonight."

"Oh, I will. Big headache tomorrow. Ciao."

PERILLO CALLED AS NICO was changing into shorts and a T-shirt to do some weeding. "I got the results on the syringe. It had traces of pentobarbital. That's how she killed herself."

"Let's say that's what probably killed her. You still need to wait for the autopsy report."

"You are splitting one hair into many, but justifiably so. Haste is not a good policy, and I now have more questions than before."

"I have only one. Why poison Mantelli with wood alcohol

when all she had to do was inject him with pentobarbital? A much faster, easier way to kill."

"I see we agree. Are you free now?"

"Give me the time to change and I'll come to the station."

"No, Daniele and I will come to you. Being in comfort is more conducive to clear thinking, and your balcony offers fresh air."

A glass of whiskey also helps, Nico thought, but said, "What about Tarani?"

"He is in Florence, convinced we have found Mantelli's killer, who is conveniently dead."

"No dinner. I have to work tonight."

"I would not presume to impose on you for food. Ivana has plans to salvage our spirits with a seven-layer eggplant and zucchini lasagna, followed by a homemade cassata. She's extended the invitation to you, but alas, it appears Tilde has you under lock and key."

"Stop expending oxygen with your fancy talk and get over here."

"At your orders."

"LOREDANA WAS NOT A stupid woman," Perillo said as he sat down on Nico's balcony and answered the question he had posed not half an hour ago. "Killing Mantelli with pentobarbital held the risk of immediately leading us to her as the prime suspect."

"You didn't know she took pentobarbital." Nico put two glasses and an open whiskey bottle out on the table. He'd dropped the last of the olives in a small bowl, which he now pushed Daniele's way. "She told Diane about taking the drug only after Mantelli's death."

Daniele kept his gaze on the fast movement of the swallows swooping across the sky. They enchanted him with their dips and rises.

Perillo poured himself two fingers of whiskey. "We would have found out quickly enough. Maybe Loredana knew Ida had heard her threat. She was right there, telling Loredana her leg was bleeding. Ida would go straight to the carabinieri once she found out Mantelli was murdered—"

"But she didn't," Daniele interrupted, clearly upset. If only he could shut them out and watch the birds.

Perillo flicked his eyes over to Daniele. Poor boy. Loredana's death had hit him the hardest. He had refused to see her body. "Loredana had no way of knowing that Ida follows her own rules. Any other housekeeper would have reported it right away. Loredana couldn't risk having us go through her belongings and finding the murder weapon. So she used antifreeze instead." Perillo drank the whiskey down. "Thank you. This is a welcome comfort. Dani, you should try some. It's soothing."

Daniele shook his head. "How many people know antifreeze will kill you? I didn't. If I'd guessed, I would think it would make you throw up instantly."

"It was in the news a few years ago," Perillo said. "Some tourists in the Caribbean died after consuming it."

"I will not believe she killed anyone," Daniele said. Her death had left him filled with sadness, anger and guilt. It was his call that had sent her running to her death.

"Not even herself?" Nico asked, settling down on the third chair with OneWag at his feet.

"Not even herself." Daniele turned to Perillo. "You saw what she was like, Maresciallo. It doesn't fit."

"Yes, I did see. When we told her about Mantelli, she put on a show. She was shocked, maybe even sad, but she was center stage, not Mantelli. She was vain and desperate for attention. Now we know she was also on drugs and very unhappy. She was fragile, as you put it yourself, Dani. That can lead to suicide. She did start to write a suicide note."

"Anyone could have done that. It's all wrong, Maresciallo. The place she died doesn't make sense. If she'd killed herself, she would have chosen somewhere beautiful where everyone could see her and mourn for her. She would have staged her own death. Killing yourself in the woods where only a dog can find you, that's not the Loredana we met."

Nico and Perillo exchanged glances. Daniele was too young, too inexperienced to know the power of desperation.

"Let's get back to Mantelli." Nico's gaze went to Perillo. "Are you convinced Loredana killed him?"

"I didn't see her do it, but she threatened him and she's got motive."

"So did Aldo, and he's been cleared. I think we need to dig a little deeper. It's not right to decide she was the murderer without being at least ninety percent convinced. I'm only at fifty."

"Zero for me," Daniele piped in.

Perillo found comfort in a cigarette this time. "I know. I have not succeeded here, not at all."

"Let's succeed now," Nico said. "Daniele, did you send me the name of the two vintners who paid Mantelli?"

"No." Daniele's face turned red. "I'm sorry. I forgot. I had their names and telephone numbers ready to send you, but," he stumbled over his words, "I had to call Loredana to make sure I didn't scare her, and then I did because she was gone, and I—"

Nico stopped him with a hand on his shoulder. "It's fine, Daniele. You had a lot on your mind. Send them to me when you get back."

"I can go now."

"No, stay here with us. We need your sharp mind. How about a glass of wine? I'll join you."

"No, thank you. A glass of water would be nice, though." Daniele got up. "I'll get it." He was eager to get away from the smoke and the banter, because that's all it was. A back-and-forth of maybe, could be. The only concrete events were Mantelli and Loredana's deaths.

"Go ahead. Help yourself. There's some bread and cheese if you want."

At the mention of food, OneWag followed Daniele in. Out of sight of the two men, Daniele picked up the dog and hugged him. They didn't believe him about her death. After talking to her awful stepmother, he'd seen Loredana as a fighter. Fighters didn't quit. Was he wrong? He didn't think so, but these two knew so much more about people than he did.

Perillo sighed. "My brigadiere needs to grow some crocodile skin. He's too upset to think straight. Why do you want those names? Are you thinking they might be suspects?"

"No, but we don't really know anything about them. There's no harm in having a chat with them." There was something Ginevra had said about Mantelli that had set him wondering about "struggling vintners."

"Diane Severson is the one I need to question more carefully," Perillo said. "She was at the villa Tuesday morning, ostensibly to let Peppino know about the sale. I've thought about the theory Dani offered in the park yesterday. It's plausible. Diane went to the villa Tuesday morning, dropped some antifreeze in Mantelli's whiskey bottle and told Peppino to get rid of it after Mantelli had his drink."

"You think there was another bottle, an open one Diane spiked with methanol, and Peppino got rid of it?"

Perillo took a drag from his cigarette. "Could be. He seemed to me to be a hardworking, honest man, but he must have been angry with Mantelli for selling the villa."

"Diane told me he's in complete denial. He thinks she'll cancel the sale."

"Maybe that's what she promised him in exchange."

"But Nelli tells me he knows he'll have to leave the villa. He's very upset about it. I saw that myself. I guess if the news is bad enough, you can hope and despair at the same time." Rita had shifted from one to the other for months after the diagnosis. "From what you've told me someone could have gone to the villa in the afternoon. Didn't Peppino say he usually takes a nap then?"

"Yes, he did," Perillo said, "and his room is far enough away that if anyone came to visit, he wouldn't have heard anything."

"Before Mantelli went to the piazza where Aldo met up with him, was he home?"

"After lunch he usually went back to Il Glicine with Loredana, but she says he told her he had work to do."

Daniele walked back out on the balcony followed by OneWag. "Peppino didn't mention the sale of the villa when he came to the station." He was holding a tray with an opened bottle of white wine and two glasses, one of which was filled with water. "He also didn't tell us that Signora Severson had paid a visit to the villa Tuesday morning. That's two important omissions." He set it down on the table and sat down. OneWag curled up at his feet. "Peppino came to the station before we knew Mantelli had been murdered. I think he helped Signora Severson kill her husband. And, if you permit me, Maresciallo, I would ask the whereabouts of the signora last night and early this morning."

"You think she helped Loredana run?" Nico asked.

Daniele drank half a glass of water before answering. "She may have killed her." Saying those five words almost made him smile. He knew he was climbing up mirrors trying to sustain his conviction that Loredana did not kill herself.

Perillo put out his cigarette in the portable ashtray and stood up. "We'll dig deeper while we wait for the autopsy results. Thank you, Nico, for your unparalleled hospitality, and for giving me the well-deserved and very necessary kick to my ass."

"Never a kick, Perillo. A suggestion."

"Call it what you wish. My ego registered it differently. My ass and my ego speak to each other daily."

Nico and OneWag walked the two men to the door. "I'll send the vintners' names and numbers as soon as I get back," Daniele said.

Nico nodded. OneWag followed Perillo and Daniele down the stairs. It was time to lift a leg. When he came back, he found his boss sitting out on the balcony, sipping a glass of white wine. No bread, no cheese. There was nothing for OneWag to do but jump up on the sofa and wait. Soon it would be dinnertime.

NICO AND ONEWAG FOUND Cinzia in the front garden with clippers, in shorts and a T-shirt, cleaning up her roses. "Ehi, Nico, I'm sorry you can't stay for dinner tonight. We'll do a repeat when you're free, although I know you could have gotten out of work. You must be upset about that woman killing herself. You met her, right?"

Nico said nothing. Thankfully, Cinzia kept going. "I can't blame you. It's hard to celebrate anything after finding a dead body in the woods. Come here." She opened up her arms, and Nico walked into them. They hugged and cheek-kissed. "Forgive me, but I'm so happy I could even hug Salvatore." Cinzia's eyes glistened, and a natural blush sat on her cheeks. Nico was glad to see her back to her usual vivacious self.

"Aldo's in the kitchen. He wants to see you."

"And I, him. Enjoy your celebration."

"Thanks. We plan to get so drunk, we've declared tomorrow a holiday at the vineyard."

Aldo was bent over the kitchen table, slicing a row of plump sausages with a six-inch knife. A large tray held two well-seasoned, spatchcocked chickens shiny with oil and spattered with rosemary sprigs.

OneWag raised his head with trembling nostrils.

"Ciao, Nico. You're going to regret missing this. So is Rocco." Aldo put the knife down, and Nico gave him a half-hug.

"I know I will. I can't tell you how glad I am to have you back where you belong."

"Thanks." Aldo wiped his hands on his green Ferriello apron and reached for a glass. An open bottle of Ferriello red was already on the table along with a half-full glass. He poured the wine into the empty glass and handed it to Nico. "Let's drink to always being where we belong."

"I'm with you on that," Nico said, happy to feel that he belonged in Gravigna. He clinked Aldo's glass. OneWag whimpered.

Aldo turned toward the counter behind him and cut off a piece from one of several raw pork cutlets, then tossed it to OneWag. The dog gulped it down.

Nico heard his phone beep. He dug into his pocket. It was a text from Daniele with the vintners' names and phone numbers. It was too late in the day to call them. He didn't want to rush through the calls, and he was overdue at the restaurant.

Aldo had resumed slicing the remaining sausages down the middle, careful not to slice all the way through. "Tell Salvatore I forgive him. I know he was following orders. And thanks for helping Cinzia."

"No thanks needed. We're friends."

Aldo pointed his knife at Nico. "Friend and landlord. Don't you forget it."

Nico laughed. "I remember every first of the month." He finished his wine in two big gulps. "Ciao, Aldo. I'll see you around. Let's go, OneWag."

The dog gave one last pleading look at Aldo. When that got him nowhere, he took his time following his boss to the car.

IVANA'S SEVEN-LAYER EGGPLANT AND zucchini lasagna had been eaten, along with the fennel and green olive salad. What was left of the cassata was back in the freezer. Daniele was now explaining to Ivana how to make the Venetian specialty dish sarde in saor.

"You deep-fry the sardines, cover them with lots of onions and marinate them in a sweet vinegar sauce."

"That sounds delicious."

The notes of "O Sole Mio" rang out loudly.

Ivana protested. "Salvo, please lower the volume on that thing. It drives me crazy."

Perillo, still comfortably seated at the kitchen table, saw it was an unfamiliar number and rejected the call. "Done."

Two minutes later, the song burst out again. He let it ring. It was the same number, but he liked the music.

"Salvo, answer it." Ivana said. "We're going deaf."

Perillo swiped and put the phone to his ear. "Perillo speaking."

"Signor Maresciallo, Ida speaking."

"Ah, I'm glad it's you. I'd like you to tell me what you meant by two and two doesn't make six or even four."

"That's not why I called, but I can tell you. It's the advice I gave Signor Mantelli when I found out he gambled on soccer matches. Same advice I gave my nephew. You can't count on things adding up the way you want."

"How do you know he gambled?"

Daniele leaned forward to listen. Ida's voice was loud.

"Every Friday morning, I'd hear him place his bets on the teams, but that's not important. I hear that poor girl is dead."

"Yes, she committed suicide."

"How?"

"We don't have the autopsy report yet."

"I also heard a syringe was found next to her body. Is that true?"

There was no point in denying; it would be in the newspapers tomorrow. "Yes."

"Oh, she liked her drugs. Right from the start I saw that. She was just as hooked as Signor Mantelli was hooked on gambling.

It was sad, such a pretty girl. She could have been in the movies. She was sorry for what she'd done. The drugs—"

Perillo interrupted. "Can we talk about this tomorrow? I'm in the middle of dinner."

"Your dinner will have to wait. This is important. The syringe you found, it wasn't hers. I have her syringe. Friday, after Signora Diane told her she had to go back to the B&B, Signorina Loredana took me up to her bedroom. She said if she didn't get rid of them, they were going to kill her. 'I can trust you,' she said, and handed me one of those fancy bags for creams and things. 'Thank you,' I said, 'but I don't wear makeup, and it's way too late for creams on my face.' Oh, she liked that. I made her laugh. Did you ever hear her laugh? It was like a little bell ringing."

Perillo looked at his wife and shrugged. She hated interruptions during meals, but luckily her attention was on Daniele, who was writing out the recipe for sarde in saor.

Ida talked right through his shrug. "Once she stopped laughing, she unzipped the bag. I saw pill bottles, cotton balls, alcohol, a syringe and little vials of some liquid. 'Please take them. Throw them away where no one can find them. They've ruined me.' She zippered up the bag and clasped my arms around it. She then hugged me. 'Even if I come begging,' she said, 'don't listen. Get rid of everything now, before I change my mind.' She pushed me out of the room and locked the door. Half an hour later, Signora Diane drove her with her suitcases to the B&B."

"What did you do with the drugs?"

Both Ivana and Daniele turned to look at Perillo.

"I kept them. The bag was pretty, so I put everything in a Coop bag. Some other garbage killed her."

"Thank you for this information. You could have told me this yesterday morning."

"Why would I have? She was still alive. I'm calling you now to save you from climbing up and down those stairs. Send your

brigadiere. His knees can take it. And I'll have a strawberry crostata waiting for him. That young man needs some looking after.
So did that poor girl. I'm sorry she didn't make it." She hung up.

Ivana gave her husband a questioning look. "I hope we can
keep the evening free of the dead."

"Of course. I am only too happy to do so."

"Now, both of you, please have some fruit." Ivana pushed a
bowl filled with peaches and apricots Daniele's way. "Next time
you come, we'll make sarde in saor together."

Perillo and Daniele eyed each other. Ivana had outdone herself
with this meal. Ida's news would have to wait.

FOURTEEN

After breakfast the next day, Nico and OneWag slowly walked Gogol back to the Medici villa that was now an old-age home. Nico had questions he didn't want overheard by the gossip mill. "I hear you go to the dog kennel every morning," Nico said. "What takes you there?"

"The animals. We are friends, as you and Nelli are friends. No different. We are all creatures of God. I know them all, and they know me. I hear them calling me sometimes. They are imprisoned and in need of stories to soothe them. They listen to the verses of the Poet and dream." Gogol chuckled. "I do it for them, but also for me. It keeps the gnawing rust far from my memory."

"Did you see anything different yesterday morning?"

"They called before the waking of the sun. When I greeted them, no dog raised its head in greeting. I understood Death was near."

"You were there before Dino?"

Gogol nodded. They had reached the entrance of the home. Just past the massive open door, Lucia, the knitting gatekeeper, was watching them. Gogol had dubbed her Cerberus, the Hound of Hades.

"Did you hear or see anything that might help us understand what happened?"

"Death is quiet. The dogs were quiet. I prayed." Gogol took a step inside the door. "Tomorrow, if I live."

"You will. Rest well."

Nico and OneWag walked back to the piazza and got into the car. Nico took out his cell phone as the bell of Sant'Agnese, the church on top of the hill, rang out nine-thirty. It was time to call the vintners.

He tried Sole d'Etna, the Sicilian vintner, first. A woman answered after a few rings. Nico asked to speak to the owner.

"That's me and my husband, Giuseppe, and Nina Mazzaro. Who is this?"

After introducing himself, he explained that he was calling on behalf of Mantelli's wife. "She found your name on her husband's computer with a list of payments you made to him. These payments ended two months ago. She was wondering what they were for and why you stopped paying."

"We stopped because we'd paid the loan back in full. I've got Signor Mantelli's signature to prove it."

Not a bribe, then. A loan. Ginevra had said Mantelli liked to help struggling vintners. Maybe he wasn't such a bastard after all. Or had it just been an ego trip? At this point, it didn't matter. "I imagine there was a written agreement."

"Certainly. I'm sure Signor Mantelli kept a copy of it, but I'll be happy to send Signora Mantelli a copy of the agreement, along with Signor Mantelli's letter stating the loan was paid in full."

"She would appreciate that. You have his email address?"

"Yes, we do, and please tell her how sorry we are about his death. We would have lost the vineyard if he hadn't opened up his wallet."

"Did you ask him for a loan directly?"

"No, I would never have had the courage. He was vacationing in Taormina and came here for a tasting. He liked our wine very much. I told him we might have to close. 'Your wine merits life,' is what he said, and he offered us a loan with very generous terms. Please tell the signora how grateful we are to him, may God rest his soul."

"I will. Thank you for clearing up the situation. Buongiorno."

He eyed OneWag, who was feigning sleep on the front seat, and scratched his ear. The call to the Piedmont vintner gave the same answer. Mantelli had loaned money to Giorgio Casagiorni, owner of the Casagiorni Nebbiolo vineyard, four years ago. He must have been very flush at the time. Casagiorni had just finished paying it back. He, too, agreed to send a copy of the original agreement and the paid-in-full letter to Mantelli's email address.

Nico dropped the phone in the open glove compartment and put the key in the ignition. "Get down."

The dog raised his head and blinked sleepily.

Nico started the motor, "Down or out. Take your pick."

OneWag unpeeled his body from the front seat and lowered himself down slowly. The pit was better than out.

ON THE WAY TO meet Perillo and Daniele in the park, Nico called Diane to tell her about the two vintners. "They both say the loans are paid in full and they have papers to prove it. They're going to email you copies."

"Thanks for letting me know." Whatever ill feelings she'd had after the pool fiasco were now gone. "I'd like to think the loans show that I loved a man who had some redeeming features, but I suspect he did it to boost his perpetually suffering ego. What made you get this hunch?"

He told her about Ginevra's comment. "Can you look through his papers to see if you find the loan agreements?"

"I've examined every piece of paper in this house. No loan agreement, no receipts for debts paid and no Swiss bank account numbers."

Her answer didn't surprise him. He suspected Loredana had found them first. "Let me know if you receive proof of payment from the two vintners. I want to make sure they were telling the truth."

"What about Luca?"

"Verdini claims it was payoff money."

"A good review from the great Michele is more important than a loan, then. Luca's folks are rich. I'll let you know. Ciao."

NICO FOUND PERILLO PACING the perimeter of the park under the splotchy shade of the oak trees.

Nico walked up the slight slope and joined Daniele. "Perillo, stop a minute. I have interesting news."

"I have better," Perillo shouted. "Two more rounds and I'm with you."

Nico sat on the bench. "What's he doing?" he asked Daniele, who was following Perillo with his eyes as if afraid he might fall down.

"He says the doctor told him the walking would loosen his stiff knee." Maybe this was true, but Daniele suspected the maresciallo was only trying to clear his head.

"Come on, sit down. He'll be fine. What is this better news?"

Daniele stayed standing. "He received a phone call from Mantelli's housekeeper last night. He'll want to tell you the rest himself." Perillo still had one more round to go.

"Maresciallo Perillo, if you don't stop this minute," Nico said as Perillo paced closer, "I'm taking my news to Tarani."

Perillo stopped on the spot. He took a few deep breaths and walked to the bench. "Loredana might not have killed herself." He sat down next to Nico. Daniele sat on the other side.

"You got the autopsy results."

"Not yet." Perillo relayed what Ida had told him. "Loredana gave all her drugs to Ida in a bag. Including the syringe. Daniele picked them up this morning."

Daniele nodded. He'd gotten a plastic bag full of drugs and two slices of Ida's strawberry crostata.

Nico leaned back on the bench. As he'd told Diane, it wasn't like Perillo to jump to conclusions. "Loredana could have gotten more drugs. She was an addict. Whatever her intentions to come clean were, her body needed the drugs to function. She was under a lot of stress."

"Pentobarbital is easy to get," Daniele admitted. Last night, after the maresciallo had given him Ida's news, he looked up the drug, not sure which was the worse end for Loredana, suicide or murder. "It's outlawed in America, but here, you can get it online."

Perillo stood and lit a cigarette. "You're probably right, Nico." He walked a few steps away to keep the smoke from bothering Daniele. "I'm getting overimaginative. I keep wondering why there was no trace of her when the hikers went back to find her. Remember, we thought someone had picked her up?"

"She hid from them."

"If she was planning to commit suicide, why take her two suitcases with her?"

"Maybe the idea of suicide came to her afterward, when she realized she really had nowhere to go. Perillo, we could debate this all day. Let's wait for the autopsy report."

"If they find she died of an overdose of pentobarbital, that won't tell us who administered it."

"Unfortunately, that's true. Did you go through the contents of her suitcase?"

"I did." Daniele said. "It was full of clothes, shoes, makeup. Women's things. She must have packed in a hurry. She didn't bother folding anything."

"Her phone?"

"It was near her body next to a sharp rock," Perillo said. "She or someone else smashed it into small pieces. The rock had tiny slivers of glass on it. That phone was pummeled with an incredible amount of rage."

Or desperation, Daniele thought but didn't say.

"Tarani took it with him to Florence headquarters to see if it's possible to retrieve any information from it."

Daniele shook his head and said to Nico, "You have news?" He hoped it had nothing to do with Loredana.

"I do. Something that might open up a new line of inquiry."

"Good," Daniele muttered under his breath as Perillo spread out his arms and looked up at a lacy patch of sky peeking between the tree leaves.

"This is important. Sit down and listen."

Perillo did as he was asked. Nico told them what he had discovered after talking to the vintners. "Loredana may or may not have killed Mantelli. Now that she's dead, we can't know for sure, which means you have to consider all the other suspects. Did you try reaching Diane?"

"She's in Florence working with Signora Della Langhe until tomorrow. I told her about Loredana. 'That's what I thought she'd do,' was her only comment. I asked her to come to the station to help me clarify a few things as soon as she got back. She's said she'll only come of her own accord if you sit in on the meeting. She's either given her heart to you or she finds Americans more trustworthy. Perhaps both."

"You never quit, do you?" Nico didn't mind. It meant that Perillo was getting back to his endearingly annoying old self. "Verdini is who you have to talk to next. Diane told me his parents are rich, but that doesn't mean they were willing to give him money or that he even asked them. After talking to those two vintners, I think Mantelli giving Verdini a loan makes much more sense than asking for a kickback."

"Signor Mantelli asked Aldo Ferri to pay," Daniele said. "Signora Cinzia confirmed it."

Nico shook his head. "That was a very different situation. He was in love with Cinzia and wanted to make both of them suffer. Verdini told me he had kept paying Mantelli even after other important wine critics were giving him great reviews. He claimed he had done it out of gratitude, knowing Mantelli needed money. I find that a little too generous of him."

"You think he was continuing to pay back the loan with interest, but Mantelli demanded the money back all at once."

"And Verdini didn't want to pay it."

"This must have been before he sold the villa."

"Maybe Mantelli wanted all the money he could get. Diane only found about the sale from her lawyer a few days before he died."

"About the esteemed wine critic needing money," Perillo said, "Ida confirmed he placed bets every Monday morning."

Daniele jumped in. "If Ida knew, I think Signora Severson must have also known. She must be very angry that her husband threw away their money like that. That gives her good motive."

Nico studied Daniele's intent expression for a moment. "You really think Loredana is innocent of Mantelli's murder, don't you?"

"Yes, and that she didn't kill herself."

Perillo shot a look at Nico, which seemed to say, *What can I do, Dani has fallen in love again.*

Not love, Nico thought. Daniele was following his instinct, and there was a chance his instinct was spot-on here. "Why would anyone want to kill Loredana?"

"She knew who killed Mantelli."

PERILLO AND DANIELE WALKED down the geranium-lined path with Contessa leading the way. Perillo had called ahead. Luca Verdini was waiting for them in one of the uncomfortable chairs by the tasting shed.

Perillo put on a smile as he approached. "Thank you for taking the time to answer a few questions."

Verdini stood, but did not return the smile. "Actually, I don't

have much time. I'm conducting a group tasting in twenty minutes."

"I shall be as brief as a Neapolitan maresciallo can be. May
we sit?"

"Of course."

Perillo picked the chair with the best view. He waited for
Daniele to sit and take out his pen and notebook. Verdini sat
opposite. Seeing all was well, Contessa took off.

"We've been wondering about the kickbacks Signor Mantelli
had asked of a few vintners, you included."

"I, too, found it puzzling at the time," Verdini said. "He was
such a well-regarded wine critic. I have to admit I was happy to
comply. He gave me the boost I needed."

"You attest that the eight hundred euros you paid Signor
Mantelli monthly was in order to get good reviews on his blog
and his magazine?"

"I do."

"We spoke to two other vintners who were on the same list
we found in Mantelli's computer. They have declared and sent
proof that the money they sent Signor Mantelli was repayment
plus interest for a loan he had given them. Perhaps he offered you
a loan also?"

There was no telltale reaction from Verdini. "No, he didn't,"
he answered calmly. "He's the one who wanted money, not me. I
needed to be put on the map, that's why I accepted the deal. Why
are you asking?" He raised a hand. "You don't need to answer.
Diane put you up to this. If Michele had loaned me money, she'd
want me to pay it back. Well, there was no loan."

"And you continued to pay him even after you no longer
needed his praises?"

"Yes. I was, still am, grateful to him. I stopped paying last
month because I discovered he was gambling his money away."

"Where were you on Tuesday last week?"

"Tuesday? I'm always here working with my men. Three Albanians who have been with me from the start. Ginevra came mid-morning. I had a lunch appointment at Cibreo with friends of mine, a couple from Paris. We did the art-in-churches tour together. Florence has the highest concentration of fine art in the world. Have you been to the Brancacci Chapel? I see your brigadiere has."

Daniele had been nodding. Now he blushed.

"Glorious, isn't it?"

Daniele nodded again. The anguish on Eve's face after being expulsed from the Garden had crushed his heart. For an instant, Loredana's face flashed through his mind with the same anguish.

"What time did you get back?" Perillo asked.

"Too late to change for dinner, unfortunately. I drove from Florence straight to Castellina to pick up Diane. She was staying at the Palazzo Squarcialupi Hotel." As his fingers combed through his hair, he smiled. "She was nice enough to forgive my disheveled attire."

Perillo leaned forward and set his dark eyes on Verdini's handsome face. For a moment, he thought how nice it would be to have his youth, his looks, his confidence. But only for a moment. "I ask again to be doubly certain: Signor Mantelli did not loan you money?"

"He did not. He asked for a kickback and I gave it to him, just as Aldo Ferri did."

"I see. I hear voices approaching. I think your clients are here. We shall leave you to your work." As Perillo stood up, he saw a flash of red running up the path. "Daniele will write up what was said here. I ask that you please come down to the station tomorrow to sign it. And please bring the names, phone numbers and addresses of Ginevra, the workers who were with you and the friends you saw that day."

Verdini got on his feet. "I have them right here." He stepped into the shed and came out with an open logbook. "You'll find what you need on the top of each worker's page."

While Daniele had copied what he needed, Verdini took out his phone, clicked on contacts and when Daniele had finished with the logbook, offered him the names and phone numbers of his Parisian friends. "They're still in Florence, staying at the Lungarno."

Perillo noticed the smug smile crossing Verdini's lips. He suspected that meant the alibi was solid. "Thank you. I expect to see you tomorrow."

Verdini nodded. "Probably in the afternoon. My morning is packed with tastings and sales. Excuse me, but I need to greet my guests before Contessa overwhelms them with her attention." He hurried up the path.

Daniele put his notebook and pen back in his shirt pocket and gave a last look at the vines receding in the distance. "I'll check the alibi when we get back."

"I think you'll find it has no leaks."

For Loredana's sake, Daniele hoped it was full of holes.

DANIELE WAS IN HIS room, spooning a ready-made bean soup he'd bought at the Coop that he hadn't bothered to heat. When the maresciallo invited him to dinner, he'd said he wasn't hungry. It was true, but it wasn't the real reason he'd turned down the invitation. He needed to be alone to understand why he was so certain that Loredana hadn't killed Mantelli or herself. It was like something was stuck in his teeth and no prodding would get rid of it. He had no proof. Was he being naïve? He knew that was what Nico and the maresciallo thought. Was it because she was so beautiful? Verdini's alibi had turned out to be as solid as Ghiberti's bronze doors.

His thoughts were interrupted by the phone. He didn't

recognize the number and clicked off. The phone rang again. Maybe it was from Vince or Dino. They'd never exchanged numbers.

"Brigadiere Donati speaking."

"Dani, my mother just told me what happened. I'm so sorry."

A soothing happiness enveloped him. "Thank you, Stella."

"I knew you'd be upset. I don't want to disturb you, just give you a hug by phone."

"I don't think she killed herself or Mantelli."

"I know. Nico talked to Mamma, and when I called her ten minutes ago, she told me. Do you have proof?"

"No. That's what's terrible. Not a shred of proof, but I can't get rid of the conviction. I think she knew who killed him and maybe tried to blackmail them, and that's what got her killed. She didn't have any money of her own."

"You must have someone in mind."

"I do, but I can't tell you."

"I don't need to know, but what are you going to do about it?"

"It's up to the maresciallo, but he doesn't believe me."

"You're his brigadiere. Maybe you can sniff around. You might find something you can show him."

He had thought of asking Peppino if he had heard Loredana's threat to Mantelli. Ida might have lied for her own reasons. "The maresciallo wouldn't like that."

"Well, sometimes he does."

Daniele's "yes" wasn't very convincing.

"Now can be sometimes. But be wise in your sniffing. I don't want you to get hurt."

"Thank you," Daniele said, too moved to say anything else.

"Come to Florence soon," Stella said. "I could use a friendly face."

"Me too."

They clicked off.

—

PEPPINO PEERED OUT OF the half-open door. "The signora is in Florence," he said and started to close the door.

"I know, Signor Risso," Daniele said. "It's you I want to talk to. You know Signorina Loredana is dead."

"Yes, Nelli told me. She was a strange one, but kind. Before she left, she wanted to give me some money. I didn't take it. I have no need for money. She said she wanted to give me something because I was nice to her. All I did was make her breakfast. Caffelatte and yoghurt with a spoonful of my blackberry jam. I have three blackberry bushes at the end of the property."

The door stayed half open. "You're lucky. My mother makes jam, but she has to buy the fruit."

"Luck is no longer with me."

"Yes, I heard about the sale. It must be very hard."

"It broke me."

"I'm sorry. May I come in? Signorina Loredana's death has shaken me, and I thought maybe you could help."

"If I can." Peppino opened the door slowly, as if its weight was too much for him.

Daniele stepped inside. "Thank you." He followed Peppino into a room just beyond the entrance hall. The kitchen was all steel and glass. At the far end of the room, between two large windows, a ceramic bowl with a utensil sticking out of it sat on the edge of a thick glass table.

"I'm sorry," Daniele said. "I interrupted your dinner." The room was very hot. The windows were closed. Peppino was wearing baggy jeans, workmen's boots and a long-sleeved shirt. He obviously didn't feel the heat.

"No bother. It's cold. Bean soup from the Coop. A lone man's feed." Peppino walked over to the table and sat on a backless metal stool.

Daniele was going to say that he'd had the same dinner, but the "lone man's feed" comment stopped him.

After a couple of spoonfuls of soup, Peppino asked, "What can I do for you?"

"May I sit?"

"If you want."

Daniele pulled out another stool from under the table and sat. "I was wondering if you ever heard Signorina Loredana threaten Signor Mantelli."

"Ida said she heard that. Not me. If the signorina said what Ida thinks she heard, she didn't mean it. You get angry and you say the stupidest things. Men and women both. That young woman depended on Mantelli. She looked at him like a new-born kitten looks at her mamma. That's not love. Need is what it is."

"The capitano in charge of the investigation thinks she killed him, and that's why she committed suicide."

"No."

"Everyone thinks that now. It's going to be in the papers." Daniele could see that Peppino was upset by what he'd just said. He was folded over himself. "That's how she's going to be remembered. I feel it's my fault. I called her to come to the station because the maresciallo and the capitano wanted to question her. I must have scared her, and she ran. That made her look guilty. I feel terrible about it. Now she's dead. Suicide, they say."

Peppino shook his head and straightened up. "A weak animal runs from danger, hoping to outsmart death. Poor little kitten."

"I think she's innocent, Peppino. I also think you know more about Mantelli's death than you've told us."

"I cannot help you. May Signorina Loredana rest in peace." Peppino bent over his soup and resumed eating.

Daniele waited. The only sound came from the spoon hitting the bottom of the bowl. There seemed to be no end to the soup.

Daniele waited a few more minutes. "The maresciallo is going to question Signora Severson tomorrow."

Peppino's spoon stopped midway between the bowl and his mouth. "The signora is in Florence."

"She'll be back tomorrow morning."

The spoon went back to the bowl. Peppino lifted his head to look at Daniele. "Why more questions?"

"Until the case is closed, there will always be more questions. Goodnight, Peppino. Thank you for listening."

AFTER A LIGHT DINNER made up of barely warm zucchini and onion soup, a spinach omelet and a fruit salad, Perillo offered to clean up, as he did every night. Ivana, as expected, told him to get out of her kitchen. With a kiss to her forehead, he obeyed and left the apartment for his nightly two-cigarette walk around the small park.

As he walked, he tried to free his mind of the image of Loredana's body, curled up as if asleep. She looked at peace, something she had clearly not been in life. Was she Mantelli's killer? Her threat, her actions suggested she was, but there was no definitive proof. He walked the perimeter of the park, and after finishing his first cigarette of the evening, he debated lighting another and walking another round. He was tired, perhaps even depressed, but at least his knee was feeling better. He checked his watch. Ivana would welcome him back now. Perhaps they'd watch a bit of television together. He looked forward to being near her, holding her hand, breathing in the lily-of-the-valley scent she had bought for herself after a church visit to Florence and the thirteenth-century Santa Maria Novella Apothecary. He would ask Daniele to get him a new bottle on one of his trips to the city. Being close to Ivana reduced whatever work problems he had to digestible nuggets. Another cigarette would be of no help at all, he decided. He really did need to quit.

As Perillo left the park and made his way to the barracks apartments, the first muffled notes of "O Sole Mio" rang out in his pocket. He answered, hoping it was Ivana calling him back for the start of a television show. He had just heard the nine o'clock church bells.

"Ciao, Salvatore. Am I interrupting something?"

It was soft-voiced Barbara, Della Langhe's very capable assistant. They had never met in person, but he considered her a friend. She had saved him many headaches with Della Langhe. "No, I've just finished my after-dinner stroll."

"Are you ever going to give up smoking?"

"How did you know?"

"Your voice."

"I'll think about it tomorrow."

"Your choice, your life. I just got home from having dinner with friends at Perseus."

"Dario Cecchini's steaks in Panzano are better." He didn't really know, as he'd never been to Florence's famous steakhouse, but he liked to one-up Barbara.

"You're just envious. But listen. Elsa's husband happens to work in the medical examiner's lab. I asked him about the autopsy on the woman who killed herself in Gravigna. He knows I work for Della Langhe and didn't want to tell me anything. Another bottle of Fontodi Chianti Classico did the trick, but you can't act on what I'm about to tell you until you get the official autopsy report. I'd like to keep my job."

"I understand." He definitely wanted the same. "I swear on the lives of my suede boots and jacket that I won't act on what you tell me."

Barbara laughed in his ear. "I didn't know you were such a fashionista. You'll have to send me a picture."

"I'm listening."

"He overheard the medical examiner tell his assistant that

your Loredana Cardi didn't have enough pentobarbital in her blood to kill her."

"Holy heaven, what are you saying?"

"She didn't die of a drug overdose. Something else killed her."

"What?"

"He doesn't know, and he thinks the medical examiner doesn't know yet, either. He did say she wasn't wounded in any way that he could see."

Perillo leaned against the barrack wall for support. "Holy Mary and all the saints," was all he could say. He reached for a cigarette and lit it. After a drag, he asked, "Does your friend have any idea of how she committed suicide?"

"He thinks she was murdered. Buonanotte, Salvatore. Again, please wait for the official autopsy report before doing anything. You don't have to thank me."

"I won't. You just gave me a sleepless night."

He put out his half-smoked cigarette. It tasted like dust. Daniele and Nico would have to wait for Barbara's news until the morning. For now, he needed Ivana.

FIFTEEN

Caught by surprise, Daniele quickly took off his headphones and stood as Perillo walked into the office. "Buongiorno, Maresciallo."

"Sit, sit," Perillo said with a wave of his hand. "What are you doing in the office at this hour of the morning?"

It was the very question Daniele would have liked to ask Perillo. It was now 8:10. The maresciallo was never in the office before nine. "I woke up early." He had tossed and turned all night.

"Well, I never went to sleep," Perillo said. It wasn't quite true. He'd managed to catch snatches between worrying whether he had another murder to deal with. Walking to his desk, he noticed Daniele's headphones were attached to his phone. "Ah, yes, music to calm the troubled soul. I should try that sometimes. What music?"

"Beyoncé."

"Ah, you have a bias for beauty. Not that I blame you. Well, I hope your soul finds some consolation in that you may be right about Loredana."

Daniele's face turned the color of ripe strawberries. "You have proof she's innocent?"

"Not proof. At the moment, it is only a possibility." He couldn't think of any reason why she would have been murdered for killing Mantelli. Much more likely that she knew who the murderer was and possibly tried blackmail—if she had been murdered, if she was innocent and if the medical examiner was right. If he was smart enough, if he still believed in himself, if he wasn't going through a midlife crisis.

"*If* is a word that should be abolished from all languages," Perillo said out loud. "We will have to wait for the official autopsy report."

Daniele swallowed. "Can you tell me more, Maresciallo? Please," he added as his color faded. His heart was banging against his rib cage, as if trying to escape.

"I'll explain on the way to the café. We both need more fuel."

After Perillo had his espresso and Daniele his apricot fruit juice, they slowly made their way back to the office. Daniele listened with bent head as Perillo told him what Barbara had said. He wanted to tell the maresciallo that there was no *if* involved. He knew he was right and Barbara had just proven it, but it gave him no consolation. He found murder horrifying. Suicide, sad as it was, was at least an act of free will, even if a desperate one.

"Maresciallo, will you excuse me for twenty minutes?"

"Of course," Perillo did not ask him the reason. "Be back by nine-thirty. I'm expecting Signora Severson to come by, and I need you with me."

"Yes, Maresciallo."

Perillo lit his first cigarette of the day and watched his trusted brigadiere walk away briskly, as if he needed to distance himself from Barbara's news. *He's going to the Basilica of Santa Croce to light another candle for Loredana.*

Back in his office Perillo called Nico to relay Barbara's news.

Nico was sitting with Gogol at their usual table at Bar All'Angolo when he took the call. "Too bad you can't bring it up with Diane."

"I can play with the fact that we don't have the results of the autopsy yet. Suicide hasn't been proven."

"Is Tarani in on this?"

"No, and I'm not telling him because I'm not supposed to know. I'm interrogating Diane Severson on my own. You will be her American witness. I'm very happy to have you. But I want no . . . what is it you Americans say?"

"Miscarriage of justice?"

"Hanky panky."

Nico's eyebrows shot up. "Where did you get that from?"

"An old tourist from Texas taught me. Whenever he saw me, he'd shake his finger at me and say, 'No hanky panky now.'" Perillo let out a long breath. "I'm sorry. I needed to put a crack in this boulder Barbara dumped on me."

"We'll smash it to pieces together once we know for sure that she was murdered. I'll see you at ten-thirty."

"Diane is coming in at nine-thirty. She sent me a text last night."

"She changed it to ten-thirty. I was going to text you in a few minutes. Ciao." Nico wasn't happy about having to be on witness duty for Diane's interview. He had planned to do his shopping before reporting for lunch at the restaurant. Nelli was coming over for dinner tonight, and he wanted to impress her with a meal she'd never eaten, a down-home American meal—Caesar salad, fried chicken and homemade potato chips, followed by apple pie and ice cream. The apple pie, he'd made late last night. All it needed was to be heated in the oven.

Nico stood up. "Gogol, I'll see you tomorrow. I've got a busy day."

The old man looked at his friend with regret on his face. "You are entering the deep and savage path."

"No, my friend, I think that path is ending. I'm about to embark on a much happier one. Arrivederci."

"I wish it for you. Tomorrow, if I live."

"You will." Nico waved at Jimmy and Sandro and walked out,

followed by a reluctant dog. A friendly lady had been feeding him bits of her ciambella.

NICO, DIANE AND PEPPINO walked into Perillo's office together at precisely 10:30. Perillo instantly stood up. Daniele did the same, his heart skipping a beat at seeing Peppino.

"I see you've brought reinforcements to do battle with a harmless maresciallo," Perillo said in a light tone. "It is to your advantage that I did not ask Capitano Tarani to join us. I bend with the wind. He does not. Signor Risso, although I did not summon you, I am glad you are here."

"I asked him to come. I think it's fairer to interrogate us together." Diane lowered herself on one of the two chairs that had been placed facing Perillo's desk. She was wearing wide purple slacks splashed with bright orange flecks. Her loose-knit top was the color of apricots. Turquoise espadrilles completed the outfit. As usual, she had on no makeup or jewelry.

Peppino, in the same work clothes he had worn on his first visit to the station, stood behind his mistress, not knowing what to do with his hands. He had not brought his hat.

"Peppino, sit next to me." She took his hand and steered him to the chair. Peppino looked at Nico. Nico shook his head. "No, please, the chair is yours."

Peppino sat down slowly, his gaze on Nico, just in case he changed his mind. Daniele had already left the room when Diane said, "Maybe your brigadiere can get another chair," in the imperious tone that came to her when she was annoyed. "I don't know why I am here again, Maresciallo. I am a working woman. As you know, Prosecutor Della Langhe is very annoyed I'm being kept from doing my work for his wife."

"I'm perfectly aware of that, Signora. You are here—" Perillo stopped as Daniele re-entered the room with a wooden chair.

Nico took it from him and placed it several feet from Diane and Peppino, angled so he could see their faces.

Perillo finally sat down behind his desk. "You are here, Signora, because I have to solve the murder of your estranged husband and find clarity in the mysterious death of his girlfriend."

Diane tossed one colorful leg over the other. "Della Langhe has declared it solved. Loredana killed Michele and then took her own life."

"That is one possibility."

"And the other possibility is that I killed Michele?" Diane laughed. "Maresciallo, you're unbelievable. What is your thought process here? Did Loredana's beauty grab your genitals so hard your brain has turned to mush?"

Daniele's eyes widened in horror. Perillo's face lost all expression. Every one of his muscles clenched like a fist aching to strike.

Nico called out softly in English. "Diane, there's no need for that."

"Shut up, Nico. I didn't ask you here to take his side."

"Actually, I'm taking yours." He said this in Italian and turned to Perillo. "Excuse the interruption." He noticed that Peppino seemed to have shrunk into himself.

Perillo relaxed his shoulders and sat back in his chair. "Signora Severson, we have no proof that Loredana killed your husband, just as we do not yet have any proof she took her own life."

"What, you think she died of a heart attack? With a syringe right next to her body?"

Perillo ignored her interruption. "Until we do, I need to pursue every possibility. You had a good motive. Your marriage was over. You weren't going to get the money he had removed from your joint bank account. If he lived, the money from the sale of the villa might disappear too. If your husband died, the money from the sale of the villa would go to your son. You went to the villa Tuesday morning with the excuse of telling Signor Risso about the sale. You knew your husband liked to drink whiskey. You doctored the bottle and then asked Peppino to dispose of it after Mantelli had his evening drink."

Peppino stood up as fast as his old body permitted. "No. No, Maresciallo. The signora did not ask me to do anything. Please, believe me. She did not ask me."

Diane took his hand. "Thank you, Peppino. Sit down. It's all right. The maresciallo is just fishing around, trying to give himself importance. He can't prove anything."

An interesting comment, Nico thought.

He wasn't going to get anywhere, Perillo realized. Not with her. He had hoped to shake her up a bit. He'd never met a woman like her. A Medusa, capable of turning men to stone. Peppino was the weak link. He would have to get to Peppino alone. It was time to change the subject. "Why do you think Loredana killed your husband?"

"He was going to leave her."

"He told you this?"

"He always left them. But no, Ida told me. She overheard him telling Loredana it was over. Heard her threatening him."

"That's the word of only one person. Daniele tells me you asked Loredana to leave the villa. You even changed the locks. Why is that?"

"She was acting as if she owned the place, dropping her clothes everywhere, ordering Ida about, sending Peppino out on errands. She must have been on some pill or other. She became manic. I'd had enough and drove her back to the B&B. She wouldn't give back the keys to the villa I'd given her, so I changed the locks. I hope my kicking her out didn't destabilize her even more. Feeling guilty is something I've always tried to avoid." She checked her Apple watch and stood up. Nico stood too. "I'm going back to Florence now to continue my work for Signora Della Langhe. If you need to interrogate me again, you'll have to charge me first. Buongiorno, Maresciallo. Brigadiere." She nodded at each of them. "Come Peppino, I'll take you home."

Peppino stood up slowly. "No, Signora. Thank you. I have shopping to do at the Coop. Nelli will take me back." He held his hands clasped tight, his shoulders tensed forward, his expression hard to read.

"Then I'll drive you to the Coop."

She's afraid he'll stay and talk, Perillo thought.

He's shaken, Daniele thought. He had kept his eyes on Peppino throughout. He defended the signora, but clearly didn't like what he heard her say.

He looks overwhelmed, Nico thought. Broken. Nico was glad Nelli was going to drive him home.

"Thanks for coming, Nico," Diane said as she walked to the door followed by Peppino.

"I'll see you to your car," Nico said.

She waved. "No need. Stay with your friends. Ciao." Out she went. A stooped Peppino followed, shutting the door quietly behind him.

"What do you think?" Perillo asked, looking both at Daniele and Nico.

"Loredana? Diane?" Nico said. "There's no proof either way."

Perillo sat back down in his chair. "We have to get Peppino back here somehow."

Nico remained standing. It was time for him to go to the restaurant. "I would wait until you have Loredana's autopsy results."

"I think you're right."

Daniele stood next to his computer in the back of the room and said nothing. He was counting on Peppino to tell the truth.

NICO WAS HELPING ALBA clear the tables when Nelli called.

"Ciao, Nelli. I was about to call you. Is eight o'clock a good time? Please just bring yourself, nothing else. Okay?"

"Nico, can you come to Greve now?"

He heard the tremor in her voice. "What's wrong? Are you hurt?"

"No, it's Zio Peppino. He wants to talk to Salvatore. He won't tell me why, but he wants me to be with him. He's very upset. He keeps saying, "It's not right, it's not right," but he won't tell me what he means by that. Maybe you can talk to him and find out? I'm scared. I feel like he's going to say something to Salvatore that he's going to regret. Can you come? Please."

"Of course I'll come. Where are you?"

"At the far end of the piazza, on the bench in front of the tourist office."

"I'll be there in twenty minutes." Nico clicked off. He grabbed as many dirty dishes as he could and took them to the kitchen. "I'm sorry, Tilde, I can't finish up. Nelli needs me in Greve."

Tilde looked up from scraping a pot. "Is she all right?"

"I hope so. I'll let you know later. Ciao." Nico lowered the dishes in the sink and rushed out.

"Give Nelli a hug for me," Tilde yelled.

"Ah, Nelli," Elvira said, looking up from her *Settimana Enigmistica* as Nico ran past her. "She finally lit a fire under your toes. About time."

NELLI AND PEPPINO STOOD up as Nico and OneWag walked across the piazza toward them. Peppino had regained his straight back, Nico noticed as he got nearer. His face looked rigid, determined. In contrast, Nelli, in her usual paint-splattered jeans and old shirt, looked diminished.

Nico kissed her cheeks and gave her hand a squeeze as OneWag stretched out his body against her legs. Nelli gave the dog a quick scratch on his head. "Thank you for coming, Nico."

"Glad to." He turned to Peppino, who impatiently shifted his weight from one foot to the other. "Salve, Peppino. Nelli tells me you want to see Maresciallo Perillo again."

Peppino stood still and nodded. "I must."

"Let's get away from here," Nico said as he took Nelli's arm.

Peppino didn't move.

"Come on, Peppino. We'll walk to the carabinieri station. It's not far."

"I know where it is. I don't need you."

Nelli freed herself from Nico's hold and tugged at Peppino's arm. "Tell Nico what is bothering you. He can help you. He's friends with Salvatore. I don't want you to have to pay for somebody else. Nico, stop him from going."

Nico took her hand again. "No, Nelli, I can't, I'm sorry. I think Peppino realized how serious his situation was during Perillo's interrogation of Diane this morning. He has something on his chest he needs to get out."

"He can tell us."

"No! Only the maresciallo and the brigadiere. I will tell them."

"We have no right to stop him, Nelli. I know you're trying to protect him, but he knows what he's doing."

Nelli's jaws clenched, her eyes coldly assessing Nico's face. He felt bad for disappointing her. "Not speaking up will only make things worse for him."

After a few seconds of assessing this man she thought she might have started to fall in love with, rethinking her feelings, Nelli shrugged and followed Peppino, who had started walking to the main street.

Taking advantage of their backs to him, Nico quickly phoned Perillo. "Peppino is coming. He has something he wants to tell you."

"Finally, the truth?"

"I hope so." Nico clicked off and, followed by OneWag, walked quickly to catch up with Nelli and Peppino. Halfway up the hill that led to the small park and the carabinieri station, Peppino started muttering, as if going over what he was going to say. Nico moved closer to him. "This morning at the station with Signora Severson was difficult for you, wasn't it?"

"She insisted I come," Peppino said. "I had the roses to clean. June is their month. They need care every day to keep them happy. The signore understood. She does not."

"Ah, that's why you looked uncomfortable. You were thinking of your roses."

"The brigadiere, he didn't take his eyes away from me. Those eyes said to me, 'Tell the truth.'"

"Now you will?"

"Yes."

"Why now?" Nelli asked.

"It's time."

When they reached the station, Peppino started to go inside. Nelli stopped him. "I'll come with you."

He lifted her arm from his. "I'm going alone."

She gave him a hug. "I'll wait for you here."

He kissed the top of her head. "Forgive me, Nelli. Take her home, Signor Nico. She likes you."

"Zio Peppino, I'm not going anywhere. Hurry up in there, and then I'll take you home and cook you the dish I made for your birthday. Ricotta ravioli with slices of pear. Remember? You practically ate the whole bowl!"

"Make that for Signor Nico, but thank you. Now, go home with your man."

"In bocca al lupo," Nico wished him.

"May the wolf croak." Peppino said before the station door closed behind him.

Nelli kept her eyes on the closed door.

"Will you come home with me?" Nico asked, touching her elbow.

Nelli flinched. "No, sorry. I'm all nerves. I'm angry with you and furious with Peppino. Maybe I'm not being fair, but I can't help it." She kept watch on the door, not noticing OneWag sitting at her feet, looking up at her. Part of her was hoping Peppino would come back out with a wave and a smile, as he had done after a visit to the cardiologist she had taken him to just two months ago. They had celebrated with his potato soup and a whole bottle of red. She knew it wasn't going to happen today. She turned toward Nico, who was standing by her side. "We'll have dinner some other time. Okay?"

Nico had looked forward to their evening. Now he found himself hurt, like a kid suddenly deprived of fun. It made him feel foolish and selfish. "Sure. Can I keep you company now? We can wait on one of the benches in the park. He might be a while."

"Forgive me, but I'd rather wait alone."

"As you wish." He walked away. After a few minutes, he looked back at Nelli. OneWag was still sitting at her feet. Nico whistled.

OneWag swiveled his head from one to the other of his favorite two-legs. "Go, Rocco," Nelli said. "I'll be fine."

OneWag ambled slowly toward Nico.

"BUONGIORNO AGAIN, SIGNOR RISSO," Perillo said from his desk as Vince brought Peppino into the office. He indicated the chair in front of him. "Please, sit." He noticed the change in the man. His tanned, wrinkled face now looked sculpted out of rock.

Peppino stopped behind the chair, standing very straight, as if at attention. He set his eyes on Daniele, who was standing in the back. Half a minute, if not more, passed in silence.

"How can the maresciallo help you?" Daniele said, keeping his voice soft to hide his excitement. It looked like his visit last night had worked.

Perillo glanced at Daniele. He sensed that there was some kind of rapport between the old man and the young one. Maybe it was best to leave Peppino to his sensitive brigadiere. He gave Daniele a nod of approval.

"You came here for a reason," Daniele reminded Peppino before sitting in front of the computer, ready to start typing.

The old man wiped his mouth with the back of his hand. "I did not believe Signora Diane when she told me about the sale of the villa." His voice was low and gruff. "I said, no, he would never do that. He promised. I worked hard for Signor Michele for fifteen years. We were friends, he said many times. Even though we are from different worlds, we are friends, he always said. In the afternoon, when he came home, I told him what the signora had told me. I said, 'She makes up stories because she is angry with you.'

"He laughed. 'You have the brain of a mule,' is what he said. 'You get an idea in your head, and no one is going to succeed in kicking it out of you.'" Peppino stopped and took a deep, shaking breath. "He said, 'Diane spoke the truth. The villa is sold. I need the money.'"

"But the promise?" Peppino spoke as if addressing Mantelli, not Daniele. His rock-hard face was transformed into a mask of disbelief. "You promised I would work here, for you, until I died." He shook his head, took another breath. "'You're a decrepit fool,' he said. 'You'll die soon enough.'"

The old man's knees seemed to give in. Perillo got out of his chair to help. Peppino raised a hand to stop him. "I will sit." He sank into the chair, bent over, his shoulders slumped, his eyes wet.

Daniele wanted to offer Peppino a glass of water, a little comfort and understanding, but he had to do his job, fingers poised on the keyboard. Giuseppe Risso was about to surrender the truth.

Peppino wiped his mouth again with the back of his hand. "What I came to say is that I am the one who killed Signor Michele." The tears his eyes had been holding back began to trickle down his rough cheeks. "I am a proud man. He insulted me. He took away my dignity, my peace. Taking care of the villa has been everything to me. It is my wife, my children, my relatives. It is my life. He took it away and made fun of me. I'm not making excuses, Maresciallo. I'm explaining why I put antifreeze in his whiskey glass. On Tuesday afternoon, he asked me for a whiskey. I would always remind him what the doctor said. Only one glass, Signor Michele." Peppino raised his index finger. "Only one glass." He dropped his hand back on his lap. "Tuesday I said nothing. Whiskey and antifreeze is what I gave him to make him sick, to have his stomach burn as he burned my heart. I wanted him to vomit until there was nothing left inside, because that was how I felt. I wanted him sick. Only sick. Not dead, never dead."

Perillo leaned forward on his desk. "What you have just told us is very interesting, but why did you wait until now to confess?"

"This morning, you accused Signora Diane of killing her husband. If not the signora, Signorina Loredana. That is not right. It is time for the truth."

"Are you certain it is the truth?" Perillo asked. "The carabinieri who came to the villa found only one unopened whiskey bottle. What happened to the bottle from which you poured the drink?"

"It was empty, so I threw it in the recycle bin."

"When?"

"Tuesday night. The recycling dumpster is cleaned out on Wednesday mornings."

Perillo sat back in his chair. No wonder the men didn't find anything. They'd gone to the house on Thursday evening. "Peppino, I'm going to ask you to repeat your confession, but before you do, I want you to think hard about the consequences. You will go to jail for a very long time. If your only crime is throwing away a tainted bottle, your jail time will be much shorter."

"I did not want him to die, but I am the one who killed him.

I am telling the truth." Peppino wiped his wet cheeks with his calloused hands and straightened his back to stare at Perillo.

Perillo reached for the office phone and called Tarani. Since the capitano was still in charge, why not let him come down and take this poor man to jail.

After checking for typos, Daniele sent Peppino's statement to the printer. He sat back in his chair for a moment. He was tired, relieved and sad. Yes, Loredana was innocent, but Peppino was a good man who didn't deserve to spend what was left of his life in jail. "Would you like a glass of water?" he asked Peppino.

"No, thank you, Brigadiere Donato, but a favor, please."

Daniele shot up. "Yes, how can I help?"

"Nelli is waiting outside for me. Can you please tell her to go home?"

"We can bring her in," Perillo offered. "Don't you want to say goodbye?"

Peppino's attention was on Daniele. "She will need your kindness."

"I will do my best."

As Daniele crossed the room, Perillo told him, "Get Vince to bring in the statement from the printer, plus the camera and the fingerprinting kit. You will have to be patient, Signor Peppino. Capitano Tarani is in Florence. It will take him an hour to get here." He leaned across his desk again. He would have liked to have Nico's courage and dismiss what this man had told him, but he couldn't. There was no weapon to hide. The only way he knew how to help him now was to say. "You must be hungry. The café next door has delicious sandwiches—what would you like?"

NICO SAT OUT ON the balcony. All that was left of the sun on the darkening sky was a thin, pink-edged fading orange streak. OneWag had been fed and was asleep at his feet; the three swallows had come home and tucked themselves between the roof and beams for the night. Usually it was his favorite time of the day. Tonight, he missed Nelli. What Peppino ended up telling Perillo would hurt her, and he could do nothing about it. He dug into the big bowl on his lap for the last spoonful of chocolate gelato, his go-to Italian pain reliever. To make things worse, Perillo was taking his bloody time clueing him in on what Peppino had told him.

The phone call came just as he got up to take the empty bowl and spoon to the sink.

He picked up the phone and swiped. "Is it over?"

"Daniele was right. It wasn't Loredana."

Nelli's anguished face flashed in front of Nico's eyes. "He's admitted Diane asked him to throw out the bottle."

"No. He's confessed to killing Mantelli."

Nico sat back down, his mind instantly refusing the possibility. "It can't be. He's covering for her."

"You're letting your emotions cloud your thinking," Perillo said.

"You believe he's telling the truth?"

"I'd like not to. Peppino Risso is a good, simple man who didn't know what he was doing. I do believe him. So does Tarani."

"Nelli was waiting for him outside. Does she know?"

"Yes. Peppino asked Daniele to tell her. She didn't seem surprised, Daniele thinks. She just nodded, thanked him and walked away."

Nico wanted to kick himself for leaving her. He should at least have stayed nearby. "It's over, then."

"The Mantelli case is over, but the outcome is not something I want to celebrate. Dani feels the same way, despite being right about Loredana. Peppino will need a very good lawyer. Maybe he can get involuntary manslaughter. He could get away with doing five years."

"Maybe Diane will help. She'll know the right people."

"I hope so."

"You have one more death to deal with. Any news on Lore-dana's autopsy?"

"Tarani thinks he'll get it tomorrow. He promised he'll email it as soon as he's read it. I'd wish you buonanotte, but I know it's not going to be a good night for you. Nelli is a good friend of yours. I can wish you some sleep."

"Same to you." He clicked off and sat back down to stare ahead at what was now blackness punctured by stars. He wanted to call Nelli, offer his shoulder to cry on, but she had preferred being alone earlier. They were not good friends as Perillo thought. They were friendly, but knew so little of each other. He had hoped dinner tonight would bring them closer to real friendship. Maybe something more.

Nico checked the time. It wasn't too late to call. He reached for the phone again. "Hi, Diane. Nico here."

"Peppino confessed?"

"Yes. You knew?"

"I suspected. I feel sorry for him. I know he didn't want to kill Michele, but I must say I am relieved for myself."

"He needs a good criminal lawyer. Can you help?"

"I do know a lot of people. I'll ask around. Peppino doesn't deserve any jail time. I'll make a few phone calls and let you know."

"Thanks, Diane. You're a good woman."

Her laughter came across the line strong and clear. "That's the first time I've ever heard that said about me. Goodnight, Nico." The line went dead.

Nico kept the phone in his hand and texted:

DEAREST NELLI, I AM SO SORRY. I WISH I COULD MAKE YOU FEEL BETTER. PLEASE KNOW THAT IF YOU EVER NEED A SHOULDER, I AM HERE FOR YOU. NICO

SIXTEEN

Ten o'clock the next morning Nico was in Tilde's kitchen cutting slices of prosciutto in thin strips to toss them with thinly sliced mushrooms into a deep pot in which butter was simmering. After he was done, he watched Tilde add cream, a small amount of tomato sauce and several fistfuls of grated Parmigiano.

Tilde stirred with a wooden spoon and stepped back from the stove. "Your turn."

Nico picked up a fat lemon and grated the peel into the skillet. At lunchtime, the sauce would coat plates of small maccheroni. "Did you come up with this dish?"

"It's a Paolo Petroni recipe. If you want a Tuscan cookbook, he's the best. Any news from Nelli?"

"She texted back just as I came here. 'Thank you.' Nothing else."

"Give her space. When her father died, she disappeared from view for over a month. Peppino was her last link to him."

"What about her mother?"

Tilde stopped stirring and looked at Nico in surprise. "You really don't know anything about Nelli, do you?"

"We don't see each other that much. She's stopped having breakfast at the café."

"Well, when you see her next, which might be a while, ask questions. Get her talking."

"I'm not very good at that. Rita did all the talking."

Tilde laughed. "I know she did." She turned off the burner. "I'll give this a rest until the orders start coming in. If you have nothing better to do, Alba could use some help setting the tables."

"What happened to Nelli's mother?"

"She died of an aneurysm when Nelli was six. She only had her father until he died about four or five years ago."

"Understood. Thanks." He walked out of the kitchen and went over to Elvira, who handed him the pile of napkins she'd just folded. Folding napkins and opinionated comments were her daily contributions to her restaurant. "I'm sorry about your girlfriend."

Nico grabbed the napkins. "Nelli's not my girlfriend."

"Your loss, then. It's time you stop—"

Nico's phone rang. He tucked the napkins under his arm and reached into his pocket. "Sorry Elvira. I have to take this."

Elvira raised her eyebrows. "You don't know who's calling."

Nico looked at the screen. "I do. The maresciallo." He walked toward the terrace.

Elvira took another napkin from the pile and started folding it on her lap. "Fine. I'll keep my lecture for another time."

A burst of sunlight hit Nico as he walked out onto the terrace. He put up his hands to shade his eyes. Alba waved at him.

"Let me start out by saying I never believed in horoscopes," Perillo said, "but holy heaven, I am beginning to think the astrologists are on to something."

Tucking his phone to his ear with his shoulder, Nico started distributing napkins. Perillo was always a talker. When he was upset, his mouth sprung a leak.

"Ivana did my horoscope at the beginning of the month. She always does that, and I ignore the results. This month, I should have listened. She repeated it last night. The sun is in reverse, Mercury is rising somewhere. The result? Bad news. I've certainly had that in the past two weeks. And now . . ." Perillo paused for dramatic effect.

"And now?" Nico dutifully asked. He pulled out a chair from a table outside and sat down. "I don't know about you, but I have work to do."

"Tarani sent the report, as promised. Loredana was suffocated. The pentobarbital was administered to make it look like a suicide. Whoever did it either didn't know how much was needed to kill and had to use the pillow or the reverse."

"Did they find any fibers?"

"They found a lot in her mouth, under her fingernails and some on her clothes. She must have bitten whatever was suffocating her. The pentobarbital looks like it came later. They sent what they gathered to the lab to be tested. It might take a few days. Today, Tarani wants to discuss possible suspects and said to bring you in for the discussion. Are you willing?"

"I can't before four this afternoon."

"Good. I can have lunch."

"Well, buon appetito. See you at four." He clicked off. He had another phone call to make. He walked under the shade of the fig tree. "Hi, Diane. Is this a bad moment?"

"Not at all. Life is looking a little brighter these days. The deposit check from the buyers just came through, and my son is coming home in three weeks. I did spread the word to my Milanese friends about a good criminal lawyer. One friend says he knows of one, but wants to check with him first before giving his name."

"That's great. That's why I called. Thank you very much."

"It's nice of you to care about Peppino, or is it because of his friend Nelli?"

Nico didn't answer.

"Sorry, none of my business. Peppino deserves all the help he can get. I'm trying to keep up his work in the garden, but I don't have his touch or his patience. I'll call you as soon as I have a name." The line went dead.

Alba came under the fig tree, kissed Nico's cheeks and handed him the basket half full of flatware. "Your turn now, Nico bello. I'll bring out the plates."

"THANK YOU FOR JOINING us," Capitano Tarani said as Nico and OneWag walked up the slight slope of the park to reach the benches sitting under the oak trees. The three men stood, all dressed casually. Tarani had a more human dimension without his immaculate uniform and boots. He no longer seemed like a store mannequin. Even the tightness of his face had eased.

They shook hands. "I'm happy to help in any way I can." Nico stepped into the shade of the trees and eyed the empty benches. "Do you mind if I sit?" After four hours at the restaurant, he was eager to be off his feet. He was also thinking of Perillo, who wouldn't suggest sitting in front of Tarani no matter how much his knee hurt. Nico sat at the far end of one of the benches. OneWag, after a quick inspection of everyone's shoes, wandered off on a longer sniffing expedition.

Tarani chose the other bench and watched the few passersby walk on the street below for a few moments. No one spoke before he did. "It is unusual for me to conduct business in a park in plain view, but then, involving an American ex-homicide detective is also unusual." He indicated the empty space on his bench. "Maresciallo, Brigadiere, please sit down. I do agree that sitting in the shade of old trees with the hint of a breeze is far more pleasant than a hot office."

"Glad you think so, Capitano." Perillo sat down on Tarani's bench. Daniele, pen and notebook already in hand, joined Nico.

"Possible suspects?" Tarani asked.

"It would be convenient to believe Peppino was responsible for Loredana's death too," Perillo said, "but I find it highly unlikely."

A fidgeting Daniele pushed himself to the edge of the bench, eager to speak.

Tarani turned to Perillo. "She might have known he had killed Mantelli and perhaps tried to blackmail him."

"Go on, Dani," Nico said in a low voice.

Color flooded Daniele's face. "If I may, Capitano, killing someone by poison is a passive gesture. You drop something in a glass or food. Time passes between the gesture and the death. You don't even have to be present. And Peppino didn't mean to kill Mantelli."

"That's right," Perillo said. "I believe he simply wanted to punish Mantelli by making him sick."

"Loredana's murder was an aggressive gesture," Daniele continued. "Whoever killed Loredana watched her die, made it happen with their own hands. I don't think Peppino is capable of being that cold-blooded."

Perillo agreed. "Well said, Daniele." He was surprised and proud Daniele had found the courage to speak up. "Now, I think Diane Severson is quite capable of watching her victim die. She's a very strong woman and has a clear motive."

Tarani leaned back and crossed his long legs as though he were sitting on a plush sofa and not on a rough wooden bench. No longer a mannequin, Nico thought, at least today, but still a man of authority.

Tarani turned his head toward Nico. "What do you think, Signor Doyle? You've spent time with her."

Annoyed, Nico managed to keep his face neutral. He'd dress down blabbermouth Perillo later. He'd been summoned here as an expert on Diane. "I've only had a few exchanges with her, but she strikes me as a very strong, capable woman. Also intelligent. She does have a possible motive, but a hard one to prove."

Perillo threw his hands up. "Money! It seems Mantelli had a gambling habit, but to lose all his money to gambling? It doesn't make sense. Even if he did, Diane Severson doesn't believe that. She thought Loredana knew where it was. Loredana didn't know or if she did, she wouldn't tell. After Daniele called her to come to the station for more questioning, she could have panicked and called Diane for help. Diane wasn't going to help her unless Loredana revealed where the money was. Say Loredana decided that being penniless was better than years in jail and told. With her beauty, she probably thought she could find another rich man to take care of her. Then Diane could have picked her up, suffocated her with a pillow she'd brought and injected her with the drug."

"It's a reasonable possibility." Tarani uncrossed his legs and leaned his torso forward, planting elbows on his knees. "Severson would have had to buy the syringe and the drug in advance."

"Not necessarily," Perillo said. "Loredana could have kept a spare of both, in case withdrawal was too painful."

"But Diane wouldn't have known that." Nico said. He thought Perillo's theory was based on too many *ifs*, not that his theory was any better. "Has anything been retrieved from Loredana's smashed phone?" he asked Tarani.

"Unfortunately, the technical lab wasn't able to retrieve anything."

"There is another possible suspect," Nico said.

Tarani gave Nico his undivided attention. "Who?"

"Luca Verdini. According to Diane, Loredana was very interested in Verdini. I saw them together once. Verdini was very happy to be rid of her."

"Why would he kill her?" Tarani asked.

"Verdini claims he was paying eight hundred euros a month out of gratitude for Mantelli putting him on the map of excellent vintners. I find that hard to believe. Mantelli had loaned money to two other vintners. The money Verdini was paying back could also be a loan. Ida and Diane both said that Loredana was going through Mantelli's drawers, closets, obviously looking for something."

"Information on his money," Perillo said. "What else is there?"

"A loan agreement with Verdini. A loan he would have to continue paying back to Diane. Loredana needed money badly. Maybe she thought she could get some from Verdini by threatening to tell Diane about Mantelli's loan. It's worth looking into."

Perillo reluctantly nodded his agreement. Diane as the culprit made much more sense to him. Daniele didn't care. Finding out who had killed Loredana wouldn't bring her back.

Tarani stood. Perillo and Daniele did the same. Nico was slower to follow. "We know what we need to do. We will check Severson's phone and her computer. I'll ask Della Langhe for a search warrant to do a proper sweep of Mantelli's villa. The prosecutor will not be happy, but it is necessary. His reluctance to accuse Severson has an advantage. It will allow me to obtain a search warrant for Verdini's property as well, even though the connection to the victim is tenuous. Maybe luck will be on our side, and we'll find a pillow or blanket with fibers matching those found in Loredana's mouth. Never discount the role of Signora Fortuna in solving crimes. I will be returning to Florence now. Thank you all." He shook hands with the three of them and walked away.

As soon as Tarani was out of sight, Perillo sat back down with a thump. Daniele sat more gently.

"You look stuffed," Nico said, sitting next to Perillo.

"I am."

"What did Ivana make you for lunch?"

Daniele smiled and wiggled his index finger in the hollow of his cheek, a gesture that meant "delicious."

Perillo grinned. "A pasticcio of penne with artichokes, shallots, mushrooms and Parmigiano, of course. What is 'pasticcio' in English?"

"A mess?"

"Pasticcio is more elegant than that," Perillo said. "A combination of ingredients held together by the miracle of a pink besciamella sauce. It is a gift from the heavens."

Nico stood up. "Sounds excellent. I suggest a long walk or no dinner. Talk to you tomorrow. I'm going back to the restaurant."

Nico and OneWag left them dreaming of their last meal.

DIANE CALLED LATE THAT night while Nico was watering the vegetable garden.

"I've got good news."

"That's always welcome. Hold on a sec." He walked over to the wall to turn off the water. "Okay, I'm listening."

"My friends found a very good lawyer who's eager to take on Peppino's case pro bono. He's been defending ultra-rich clients; he's swimming in money and loves the idea of defending a gardener. Says it will give him good publicity. I'm assuming you don't care about his reasoning."

"I don't, as long as he's good."

"He'll get Peppino the minimum sentence."

The tension Nico had carried inside him since Peppino's confession eased. "This is wonderful news. I don't know how to thank you."

"I could ask you to seduce me, but that's only fun if we both want it, so maybe we can have a drink together instead—somewhere that doesn't need your waiter services. I'm leaving the villa in two weeks, so before then?"

"Of course. You pick the place. Again, I'm very grateful."

"Don't be. Gratitude makes an evening drink awkward. Sweet dreams." She clicked off.

Nico whistled. OneWag took his time to appear. "Come here, you mutt." He picked up the dog and gave him a hug, one he would have liked to give to Nelli with the good news. But it was past midnight, too late to call.

SATURDAY MORNING, GOGOL DIDN'T show up for breakfast. Nico waited until nine o'clock. At least now, he could go ahead and call Nelli. He'd check on Gogol at the old-age home after the call. He walked out into the piazza. The Bench Boys greeted him with raised hands. He called out, "Buongiorno. Beautiful weather, isn't it?" All four looked up to check the sky, which was as blue as it had been the whole month.

"It's cooler today," Nico said. A strong breeze was swaying the leaves and flowers of the two linden trees. He breathed in the scent.

"At our age, we like the heat," Gustavo said. "It cushions our bones." All four wore sweaters.

One day, his bones would need cushioning too, but today, Diane's good news and the cooler weather made him feel that day was very far away. He sat on an empty bench on the other side of the piazza and called Nelli.

"Ciao, Nico." Her voice was soft and low. "I'm sorry I disappeared that day. I was going to text you."

"There's no need to apologize. I hope I'm not disturbing you, but I have some good news." He told her about the lawyer Diane had found for Peppino. "He'll do it for free."

Nelli let out a long sigh. "Thank you for telling me." He had refrained from mentioning his involvement in procuring the lawyer. "I'm in my studio next to the art center. Come by."

Two heart-warming words, and yet he hesitated. He convinced himself it was for a good reason. "I should check on Gogol first. I'm worried about him. He stood me up this morning."

Over the phone came the wonderful sound of a small laugh—a giggle, really. "Gogol is here with me."

Nico laughed too. "I'll be right over."

NELLI, IN HER USUAL painter's attire, stood in a corner of the small room watching over a large gurgling moka sitting on a hot plate. Nico wanted to walk over and at least give her the usual ciao with the double cheek kiss, but didn't know if it would be welcome. OneWag had no hesitations. He stretched himself up against her legs.

She scratched the dog's head. "Missed you."

"Ah, to be a dog," Gogol said.

"Want some coffee?" she asked Nico with a half smile on her face. OneWag had settled at her feet. "There's enough for all three."

"Thank you, no. I've had enough waiting for this gentleman." Gogol was perched on a stool, arms crossed over his thighs, his coat hanging down to the floor. "Nelli beckoned me."

"I did not, but I'm glad you came. You cheered me up with your lovely quotes. I'm grateful."

"'Great sorrow took hold of my heart when I heard her.'"

"It's him, not her," Nelli corrected. "*Inferno*, fourth canto."

"Brava." Gogol held out his hand to take the cup. "I adapt for the occasion." He looked at Nico. "She gives satisfaction." With full cup in hand, he carefully slid off the stool. "I will take my coffee for a walk to cool it down."

"Don't forget to bring back the cup," Nelli told his back. "And thank you for the visit."

"'After I let my tired body rest awhile, I took to the road again.'"

"See you Monday," Nico said.

Gogol didn't answer.

"Sit," Nelli said pointing to the vacated stool. There were no chairs. The space was small and simple. The walls were covered with Nelli's small abstract paintings of a barely recognizable Tuscan countryside. More paintings were stacked vertically underneath the table. A table pushed against a wall had tubes of oil paint scattered over it. The hot plate rested on the far end. Above the table, three small open windows looked onto a patch of dirt and weeds. A small refrigerator in a corner. A wooden easel faced the windows. Nelli moved to her painting stool with her big cup of coffee. OneWag followed, while Nico replaced Gogol on the other stool.

"I owe you an apology," she said.

"You do not."

"Nico, please be quiet and listen. I was very angry with you for not helping me stop Peppino. You see, I knew what he was going to say, or at least sensed it. He was so upset after Mantelli's death. He blamed it on the sale, but if that was the reason, where was his anger? I saw only pain, too much of it, and then I began to see guilt. The more I tried to help him, soothe him, the more he turned away from me with furtive looks. It's hard for me to explain, and I suppose hard to understand. I saw it in his eyes. He's such a good man, a pure heart. I had no doubt he didn't mean to kill the man. I didn't want him to suffer for a mistake, even a fatal one, and I stupidly tried to stop him. You were right. Not telling would have made him suffer even more than being locked up in jail." She took a long sip of her coffee.

Nico stood up and opened up his arms. "Can I please give you a hug?"

Nelli shook her head. "I'll spill the coffee, and what's worse, I'll crumble, and you'll have to sweep me up from the floor. I haven't cleaned it in weeks." She looked at his face. She was no longer angry. She missed him, but she felt too in need now. She must not lean on him. "We'll have a nice dinner together soon."

"That sounds good. I put the apple pie in the freezer." He smiled to hide his disappointment. "Let me know."

"I will."

Nico left the studio. The fact that OneWag stayed with Nelli filled Nico with almost parental pride. His mutt understood when one needed comfort.

THE SEARCH WARRANTS CAME through on Monday. So did

the lab report on the fibers. Instead of calling Nico with the information, Perillo decided to surprise him at Sotto Il Fico.

"Ehi, Perillo, ciao." Nico was at the bar right by the entrance, filling a tray with six espressos Enzo had just made. The lunch service was almost over. "News?"

Perillo didn't answer. "Ciao, Enzo. Can I have one of those?"

"Coming up," Enzo said, wearing his usual Florentine soccer shirt. "Glad to have you here. It's been a while."

"They keep me busy in Greve. Nico, do you have much longer?"

"These six are my last diners."

"I'll have my coffee outside while I wait for you."

Enzo handed over the coffee. "Have you found who killed that poor woman yet?"

"Getting close."

"Good. Can I get you anything else?"

"No thanks. Say hello to your mother."

"She's fast asleep in the back. She'll be sorry she missed you."

Tilde rushed into the front room. "I heard your voice. Ciao, Salvatore." She kissed his cheeks. "How is Ivana?"

"Doing well."

Tilde punched his arm lightly. "Damn it, let her out of the kitchen for once. Bring her here one night."

"I'll do that."

Tilde studied him for the few seconds it took him to drink his espresso. "You look like you've swallowed a firecracker."

The firecracker in his pocket was about to light up the night sky. "A little bit of indigestion, that's all."

"Not on Ivana's food," Tilde said. "I guess we'll find out soon enough. I've got a kitchen to clean. Don't forget to bring Ivana."

On the way to the kitchen Tilde crossed paths with Nico. "I hope I won't have to wait for the newspaper to find out."

"Find out what?"

"Salvatore will tell you."

"Are you all right?" Nico asked Perillo after they stepped outside the restaurant. His eyes looked feverish.

"Tired, relieved, excited."

"You have news."

"We can talk in the church. Don Alfonso just reopened it." The church doors of Sant'Agnese closed at noon and reopened at two.

They walked up the three ramps of stone stairs. Cool air enveloped them as they stepped into the darkness of the church. The only other living creature inside was OneWag, asleep at the foot of St. Francis. At the sound of footsteps, he lifted his head. He blinked sleepily at Nico with a wag of his tail.

"What are you doing here?" Nico whispered. "Shame on you. Get out." OneWag blinked again.

"Leave him be. Sit down and read this." The dog went back to sleep on the cold marble floor. Perillo dug into his jeans and came out with a folded white piece of paper. He unfolded it and handed it to Nico.

Nico read it standing up. Read it and reread it. "It's done."

"Yes. Daniele and Tarani's men went over there this morning with the search warrant. They found everything they needed. Now I'm going to light a candle to thank whatever saint brought us such luck."

"This was solved by arrogance, not luck."

"I guess you're right. To the devil with the candle. Let's go to Bar All'Angolo with your blasphemous dog and have a glass."

"A very good idea. Come on, OneWag, back into the heat."

SEVENTEEN

Saturday night, four days after Loredana's killer was arrested, Nico and OneWag walked over to the Ferriello vineyard for Aldo's second out-of-jail celebration. He had picked a good night, Nico thought. The unusual June heat had suddenly retreated midmorning, as if finally conceding that the Tuscans needed a breather. As he walked across the vineyard's parking lot, he met up with Daniele and Stella, who had come up from Florence for the night. She gave Nico a hug. She looked pretty in wide calf-length white slacks and a loose sleeveless turquoise tunic that made her green eyes shine.

Daniele and Nico greeted each other.

"Is Nelli coming?" Stella asked as they walked to the Ferri house at the end of a short graveled road.

"She said she wasn't quite up to celebrating yet."

Daniele reached his arm out to Nico. "But didn't you tell her about Peppino's case getting a big boost?"

"I did, but she knows murder is going to be talked about tonight. She'd rather not hear."

"The maresciallo convinced his wife to come," Daniele said, "and she hates anything to do with death."

"I guess I'm not as persuasive."

Stella slipped her arm in Nico's. "I'm sorry, Zio Nico. I was so looking forward to giving her a big hug."

Me too, Nico thought.

Perillo and Ivana waited for them before going to the garden behind the house. Instead of his usual jeans, Perillo wore pressed navy slacks with a blue and white striped shirt with rolled-up sleeves. Ivana had dressed in a straight red skirt and a white linen blouse trimmed with lace.

"Buonasera, Signora," Nico said, feeling awkward. He didn't know whether to offer his hand or kiss her cheeks.

"Ivana, do you remember Nico?"

"Of course, we met last year at your party. Buonasera." She was too short to reach his face and blew him a kiss instead. "Salvatore, Daniele and you are the three musketeers of Chianti. At least that's how I think of you."

"One for all," Daniele chimed in, "and all for one."

"Thank you. I consider that a compliment," Nico said. Her soft round face broke into a smile.

"Ehi, what are you waiting for?" Aldo walked toward them, his vast white apron flapping with each step. "I heard your voices and popped the champagne."

They walked to the back garden, a large square space covered in grass and flagstones. On one side, a wide, waist-high fireplace was embedded in a thick stone wall. Thick logs burned under a coating of ash.

Nico went over to look at the amount of meat on the grill. Pork chops, sausages, steaks, chicken. A mesh sheet was covered in blistered peppers, charred eggplant slices, whole carrots and fat slices of onions. A basting brush rested next to a bowl of oil, garlic and chili peppers. To one side, thick slices of bread waited to be brushed with oil and garlic. Chopped tomatoes sat in a blue bowl. That meant bruschetta—the *ch* pronounced like a *k*, as Rita often had to remind him.

Nico looked back at Aldo, who was pouring champagne into seven flutes on a round wooden table already set. "Aldo, we're going to have to eat until morning to finish all this," Nico said.

"My wine will help to digest it all, but first, a toast."

Everyone picked up their flutes.

"Cinzia, come out here," Aldo shouted.

Cinzia walked out of the kitchen, holding a large red and blue patterned bowl with a towel, which she placed on the table. "The beans had to finish cooking." She looked radiant in a white dress with a single row of blue flowers and leaves along the hem and low neckline.

Aldo handed her a flute and raised his own. "I toast Nico, for believing in me and working hard to prove my innocence."

"Thanks, Aldo. I only did it to get a break on rent." He got laughs. Aldo had in fact offered to lower his rent out of gratitude, but Nico had refused. His rent was already low, and last year had been a shaky one for the vineyard.

Aldo toasted Perillo next. "I know arresting me was Capitano Tarani's doing, not yours, and you worked hard to solve the case, which means I must forgive you."

"Thank you," Perillo said. "I regret not having the choice."

"I didn't want to forgive you," Cinzia added with one of her roguish smiles, "until I met your wife tonight." She raised her flute. "Ivana, I toast you for having to forgive him every day."

Ivana covered her laughter with her hand.

"And to Daniele," Aldo added, "the quiet young man who gets the work done."

Daniele clasped Stella's hand as he turned fiery red. His reaction brought laughter, deepening the bloom to purple.

Aldo spread out his arms. "Now that we all get along again, please, to the table. Nico, a hand?"

"Sure." They walked over to the fireplace. Aldo handed Nico a large platter on which he dropped the grilled meats and vegetables, surrounding them with the bread and tomatoes. OneWag had followed Nico and now sat at Aldo's feet, his nose raised high to inhale the scrumptious smell.

"You're going to tell us how it ended, aren't you, Nico? The papers only told us about the arrest. We want all the details."

"Ask Perillo. It's his story—his and Daniele's."

Aldo, his face red from the heat of the fire, eyed Nico skeptically. "You're telling me that you had nothing to do with it?"

"Very little."

"That I don't believe." Aldo took the platter from Nico and held it high. "Here it comes. I want no leftovers." Cinzia moved her bowl of steaming beans with garlic cloves, fresh sage and olive oil to one side to make room for the platter. She started pouring Ferriello Riserva in everyone's wine glass amidst sighs, laughter, remarks. "Mamma mia, you emptied the butcher shop." "The smell alone is enough to fill you." "I won't eat again for a week." And a chorus of "Buon appetito."

Time passed. The sun's color deepened as it dipped closer to the horizon. The sky picked up streaks of pink and orange, the color of ripe peaches. The platter was emptying out. More bottles were uncorked and poured. Stella fed OneWag tidbits under the table. Daniele wished Stella would never go back to Florence. Ivana wondered if she ever would have a real home with a cooking fireplace. Nico and Perillo waited. Nico had already told Perillo earlier to keep him out of the story.

"Maresciallo Perillo," Aldo said after wiping his mouth with a cloth napkin. "Please tell us how you found Loredana's murderer, Luca Verdini."

"Yes, please," Cinzia and Stella said, almost in unison. Ivana remained quiet. Her husband had warned her. She had come anyway because she was proud of her Salva.

"Arrogance." Perillo wiped his mouth, and pushed his chair back a few inches from the table to see everyone better. Ivana brushed his hand lightly. He understood. Don't be pompous. "The medical examiner found fibers and hair in her mouth. Hair also on her clothes. The hair turned out to be from an Irish setter.

Verdini owns one. Armed with a search warrant, we went through his home and his property. This is where his arrogance comes in. Instead of destroying the pillow he had used to suffocate the poor woman, he was sitting on it in a chair next to his tasting shed. The fibers matched. So did the hair. He was surprised when we arrived with the search warrant. He had no doubt that we would think Loredana had committed suicide."

"I heard she was a drug addict," Cinzia said.

"She was. That's what made him think he would get away with her murder."

Aldo put his wine glass down. "The reason?"

"Loredana knew Mantelli had loaned Verdini a lot of money to get him started on ColleVerde. Mantelli's wife did not. With Mantelli now dead, Verdini could keep the money he still hadn't paid back."

"How much?" Aldo asked.

"A hundred and fifty thousand euros, given to him in cash. Mantelli's bank manager gave us that information. The withdrawal was made exactly one month before Verdini sent his first payment to Mantelli. Verdini had paid back a little more than nineteen thousand when Mantelli was killed. We think Loredana had found the loan papers to prove it, and she wanted a share of the money owed, or she'd tell the wife. Verdini would then have had to keep paying off the loan to her son, who had inherited Mantelli's estate."

"Why did he need a loan?" Cinzia asked. "His father owns a slew of five-star hotels all over Europe."

"Verdini's father had broken off relations with his son, though he has hired a big lawyer to defend him."

"How did he get the pentobarbital?" Aldo asked, reaching over to refill Perillo's glass.

Perillo covered the glass with his hand. He'd had enough wine, food and talking. "Daniele is the man who discovered how.

Behind his young blushing face is an impressive mind, which takes over when mine sputters." Under the table, he reached for Ivana's hand. "Tell them, Daniele."

Daniele blushed. Perillo had warned him he would have to speak. He had rehearsed his lines, gone over them while playing with the vegetables that had been cooked too close to the meats for his comfort. He hadn't touched his wine.

Stella tugged at his sleeve. "Go on."

He sat up. "In this country, you can get the drug online on some end-of-life sites," Daniele said, "but it takes time to receive them. Verdini was in a hurry. The drug is also used by veterinarians to put animals to sleep. I decided to pay a visit to the vet in Greve on Monday and asked if he had recently examined a female Irish setter. I was lucky. Verdini had brought in his dog a week before. I asked what was wrong with the dog. The vet answered he had no idea why the dog had been brought in. She was in perfect shape. That led me to ask if he was missing any pentobarbital. He keeps it locked away, with the key in a drawer in his desk. Verdini could easily have taken it."

Nico stepped in. "When I visited Verdini and complimented his dog, he told me he'd had to put down her mother just a few months earlier. He must have seen then where the key was kept."

"A bottle was missing." Daniele said before sitting back down with relief. It was over.

"Well done," Stella whispered.

"Thank you for telling us," Aldo said. "I'm happy to know we are in very good hands with Salvatore and Daniele," he turned to Nico, "with some helpful advice from our American friend."

The garden lights turned on automatically. Ten minutes after nine, and it was now finally dark.

"It's the longest day of the year," Ivana said.

It certainly felt like it, Nico thought. The three women got up to clear the plates and bring in new ones. Aldo went to get some cognac and his dessert wine.

Stella and Ivana came back from the kitchen and sat back down at the table.

"I have no more room," Nico said.

"Without dessert, no good meal is complete," Perillo said. Stella patted her flat stomach. Ivana beamed. Daniele blushed for seemingly no reason.

"Here it comes," Aldo announced after filling everyone's small dessert glasses. Cinzia walked out of the kitchen, holding a round platter. "Ivana and Daniele made this together."

"No, no," Ivana said. "Daniele made it." Cinzia lowered the platter to show off a tiramisù covered in cocoa powder.

"I watched to learn," Ivana said. "Tiramisù is not a Neapolitan dish. We have sfogliatelle, babà au rhum, pastiera."

Cinzia went around the table and kissed Ivana's cheek, then Daniele's. "A wonderful gift, thank you."

Nico slipped his fork in the soft layers of espresso-soaked cookies, cocoa powder and mascarpone mixed with eggs whipped with sugar. The tiramisù was the best he'd ever eaten, but he couldn't take another bite. He was half-drunk, his stomach stuffed even though the rest of him felt empty. It was a feeling that he remembered from his New York days. When a case was over, the guys would go out for a drink to celebrate, feeling satisfied yet empty. Once he was home with Rita, that feeling disappeared. He'd been lucky. Now he was alone with a dog. Nico realized the wine was making him feel sorry for himself. *Get a grip*, he thought.

He sat in his chair and watched the others enjoying themselves. These were his friends. This was his new life. Tomorrow he'd help out at the restaurant. Monday morning, he'd meet Gogol again and listen to Dante quotes he didn't understand.

He'd help out at the restaurant, Alba teasing him and Tilde and Enzo grateful for his much-needed help. In the afternoon, fresh flowers for Rita. He had a good life.

"Before everyone staggers home," Aldo raised a fork, "my mother always said that there is no such thing as a coincidence, and I have always believed her, God rest her soul." He blew a kiss to the sky. "Doesn't everyone think that the gardener killing Mantelli was very convenient for Verdini?"

"Nico, this one is yours," Perillo said, happy he could finish off the big mound of tiramisu on his plate.

"In this case, your mother was right," Nico said. "Fortunately, Peppino has a very good lawyer, thanks to Diane Severson. During their meeting in jail, Peppino said, 'He didn't tell me it could kill.' The lawyer wanted to know who 'he' was. Peppino told him. Verdini had called the villa on Tuesday. Peppino apparently answered gruffly—he'd just found out about the sale. Verdini asked him what was wrong. Peppino explained and added how upset he was. Verdini saw his opportunity and told Peppino a long story about a friend paying back a man who had insulted him by putting a hundred milliliters of antifreeze in his drink. He said the man was sick for a few hours then apologized."

"The seed was planted," Aldo said. "But if Peppino hadn't gone through with it?"

"Verdini would have killed Mantelli himself," Perillo said, leaning into the table and getting cocoa powder on his shirt. Ivana shook her head with a sigh. "We looked into ColleVerde's finances. Sales were good, but a lot of distributors owed him money. Some had no intention of paying him, claiming he had sent them inferior wines. He couldn't afford to keep paying back the loan and interest. This is the end of the story."

"I want to know what will happen to his Irish setter," Stella said.

"His ex-wife took her," Nico said. OneWag started barking.

Nico tried to quiet the dog without success. "I think he's trying to tell me something."

"Perhaps that it's time to go home," Ivana said.

"I think you're right." Nico stood up. The others got up too. OneWag took off. "This was wonderful. Thank you both."

"Leave everything on the table, please," Cinzia said. "I have someone in the kitchen to help."

There were many thank-yous and buonanottes exchanged, cheeks kissed, hands shaken. Perillo offered Nico a ride home.

"Thanks, I need to walk it off."

WHEN NICO GOT HOME twenty minutes later, Nelli was sitting on the steps of the house with OneWag in her lap. The lamp above the door kept her face in shadow. She had chosen that spot on purpose. She felt bold, and at the same time as shy as a sixteen-year-old. "Today was the first day of summer and the longest day. I wanted to celebrate it, so here I am."

Nico felt his whole body smile as he sat next to her. He looked at his watch. "We only have five minutes left."

"Then hurry, give me a hug."

OneWag slipped off her lap to give them room.

Sitting on the steps, they came together in an awkward hug, their backs twisted and their chests not touching.

Nelli pulled back and held her face up to the light. The shyness was gone. "Maybe we can celebrate more comfortably?"

"Good idea," He lifted her up and didn't hug her again, in case standing was what she meant by comfortably. She took his hand and led him up the stairs.

OneWag, being a wise mutt, chose the sofa as his bed that night.

ACKNOWLEDGMENTS

COVID-19 HAS KEPT ME away from my friends in Chianti, but they were with me nonetheless as I wrote this new story. They whispered in my ear, urging me on, bringing life to my words. I especially send grazie to Lara Beccatini, Ioletta Como and Andrea Sammaruga for their friendship. I will forever be indebted to Maresciallo Giovanni Serra, who continues to answer my questions virtually. I miss all the Panzanesi friends I made writing this series. I wish them good health and hope to see them very soon.

In New York, I thank Barbara Lane for her unerring eye. There is not a typo or misplaced comma that she doesn't catch. Misha Meisel deserves a special thanks for inspiring me to get certain details right. I am grateful to Dr. Lee Goldman for answering the most important question.

I am blessed with a wonderful editor, Amara Hoshijo, who makes my story so much better. I thank Daniel O'Connor for his sharp eye. Publicist Alexa Wejko is great at spreading the word. Thank you to the three of you.

I thank my husband, Stuart, for his support and undying patience.